Hearts
ENTWINED

Hearts ENTWINED

A Historical Romance
NOVELLA COLLECTION

The Love Knot · KAREN WITEMEYER

The Tangled Ties That Bind · MARY CONNEALY

Bound and Determined · REGINA JENNINGS

Tied and True · MELISSA JAGEARS

BETHANYHOUSE
a division of Baker Publishing Group
Minneapolis, Minnesota

The Love Knot © 2018 by Karen Witemeyer
The Tangled Ties That Bind © 2018 by Mary Connealy
Bound and Determined © 2018 by Regina Jennings
Tied and True © 2018 by Melissa Jagears

Published by Bethany House Publishers
11400 Hampshire Avenue South
Bloomington, Minnesota 55438
www.bethanyhouse.com

Bethany House Publishers is a division of
Baker Publishing Group, Grand Rapids, Michigan

Printed in the United States of America

ISBN 978-0-7642-3032-5 (trade paper)
ISBN 978-0-7642-3149-0 (cloth)

Library of Congress Control Number: 2017950630

Scripture quotations are from the King James Version of the Bible.

These are works of fiction and/or historical reconstruction. In historical reconstruction (*Bound and Determined*), the appearances of certain historical figures are therefore inevitable; all other characters are products of the author's imagination, and any resemblance to actual events or persons, living or dead, is entirely coincidental. In works of fiction, the names, characters, incidents, and dialogues are products of the author's imagination and are not to be construed as real. Any resemblance to actual events or persons, living or dead, is entirely coincidental.

Karen Witemeyer is represented by Books & Such Literary Agency.
Mary Connealy and Melissa Jagears are represented by Natasha Kern of the Natasha Kern Literary Agency, Inc.

Cover design by LOOK Design Studio
Cover photography by Mike Habermann Photography, LLC

18   19   20   21   22   23   24   7   6   5   4   3   2

Contents

A LADIES OF HARPER'S STATION NOVELLA

THE *Love* KNOT

KAREN WITEMEYER

To all my readers in the Netherlands.
You welcomed me so warmly into your country
and inspired me to bring home a piece of Holland
to incorporate into my stories.
This hero is for you.

Judge not, and ye shall not be judged: condemn not,
and ye shall not be condemned: forgive, and ye shall
be forgiven.

—Luke 6:37

Chapter

1

May 1895
Harper's Station, Texas

*C*laire Nevin frowned at the cheerful white clouds frolicking across the blue sky and tried to close her ears against the melodies the birds insisted on singing in response to the deceptively fine morning. Ignorant creatures. Could they not sense that this day held no cause for celebration? Cause for *trepidation*, aye. The letter in her reticule felt like a stone weighing on her wrist, demanding sacrificial action with no more than veiled hints for explanation. Yet family was family. Claire would do her duty. She wouldn't abandon them in their time of need.

And if she secretly grumbled about her flighty sister jumping into trouble *again* without once considering the consequences, leaving her older sister to clean up her mess from half a continent away? Well, no one need be privy to that wee detail.

Claire set her chin and straightened her spine against the hard bench outside Harper's Station's general store and smoothed the fabric of her myrtle green traveling dress over her knees. She wouldn't feel guilty for her uncharitable thoughts. Polly was sixteen, no longer in short skirts and pigtails. It was high time she learned a thing or two about responsibility. Claire had been working in Miss Fester's embroidery shop for two years by the time she turned sixteen. She'd left school—though not her books, heaven forbid—to work in a dark little room at the back of the shop, pricking her fingers constantly as she dressed up handkerchiefs and hemlines with tiny flowers and French knots for a trifling wage. Her earnings might have been piddling, but she'd managed to put food on the table when her da drank away all his wages at the pub.

She still sent money home every month. With seven Nevin daughters still filling the nooks and crannies of their New York tenement apartment, and her da with no intention of denying his insatiable thirst, her mam needed all the help she could get. Claire was glad to do it. Glad to help in any way necessary—unless it required her to travel to Seymour. In that case, *glad* was the precise opposite of what she felt.

Where was Benjamin Porter? Claire tapped her toe on the wooden floorboards beneath her feet, then cast a glance over her shoulder toward the store entrance. The freighter had always been the punctual sort, until he married. Lately he seemed to prefer lingering over breakfast with his wife to running his routes.

Claire's shoulders sagged. When had she become such a shrew? Ben and Tori had been married barely a fortnight, and here she sat casting silent aspersions on their character. Mr. Porter *should* linger over his breakfast. Kiss Tori on the cheek and ruffle little Lewis's hair. He was a family man now, and family came before business. Always. In truth, she dreaded this excursion to Seymour so much that she'd forced herself to arrive far ahead of the appointed time in order to sidestep the temptation of not arriving at all. Mr. Porter probably didn't even realize she was waiting for him.

At the quiet click of a door handle unlatching, Claire pasted on a bright smile, determined to be a pleasant traveling companion for the man who had been kind enough to offer her a ride to Seymour before making his usual deliveries. Only it wasn't Mr. Porter who glided through the doorway, but Mrs. Porter.

"Claire? Why didn't you knock? You would have been welcome to join us for a plate of biscuits and gravy." Tori extended a china teacup with a moss rose design toward Claire. "With Ben in the house now, I make enough to feed an army. I swear he can put away more food than those giant horses of his do. And Lewis is determined to follow his new pa's example, though I think he shares half of his plate with Hercules."

Claire's smile softened into something much more genuine as she pictured the towheaded boy slipping his dog treats beneath the table. Her second-youngest sister, Brigid, would be about Lewis's age now. She used to sneak crumbs from her own meager supper to a skin-and-bones tabby that wandered the alley behind their building. Did she still? A twinge of homesickness pricked Claire's heart with unexpected sharpness. Leaving Mam and the girls last summer was the hardest thing she'd ever done. Yet it had been the best thing, as well.

"I don't want to be intrudin'," she said, her Irish brogue thicker than usual on her tongue, no doubt exaggerated by thoughts of home. She accepted the tea Tori offered and scooted over to make room for her friend on the bench. "I had a bite with Maybelle afore I left the clinic."

Tori sipped her own tea and gazed into the blue sky, affording Claire companionship yet privacy at the same time. "Ben and Lewis are out back, loading the supplies for today's deliveries. He'll bring the wagon around shortly."

"'Tis kind of yer man to see me to town."

"He's glad to do it. Though I admit I was surprised when he told me about your request." Tori kept her attention on the sky, but Claire felt the gentle prodding rub against her already tender soul. "I haven't known you to leave Harper's Station even once since the day you arrived." Tori lifted her teacup to her mouth. "Not beyond a short jaunt to one of the area farms to tend an illness, anyway."

Unasked questions hung in the air between them. Tori wouldn't press for answers, yet the urge to share swelled in Claire like an overfilled hot-water bottle threatening to burst.

11

She set her teacup on the wooden bench seat and reached into her reticule to extract the letter. Her fingers trembled just enough to rustle the paper as she handed it to her friend. "I'd not be visitin' Seymour if I had any say in the matter, but me sister's in some kind o' trouble."

Tori met Claire's gaze, her brows lifted in a mix of concern and curiosity. "What kind of trouble?"

Claire shrugged. "I don't know. She doesn't spell it out, just begs me to meet the mornin' train on this particular date. Read it for yerself. See if ye can make any sense of it."

Tori set aside her tea and reached for the letter. Claire reclaimed her cup and took a long, slow sip. Perhaps the warm liquid would soothe her frazzled nerves. As the tea slid down her throat, she closed her eyes. Polly's looping penmanship rolled before her. She'd read the letter so many times since it arrived four days ago that she had it memorized.

Dearest Claire,

You are the only one I can trust. Mam has done what she can, but you know how stubborn Da can be when he sets his mind to something. And he's set it to cutting me off. Home is lost to me.

I know you're probably shaking your head and clicking your tongue about whatever folly I've gotten myself into this time, and you'd be right to do so. As usual, I failed to think through the consequences before I ran headlong into trouble. But I'm praying that as much as you are shaking your head, you're also opening your arms to embrace me as you've done so many times before. You've always been my anchor, Claire, and I need you now more than ever.

I'm not asking for money. I'll find some way to get by. I'm hoping to convince Miss Fester to take me on. My embroidery is not as fine as yours, but I've a deft hand when it comes to beading and piecework. Perhaps I can earn a place crafting handbags for her shop. But without enough coin for respectable lodging, I'll have no place safe enough to store my treasure. Mam cannot keep it for me any longer. That's why I'm sending it to you.

You've made such a life for yourself, Claire, just as I always knew you would. A healer! Could you have imagined such a thing even a year ago? Mam is so proud of you. And the women you live with sound so strong and supportive and forward-thinking. I know that, for once, I'm doing the right thing.

It's a lot to ask, considering how you came to be in Texas, but I'm begging you to meet the train in Seymour at ten o'clock on the second Tuesday of May. I've entrusted my trousseau to a family friend you will recognize. Take it home with you. Make it your own.

Thank you, Claire. I love you. You'll never know how much.

Polly

The paper crinkled as Tori carefully folded the letter into thirds and handed it to Claire. "I see why you're going, though I find it odd that your sister is going to such lengths to protect her trousseau. Would your father really forbid her from keeping it at home?"

Claire thought about her father and his unpredictable rages. "Aye. Though I imagine Mam tried to hide it from him as long as possible. If Polly did something that warranted expulsion from the family, Da would not want any of her things left behind to remind him of her."

A picture of the battered steamer trunk she and Polly had used to store their trousseau rose in Claire's mind. A broken clasp that wouldn't lock. A dent in the lid. Rust on the hinges. Yet together they'd placed all their dreams for the future inside. Pillowcases Claire had lovingly embroidered as she imagined her future husband lying beside her. Quilts Polly had pieced out of dress scraps destined for the rag bin. They'd been beautiful. Her sister might

13

be flighty when it came to most responsibilities, but she was a craftswoman when it came to quilting. Her stitches precise, her appliquéd edges flawless. Miss Fester would be lucky to have her.

"The two of us had such romantic dreams." A wistful smile curved Claire's mouth. "Most of it pure foolishness, but it got us through the lean times."

At least until the day Claire realized that dreams couldn't be trusted. Practicality was the only way to ensure one's future.

She'd left most of her trousseau behind when she answered Stanley Fischer's advertisement for a mail-order bride, not wanting the sentimentality that had inspired their design to follow her into her sensible marriage. Then, of course, she'd *met* Mr. Fischer, and all thoughts of marriage, sensible or otherwise, had run screaming into the abyss.

"I can understand Polly wantin' me to keep her trousseau, but why insist I meet the train in person? Could not the box simply be shipped to me and brought in by Mr. Porter? There's something more to this story. Something me sister's too ashamed to admit, even in a letter. Whoever's bringin' the box must be bringin' explanations, as well. 'Tis the only thing that makes any sense."

Tori's hand covered Claire's and squeezed. "I remember well what it was like to be young and foolish, but no trouble is insurmountable. She'll survive, Claire."

"But she must be so frightened." Claire grasped Tori's hand with a desperation she'd been denying for days. "No home. No family. She has friends, but they're all as flighty as she is. They'll be no help." She yanked her hand away and pushed to her feet, then paced in front of the bench, her boot heels clicking a sharp staccato rhythm as she moved. "The day I received her letter, I wrote back, urging her to come here to Harper's Station. I even sent her funds for train fare. Whatever trouble she's in can't follow her here. Surely." Her pace slowed as she lifted her gaze to the east, blinking against the glare of the morning sun, and then she stopped altogether. "She won't come, though. I know it in me bones. There's a lad she's fond of back home. A scoundrel for certain, but she loves him with all the dramatic devotion of a sixteen-year-old's heart." She shook her head, as much to wish the truth away as to acknowledge it. "No. She'll not be leavin'."

Tori stood beside her and placed a hand on her shoulder. "Then you should go to Seymour and learn all you can from this family friend your sister has entrusted with her secrets. Perhaps then you'll know how best to help her."

Claire nodded. "'Tis all I can do."

An hour later, the outskirts of Seymour rolled into view, and Claire's grip tightened on the arm of the freight wagon's bench.

"Almost there." Ben Porter turned a friendly smile in her direction, but all Claire could manage was a sickly twisting of her lips in response.

Why couldn't the road be longer? No, that wouldn't be sufficient. Getting mired in a bog would be better. Or set upon by masked bandits. Then she'd not be at fault for missing the train. She would have made an effort in good faith, after all. Done her duty. But the Lord had cursed her with sunshine, good roads, and peaceful travel. She eyed the one cloud overhead that contained a touch of gray along its belly.

It's not too late for a lightning strike and runaway horses, Lord. Really. I wouldn't mind. Not that I want any harm to come to Mr. Porter, mind ye. Just turn his massive beasts around and run them back toward home.

Sunlight glistened off the gray-rimmed cloud and bleached it white.

Claire dipped her chin, her spirit chiding her. She was being cowardly. Such wishes belonged to a child, not a woman of eighteen. God had not given her a spirit of fear, but one of power and love and a sound mind. 'Twas high time she put that sound mind to work and focused on her Lord's power and love instead of the spiteful nature of a particular mercantile owner.

"You sure you don't want me to stay with you?" Mr. Porter's

brow puckered with concern. "I can postpone my deliveries until after you've met the train."

His kindness shamed her. Forcing her fingers to uncurl from around the bench handle, Claire folded her hands in her lap, then slowly raised her gaze and shook her head. "'Tis no need. Ye've already gone out o' yer way for me as it is. Besides, there's no tellin' how long I'll be visitin' with the friend me sister sent. I haven't seen a body from home in months. 'Twill be good to swap stories and hear how me family fares."

Her escort eyed her doubtfully. "You sure?"

Bright red lettering swam into the corner of Claire's vision as they passed the first few buildings of town. Claire swallowed hard. *Don't look. Don't look.* But her glance defied her mind and darted around Mr. Porter's broad shoulders to dance over the large, imposing sign. *Fischer's Emporium.* Claire shuddered.

"Miss Nevin?"

She jerked her attention back to the man at her side. "Sorry." She forced a smile. "Go on and tend to yer business, Mr. Porter. I'll be fine."

He frowned but thankfully didn't argue. "You know where to find my brother's livery, right? I spoke with him yesterday and reserved a horse cart for you. He'll have everything ready whenever you decide to head back."

"I know where to go. Tori wrote out the directions for me."

The freighter nodded. "Good. If you need anything—" he paused to glare at her—"*anything*, you head to the livery. Bart and Addie will take care of you."

"Thank ye. I'll remember that." Mr. Porter meant well, she knew. But going to Bart Porter's livery was going to be hard enough without lingering for an extended visit. The stables stood only a block from the emporium.

She'd already plotted a route to get from the depot to the livery via side streets so she could circumvent Fischer's store. If the horseflesh Porter's brother rented her was half as good as he claimed, she'd be able to rush past the emporium in a blur on the way out

16

of town and neatly avoid any contact with the man she'd jilted nine months ago.

It wasn't cowardly. It was . . . intelligent. No one with half a brain poked a rabid wolf just to prove herself brave. Much wiser to evade the beast's vicinity altogether.

"Here we are." The wagon slowed as Mr. Porter brought his draft horses to a halt.

Claire's stomach swirled, and her head grew light. Avoiding the wolf was all well and good, but there'd be no avoiding whoever stepped off the train that had just pulled into the station. No avoiding the truth about her sister, either. As much as Claire wanted answers, she dreaded them with equal fervor.

Mr. Porter came around to her side of the wagon and helped her down. Once on the ground, she thanked him for his assistance, then turned to face the depot. Hands quaking slightly, she smoothed her bodice and touched her hat to ensure it remained straight. Setting her shoulders, she lifted her chin and strode forward. Polly was counting on her. Whatever trouble stepped off that train, she'd handle it with calm efficiency and sensible practicality. Just as she always had.

Weaving through the drummers and departing passengers who milled about on the platform, Claire made her way to the train. Steam hissed. The conductor shouted instructions. Porters jumped to obey. And amid the chaos, people trickled out of the front railcar.

One stranger after another exited to clutter the platform. Claire inched forward, determined not to miss whomever her sister had sent.

The top of a man's hat protruded from the doorway. A hand reached for the bar alongside the opening to steady his descent. Claire stilled. Her mouth turned to cotton wool, and her heart thumped in her chest. As if time had been mired in molasses, a chin gradually appeared. A strong, square chin. A clean-shaven chin. An impossibly familiar chin. The rest of the man's face remained blocked by the brim of his hat as he ducked.

It couldn't be. Saints preserve her. Polly could never be so cruel.

Her knees weakened, and Claire staggered, but there was nothing to grip for support. Only her own hand. So she clasped her fingers together and willed her spine and legs to straighten.

The man's foot reached the first step, and finally, his hat lifted.

Instinct might have warned her what was coming, but nothing could stop the burning jolt that seared her soul when Pieter van Duren's honey-brown eyes locked on hers.

Chapter

2

*C*laire stared at the man who had broken her heart. Why? Why had Polly sent him of all people? The van Durens had been neighbors, fellow immigrants, though from Holland instead of Ireland. While most of the Nevins' non-Irish neighbors looked down their noses at them and others of their *kind*, the van Durens had been different, inviting them to church services and sharing food during the harsh winters. It was their kindness that had drawn Claire's mam to accept Mrs. van Duren's invitation to worship, but it had been the warm fellowship of the small congregation and the simple, practical teachings of biblical truth that kept them coming back. It was in their Sunday school that Claire had come to know Jesus and to believe in his love for all mankind, even the despised Irish.

As the two families grew closer, the elder Nevin girls played with the two van Duren boys. Went to school with them. Fell in love with them. Polly with the younger of the two, Diederick, who could wrap the world around his finger with nothing more than some blarney and a smile, and she with the older, more serious Pieter.

Four years had separated Claire and Pieter in age, but she had adored him, following him around the schoolyard, the neighbor-hood, pretty much everywhere. He'd treated her kindly, never teasing her or poking fun at her freckles or calling her *carrot head* as the other boys had. In fact, he'd looked out for her like an older brother, even going so far as to meet her after work at Miss Fester's shop in order to walk her home. But the winter she turned sixteen, something had changed between them. Deepened. Brotherly affection transformed into manly interest. Girlish fancy matured into deep-seated love.

Until his betrayal ripped apart the seam binding them together, leaving her edges ragged and threadbare.

And now he was here. In Seymour. Less than ten feet from where she stood. Holding some kind of small bundle firmly against his chest, his left arm cradling it like a . . . a . . . *babe*. The heart fractures Claire thought long healed cracked open and bled inside her chest.

She tore her gaze from his and stared at the ground to center herself. This wasn't about her. It was about Polly. Claire need only speak to him for the briefest of moments. Glean what she needed to know, then send him on his way.

When she lifted her eyes again, he had turned to face the railcar and held his hand out expectantly. Claire's chest throbbed, the ache nearly unbearable as she braced herself for the wife he was no doubt preparing to hand down. But instead of a beautiful, wil-lowy blonde with sparkling green eyes and a dowry to make any man salivate, even a sensible Dutchman who'd sworn he preferred freckly redheads, all that emerged was the handle of a well-worn carpetbag—one that bore a remarkable resemblance to the one Polly used to tote around her quilting supplies.

Claire couldn't seem to move. She barely breathed as Pieter collected the bag, then made his way toward her. One solid stride came after another, his sensible work boots even more scuffed than she remembered, the heels worn down in back. His tan trousers were creased from the long journey with a few dark spots of un-decipherable origin around the knees. Probably the babe's doing.

He wore a blue shirt . . . nay, he wore *the* blue shirt. The one she'd sewn for his twenty-first birthday. The one she'd pieced together from remnants purchased at a discount from the seamstress whose shop stood two doors down from Miss Fester's. Durable denim, since he tended to wear clothes until they fell off him, his father's thrifty nature deeply embedded in Pieter's character. Yet this shirt, nearly two years old now, looked new. As if he'd not worn it since they separated. As if he'd saved it. For today.

Her mind too numb with shock to process the ramifications of that observation, Claire focused on keeping her legs beneath her as Pieter halted in front of her. She tilted her head slightly upward—he stood a good five inches taller—and stared into eyes she never thought she'd see again.

He smiled, the subtle movement barely curving his mouth, yet the expression was so quintessentially Pieter that a wave of homesickness broke over Claire, nearly drowning her in memories of what had once existed between them.

He had no right coming here. Stirring up feelings. Looking so steady and sure when he was nothing but a philandering ne'er-do-well.

Pieter bent sideways to lower Polly's bag to the ground, then lifted his hand to remove his hat. The circular crease in his blond hair tempted her to brush it out with her fingers. She fisted her hands against the impulse. There'd be no touching. Her nerves were too raw just from the sight of him. Touching him would be catastrophic.

"Claire." He dipped his chin in greeting, his voice soft and velvety, just as she remembered.

She said nothing in return. Mostly because her tongue was stuck to the roof of her cottony mouth. Yet she also remained quiet out of fear that once she started talking, all the anger and pain she'd clamped off for the last year would gush out of her like blood from a freshly opened wound.

So they stared at each other. Pieter never had been one for stringing words together. Then a train whistle pierced the air. The baby twitched, one tiny leg kicking out of the blanket. Fussing quickly followed.

Pieter jammed his hat back onto his head and shifted his grip on the babe, making little hushing sounds that turned her heart to mush. She'd always known Pieter would make a wonderful father, and now the proof stood right before her eyes. It hurt. Saints above, it hurt. He was supposed to father *her* children, not some other woman's.

After he settled the little one, he reached into the pocket of his jacket and pulled out an envelope. He met her gaze, his eyes seeming to stare into her soul, communicating support, steadfastness, and . . . sorrow? Claire gave her head the tiniest of shakes. No, that couldn't be right. She was reading old dreams into nothing more than a stare. He didn't care about her. Not like that. Perhaps as an old friend who shared companionable memories, but nothing more. Nothing deeper.

He held out the envelope to her. "From your sister."

Those three words burst through her brain like gunshots. Polly. Yes. That was why she was here. The messenger didn't matter. Only the message.

With shaking fingers, Claire accepted the letter from him, careful to touch only the paper. Looking around for a place that would afford a bit of privacy, she spotted a bench on the west side of the depot, away from the bustle surrounding the train. "Perhaps we can sit?" Thankful that her voice sounded nearly normal, she nodded toward the bench. But then she glanced back at him. "Unless you need to wait for your wife. Was she delayed on board?"

Pieter's brow furrowed. "Wife?" He looked behind him as if he feared some woman was about to sneak up on him and slip a yoke around his neck. "I have no wife."

"Then where did . . ." *The babe come from?* Claire shook the thought away with a wag of her head. "Never mind. It's none of my concern. I'll just . . ."

He has no wife. The insidious little thought drove all other words

22

from her mind. She gave up on speaking and marched toward the depot. Let him follow or not. She had a letter to read.

Taking a seat on the bench, she dropped her reticule onto her lap, then broke the seal on the envelope and pulled out the letter from her sister. The ink had run in a few places thanks to round droplets that marred the paper. Tears? Claire's stomach dropped. What had happened to her beloved Polly?

Claire,

Please forgive me for my secrecy, but I feared if you knew what I planned to send to you, you would not accept it. But I'm sure that the instant you look into little Liam's eyes, my son will win you over. Yes, he's my son. I didn't realize I was carrying him until a few weeks after you'd left. At first I was elated, sure his father would do right by me, but after I told him about the babe, Dirk left town. Left me. Left our child.

Vision blurring, fingers trembling, Claire lifted her gaze to the man standing in front of her, the one gently rubbing the back of a sleeping infant. Her nephew. Claire sucked in a breath. The child was *Pieter's* nephew, as well. No wonder Polly had chosen him to carry out this task.

Pieter's eyes met hers, his warm brown gaze full of the same heartbreak and disappointment that threatened to swallow her.

Clearing the thickness from her throat, Claire turned back to the letter.

I hid the fact that I was carrying from Da by staying out of his sight and wearing baggy clothes, but as much as I hoped to finish the birthing before he came home from the pub that evening, first babes are never much in a hurry. Da tried to toss me out that very night, but Mam threatened to clobber him over the head with her rolling pin if he so much as touched me or the babe. But I knew she couldn't hold him off forever.

I tried everything I could think of to keep Liam, to find someone to watch him while I looked for work. But you know what it's like here. All the families in our area are too poor to feed their own children. I can't ask them to take in mine. Yet I couldn't bear the thought of leaving him as a foundling. Growing up in an overcrowded orphanage with no mother to love him.

Please, Claire. Take Liam into your heart. Into your home. Love him as I do. Be the mother he needs. I trust you as I trust no other.

And maybe . . . you might tell him stories about me. Stories to make him smile. Maybe someday, if the Lord sees fit to bless me, I can come for a visit and feast my soul on the lovely young man he is sure to become under your guidance. Aunt Polly will dote on him and spoil him terribly, ensuring I will be his favorite of all the aunts. For he is to be your son from this day forward, not mine. Don't hold back any love from him in fear that he will be taken away from you. Give him everything in your heart, Claire. As I have.

Polly

A child. Her sister had sent her a child.

A thousand practicalities flooded Claire's mind, as they always did when a predicament arose unexpectedly. She could handle any problem if she broke it down piece by piece and made a plan. A goat for milk. Diapers. A bed. She'd have to rig some way to keep him occupied and safe while she worked at the clinic. Maybelle shouldn't mind having a child about. The old midwife was always complaining about how Harper's Station needed more babies. All those single women and no men. Although Maybelle had been eyeing Emma Shaw's midsection rather closely lately. Their banker and colony founder had married the town marshal last fall. Perhaps little Liam would have a playmate before the end of the year.

Liam. Named for their grandfather. The kindly man who had

wept when his daughter told him her husband had decided to emigrate to America. It was the only memory Claire had of Ireland. The small cottage with a thatched roof. Grandfather in the rocker, holding baby Eileen, Polly standing at his knee, sucking on her fingers, while Claire rubbed his arm in a childish attempt at comfort as tear after tear rolled down the old man's weathered cheeks at the impending loss of his faery girls.

Liam.

Polly's son.

Her son.

Claire lifted her gaze once again to Pieter, then shifted it to encompass the bundle he cradled against his chest. Practical concerns dissolved. Sentimentality faded. A single thought radiated with the brightness of the sun, shoving all else into shadow.

"May I hold him?"

Chapter
3

$\mathcal{P}$ ieter stepped forward and gently transferred his nephew to Claire's arms. The instant her eyes met Liam's dark blue gaze, her face transformed. Heartbreak gave way to wonder as she dug his little fist out of the blankets and gave him her finger to hold. That was all it took. The two fell instantly, madly in love.

Pieter recognized the look on her face. It used to be aimed at him. And oh, how he wanted it back. Wanted *her* back. She was the only girl he'd ever loved, and he wasn't about to let her slip away from him again. God had given him a second chance. He wouldn't waste it.

His chest ached, full of all the things he wanted to tell her, to explain to her, but he'd probably be better served by letting Liam soften her up first. He moved the bag of infant supplies close to the bench, then mumbled an excuse about needing to fetch the rest of the luggage.

Not that Claire paid him any heed. She was too caught up in the *kleintje*. Understandable, Pieter acknowledged as he strode across the platform to where the porter was unloading trunks and cases from the train. Even at three months, Liam had all the charm of his father and the winsome smile of his mother. Pieter had fallen hard for the little man himself over the course of the train ride. Liam was blood. Family. No matter what happened with Claire, this boy would not grow up without a van Duren in his life. Since Pieter's wastrel brother was too focused on his own pursuits to fill the role, Pieter would volunteer.

"All this belongs to you?" A uniformed porter raised a brow at Pieter when he began separating and stacking his trunks and crates into a neat pile to the left of the rest of the luggage.

Pieter nodded. "*Ja.*" A man making a new life for himself needed to be prepared. One crate held his grandmother's wooden cheese molds, which his *moeder* had brought over from Holland. Another held churns, paddle spoons, bowls, and a set of decorative butter molds.

Texans might prefer beef cattle, but Pieter had come from generations of Dutch dairymen and had apprenticed with a cheese maker in Rochester. He had a plan, and after five years of working and scrimping, he had the money and skill to make it a reality. Yet the victory would be hollow without Claire by his side.

He glanced back toward the bench where she sat, her head bent close to Liam's, her smile soft and sweet. Longing speared Pieter through the chest. He had a steep climb before him. Yet standing at the base of a cliff and wishing to be at the top wouldn't get him there. He needed to dig in his toes, grab a handhold, and start the ascent.

He faced the porter. "Is there somewhere I can store these for a time?" He gestured to the crates and his trunk of personal belongings. The smaller steamer trunk Polly had sent would go to Claire.

"We have a storage room in the depot, sir. We can put your things there, if you like. I'd be happy to cart them for you." The porter's eyes brightened, no doubt anticipating a healthy tip.

But Pieter had been scrimping too long to start tossing money around now. He hefted the first crate up to his shoulder. "I'll see to them."

Once the luggage was settled, Pieter collected his small satchel of personal items, slung the strap over his head to lie across his body, then grabbed Polly's steamer trunk. The poor thing had been battered when his journey began, but after a few days in a baggage car, it barely held together. As much as Pieter appreciated the thrift in continuing to use such an item, if it failed to hold its contents, it wasn't serving the purpose for which it was intended. He'd have to get Claire a new one.

If she chose to join him in Snyder. Pieter frowned a bit as he walked back to the bench. He probably shouldn't get ahead of himself.

"Oh good, ye're back. I think Liam needs a change of his napkin." Claire ceased digging in the bag he'd left with her and eyed the trunk he carried. She pushed to her feet in expectation and shifted the babe to lie on her shoulder.

Pieter set the trunk on the bench beside her, but he knew she wouldn't find what she was looking for. "It only holds linens and trinkets. No diapers. I checked at the last stop."

Claire lifted her hand from the trunk lid and turned to look at him, her blue eyes luminous. His heart thumped. Heavens, but he loved her eyes. So bright. So full of life. Open and honest. And at the moment, flummoxed.

"What d'ye mean, there's no diapers in the trunk? There be none in the bag, neither. I know me sister can be a bit irresponsible, but surely she did not send ye all this way without a change of underthings for the baby."

"*Nee.* She sent just enough. I put the last one on him this morning." And seeing as how before this trip he'd never diapered a babe on his own, he thought he'd done a pretty fair job of it.

Claire stared at him, and not in the way he would have wished. "So where be the soiled ones?"

"I disposed of them." The foul-smelling cloths had made him gag. He hadn't wanted to subject the other passengers to such a vile odor. Especially not in the stuffy, enclosed space of a railcar.

Her eyebrows arched upward. "Ye *disposed* of them."

Why did she make it sound like a crime?

28

"And here I always thought ye the thrifty sort. Should've known all that hobnobbin' you've been doin' with the fancy folk over in Rochester would change that about ye, too."

"What fancy folk? I worked at a dairy, Claire. Shoveling manure and making cheese." And learning every inch of the business so he could duplicate Mr. Ellmore's success when he started his own enterprise. What did she think he'd been doing the past three years? Wining and dining with the social elite? That was his brother's angle, not his.

Well, except for that one time.

That one disastrous time that drove Claire out of his life. To another man, a stranger. How Pieter had died inside when he learned that she'd left New York to become a mail-order bride to some shopkeeper in Texas. She'd chosen a complete stranger over him. A man who didn't love her, who didn't even *know* her. It was only when Polly explained that Claire hadn't gone through with the marriage and instead had been living in a women's colony, apprenticing as a healer, that Pieter's hopes had revived and his plans had begun in earnest. Plans he was determined to carry out no matter how much the lady in question glared at him and muttered under her breath about daft men and their tiny brains.

"He shovels manure but can't be bothered to rinse out a soiled napkin?" she grumbled. "Does he think diapers grow on trees, that he can just pluck another whenever the need arises?" She dug through the trunk herself, tossing quilts and baby clothes to and fro in search of the cloths he'd already told her were not inside. She pulled out what looked like a pillowcase with an embroidered hem and froze. Pink rose to her cheeks before she stuffed the bed linen deep into the trunk.

He had no time to wonder over that odd behavior before she slammed the lid shut, picked up Polly's bag, and started marching down the street. "I'll need to purchase some diaper cloth before I can be on my way. Why don't you stay with the trunk? I'll be back shortly."

Her words insisted he keep his distance, but the trepidation lining her face as she gazed down the street fired his protective instincts. Something was wrong.

"Wait." Pieter grabbed the trunk and hefted it up to his shoulder. "I'll store this at the depot and join you."

"No!" She pivoted so fast, her skirts whipped around her legs. "There's . . . there's no need."

What was going on? Claire had always been independent and capable. Stubborn, even. But it wasn't any of those qualities he saw reflected in her eyes as she backed away from him. It was something secretive. And fearful.

Pieter's jaw tightened. He'd come here to end the secrets between them, to get everything out in the open and reestablish a foundation of trust—one they could build a future on. There was no room for new misunderstandings or suspicions, not if he hoped to regain what he'd lost. However, as she lifted her chin and marched down the street without him, it wasn't a need to expose her secrets that made him follow. It was the apprehension lingering in her eyes.

Claire Nevin might be a feisty, hotheaded Irishwoman and the backbone of her family since her youth, but she was still only eighteen. Young, vulnerable, and with a babe to hinder her should trouble erupt. Pieter would hang back, give her the freedom to handle things on her own, but there was no way under God's blue sky that he would let the woman he loved walk into a situation that frightened her without his support.

Claire strode down Main Street, weaving a path to avoid parked wagons, men on horseback, and townsfolk who loitered on the boardwalk. She finally halted in front of a large storefront painted bright red. A plate-glass display window stretched wide in front of her. Yet she hesitated to go in.

That was all the signal Pieter needed. He jogged the trunk back to the depot, stored it in the back room with the others, then loped down to the store. Peering through the same window where he'd last seen Claire, he caught a glimpse of her in the back of the shop, fingering a bolt of white cotton. She glanced over her shoulder.

Once. Twice. Then a third time. Pieter opened the door and walked into Fischer's Emporium.

"I'll be right with you, sir," the proprietor called from behind a counter at the front of the store, where a matronly woman was rearranging her purchases in a large basket.

Pieter waved noncommittally at the clerk, not wanting to encourage his attention. Wandering down an aisle with an assortment of fishing gear, pipe tobacco, and match safes on display, Pieter positioned himself near the end so that he had an unobstructed view of the fabric table across the way. He pulled a box of fishhooks from the top shelf and pretended to examine them while keeping his focus on Claire.

When the bell above the door jangled and announced the departure of the lady with the basket, Claire jumped. Her gaze darted to the counter, then back to the cloth. She shifted, aiming her back toward the front of the store and hunching her shoulders as if trying to hide. He'd never seen her so timid. She'd always approached life, whether in good times or bad, with energy and a take-charge attitude. Something about this place definitely had her rattled.

The shuffle of footsteps and a wheezing breath behind him alerted Pieter that he was no longer alone. He pivoted to find the paunchy shopkeeper making his way down the aisle toward him. The clerk's welcoming grin dimmed somewhat when he noticed Pieter's interest appeared to lie in a ten-cent box of fishhooks.

"An outdoorsman, I see." The proprietor puffed up his chest and thumped Pieter on the back. "I have some excellent new reels in stock." He stepped back a pace and pulled a box off the top shelf. He opened the lid for Pieter to view. "Nickel-plated with a range of up to two hundred yards. Best quality you'll find anywhere."

"Not interested." Pieter tipped his head in Claire's direction, irritated that the shopkeeper had addressed him first when Claire had entered before him. "I think that lady could use some assistance, however."

The clerk's face scrunched up in confusion. "Lady?" He looked in the direction Pieter had indicated. "Ah." His features cleared.

31

"I didn't realize . . . She must have come in while I was fetching Mrs. Gordon's order from the back room." He bowed his head slightly to Pieter. "If you'll excuse me?"

Pieter nodded in answer. The shopkeeper was a little oily for his liking, but he seemed attentive to his customers. He should get Claire what she needed in quick order. Then they could leave this place and whatever odd hold it had on her. And maybe they could finally have the discussion Pieter had traveled halfway across the country to instigate.

"How may I be of serv—you!" The clerk's strident tone brought Pieter's head up. The man's face darkened as he yanked the bolt of white cotton away from Claire and threw it back on the table. "Get out of my store," he gritted through a clenched jaw. "You're not welcome here."

Pieter dropped the fishing hooks and strode across the store.

Claire's chin came up. Pieter expected to see fire sparking from her blue eyes, but she barely lifted her lashes. "Mr. Fischer, I'll just be needin' a few yards of diaper cloth, then I'll be on me way. Believe me, my desire to be gone from here is as strong as yours to be rid of me."

"Diaper . . . ?" Fischer's gaze finally seemed to register the babe Claire held. "Ah. Of course. Now everything becomes clear." Some of the anger faded from his face, but the scorn that replaced it did nothing to alleviate Pieter's growing agitation. "So that's the way of it, is it? I should have known. *Hussy*," he spat. "Found yourself with child and tried to foist it off on the first decent man to offer for you, didn't you? Guess I should be glad I had the good sense to send you away nine months ago. Otherwise I'd be stuck raising another man's brat."

Searing rage burned through Pieter's brain. *This* was the man she had pledged to marry? This foul-minded prig who cast aspersions on a lady's good name based on unfounded assumptions and personal prejudice?

Pieter closed the remaining distance between himself and the shopkeeper in three steps and pushed his face close to Fischer's. "Apologize to the lady."

Fischer leapt backward, his face paling until he realized Pieter wasn't about to strike him.

Not that Pieter didn't want to. Never had he wanted to hit a man more. But his faith demanded turning the other cheek and loving his enemy, and while the last thing he felt at the moment was *love* toward the potbellied skunk in front of him, he wouldn't forfeit his self-discipline for temporary physical satisfaction. His fists remained lowered, though clenched, at his side.

"I'm sorry you had to hear that, sir. This"—he raised a brow at Claire—"*person* was just leaving."

Pieter nearly forgot his morals altogether at Fischer's pointed refusal to acknowledge Claire as a lady, but he held his temper— and his fists—in check. Barely.

"There's no reason for you to get involved," Fischer continued in that irritating tone that scraped like fingernails on a slate against Pieter's already taut nerves. "I'll just escort Miss Nevin out, and then we can put this unpleasantness behind us."

Fischer reached for Claire's arm, and without thought, Pieter's hand shot out and clasped the other man's wrist. "Don't touch her."

He stole a glance at Claire to make sure she was all right. She wouldn't meet his gaze. Humiliation stained her cheeks, yet she held her head high with dignity and stubborn Irish pride.

"I'll see meself out, gentlemen." Then, in a move that had Pieter inwardly cheering, she dropped Polly's bag at Pieter's feet, grabbed up the entire bolt of diaper cloth, and marched up to the counter.

"Hey! You can't take that." Fischer struggled against Pieter's hold to no avail. He wouldn't be getting anywhere near Claire. "I'll bring you up on charges of thievery!"

Claire ignored his bluster, plopped the fabric bolt on top of the counter, and with one hand unwound about three yards. She shifted Liam to her left arm, then took up a pair of shears that had been left on the counter near the butcher paper and roll of string used for wrapping parcels. With an embroiderer's precision, she snipped off the length she wanted, cut off a smaller piece for immediate use, then pulled out a handful of coins and laid them on the counter with a gentleness that echoed through the store with all the power of a shotgun blast.

After a quick fold of the cloth, she collected her reticule and swept out of the store.

Now *that* was a woman.

Fischer's renewed struggles brought Pieter's attention back to the weasel stuck in his grip. "Unhand me, sir. I have to make sure she left sufficient funds. Otherwise I'm going to fetch the sheriff."

Pieter only tightened his hold. "The money's all there, and if it's not, I'll pay whatever she lacks."

Fischer's eyes widened in incredulity. "Why? Look, mister, I don't know what she promised you, but she ain't nothing but a two-bit hustler. She cheated me once, and I'm sure she'll cheat you, as well, if given half a chance. She's not to be trusted."

Pieter's eyes narrowed. "Claire Nevin is the most honorable *lady* you've ever had the good fortune to meet. She's kindhearted, self-sacrificing, and someone to depend on when trouble arises. And that babe she carries—her nephew. Taken in out of the goodness of her heart. So perhaps in the future, you'll spare a moment to learn the facts of a situation before spewing your slanderous poison in public."

Pieter tossed the shopkeeper's arm away from him as if it were contaminated with gangrene, pinned the despicable man with a final glare, then picked up the bag Claire had left for him and strode out of the store without once looking back.

Chapter
4

Claire clutched Liam to her chest and nearly ran down the street toward Bart Porter's livery. It didn't matter that she didn't have Polly's trunk or even the bag of infant supplies. All that mattered in that moment was escape.

Facing Stanley Fischer had been bad enough. Just as she'd known it would be. The sour man held on to a grudge as if it were the last coin in his cash box. But having Pieter witness her folly? Her pride couldn't bear it.

And that was the issue, as always. Her pride. As much as she wanted to cast all the blame for the destruction of their relationship on Pieter's shoulders for stepping out with another woman, she'd contributed, as well. Devastated by his betrayal, she'd turned her back on him. So sure was she that any explanation he could give would be woefully inadequate, she'd refused to see him and returned each of his letters unopened. There'd been no forgiveness. No fighting for the man she claimed to love. Just fleeing. And fleeing in the rashest manner possible—by answering the ad of a stranger in Texas and pledging to become a mail-order bride.

She'd always been the wise sister, the one with both feet planted firmly on the ground. How many times had she advised Polly that

Diederick was no good for her? That he was a charmer seeking an easy life, not a man a woman could depend upon? And then, just like the Bible warned, while she'd been trying to remove the speck from her sister's eye, the log in her own eye had crushed her. Her heart took the brunt of the blow, but it had been the blow to her pride that sent her running.

She couldn't bear to see the pity in her mam's eyes, the *I-told-ye-so* in her da's. And worst of all, she couldn't stand to listen to Polly pleading with her to hear Pieter out, reminding her of his character and steadfast ways, insisting that there must be a logical explanation. Because if Claire gave in, she'd have to admit that her flighty, lead-with-her-heart-and-not-with-her-head sister might actually be right.

So she'd run. Just as she was running now.

"Claire! Stop!" Pieter called out behind her, his voice too close. He'd catch her before she reached the livery, before she could block his questions and accusations with the presence of others.

Claire accelerated from a hurried walk to an actual jog. But Liam started to fuss, his whimpers abrading her conscience. Immediately, she slowed. Was her pride really so important that she'd risk the baby's safety? Heaven preserve her! One misstep in her ill-advised haste, and she could have fallen. Liam could have been injured.

Lord, forgive me!

A strong hand grabbed her upper arm. He didn't yank her around to face him. His grip didn't bruise. Yet neither did it allow her to pull free. It simply held her. Supported her. Offered an anchor in the midst of her storm.

Claire's eyes slid closed, and for just a moment, she began to relax, to lean back against him. But then she remembered another woman whose arm had rested on his. A wealthy, beautiful woman whose father could offer Pieter everything he'd ever wanted. Success. Respect. A partnership in a thriving business. All things Claire lacked.

Her spine locked back into place.

"Fischer's a buffoon, Claire. Don't let him upset you."

Claire spun around and glared up at Pieter. "He might be a buffoon, but he's ne'er lied to me, Pieter van Duren. Never promised to marry me in one breath, then scampered off to court a better candidate in the next."

Pieter's eyes widened, and his hold on her arm loosened. She took advantage of his shock and yanked free.

"I did Mr. Fischer a bad turn. He has every right to be angry with me. Just as I have every right to be angry with you."

Pieter stared at her for a long moment, his eyes narrowing as they peered into places she strove to keep hidden. "And does he have the right to nurse that anger and treat you no better than the dirt under his feet even after nearly a year has gone by?" He paused, his voice softening to a near whisper. "Do *you* have that right?"

The soft words struck her like arrows to the chest. "Th-that's unfair," she murmured.

But was it?

Pieter said nothing. Just looked at her, his gaze illuminating his hurt. Was that how she'd been acting? As harsh and intolerant as Stanley Fischer? Surely not. She'd never been cruel. Never treated Pieter or anyone else with anything less than common courtesy. Yet neither had she extended forgiveness. In fact, ever since he'd stepped off that train she'd been trying to push him back out of her life just as Stanley Fischer had tried to push her out of his store.

The bitter taste of shame soured her mouth. All this time she'd taken refuge in being the wronged party, casting all the blame on Pieter and making herself at home in her lofty tower of self-righteousness. She truly *was* no better than Stanley Fischer.

Moisture coated her eyes as she faced the man who had once been her entire world. "Pieter. I'm sorry." She blinked against the tears that threatened to fall and patted the baby whose discontent grew louder by the moment. As tempted as she was to use the babe as an excuse to escape Pieter, she held her ground and his gaze. "I've not treated ye well, have I? Runnin' off without a word. Returnin' yer letters. Refusin' to see ye. 'Twas cowardly. I let the hurt dictate my actions. After all the years we've known each other, ye deserved better than that. And as much as I've grown during me time in Harper's Station, the moment I saw ye step off that train, all the pain came rushin' back, and with it my desire to shut ye out and flee."

Claire used the edge of the diaper cloth she'd just purchased to rub away a tear that escaped her lashes, sniffed once, then inhaled a shaky breath and lifted her chin. She'd never been one to shirk her duty, no matter how difficult. She wouldn't start now.

"Ye didn't have to come, Pieter," she acknowledged. "Ye must've known how awkward things would be between us, yet ye came anyway. To bring me my nephew." She glanced down at the squirming infant in her arms, then tipped her head to hug him into her neck. "My son." She looked up at the man before her. "Thank ye."

Pieter held her gaze for a long moment before nodding slightly. Then, apparently realizing they were starting to draw a crowd, he gently took her arm and steered her down the street in the direction she'd been heading. They walked in silence until they reached the livery.

She drew to a halt in front of the open barn doors and mumbled a quiet explanation. "Mr. Porter, a friend from Harper's Station, gave me a ride to town this morning, but since he had deliveries to make for his freight business, he made arrangements with his brother for me to borrow a horse and cart from his livery for the drive home. I should probably be checkin' on it and seein' about returnin' to Harper's Station. That way ye can get on with the rest of yer business."

"You *are* my business, Claire."

She jerked her head up, questions racing through her brain. Questions that must have shown on her face, for Pieter smiled. That small, private half-smile of his that never failed to turn her insides to mush.

"Delivering Liam wasn't my only reason for coming." He ran a finger along the edge of her face, tucking a loose strand of hair behind her ear. Her skin tingled at his touch. Then he moved on to the babe, gently cupping the lad's downy head and rubbing back and forth.

The contact soothed the boy, but it had the opposite effect on Claire. For as Pieter stroked the child, the back of his knuckles also brushed the underside of her chin, leaving not only her heart in a puddle from his tender, fatherly treatment of Liam, but the rest of her longing for another caress meant just for her.

Once the baby ceased his fretting, Pieter withdrew his hand. "When Polly finally admitted to me that your mail-order marriage never took place, I began making plans." He met her gaze, his eyes clear and intent. "Plans to win you back, Claire. To prove myself worthy of you." He retreated a step and shifted his weight, but his eyes never left hers. "When Polly approached me about Liam, I already had a train ticket to Texas in my possession. I would have come for you with or without the little man as an excuse."

He'd been coming for her all along? Even after the way she'd sliced him from her life? Her heart gave a leap, yet her head argued caution. He'd hurt her before. He could hurt her again.

"I'm not asking you to forget all that's happened between us. I'm simply asking you to give me a chance to explain and own up to my failures. After you've heard what I have to say, if you still want no part of me, I'll respect your wishes and leave you to your life in Harper's Station with no more than monthly visits to remain connected with Liam."

Claire's forehead scrunched. *Monthly visits? From New York?*

"I have no doubt that you'll be a wonderful mother to him," Pieter hurried to reassure her, as if he feared he'd insulted her with his comment. "But Liam is a van Duren. His father might have abandoned him, but I will not. He's my blood. I intend to see that he receives the love and support such a connection deserves."

This was the man she had fallen in love with, a man of deep honor and commitment, a man she had always been able to depend on. Had she painted him a full-fledged villain when perhaps he'd simply been a good man who'd temporarily stumbled? No one could be perfect all the time. Yet that was what she had expected of him. To never let her down. Ever.

"I would be glad to have ye involved in Liam's life." She swallowed another chunk of pride. It scratched as it went down, but it lightened her soul a little. "He'll need a . . ."—she nearly said *father*, but that would be inviting too many pictures of domesticity that she wasn't yet ready to contemplate—"a strong man in his life to look up to as an example. But I don't understand how ye think to visit every month. The time away from work plus the train fare would make visiting once a *year* barely feasible."

Pieter grinned and rocked back on his heels. "It won't be so bad. I thought to visit over a Sunday, get a local lad to milk the cows for me while I'm gone. And if the cheese and butter business goes as well as anticipated, I'll have extra ready cash for the train fare."

"Extra cash? Have ye gone daft, Pieter? I had to pay Mr. Fischer seventy-five dollars to reimburse him for the ticket he purchased to bring me out here. And 'twas only one way!"

Something lit Pieter's eyes. A sparkle—dare she believe it was a touch of mischief? "Don't worry. The fare will be manageable. The trip's only a couple hours."

"Whisht! Now I know ye're daft."

He chuckled. "No. Not daft. Only calculating distance from a different starting point." His face grew serious. "I bought a piece of land, Claire. And I've money to start a small dairy herd."

His own land? Heaven be praised. He'd worked so hard for so long. She knew how much that meant to him. To his family—to be the first to own land in the New World. To escape the tenements and make a life for himself. No matter what trouble had come between them, she was truly proud of his accomplishment.

"Oh, Pieter, I'm so happy for ye. I know 'twas yer dream."

"*Part* of my dream," he corrected, and a little shiver danced along Claire's nape at the implication. "I didn't just bring Liam with me on that train. I brought all my worldly goods. The land I bought is in Texas, Claire."

Texas? Who ever heard of a Texas dairy? Dairies belonged in places like New York and Wisconsin. Why in the world would he choose Texas?

40

But as her heart thumped in her chest, she recognized the answer. He'd come for *her*. To prove himself. Hadn't he said as much? Yet to go so far as to purchase something as permanent as land with no guarantee that she'd change her mind. 'Twas like throwing the deed to the farm into a poker pot when the final cards had yet to be dealt. Unaccountably foolhardy.

Yet incredibly romantic.

The blighter was cheating. Trying to manipulate her.

Or maybe he was sacrificing everything he had for love. Not only for her, but for the nephew they shared.

How could she possibly be expected to remain unaffected by such a grand gesture?

Claire stared into the tender brown eyes of the man she'd loved for half her life and felt the stone of her heart start to soften and yield. Remaining unaffected was obviously not an option. But keeping her wits about her was. She would listen to his explanations. Perhaps even offer forgiveness. Heaven knew her soul could benefit from the release of that burden. But it would be her head, not her heart, that would decide how they moved forward. Her heart had led her astray once. She wouldn't make the same mistake twice.

Chapter

5

An hour later, Claire had decided that Bart and Addie Porter were ministering angels sent by God to ease her way through the cyclone of change whirling through her life. Not only did Bart have the horse and cart ready for her, but while the men were off collecting the luggage from the depot and tracking down a goat she could purchase, Addie gave Liam what Claire could not—mother's milk. While her own six-month-old daughter rolled about on the bedroom floor, exploring table legs and sucking on blanket corners, Addie nursed Liam and freed Claire to cut the diaper cloth she had purchased into ready-to-use squares. She even had time to hem them on Addie's Singer sewing machine.

By the time Pieter returned and stored his extra trunks and crates in a back corner of Mr. Porter's livery, Liam was fed, changed, and fast asleep in a padded baby basket Addie had insisted on loaning them. With no other baby details to address, Claire was free to relax.

Only she couldn't. As soon as Pieter climbed up beside her on the small, two-person cart seat, his wide shoulders and long legs taking up more than his fair share of the space, all she could think about was him. The feelings he stirred confused her, despite her efforts to maintain a practical perspective. As her feet straddled the baby basket on the floorboard, she became far too aware of his thigh pressing against hers. And his smile—hopeful, yet a tad nervous—had an unsettling effect on her pulse.

It was too much. Too familiar and comfortable. Too reminiscent of other times they'd been together. Walks home after work, church picnics where she'd sat close enough to brush his arm every time she reached for her plate. Even now she wanted to touch him, to reassure him that he had nothing to be nervous about, that she would always stand beside him. Yet it was his very failure to stand beside *her* that had brought them to this particular juncture.

Desperate to busy her hands and distract her mind, Claire reached into her handbag for a piece of embroidery. She always stashed a small project in her reticule, hating to be idle. She was working on a bread cover for Bertie Chandler's birthday next month. In each corner of the linen cloth she'd fashioned stalks of wheat in golden-brown thread, waving in imaginary wind. She'd finished three of the corners already and started the fourth this morning—started but quickly abandoned. Her anxiety about her errand combined with the jostling of Ben Porter's freight wagon had made it nearly impossible to stitch with any level of precision. Thankfully, the plodding pace Pieter had set in order to allow the goat to keep up with their cart offered more stability.

Sliding the threaded needle from the fabric, Claire eyed the base of the wheat stalk she'd started that morning. Only three back stitches tall, poor thing. Time to fill it out with some satin-stitched leaves and grain heads. Yet when she set her needle to the linen, her fingers trembled enough to require three attempts before she found the right hole. All because the man sitting next to her chose that moment to inhale in a particularly portentous manner.

She held her breath with him, not even realizing she did so until he finally exhaled and freed her to breathe on her own. Little good it did her, though, when he opened his mouth and stole her breath altogether.

"I love you, Claire."

The quiet words caught her so off guard, she jabbed her needle into her finger. She'd been expecting explanations, apologies, pleas for forgiveness. Not a declaration. Especially not one that made her heart weep and sing at the same time.

Pieter turned to look at her. She could feel his regard, though she kept her gaze focused on her needlework.

"I know I have much to explain," he said, "but I wanted you to hear that truth first. I love you. *Only* you. I've never loved another."

Claire tightened her left hand into a fist, her injured finger throbbing just as her heart throbbed with a betrayal that had never fully healed. "Then why did ye spend all of last spring escortin' Miss Josephine Ellmore about town as if ye were courtin' *her*?"

She hadn't believed the rumors at first. The Pieter she knew would never be so shallow. So deceitful. He'd gone to Rochester to learn the workings of the dairy industry, to make business connections, to earn the funds he needed to buy his own land. For their future. He'd gone to better himself, and she'd trusted him. Even when the neighborhood girls delighted in reminding her that the best way for Pieter to better his prospects was to leave the Irish trash that persisted in clinging to his shoe in the gutter where she belonged.

Not Pieter, her soul had cried. Not steadfast, steady, dependable Pieter. His word was his bond, and he'd vowed to come back for her. To marry her. As soon as he had the money put by to provide the life they had planned.

Yet when Polly came to her, concerned about something she'd overheard Pieter's brother Diederick saying to some friends about Pieter finally figuring out how to get ahead in life, Claire had no longer been able to sustain blind faith in her man. She'd craved validation. Vindication against the cruel taunts and salacious gossip. She'd taken half a day off work and traveled to Rochester. Wearing her best dress, her hair twisted in a fancy style that had taken Polly an hour to arrange, she'd stepped off the train and walked through town, determined to prove her man faithful.

Only to prove the opposite.

She'd found them exiting an ice cream parlor. Pieter, solid and stoic as an oak, while a vibrant butterfly clung to his arm. The beautiful blonde laughed and fluttered and leaned intimately close, her expensive blue walking gown floating about her like delicate wings. She teased and cajoled and slapped Pieter playfully on the arm, as if scolding him for being too serious. And he'd smiled. A wide, toothy grin, bigger than the paltry half-smiles he'd always bestowed on Claire.

Never had she felt so shabby. So . . . second-class. Her Sunday dress, which had filled her with confidence a few hours earlier, now seemed faded and lifeless. She swore she could feel every last one of her freckles pushing out from her skin, announcing her flaws and imperfections to the world.

And in that heartbeat of keenest vulnerability, Pieter had glanced up and seen her. The color had drained from his face, and his eyes had gone as wide as silver dollars. Fitting, since dollars were apparently what he'd had his eyes on all along.

He had called her name and taken a step toward her, but she turned her back and ran. Less than a hundred feet had separated them on the boardwalk, but it had been crowded, and she eluded him by ducking into a millinery shop with a group of giggling girls, then disappearing out the back. He hadn't caught up to her that day. Nor any day since. Until now.

Pieter's gaze continued searing the side of her face, willing her to look at him. She felt the heat of it. Even saw a hint of his intensity through the corner of her lashes, but she refused to give in. A girl could get lost gazing into those earnest, honey-brown eyes. She needed all the control she could muster if she hoped to keep her mind functioning at full capacity. She jabbed her needle through the fabric and ignored the knot in her midsection that matched the tangle she'd just created in her thread.

A heavy sigh was Pieter's only response to her stubbornness. He turned away to face the road, and Claire swore the temperature of her cheek fell several degrees at his action, as if the sun had moved behind a cloud.

"I was never courting Miss Ellmore," he finally said. A long silence stretched after that pronouncement, only the creak of wagon wheels and an occasional birdcall meeting Claire's straining ears. Then he cleared his throat. "But I did make an effort to curry her favor."

Claire snuck a peek at his profile. His nape had a ruddy glow to it, his head hung low, and his shoulders slumped. He must have sensed her attention, for he started to crane his neck toward her. She yanked her eyes back to her embroidery and thrust her needle into another stitch, uncaring that it wasn't in the right place and that she hadn't yet untangled the thread from her last attempt.

She wanted to shout at him. To accuse him. To beg him to explain how he could love her while flirting with, if not outright pursuing, another.

But she held her tongue, as much out of fear of what she might reveal as a desire to make the telling just a bit harder on him. She'd decided to listen. She hadn't promised to pave the way with rainbows and rose petals.

"It was during my second year of apprenticeship at the Ellmore Dairy that Jo started acting odd."

Claire cringed at the nickname. What happened to *Miss Ellmore*? Now she was *Jo*. Claire pushed her needle upward into the fabric, huffing out an impatient breath when the knot she'd created on the back side refused to allow the thread to pass through.

"At first, she just looked at me differently, smiling far too often and too . . . brightly." The discomfort in his voice soothed her pride a bit, but the memory of his own bright smile—aimed at *Jo*—kept her from softening her stance. "Then she started coming by the dairy late in the afternoons, supposedly to visit her father, but it was *my* aid she enlisted in helping her return to the house without soiling the hem of her fine gowns. Why she wore such garments to a muck heap in the first place never made a lick of sense to me, but I couldn't ignore her request. Especially not with her father looking on."

Claire shook her head at Pieter's ignorance of feminine wiles.

True, she'd never been one to employ them herself, much preferring to speak her mind than play games, but even an innocent like Pieter must have caught on eventually that Josephine Ellmore had been angling for a strong arm to lean on.

"During the rainy months, it was faster just to carry her back to the house and avoid the mud altogether."

Claire rolled her eyes as she flipped her fabric over and started picking at the knots. "Yet somehow she managed to get *to* the dairy without assistance," she muttered under her breath. "Daft man."

"Did you say something?" Pieter's gaze warmed her cheek again.

Claire wagged her head from side to side. "Continue on with your woeful tale of carryin' fine ladies in your arms. 'Tis surely warmin' me heart towards ye."

And that was why she needed to keep her mouth shut. He'd be a fool not to hear the jealousy behind the sarcasm. Then again, he'd been fool enough to fall for the *Oh, I can't possibly dirty my hem* ploy.

"Well, anyway . . . it became apparent that she harbored some . . . interest in me."

Ye think so? Claire ground her teeth together and jerked her needle. A separated thread pulled without its partners, increasing the size of the knot. Good grief. Why would this thread not cooperate? No matter how she picked at the loose ends, the tangle only grew worse.

"And her father seemed to approve, despite the fact that I had mentioned having a girl back home."

As if that would matter. Pieter was intelligent—about *most* things—driven to succeed, and the hardest worker in ten counties. Ellmore would have recognized that right away. He'd no doubt been grooming Pieter to become a partner in his business. How better to solidify the future of Ellmore Dairy than to tie Pieter to it through marriage to the man's daughter?

"Then I made the mistake of listening to my brother."

"Diederick?" Claire's head came around at the tightness in Pieter's voice. His disapproval and disappointment in his sibling could not have been more evident. Yet judging by the way he lifted a hand from the reins to tug at his collar, there was some disapproval and disappointment aimed at himself as well.

Pieter nodded. "He came to see me one weekend, and we got to talking. I complained about how uncomfortable Miss Ellmore's . . . flirtations were making me. How trapped I felt."

Glad Jo was back to being Miss Ellmore, Claire opted to keep her gaze on Pieter's face. The way his jaw clenched when he talked about Miss Ellmore lent authenticity to his story. Claire knew Pieter. His kind nature. He'd never rebuff a woman or fail to offer assistance. He was too much the gentleman. Maybe he *had* been trapped.

Claire turned back to her needlework and ordered her heart not to soften. Trapped or not, there was no excuse for what she'd witnessed at the ice cream parlor. Pieter hadn't been carrying Josephine Ellmore's parcels or protecting her from a runaway wagon. He'd been stepping out with her. In public. Shaming the poor Irish girl he'd left behind in the tenements of New York.

"Dirk always has an angle." Pieter ground out the words between clenched teeth. "He said he'd overheard Jo complaining to her father about me ignoring her and being so rude as to leave a room whenever she entered. He said Ellmore was angry and threatened to send me packing without a reference."

An outcome that could have negated all the work Pieter had done to establish a reputation for himself among the area dairymen.

"Dirk suggested I humor the girl. Pay her some attention. Take her out a few times and let nature run its course. She was bound to tire of me, boring stiff that I am."

Claire frowned at the unflattering phrase Diederick always tossed in his brother's face whenever Pieter attempted to rein in Dirk's adventurous tendencies. Pieter might not be flamboyant or boisterous, but he'd never been boring. Not to her. Besides, what good was a bright red circus tent that flapped free of its moorings the first time a bit of wind kicked up? She'd much rather have a stone wall sheltering her, stalwart and dependable. If Josephine had half a brain, she'd recognized that truth, as well.

"Then, after the infatuation faded," Pieter continued matter-of-factly, as if such a result was a foregone conclusion, which ironically stirred Claire's temper, "I'd be free to return to you with better prospects. Perhaps even a partnership."

He fell silent for a moment, then guided the horse to the side of the road and halted the wagon. Claire's feet squeezed the basket on the cart floor at the unexpected change in direction, but she needn't have worried. Liam slept on.

Pieter turned in his seat, or tried to. There was so little space that his knees simply knocked against hers as his torso twisted. He covered her hand with his own, needle and all.

"I gave in to temptation, Claire. I knew better than to listen to Dirk's schemes, but I wanted that partnership so badly."

She understood that drive. The same need to succeed burned in her chest, too. She just never thought he'd choose the easy way over the honest way. Diederick, yes. But Pieter? Never.

"Losing my position at Ellmore's would have put me back at least a year, if not more, from my goal," Pieter said. "I couldn't bear to put off our wedding that long."

Our wedding? Claire pulled her gaze from his hand to focus on his face. His beautiful, rugged, weather-worn face.

"The separation was already tearing my heart out. I would have done anything to speed the day that would make you mine. So I . . . I gave in. With Dirk's idiotic promises of '*no one will get hurt*' and '*Claire will never even know*' scratching my itching ears, I agreed. I stopped avoiding Jo. I never sought her out, but neither did I turn down any of her requests. If she wanted me to take her to town, I took her as soon as my work at the dairy was done. I sat with her in church. Held her knitting yarn so she could roll it into a ball, and tried to look interested when she prattled on about fashion and people I knew nothing about. I even made myself smile at her with one of those ridiculous giant grins that Dirk insisted made the ladies happy."

Claire's heart seized before galloping away with her breath. Had . . . had she understood him correctly? He'd gone along with Diederick's scheme *not* because he'd wanted to find success in business, but because he wanted to find a way to make her his wife sooner? The irony was too much. He'd danced attendance on another woman in order to be with her. Heaven preserve them.

"I was stupid, Claire. Stupid and impatient. It wasn't fair to Jo for me to pretend an interest I didn't feel, and it was hurtfully disloyal to you. The moment I spotted you on the street in Rochester, I recognized my error. You were everything to me. All that I'd been working for was for you. For our life together. But by using dishonorable means to achieve an honorable end, I corrupted something beautiful and made it ugly.

"That very day, I told Jo about you and apologized for not being honest with her. She was angry and hurt, but she didn't have her father send me packing, which made me wonder if the conversation Dirk had supposedly overheard had ever really happened in the first place.

"Every weekend I returned home, praying you'd let me apologize, let me somehow put things right. But you refused to see me. Returned my letters without reading a single word. Then one weekend you were simply gone." Pieter fell silent for a moment, then slowly pulled his hand away from hers. "After all we had meant to each other, Claire, you just gave up on me. Worse—you ran off to Texas to marry a stranger."

The hurt in his voice made her heart bleed, but it was the betrayal shining in his eyes and the loss of his touch that cut the deepest. She hadn't been the only one betrayed. He'd used a woman to ease his path to success, but hadn't she done the same? Used a man to salvage her pride and escape her pain? She'd taken the easy way out, too. With disastrous results.

"Oh, Pieter," she said softly, regret thickening her voice, "we're a pair of fools, aren't we?" She fiddled with her embroidery, lamenting the jumbled mess she'd made of the threads. "Our pasts are so tangled and snarled, I doubt we'll ever be put to rights. We've too many knots in our way."

"Good."

Her eyes jumped to his. "Good? What d'ye mean, good? Knots are a bad thing."

"Not to my way of thinking." Something fierce lit Pieter's eyes as he leaned closer to her. She backed away slightly, but he followed, bending even farther toward her. "I want to be so tangled and knotted up with you that nothing will ever pull us apart again. Not anger, nor hardship, nor hurt, nor even some dunderhead's idiotic mistakes. No matter what comes, we stick together and work it out."

Her stomach ached with yearning. He made it sound so easy. It wouldn't be.

But maybe, just maybe, it wouldn't be impossible, either.

Chapter —

6

*P*ieter hadn't known quite what to expect from a women's colony, but the speed at which news spread about Claire's return was truly remarkable. Ladies poured out of every nook and cranny to swarm the clinic. Nothing stirred a female's curiosity more than a new man in town.

Pieter shook his head as the latest woman brushed past him. *He* wasn't the new man causing the ruckus, of course. Nope. Liam claimed that honor all by himself. The sheer volume of feminine cooing and high-pitched nonsense words being tossed about inside the clinic would have made Diederick proud.

Or jealous. Dirk never had enjoyed anyone else being the center of attention.

Pieter's smile slipped as he finished unharnessing the rented horse from its cart. How could Dirk turn his back on Polly and the child he'd fathered? The depth of his brother's selfishness sickened Pieter. Last he'd seen Dirk, he had been pursuing some textile heiress, sure he'd be able to convince the plain, plump young woman to marry him and thereby provide not only a managerial position for himself within her father's company, but a healthy fortune at the onset thanks to her significant dowry.

Her doting father wouldn't want his only daughter living in any discomfort.

Pieter couldn't help but secretly wish for the girl's father to beat Dirk at his own game. Perhaps when negotiating the marriage contract, he would offer a modest dowry and a position within the company only to reveal after the vows had been spoken that the position entailed the lowest, most menial labor. Pieter couldn't think of a punishment Dirk would hate more than actually having to work for his own advancement. It would serve the bounder right to be cut off from the golden goose he coveted so strongly that he had abandoned his own child to chase it.

Having already secured the goat in the fenced yard behind the clinic, Pieter took one last look at the building before leading the horse back toward town and the water pump he'd spotted near a garden area.

Despite having said the piece he'd traveled halfway across the country to say, nothing had been resolved between him and Claire. She probably needed time, but he didn't have a lot to offer. He was expected in Snyder in a week, to accept delivery of his dairy cows. He'd hoped to take Claire with him. As his wife. Yet impatience had bungled things for him before, and he'd vowed not to make that mistake a second time. If he had to woo her over the next three years, one day at a time when he came for his monthly visit to see Liam, that was what he'd do. Jacob worked for Rachel for seven years, after all, his love for his woman making the time pass like mere days. Pieter could do the same.

"There's water and pasture you can use at the station house."

The deep voice startled Pieter out of his mental wanderings. He jerked his head toward the sound and spotted a man with a gun holstered on his hip leaning casually against a large oak tree beside the local café.

The man pushed away from the tree and strode forward, sunlight glinting off the star on his vest. "Malachi Shaw," he said as he stretched out his hand.

Pieter returned the handshake, making sure his grip was firm and steady. "Pieter van Duren. I'm a friend of Claire's."

"Can't say I've heard her mention you." Shaw clasped Pieter's hand longer than necessary, his hold tightening as his gaze probed Pieter's face.

Pieter endured the scrutiny, straightening his shoulders and lifting his chin. "Our families know each other in New York."

"How long you planning to stay?"

Pieter squeezed the marshal's hand, then tugged free. He didn't mind being measured, but he wouldn't be intimidated. "I've got a room in Seymour for the week. I'll be making daily visits to Harper's Station in the interim. Making sure Claire has everything she needs for the babe."

The marshal hooked his thumbs into the small pockets of his vest, his relaxed stance at odds with the intensity of his stare. "That kid's arrival has certainly caused a stir. Especially since no one—including Miss Nevin, apparently—knew he was coming."

He was fishing for details. Pieter wouldn't be supplying any. He could understand Shaw's dedication to his duty. Protecting the ladies of Harper's Station included protecting Claire, and Pieter applauded him for that. But he wasn't about to spill personal details just to ease this man's curiosity. He took refuge in silence and an *it's-none-of-your-business* stare.

The marshal seemed to accept the closure of that particular road but didn't give up his questioning. Just jumped to a different path. "So you'll return to New York after you see the boy settled?"

Pieter crossed his arms over his chest. "No."

Shaw waited several seconds for Pieter to elaborate. He didn't. "So where ya headed?"

"I don't believe that is any of your concern."

Something sparked in the marshal's eyes. In a blink, his casual stance vanished. He stood ramrod straight, hands balled into fists and jaw clenched in warning as he stepped close enough to Pieter to bring their noses barely inches apart. "Everything that could impact the well-being of the women in this town is my concern. I saw the way your eyes followed Claire into the clinic. You're not just here for the babe. You're here for her. She came to us last year, fleeing an unwanted suitor. I aim to see she doesn't fall prey to another. If she lets me know you're not welcome, you might as well get comfortable in Seymour, for you won't be visiting that babe or anyone else in Harper's Station."

Pieter bit back a defensive retort, stilled his riled pulse, and gave a sharp nod—one of understanding, *not* agreement. He'd never force his attentions on Claire, but neither would he let this meddling marshal dictate his future. "I appreciate your looking out for Claire's best interests, Mr. Shaw. And while my personal reasons for being here are none of your business, I'm glad you care enough about Claire to stick your nose where it doesn't belong."

The marshal stepped back and grinned. "Nosy, huh? Well, I've been called worse." He gestured across the street toward the old station house. "Come on. Those women will be oohing and aahing for hours yet. After we rub your horse down and turn him out in the paddock, I'll heat up some of Bertie's coffee, and we can sit a spell."

Pieter raised a brow. "You planning another round of interrogation?"

Shaw held his arms up, palms out. "Nope. Just two men chattin', I swear. Male conversation is a rare commodity in these parts, believe me. I aim to take full advantage of you." He chuckled and slapped Pieter on the shoulder.

"That's the prettiest baby I've ever seen," Maybelle declared as she wrapped Liam in his blanket and handed him back to Claire after doing a quick exam. "And healthy as can be, too." Maybelle winked. "He'll be running you ragged before you know it."

Claire thanked her mentor and snuggled Liam close. He grinned up at her, his toothless gums shining with baby drool, his eyes dark blue and so jolly, she couldn't help but smile back. "Oh, ye little heartbreaker. What am I to do with ye?"

Give him everything in your heart, Claire.

She bent forward and touched a kiss to Liam's downy head. His tiny fist poked out of the blanket and flailed about as if he couldn't quite contain his excitement at being back in her arms. She held a finger out to him, and he clutched it, bringing it to his mouth. Claire's chest swelled. Such a precious child. So innocent. So sweet. It would be impossible not to love him.

I give ye my solemn vow, Polly. I will hold him dear to me heart and pledge all that I have to keep him safe.

"He's a little darling," Bertie Chandler crooned, moving in for a closer look. The rest of the ladies followed suit, surrounding Claire. How they had all learned of Liam's arrival when she'd only been back in town for fifteen minutes, she had no idea, but nearly a dozen of Harper's Station's citizens filled the clinic's waiting area, eager for a turn to hold the baby.

Part of her wanted to shoo them all away, to dash down the hall to her room and latch the door against them. Liam was hers, and hers alone.

Only he wasn't. He belonged to Pieter, too.

Pieter. What was she to do with all he'd told her? His declaration of love. His explanations. His dairy farm in Snyder. Saints above. He had moved to Texas for her. For Liam. He deserved to be a part of the child's life. But could she trust him enough to be a permanent part of hers?

"May I hold him?" Bertie asked, breaking Claire out of her thoughts. The older lady reached for Liam, and with great reluctance, Claire handed him over.

Most of the ladies shifted to Bertie's side, all mesmerized by the boy, but Tori Porter and Emma Shaw stayed with Claire.

"Your poor sister," Tori said, taking Claire's arm and steering her toward a sofa along the far wall. "How desperate she must have been to send her child away." The normally stoic shopkeeper's eyes misted. "I remember how hard it was when Lewis was first born. If I hadn't found that position tending house with Mrs. Barry, I might have been faced with a similar choice. Thank God she had you to turn to, Claire. I can't imagine how devastating it must have been to give up her son."

The three sat, Claire sandwiched between Tori and Emma. It reminded her of the day she'd first arrived in Harper's Station, distraught and desperate to escape marriage to Stanley Fischer. She and her sister might be in very different situations, but she understood what desperation could lead a person to do.

"Da cut her off," Claire explained in Polly's defense. "Turned her out. She had no way to provide for the babe." Her gaze found Liam, who was being passed from Bertie to her sister, Henrietta. "It was either leave him in a foundling home or send him to me."

"Then she made the right choice." Emma patted Claire's knee and smiled warmly. "You'll make a wonderful mother, Claire. You love him already, I can tell."

Claire grinned as Liam grabbed a fistful of Henry Chandler's gray hair, earning a muffled screech from the spinster. "I do."

"And what of the man who brought him to you?" Emma's arched brows and twinkling eyes didn't bode well for keeping secrets. "Mal and I saw him driving and followed you to the clinic. The man could barely take his eyes off of you."

Heat flushed Claire's cheeks. "His name is Pieter van Duren. He's a friend from back home. We . . . ah . . . courted once upon a time."

Emma leaned her shoulder against Claire's in a sisterly fashion. "He seems a much better candidate for husband than Stanley Fischer."

Claire ducked her head and fiddled with her skirt. "Pieter's a good man. A man I once loved to distraction. But he broke me heart. Quite unintentionally, it turns out, but at the time, the wound was so deep that I deemed marriage to a stranger preferable. Marriage where me heart would be safe from harm."

"Yet you couldn't go through with it," Emma said.

Claire shook her head.

"And now he's back," Tori added. "And you have another choice to make."

Claire bit her lip and looked from one friend to the other before her gaze drifted over to Liam. "Aye. And I have more than just meself to consider this time around."

An hour later in the station house kitchen, after three cups of coffee and a half-dozen molasses cookies—one of which Pieter was fairly certain he saw the marshal tuck inside his vest—very little, if any, tension remained between the two men. Malachi Shaw listened with interest to Pieter as he rambled on about his dairy prospects, and Pieter found the tales the marshal told about masked outlaws and gunmen disguised as detectives as fascinating as they were horrifying. Apparently the quiet little women's colony Claire had been living in for the last nine months had been far from quiet. Or safe.

Pieter forced himself not to think about all the terrible things that could have happened to her since she left New York. She was alive and well and only a few buildings away. But a shiver ran through him anyway. Along with a prayer of thanksgiving for the Lord's protection.

"After the Pinkertons tracked down the rightful heir to the Haversham fortune," the marshal continued, "the gal was so grateful, she insisted on sending a sizable chunk of funds to Grace as a reward. Miss Mallory—Mrs. Bledsoe now—donated every last penny back to the town, asking that we build a permanent women's aid refuge."

Pieter set down his coffee cup and leaned back in his chair. "I thought this whole town was a women's aid refuge."

"It is, to an extent." Shaw drew his leg up and balanced his ankle on his knee. "Emma and the aunts started Harper's Station as a place for women to get a fresh start, no matter their reason. Females escaping abuse. Widows or unmarried women on their own with no way to support themselves. Even ladies who simply wanted a chance to prove themselves in a trade dominated by men. This is a place where they could be safe while earning a living and contributing to a community that accepted them. But it's changing, little by little. It's really not a women's colony anymore. First Emma and I married. Then Ben and Tori Porter hitched up. Grace and Helen both found husbands and left town. Ned Johnson's already in his teens, and there are other boys who will outgrow their mama's apron strings before much longer.

"The town is changing, and Grace's gift will allow us to preserve the heart of our mission well into the future. Emma intends to break ground on the Grace and Amos Bledsoe Home for Women next month."

"Sounds like a worthy endeavor."

Shaw grinned. "Yep. My Em's already got plans for the place, endowments set up with her investors, the works. She's not one to let an idea or a dollar sit idle."

"I heard that, husband," a decidedly feminine voice called out as the back door opened. Both men scooted their chairs out and got to their feet. Emma Shaw swept into the kitchen, a wide smile on her face and a familiar youngster cradled in her arms. "It's poor manners to discuss one's wife when she's not around to defend herself."

Shaw wrapped an arm around the lively brunette's waist and dropped a kiss on her cheek. "Not if I'm payin' you compliments, angel." His gaze moved to the babe. He lifted a hand to touch Liam's back but never quite made contact. The uncertainty clouding his eyes shocked Pieter. The marshal had oozed confidence since they'd met outside the clinic. Why would an infant lay him low?

"Isn't he the most precious thing?" Emma held Liam up in front of her, grinned at him, and jiggled him gently until he grinned back. "Here. Hold him." She extended her arms.

Malachi Shaw lurched backward and waved her off. "No way,

Em. I don't know anything about babies. I'll probably tangle his booties in his bib or something."

"Nonsense. It's easy. He's already holding his head up. All you have to do is support his middle. Pretend you're holding a puppy or something." She advanced on him, turning a giggling Liam around to face him as she went. "Come on, Mal. He won't bite. He might drool on you, but big, strong man that you are, you can handle it."

The marshal shot Pieter a silent plea for help.

Pieter shrugged. "Hold him under his arms and bounce him on your knee. He likes that."

Shaw narrowed his eyes in a message that obviously declared Pieter a traitor, then tried one more time to step away. Only to run into the wall.

"Take him, Mal." Mrs. Shaw's voice was softer this time. "You need the practice." Only then did Pieter notice the roundness at her waist. "You're going to be a great father. Trust me."

"But my old man—"

"Was a drunken lout, I know." She pressed Liam into the marshal's chest and waited until his hands slowly came around to clasp the baby's sides. "You're nothing like him. You're going to love our child so much that your heart will nearly burst, and everything else will take care of itself."

"Except the diapers," Pieter said.

Shaw's wife laughed at that and turned to Pieter for the first time. Striding away from her husband despite his panicked gaze, she offered Pieter her hand in greeting. "Thank you for delivering such a delightful new citizen to Harper's Station. There hasn't been this much excitement in town since Amos Bledsoe's bicycle order arrived."

Pieter shook her hand, her kindness instantly putting him at ease. That and the fact that she didn't seem to need him to contribute anything to the conversation.

"Claire gave me permission to get in some practice time with the baby while the two of you talk."

Pieter straightened. "Talk?"

Mrs. Shaw nodded. "She's waiting outside for you." She tipped her head toward the door she had entered from a few minutes ago.

Pieter didn't wait for any further explanation. He dipped his head to Shaw's wife, grabbed his hat off the table, and made a beeline for the back door.

Chapter
7

*C*laire pushed away from the paddock fence when she saw Pieter exit the station house. Her heart ached with yearning at the sight of him. She still loved him. Desperately. But she wouldn't pledge her life to a man until she was certain of him. Just look what had happened to her mam. She'd tied herself to a jolly man with wanderlust in his veins and ended up far from home, chained to a drunkard who spouted ugliness at his own kin as if they were the enemy. Her mam never spoke ill of her da, but every time he drank away his earnings or lost his temper with one of the girls, Claire could see the heartbreak and regret in her mam's eyes.

Marriage was a leap of faith, and Claire wouldn't be makin' the jump blindfolded.

Pieter's eyes sought her out, then lit up when he spied her near the barn. His long legs ate up the distance separating them in a flash, yet once he was in front of her, he said nothing, just crushed his hat in his hands.

"Is Liam all right?" Claire scuffed her foot on the hard-packed ground, her gaze dodging away from Pieter's.

"*Ja.*"

That was it? Just one word? Well, of course. This was Pieter, the master of concise expression. Although he had strung together a pretty impressive set of words during their cart ride. Words she was still processing.

She nodded her head toward the road behind the barn. "Walk with me?"

Pieter nodded and shoved his hat back on his head. His hands hung free at his sides as he strolled beside her, but she didn't fit her palm into his as she'd done when they were courting. Touching him would scramble her brain, and she needed to think clearly. Eventually his right hand clenched into a fist. In the next breath, he shoved it into his trouser pocket as if the enforced emptiness pained him.

Guilt pricked her conscience as they meandered past the garden, but she remained resolute. They couldn't simply pretend like nothing had happened and go back to the way things were before. They had to find a new way.

A way that entailed getting past a big, ugly knot.

However—Claire speculated, her mind taking a more hopeful turn—a seamstress couldn't sew a garment without first knotting the end of the thread. Joining two pieces of fabric required an anchor. Their anchor might be different than what it once was, but one knot didn't mean their future was destined to be a tangled snarl.

After they passed the church and the new house Malachi was building for Emma, Claire guided Pieter through the adjoining field to a lopsided oak tree that had been struck by lightning at some point years ago. One large limb had been sheared off and lay on the ground. The wood had decayed somewhat but still maintained enough solidity to serve as a bench. Claire settled on one end, then invited Pieter to join her.

His jaw twitched as if he wanted to refuse, but, as usual, he held his tongue.

Claire turned her face up to him. "Please."

He blew out a breath, pulled his hand from his pocket, and

lowered himself to the log. His knees poked up like twin mountain peaks in front of him. He rested one arm across them and waited.

Swallowing the urge to continue protecting the tender places inside, Claire steeled herself to say what needed to be said. Pieter had bared his heart to her. She must do the same. "I still have feelings for ye, Pieter. Those ne'er died, despite my best efforts to bury them."

His eyes slid closed as if he were savoring the words, and when he turned to face her, a hint of a smile played at one corner of his mouth. She shook her head, trying to warn him there was more to come.

"Lovin' ye's not the problem, Pieter. It's the trustin' part that's holdin' me back."

Some of the warmth left his eyes, but he nodded in understanding.

"Before me da started drinkin', I thought him the grandest man in all the world. He was so tall and strong and had a knack for makin' me laugh. As much as I hated leavin' Ireland, I trusted me da and followed without fear. I knew he'd always keep me safe. Until the day he lost his job at the docks and came home three sheets to the wind." Claire paused to steady her voice. She clutched her hands together in her lap and bit her lip.

"He staggered home, angry, sour, and smellin' like a brewery. He started yellin' at Mam, and I tried to fix it by gettin' between them. Not the best choice. But ye know how stubborn I am. I held me ground and told him to stop bein' mean. He slapped me. Right across me face." She lifted her hand to rub her cheek, the memory of the sting fresh and sharp. "It hurt like the dickens, but it was the pain to me heart that cleaved me in two."

Pieter sought out her gaze, his eyes mournful yet fierce. "I'd never raise a hand to you, Claire. I'd sooner cut off my arm than strike a woman."

"Ye don't understand." She lowered her hand from her cheek. "When I saw ye with that woman in Rochester, it was a slap to me face. Just like the one me da delivered. It stung like a searing fire."

Pieter straightened. "Claire, I . . ."

"I know ye'd never strike me," she hurried to clarify, the wounded look in his eyes tearing at her conscience. "Ye'd never turn to drink like me da did, either. But, Pieter . . . Da shattered my illusions of him when he hit me, and you shattered my illusions when ye cozied up to Josephine Ellmore."

Pieter's throat worked as he swallowed. "I'm just a man, Claire. I'm not perfect." His quiet voice prodded her spirit. "Any man placed on a pedestal is doomed to fall eventually."

"Aye. Women, too." Inhaling a shaky breath, she reached for his hand where it dangled from his knee, and clasped it gently. "I let ye down, too, Pieter. I know it. I ran when I should've fought for the man I love."

He turned his hand and laced his fingers through hers. Warmth spread up her arm and into the cold recesses of her heart.

"I forgive ye for what happened in Rochester," she said, dropping her gaze to her lap. Coward she might be, but he would weaken her resolve with those soft, love-filled eyes of his if she gave him the chance. "But I'll not marry ye until I trust ye."

"Then I'll just have to prove myself trustworthy." He tightened his grip on her hand, and she felt the promise traveling from his skin to hers. *I won't let you down again.*

Her heart already believed him, but her stubborn Irish mind still needed convincing. "Time will tell," she said as she slid her hand from his hold and stood. She rubbed her palm along her skirt, but she couldn't erase the impact of his touch. The effects lingered. Warming her skin, fluttering her pulse. Slowly, she curled her fingers into a fist. "Time will tell."

Later that evening, after settling Liam down for the night in the basket she'd borrowed from Addie, Claire left her small room at the back of the clinic and went to the kitchen to fix herself a cup of tea. Dressed in a cotton nightgown and wrapper, with a pair of thick stockings on her feet, she laid the Bible she'd brought with her on the table before padding over to the stove. She moved the kettle to the left side of the hob, where the stove emitted the most heat, then pulled out a chair and slid onto the sturdy wooden seat.

No single day in the entire course of her life had brought as much change and emotional upheaval as this day. Not leaving Ireland. Not abandoning school to work in the embroidery shop. Not even that dreadful day in Rochester. She felt as wrung out as an old petticoat on washing day. One more tug, and she just might tear to pieces.

Only she couldn't afford that luxury. Not with Liam depending on her. The little lad needed her, and deep in her heart, Claire suspected she might just need him, too.

Leaning her forearms on the table, Claire finally gave in to temptation and folded. Her shoulders slumped, her spine sagged, and her neck wilted, letting her head plop onto the leather Bible resting on the table.

What if I'm not strong enough?

The insidious thought wormed past her defenses to burrow in her mind. She'd always been the strong one. The one the family depended on. Never afraid to roll up her sleeves and do what needed to be done. But a babe? She might know how to tend to his physical needs after taking care of her younger sisters as they'd come along, but being a mother? That was different. More important. Easier to get wrong.

Pieter could help. He wanted to be involved in Liam's life. But after the fiasco with Stanley Fischer, she'd vowed never to marry a man simply to make her life easier. So where did that leave her?

Confused.

Exhausted.

Overwhelmed.

Cast thy burden upon the Lord, and he shall sustain thee.

Her mam had quoted that verse from Psalms whenever one of her girls complained about hardship or cruelty or the injustice of people treating them poorly just because they were Irish. Mam probably clung to that verse in order to deal with Da, as well. Claire could think of no other way her mam could endure all she had without leaning on the Lord.

Now that same verse rose to encourage Claire. She curled up from the table, one vertebra at a time, until her face hovered above the Bible lying between her arms. She reached for the cover and thumbed the pages. She didn't recall the precise reference for her mam's verse, but she knew it was from one of the Psalms.

She opened to chapter 28, and while she didn't find the verse she sought, another leapt from the page to grab her attention.

The Lord is my strength and my shield; my heart trusted in him, and I am helped.

Trust. It always came back to that, didn't it? Claire ran her finger over the word at the heart of the verse. The Lord possessed all the fortitude she could ever need, and he offered her an abundant supply—offered to be her strength and her shield through all the upheaval she faced. Yet she wouldn't be helped unless she trusted him.

"I'm so used to relying on meself," she whispered into the dim room, "on my own strength, my own abilities. 'Tis hard to trust another with my troubles. Even you." She pressed her palm to her chest. "Help me," she pleaded. "Help me trust ye more."

The hiss of the kettle brought her back to her surroundings. Claire opened her eyes and pushed to her feet. She collected a large mug from the cupboard and pulled out the tea tin. Wrapping a towel around her hand, she reached for the kettle's handle, only to jerk her hand back when a sharp rap sounded on the front door. Her heart pounded at the unexpected sound.

Afraid the knocking would wake Liam, she scooted the kettle to a cooler part of the stove, then hurried to the door. Taking a moment to tighten her wrapper, she held the collar closed at the neck, then eased the door open a couple inches.

"Yes?"

"I need Maybelle. All my young'uns are ailing something fierce." Beulah Clark, a new resident living in one of the poorer houses

on the outskirts of Harper's Station, wrung her hands, her countenance even more haggard than Claire's. "Please, miss. I don't
know what else to do for 'em."

Claire glanced back toward her bedroom, where Liam slept . . .
and sighed. There was nothing for it. What needed to be done,
needed to be done. Hadn't she just asked the Lord for strength?
She guessed he'd decided she needed to practice leaning on him
right away.

"Maybelle's out at the farm." Another new resident had come
to them six weeks ago, heavy with child. Betty had taken Susannah under her wing, eager for a new girl to cluck over after Helen
left to marry her Pinkerton. Susannah had gone into labor right
after supper tonight. Maybelle would be busy with the birthing
until well after dawn. "Give me a minute to dress," Claire said,
"and I'll come."

"Thank you, miss. Thank you."

Claire nodded. "Go on back to yer little ones. I'll be along in
a blink."

Beulah thanked her one last time, then scurried away, her lantern
lighting her path. Claire closed the door, hurried to her room, and
changed into a loose-fitting calico dress that wouldn't require a
corset.

A mother's worst nightmare—a sick child. Or children, in Beulah's case. She had three. Darting a glance toward Liam, Claire's
heart squeezed. Such a precious, fragile life. She whispered a prayer
for the Clark children, then gathered the bag Polly had sent her
and restocked it with diapers, Liam's bottle, and two clean gowns.

"Sorry, me darlin', but duty calls." Claire gently eased the baby
basket off the floor, careful not to disrupt the sleeping babe. "Aunt
Emma will take good care o' ye while I'm away. There're other
children needin' me tonight, but I'll be back soon, me love. Have
no fear."

She moved quickly through the house, stopping by the examination room to grab the doctor's bag she always kept packed and
ready. Next to the medical bag was a small barn lantern. She lit

the wick and fit the globe into place. Then, with the baby basket in one hand and the medical bag, baby supplies, and lantern in the other, she made her way to the station house.

Bertie Chandler, one of Emma's aunts, answered Claire's knock and gladly took charge of Liam.

"Don't you worry about a thing, now," Bertie said as Claire tried to give her advice about everything from changing a nappy to milking the goat. "Between Emma, Henry, and me, this little man will want for nothing. You go on and help poor Beulah. We'll take care of Liam."

Something pinched Claire's chest as she turned to leave. How had she become so attached to the boy so quickly? Liam had been in her life less than twenty-four hours, yet he'd already taken up permanent residence in her heart.

Hesitating, she pressed a kiss to her fingertips, then touched them to his forehead. "Mam'll be back soon, love," she whispered. Then she pivoted away from the door, held her lantern aloft, and strode down the road with purpose. The faster she tended to the Clarks, the faster she could return to Liam.

When she reached the ramshackle house that served as the Clark home, what she found made her heart sink. Three children, aged four to ten, shared a bed. Each was feverish, coughing, and covered in a red rash that could mean only one thing—one of the most infectious diseases in existence, and one that could prove fatal to infants and adults who'd never developed an immunity. Adults like Claire.

Oh, Liam, me love. Mam won't be seein' ye as soon as she hoped.

Not when she'd just been exposed to the measles.

Chapter

8

W hat do you mean, she won't see me?" Pieter glared at the matronly woman barring his path into the Harper's Station clinic.

After his conversation with Claire yesterday, he'd believed she was going to give him a chance to win back her trust, to prove his dedication. He couldn't believe she'd shut him out less than twelve hours later. It wasn't her nature to be so mercurial.

"She's quarantined herself in her room," Maybelle Curtis explained. Circles darkened her eyes, and her hair frizzed out around her bun as if she hadn't seen her bed in days. "Won't let me in, just shoved this letter under the door and out into the hall where I could find it."

The midwife pulled two folded pages from her apron pocket and handed them to him. Pieter scanned the familiar handwriting, his heart aching and then pounding in concern. Claire had been exposed to the measles and was taking precautions to contain the spread of the disease.

She mentioned a family called Clark, outlining the care she'd given them and instructing Maybelle to inform Emma Shaw of the danger so the town could be warned. All people not previously exposed to the measles should avoid the Clark house for at least three weeks until the fever and rash had fully dissipated.

Then his gaze caught on his own name.

Tell Pieter I can't see him. If complications arise, I might not be able to care for Liam. The lad will need his uncle.

Pieter glanced up at the healer. "What complications?"

Mrs. Curtis sighed and took the letter back from him. "Measles is considered a childhood disease. Usually nonfatal."

Usually. Pieter's jaw clenched. He recalled having the measles as a boy. The fever, the rash, the itching. The disease had swept through the tenement the year before Claire's family arrived. Hundreds of people had fallen ill. Many had died, including a little girl who lived two doors down from his family.

"Most adults are immune after having measles in childhood," Mrs. Curtis continued, "but children under age five and adults not previously exposed run a higher risk of complications."

"Like death." The word nearly choked him.

"Unfortunately, yes. Lung fever can develop, or even a swelling of the brain. Claire is still young, though," the healer hurried to reassure, "only eighteen. Usually the worst cases afflict those much older. She's just taking precautions. In a few weeks this will be past, and all will be well."

In a few weeks . . . Pieter frowned, his mind spinning with all that would need to be done. Claire might have quarantined herself, but there was no way he was going to leave her to fight this battle alone.

He hated to keep the weary midwife from the bed she obviously longed to find, but he needed one more thing before he could go. "Can I borrow some paper and a pen?"

❧

Claire sat at the small writing desk in her room, penning a letter to her sister. She told Polly that Liam had arrived safely and gave her promise to care for him with all the love in her heart. She made no mention of measles, not wanting to cause undue concern. After all, there was a tiny chance she wouldn't contract the disease.

Ten days. That was how long she had to wait, locked up in this room. If she had no fever, no ulcers in her mouth after that time, she could break the quarantine. Until then, she'd have to find a way to stay busy in this tiny room without going crazy.

At least she'd have plenty of time to finish Bertie's bread cover. She glanced up at the dresser where she'd stuffed the bit of embroidery into the top drawer. A pang hit her chest at the thought of undoing the knots. Of cutting the threads—threads Pieter had likened to the ties that bound the two of them together.

She couldn't snip those strings as if they meant nothing. They'd become a symbol, a talisman, almost.

It wasn't as if she didn't have plenty of time on her hands to start over on a new cloth. Bertie would still have her gift, and Claire would have her knots.

"Whist! Ye silly goose. Savin' knots. Yer turnin' into a senti-mental fool, ye are." And talking to herself, too. Goodness. The craziness had started already.

A knock on her door brought her head around. "Yes?"

"I'm headed to bed," Maybelle announced through the door. The poor woman had been up all night with the birthing.

Claire dearly wished she could do more to help her mentor, but she dared not risk leaving her room for anything but the outhouse. And even then, she intended to wear a scarf over her mouth and nose. Thank heavens the Clarks were already isolated from the rest of town by a good two miles. She trusted Emma to get the word out and Malachi to enforce the quarantine. Harper's Station would not fall prey to an epidemic on her watch.

The sound of paper sliding against wood brought Claire's attention to the floor, where a white sheet was being pushed under her door.

"Your man left a note for you. Didn't like me turning him away." A soft chuckle filtered in from the hall. "Left here like a man on a mission, he did. All fired up, energy vibrating the very air. If I were a betting woman, which I ain't, I'd lay good odds on him bein' back sooner rather than later."

Not knowing how to respond to Maybelle's prediction, Claire remained mute. Slowly, she stood and collected the paper from the floor.

"Good ones are hard to find, Claire," Maybelle said in a quiet voice. "If you're blessed enough to find one, don't let fear steal him from you. Hold on for all you're worth."

Claire's grip on the folded page tightened without her even realizing it, crinkling it into creases.

"All right. Well . . . enough meddling. These old bones need rest. I'll bring you a supper tray later this evening."

"Thank you," Claire finally managed.

She waited until Maybelle's footsteps faded, then sat on the edge of her bed and unfolded the letter. A smile curved her lips as she saw only four short lines. Ah, Pieter. Never one to draw a conversation out with unnecessary words.

> *I'll make sure Liam has everything he needs. Mrs. Curtis told me you won't know right away if you have the measles, so I'm going to tend to some business in Snyder, then be back for you. We'll fight this together, Claire. You're not alone.*
>
> *Pieter*

A poet he wasn't, but no amount of fancy verse could have touched her heart as deeply as those last few words. *We'll fight this together. You're not alone.*

He was knotting the threads again, and heaven preserve her, she longed to pull them tight.

Seven days later, the first ulcer appeared in Claire's mouth. Two days after that, fever arrived, and with it, one stubborn Dutchman. No woman wanted her man to see her sweaty and ill or covered with a blotchy red rash, but Pieter would not be deterred. He barged into her private quarters and quarantined himself inside with her.

"Ye can't be in here," Claire protested weakly from beneath the thick pile of quilts that couldn't seem to keep her warm. "Ye need to tend to Liam."

Pieter crossed his arms over his chest and braced his legs apart as if he expected her to jump from the bed and physically push him out the door. As if she could move that solid oak of a man even when she wasn't shaking with chills.

"We're in a town full of women," he stated as if she were the daft one, not him. "The boy has at least a dozen caregivers lining up to take turns with him. He's fine. You're the one I need to be tending."

"But I'm miserable and grumpy and ugly as a speckled toad." A coughing spasm interrupted her pitiful whining.

A strong arm supported her back and raised her to a sitting position. A glass of water appeared in front of her pouting, rash-covered face. After her chest stopped seizing, she lifted her gaze to his. Those golden-brown eyes. So serious, so intent. So full of compassion and love. She accepted the glass. And him.

"I can handle miserable and grumpy," he said as she sipped the water, his eyes dancing slightly. "And while those spots *do* clash with your hair and hide the freckles I love so much, I can look past that." He smiled. That sweet half-smile that lit up his eyes and made her heart melt.

When a bout of shivers wracked her body and set her teeth to chattering, he stretched out beside her on top of the covers, fit his body against her back, and curled an arm around her, tucking her close to his wonderfully warm frame. A sigh of pure pleasure escaped her as his heat seeped into her fever-chilled bones. She relaxed against him, the shivers slowing, then stopping altogether.

As sleep claimed her, only one thought penetrated her fevered mind—*this* was where she belonged.

A week later, Pieter stood with arms braced on Claire's dresser, trying to dredge up the energy to shave. Mrs. Curtis had pestered him again this morning to get out of the sickroom and take in some fresh air. He'd refused, of course. Nothing was going to take him from Claire's side while she was so ill. The midwife had dubbed him a muleheaded clodhopper, but she'd left, so he hadn't thought any more about it. Until she barged in with a basin full of hot water and a demand that he clean himself up.

He bent down to peek in the oval mirror above the dresser. Thick, blond stubble covered his sunken cheeks. Dull, haggard eyes stared back at him. No wonder Mrs. Curtis had been harping. He looked like one of the disreputable fellows who loitered in alleyways behind saloons. Undernourished, unbathed, and beaten down by life.

How was he supposed to encourage Claire to fight for their future together, for her very life, when he looked half dead himself?

After a quick scowl at his reflection, he turned away and stripped out of his shirt. He soaped up a washrag in the basin, then scoured his skin, determined to be clean and fresh when Claire awoke. It might seem a small thing, but at this point, he'd take any advantage he could find.

She'd been growing steadily weaker and spent more of each day asleep, when she wasn't coughing or scratching at her rash. Mrs. Curtis bathed her once a day and used talc to help battle the itch, but Claire still suffered.

Those beautiful blue eyes of hers had gone bloodshot and lost their spark. Her face had grown thin and pale, and her arms had weakened to the point that she couldn't even hold up a book to read any longer. He read aloud to her, silently mourning the loss of the unflagging vigor and vitality that had always been her hallmark. The red spots on her skin were turning brown, which Mrs. Curtis claimed was a sign that the disease had nearly run its course, yet Claire's cough only seemed to worsen.

Pieter prayed while he shaved, begging the Lord with every stroke of the razor to heal the woman he loved, to strengthen her body and her spirit. *Please. I can't lose her again.*

"This fever is playin' interestin' tricks with me mind," a voice rasped from behind him, "for I swear I see Pieter van Duren half dressed in me bedchamber."

He turned, reaching for a towel to wipe the last of the shaving soap from his jaw, an embarrassed flush heating his neck. Where was his shirt? He scanned the floor, found the discarded piece of clothing, and held it up in front of him.

"Don't go coverin' up on my account." She wagged a hand as she scooted around to lay on her side. On a diagonal. Facing him. Was she . . . trying to get a better view? "'Tis the best thing to happen to me since this dratted sickness started."

Apparently so.

Pieter couldn't quite tame the smile that crept onto his face. He'd never been a vain man, but he had to admit that knowing Claire admired his physique was rather invigorating.

Claire eyed him up and down, then her brow puckered into a small frown. "Why aren't ye in Snyder? I thought ye had dairy cows comin' in."

Tossing the old shirt into a corner, Pieter let her look a little longer as he rummaged through his satchel for a clean one. "They came in last week."

"Last week!" she screeched, then immediately started coughing. Hard.

Pieter ran to the bed and helped her sit up, alarmed at the way she grabbed at her chest. "Easy," he crooned. He cradled her cheek against his torso, wrapped his arms around her, and rocked. "Don't try to talk."

As soon as the spasm relaxed, she pushed away from him and glared. "Don't ye be tellin' me not to talk, ye daft man. I'll say me piece, and ye won't be stoppin' me." The glare softened, and her hand clutched at his arm. "Please, Pieter, don't throw away all ye've worked to build. I'll be fine. Go to Snyder. Get yer cows. Set up yer dairy. I'll bring Liam to see ye when I'm back on me feet again. I swear it."

Her hand on his arm was warm. Too warm. He frowned. "I spent a few days in Snyder before your fever hit, remember?"

Her brow crinkled again.

"I met a family at the church there who live just a mile down the road from my place. They got a boy, fifteen, who agreed to tend my cows and milk them twice a day. Told him he could sell the milk and keep the money as recompense."

"Ye're trusting complete strangers?" She sounded incredulous.

He couldn't blame her. He'd never been one to delegate responsibility to others. He preferred doing things himself to ensure they were done right. This situation was far from ideal, but God had provided neighbors with a heart to help, and he'd stepped out in faith. He'd had no choice, really. He couldn't be in two places at once, and he *had* to be here.

"The Muellers are good folks," he said. "Their own farm is in fine repair, barn clean, animals well tended. My girls will be fine."

Claire fell silent, and a tear rolled from the corner of one red-rimmed eye. "Ye chose me over yer future," she whispered.

"You *are* my future, Claire. Nothing is more important to me than you."

She shook her head. "I've been such a stubborn fool, Pieter. I've wasted so much—" Another spasm of coughing hit her. Harder this time. So fierce she doubled over and moaned at the pain.

Nothing Pieter did seemed to help. Holding. Rocking. He even tried lifting her arms above her head like his *moeder* had done for him when he was a boy. It did no good. She kept coughing, spitting up yellow phlegm, then started to wheeze. His heart pounded. Something was seriously wrong.

Suddenly her hand grasped his arm again. Nails biting into his skin. "Can't . . . breathe . . ."

Pieter set her away from him and ran out of the room. "Mrs. Curtis!" he yelled at the top of his voice, praying she wasn't out on a house call.

The sound of hurried steps shot relief through him. He headed toward the sound and nearly ran the healer down outside the kitchen. She jerked backward, blinked once at the sight of his bare chest, then moved around him.

"She can't breathe," Pieter said as he followed her back to Claire's room.

"The fever's moved to her lungs." Her pronouncement shot terror into Pieter's heart. *Complications.* "Bring the kettle from the stove. We'll fill the basin and prop her head over it. Inhaling the steam should help calm the spasms."

Pieter dashed back to the kitchen to fetch the kettle. Within minutes, Mrs. Curtis had Claire bent over the steaming basin, a towel covering her head and draping down over the bowl.

Gradually Claire's breathing calmed, and with it, Pieter's pulse.

"I'll make a garlic paste to rub on her chest," Mrs. Curtis said, more to herself than to Pieter. "I'll fix a tonic of water, lemon, and cayenne pepper, too. If you can get her to drink a dose four to five times a day, it might help clear her lungs."

Pieter nodded. He'd see it done. "What else can I do?"

She met his gaze over Claire's bent head. "Pray, Mr. van Duren. Pray."

Chapter

9

laire woke up clearheaded for the first time in . . . well, she couldn't recall precisely how long it had been. The first thing her clearheaded mind registered was a stiffness in her limbs that demanded release. She slowly uncurled her legs, sighing slightly at the delicious stretch. As she added her arms, she became aware of a low rumbling sound vibrating somewhere beneath her. Frowning, she rolled onto her side, lifted up on one elbow, craned her neck toward the floor, and found the source of the rumble.

Pieter.

She smiled. He was snoring.

He lay sprawled on a pallet of Maybelle's quilts, rolled toward her, one arm stretched toward the bed as if even in sleep he strove to be close to her. Her heart gave a little kick. Her gaze roamed his face, so relaxed in sleep yet still bearing evidence of his fatigue. Dark smudges beneath his eyes. Lines across his forehead. His stubble had grown along his cheeks and chin, giving the straight-laced, devout man she loved a touch of ruggedness. She rather liked it.

What an ordeal she'd put him through. Yet he'd done exactly

what he'd promised. He'd stayed by her side every minute. How had she ever doubted his commitment, his steadfastness? One mistake did not define a man's character. Actions over a lifetime did. And Pieter van Duren was nothing if not dependable, faithful, and honorable to the core. Maybelle was right. She'd be a fool to let fear steal him away.

Claire sighed. Then wrinkled her nose as a horrid smell wafted upward into her nostrils. What *was* that? She sniffed again. Garlic. She tilted her chin down to examine her chest. A garlic plaster. Smeared from her neck to places unknown beneath her nightgown.

She couldn't tell Pieter she'd changed her mind about marrying him while covered in dried sweat and garlic. A woman had her standards.

Rolling quietly out of bed, she stood on legs as wobbly as a new foal's but managed to maintain her verticality long enough to fetch a clean dress from the wardrobe and undergarments from the dresser. An urge to cough rose in her chest, but she managed to restrain it until she was in the hall and had closed the door behind her. She lifted her arm to muffle the rasping as the spasm wracked her chest. With much less pain than she'd previously experienced. In fact, besides a slight rub in her throat, it didn't hurt at all.

Thank ye, Lord. Then, thinking of Pieter and the noise she'd just made, she added to her petition. *Let him sleep. Please. He needs the rest.*

And heaven knew, she needed a bath.

Pieter rolled onto his back and froze. Instantly awake, he tore open his sleep-roughened eyes, heart pounding.

Claire.

He couldn't hear her. He jolted to a sitting position and scanned the bed. Empty.

"Claire?"

Where was she? He scrambled to his feet and hurried to the opposite side of the bed. No, she hadn't fallen onto the floor.

So where had she gone? And how could he have slept through her leaving? For two weeks he'd been attuned to every breath she took. Every twitch of muscle. Every sound. How could he have just . . . lost her?

He rushed to the door, tore it open, and bellowed for Mrs. Curtis as he raced down the short hall to the kitchen. The sight there pulled him up short.

"You know, Claire," Mrs. Curtis said idly as she lifted a spoonful of soup from the bowl sitting on the table in front of her, "you really ought to train that man of yours to keep his voice down. This is a clinic, after all. It's not good for our patients' nerves to have wild men running about unshaven and rumpled. It's unsettling."

"I don't know about that," Claire said, her gaze drifting to Pieter as her lips quirked in a smile. "A bit of wildness now and again can be good for the circulation. Gets the heart pumpin', ye know."

Pieter just stood there, drinking her in. Claire . . . healthy, beautiful Claire. Alive. Radiant. Perhaps still a tad pale and thin, but that would right itself with time. Her fiery hair glowed in waves down her back, damp and drying in the heat emanating from the kitchen stove. The red measles spots had finished fading away, leaving only her adorable freckles to dance across her cheeks.

He blinked against the overwhelming gratitude threatening to spill from his eyes. She had made it through. He'd never be able to thank the Lord enough.

Mrs. Curtis stood and walked to the stove, taking a third bowl from a nearby cupboard on her way. She ladled out a healthy serving of what smelled like chicken soup, though Pieter didn't take his eyes off Claire to verify. The healer strode up to him and pushed the bowl into his hands.

"Her fever broke sometime last night," she said in a low voice. "I listened to her lungs after she finished her bath, and they sounded clear. She might have a lingering cough for a few days, but she's on the mend. The worst is past."

"Thank God." Pieter fit his hands to the bowl, the warmth traveling from his fingers to his heart, melting away the fear he'd tried so hard to ignore during the last fortnight. Finally, he turned his attention from Claire to the woman before him. "And thank you, ma'am. I wouldn't have known what to do. If there's ever anything I can do for you . . ."

She touched his arm. "Just take care of my girl, Mr. van Duren. That's all I ask."

He nodded solemnly. "I will, ma'am. You have my word."

She patted his arm, then turned and moved toward the front room. "I'll be in the clinic if you need me, Claire." She tossed a wink over her shoulder at Pieter. "But something tells me you won't."

Feeling grubby compared to the sweet vision sitting at the table, Pieter needed a moment to get his feet to work, but his compulsion to celebrate Claire's recovery eventually drove all self-consciousness from his mind. He pulled out the chair next to hers and folded himself into it. Glancing at her bowl, he noted that she'd eaten almost its entire contents, and another wave of thanksgiving swelled inside. Fever gone. Appetite returned. And her bright blue eyes had reclaimed their sparkle. His world was back on its proper axis.

His stomach rumbled, but before he reached for a spoon, he covered Claire's hand with his. "Thank you for not leaving me." His rough, emotion-clogged voice shook slightly as his heart poured out its raw truth.

She squeezed his hand, tears shimmering in her eyes. "I'll not be leavin' ye ever again, Pieter. I swear it." Her vow, so fervent and heartfelt, made his blood surge with triumph. Then that sassy smile he loved so well flashed at him. "All ye got to do is put a ring on me finger, and I'll be yours forever."

His breathing stilled. "Does that mean . . ."

"Aye, ye daft man. I'll marry ye. If'n ye'll still have me. There's no one on this earth I trust more with my future than you, Pieter van Duren. It's always been that way. I simply . . . forgot for a while, is all."

Pieter beamed at her, his smile wide enough to swallow his ears had they not been attached to his head. Then he yanked his hand away from hers, jumped to his feet, and dug into his trouser pocket for the item he'd carried on his person since the day he left New York.

"Heaven preserve us, Pieter. What kind of strange jig are ye—"

Her words died away as he finally grasped what he'd been searching for and dropped to one knee.

Between thumb and forefinger, he extended the silver ring he'd purchased nearly a year ago, the one specially crafted into the shape of a Celtic symbol Polly had told him about.

Claire's blue eyes misted over and her hands trembled as she reached out to cup both sides of his proffered hand. "'Tis a love knot," she whispered, one finger tracing the simple figure-eight design at the center of the ring. "Oh, Pieter. 'Tis the most perfect thing I've e'er seen."

"I've carried it with me every day since I left home. And while I understand we need time for you to fully recover and for me to find a parson before we wed, would you let me put it on your finger now? So I can make you mine forever, just as you said?"

Her gaze melded with his. She bit her bottom lip, then nodded. "'Twould be me honor to wear yer ring, Pieter. To tie my future to yours and follow ye all of my days."

Gently, Pieter clasped Claire's left hand and slid the ring onto her finger. "I love you, Claire Nevin. And I pledge to do everything in my power to make you happy as we live out our days together."

She watched the ring slide into place, then lifted her face to meet his eyes. "Just love me, Pieter. That's all I need."

Pulse pounding, blood thrumming, Pieter pushed to his feet and swept Claire along with him. Holding her close to his heart, he bent his head and kissed her with all the love surging through his veins. Her arms wound around his neck as she leaned into his chest, her head tilting back to give him better access.

The girl he'd loved for half his life was finally his, and he would never let her go.

Epilogue

ONE MONTH LATER

Dearest Polly,

Two weeks after the wedding, I'm still not used to people calling me Mrs. van Duren. After nearly nineteen years with one name, it feels odd to be addressed by another. Yet I couldn't be happier about the change.

You were right all along, sister. Pieter is everything I ever wanted in a man. Not perfect, but wonderful just the same. And Liam is such a blessing to us. He's pushing up on his elbows these days and has figured out how to roll onto his back. Such a clever lad. Soon he'll have the entire roll mastered, and I'll really need to stay on my toes.

Life in Snyder is good. It's a rougher town than Harper's Station, but that's to be expected in a place founded by a former buffalo hunter. Word has spread about my work as a healer, though, and some of the women around town are seeking my advice.

Pieter's dairy business is gaining ground. He wants to teach me how to make cheese. Can you imagine? An Irish-woman making Dutch cheese. I told him he's daft, but I think he believes that to be a term of endearment, for he just smiles and drops a kiss on my cheek whenever I call him that.

I was so thankful to hear that Miss Fester took you on. Not that I doubted she would. She recognizes a fine hand when she sees it and knows your beadwork will fetch her a pretty penny. I pray for you often and hope one day you'll find—

Liam began to fuss, waking from his morning nap earlier than expected. Claire set down her pen and started to get up from the desk, but Pieter was faster.

"I've got him," he said, picking up the baby from where she'd laid him in the middle of the bed. Pieter made shushing noises and cradled the child in his arms. He paced the small room, his deep voice crooning a Dutch lullaby.

> Slaap, kindje, slaap.
> Daar buiten loopt een schaap.
> Een schaap met witte voetjes,
> Dat drinkt zijn melk zo zoetjes.

Something about a sheep with white feet walking and drinking sweet milk. Claire smiled to herself as she listened to her husband's fine voice. 'Twas a fitting song for a dairyman's son.

Her old room at the clinic was barely large enough for her husband to take four steps before he had to change direction, but Pieter didn't seem to mind. They'd arrived in Harper's Station last night for the groundbreaking ceremony scheduled for this morning, and Maybelle had been kind enough to welcome them back to the clinic.

Claire glanced around the small space. So many memories in this room. In this town. Dear friends—some of whom she hadn't seen in months.

"Is he settled enough for an outing?" she asked, suddenly

desperate to reunite with the women who had meant so much to her when her life had been falling apart. She crossed the floor to meet Pieter pacing back from the door. "I know it's a bit early yet, but I'm dyin' to see everyone. Surely at least Emma will be out and about, settin' everythin' to rights afore the ceremony. Would ye mind if we took a stroll through town to see?"

Pieter smiled that heart-melting half-smile of his and pressed a soft kiss to her forehead. "Lead the way, my love."

Oh, how she loved this man. On impulse, she rose up on her tiptoes, grabbed his face with both hands, and kissed him. He cooperated with admirable enthusiasm, despite the fact that his hands were tied up with Liam. By the time she pulled away, both of them were breathing a touch more raggedly than before.

Claire laughed, then spun away from him, dancing toward the door.

"It's not nice to tease a man like that, wife," Pieter growled.

Full of mischief, Claire twirled back to face him, a saucy retort on her tongue. A retort that never made it past her lips, for her husband had deftly shifted their son to one arm, freeing his other to wrap around her waist with unyielding strength. He pulled her tightly to him and took his turn in their war of kisses.

A war that raged far longer than either of them had intended. By the time they finally left the clinic, Liam was wide awake, and all of Harper's Station had gathered at the groundbreaking site— including the Clark family, Claire was happy to see, fully recovered from their own bout of measles. She waved to Beulah as she walked past the station house where the children were climbing the fence, trying to pet Malachi's horse.

"Claire!" Helen Dunbar, the dark-haired woman who had always been so reserved and somber, grinned wide enough to rival the Wichita River as she approached. "Look, Lee."

The tall man at Helen's side pivoted to face the late arrivals. "Miss Nevin." He dipped his chin. "Good to see you again."

"'Tis Mrs. van Duren now," Claire corrected, nodding to the man at her side. "This is me husband, Pieter, and our son, Liam."

Helen frowned. "But you weren't expecting when I left town a few months back. How . . . ?"

Claire smiled, not embarrassed in the slightest. How could she be, when her sister's gift had granted her the family she'd always longed for? "Liam is my nephew by blood but the son of me heart."

Mr. Dunbar limped slightly as he made his way to Pieter's side and extended his hand. "Good to know you, sir. Did your wife tell you about the time she saved my life?"

Pieter's eyes widened as he shot Claire a look.

"Don't be lookin' at me like that, Pieter van Duren. A girl has to have a few mysteries about her to keep life interestin'. Besides, Helen did all the real nursin'. I just sewed him up and applied one of me mam's bread poultices to help clear out the infection."

The Pinkerton grinned. "I don't think either of us will have to worry about life ever being dull with these two spitfires running circles around us."

Pieter nodded, his eyes warm as he met Claire's gaze. "Nope."

Emma Shaw surged into their midst, making an immediate grab for Liam. "Give me that boy, you thief." She mock scowled at Pieter before turning her full attention on the babe who had lived with her for nearly a month during Claire's quarantine. "Auntie Em missed you, Mr. Liam. Yes, she did." She held him in front of her face and buried her nose in his belly, cooing all the while. "I can't believe your mean old daddy stole you away from me and took you off to Snyder. So far. You better make him bring you back to see me on a regular basis, or I'll sic Uncle Mal on him. Yes, I will."

Everyone chuckled, including Malachi himself, who traipsed up behind his wife and slipped one arm around her thickening waist while offering a finger to Liam to grab. The babe giggled and clasped the offering, shaking his prize as if he'd just captured a dragon's tail.

"Can I play with the baby, Ma?" A young lad bounded up to the group, headed straight for Emma and Liam.

"Maybe after the ceremony, Lewis. If his mother says it's all right." Tori Porter smiled an apology to Claire as she followed in her son's wake. "He's missed having Liam to boss around and share all his manly wisdom with."

Claire chuckled softly, and Liam gave a squeal when Emma lowered him to Lewis's level. "Judging by the sound of things, I'd say the missin' was mutual. We'll definitely get them together after the groundbreakin'." Claire leaned close to Tori and whispered, "Get Lewis some practice for bein' a big brother, hmm?"

Tori's fair skin turned pink. She hadn't intimated anything, but there was a secret glow about her that made Claire's imagination spark.

A newcomer approached the group, sparing Tori from having to answer—a quiet, petite woman escorted by a man in a dapper suit and spectacles.

"Grace!" Claire cried and immediately moved to embrace her friend. "I haven't set eyes on ye in ages! 'Tis so good to see ye. And on such a wonderful occasion." She stepped back and motioned to the shovel that someone—Emma, no doubt—had tied a giant red bow around and propped against the west end of the station house paddock fence. "This women's aid refuge is such a grand idea."

Grace blushed prettily, then nodded toward her husband. "Amos is the true mastermind. I wanted to donate the funds back to the town as thanks for being my sanctuary for so many months, but Amos came up with the idea for a building to provide shelter for ladies in similar circumstances. He's quite clever with things like that."

Mr. Bledsoe covered the hand Grace had laid upon his arm with his own, the movement brimming with such affection that Claire couldn't help but move a step closer to her own man, seeking the same connection—one Pieter readily supplied by placing his warm hand on the small of her back.

"A refuge seemed like the best way to honor what Harper's Station stands for, especially now that citizens of the male persuasion are working their way into the community," Amos said, his eyes lighting with humor as he glanced from one man to another in their circle.

Grace grinned at the ladies. "My Amos is very forward-thinking."

"He rides a mean bicycle, too," a crotchety voice added to the convivial gathering. "And don't think I'm going to let you leave without giving me another lesson, young man." Henry Chandler shook a scolding finger at Amos Bledsoe. "You still haven't taught me how to do those leaping stops of yours."

"Heaven forbid, Aunt Henry," Emma exclaimed before Mr. Bledsoe could give an answer. "You'll give me heart palpitations. And you know that's not good for me in my condition."

"Bah! Your condition's as hearty as ever. You take after my side of the family."

Claire grinned at the two older ladies who'd joined the group. As the elder Chandler sister matched wits with Emma, Claire focused on the younger. "How I've missed ye, Bertie."

"And I've missed you, dear. *All* of you." Bertie Chandler, the rounder, softer of the two Chandler sisters, embraced Grace and Helen on her way to Claire. She encircled Claire in a warm hug, then released her to clasp her hand. "I think of you every time I use that beautiful bread cloth you embroidered for me, but it's not the same as seeing your lovely self in person. Still knotted to that young man of yours, I see." Her knowing smile brought an answering grin to Claire's face. After her recovery from the measles, she'd shown Bertie the original bread cloth covered in knots and explained why she'd not had the heart to take them out.

Bertie had encouraged her to keep the cloth tucked away in a special place to bring out whenever times grew rough or even just when Pieter started grating on her nerves. It would serve as a reminder of her commitment, her choice to bind herself to this man and hold fast to him.

"Adding new knots every day," Claire said. "I do believe we're so well tangled we'll never be free of each other."

Bertie's eyes glowed with pleasure. "Exactly as the Lord intended. '*What therefore God hath joined together, let not man put asunder.*'"

"Aye, there'll be no asunderin' with us," Claire vowed, seeking Pieter out where he stood among the men. His head turned as if he sensed her regard, and the heat of his golden-brown gaze warmed her down to her toes. "Just love, trust, and enough forgiveness and laughter to keep us smilin' the rest of our days."

A KINCAID BRIDES NOVELLA

THE *Tangled* TIES THAT BIND

MARY CONNEALY

Chapter

1

*H*ome. One more hour on the trail and Connor Kincaid would be home for the first time in five years. Only he realized he wasn't thinking of Pa and Ma and their house. He was thinking of Uncle Ethan's place. Maybe because it was closer and he'd go right by—so of course he'd stop. Maybe because once he got to Uncle Ethan's, he was on Kincaid land and that meant home.

Or maybe he was just wanting to see Maggie again. His childhood best friend. The beautiful fifteen-year-old girl who made Connor feel things he had no business feeling for a cousin—who was in no way a real cousin.

Those unruly feelings were a big part of why he'd ridden away. But he was all grown up now, and she'd be grown up, too, and he could feel anything he wanted.

It was a perfect day in the Rockies. He rode along the stony trail, trees thick on both sides, skirting around the northern base of Pike's Peak, daydreaming about a grown-up Maggie.

A strange, unnatural rasp jerked his thoughts back to the present.

Between one heartbeat and the next he drew, cocked, and aimed his pistol.

A twig snapped.

"Who's there?" A woman hollering was a whole lot more than a snapping twig to get a man's attention.

Then she shouted, "Be careful!" A short scream stopped any more words from being voiced.

"Be careful of what?" He holstered his gun. He wasn't going to start shooting until he knew what he was aiming at.

Through the thick leaves he saw the branches of a skinny oak tree shake like they were caught in a cyclone.

He ground-hitched his horse just in case the gray needed to make a run for it from whatever was snorting in the thicket over there.

Picking his way into the forest, he wound past a couple of trees and came face-to-face with a buffalo.

Connor could have reached out and touched its horns.

The huge cow was scratching her backside against a slender tree, which explained the image of a cyclone. Then she spotted him and snorted hot breath and buffalo spit in Connor's face.

The buffalo swung its massive head at Connor, who threw himself backward. He crashed into a tree, so he didn't get that far back. The horns barely missed him.

"Climb!" The screaming cut through his panic. He leapt, grabbed a branch, and swung his legs up. A slashing horn caught his left foot and ripped the boot right off.

The blow almost knocked Connor out of the tree. The bark scraped up both hands, and he banged his head against the bottom of the limb. But he had the grit to hang on, wrapping his legs around the branch.

The buffalo lifted its head high, missed him with her horns but cracked into Connor's back. It sent him flying, except he somehow was able to cling to the branch. The painful whack had flipped him over the limb so that now he was on top of it and out of the buffalo's reach.

He hoped, anyway.

He grabbed the branch above him and stood, finally able to quit fighting for his life, which gave him time to ache in every muscle and joint. He looked down, between the toe of one boot and the sock on his other foot. The cow looked up. Connor's Stetson hung from one horn. The lousy hat thief.

The cow wasn't that far below. Connor crouched, made a swipe, and snatched up his hat. She slashed at him with her horns and nearly snagged his arm. He decided he wouldn't be so brave trying to fetch his boot.

He plunked his hat on his head with hands he noticed were shaking.

Then he heard, "I told you to be careful."

He lifted his head and looked straight into a pair of pale blue eyes, rife with irritation and maybe a little panic.

"Maggie?"

"Connor!" A bright smile bloomed on her face. "Welcome home."

It was Maggie all right, and she sure had changed. Great land of milk and honey, cute little Maggie had grown all the way up into the most beautiful woman who could possibly walk the earth—or in this case, walk the tree limbs.

"That buffalo's had me treed for almost an hour," Maggie said.

Connor grinned. "Next time don't yell, 'Be careful.' Instead yell, 'Be careful of the *buffalo*.' Things might've ended different, you know."

The huge cow poked her head past the stand of trees lining the trail. She bellowed mighty loud.

Hoofbeats pounded away. Unfortunately not buffalo hooves.

"And there goes my horse." That was all this mess needed. "Now I've got to walk this mountain trail another hour to Ethan's house."

"Assuming we ever get down from here."

He glared at the little pessimist, then quickly perked up. "Unless you have a horse!"

He wouldn't mind riding double with her.

"Nope. My horse ran off just like yours and for the same reason. It's almost certain my horse will go on home. I honestly expect Pa here any second now."

Her Pa was Ethan Kincaid. Uncle Ethan coming was a fine thing.

"He'll be hunting me," she said.

"Maybe my pa will come along, too." Connor sure hoped so, as he couldn't wait to see him. "I've missed him and Ma something fierce. I can't believe how long I've been away. How did the years go by so fast, anyway? Yep, I can't wait to see everyone again."

"Oh, I should tell you: Julia was invited to the grand opening of a dinosaur museum. They promised her time to study the bones, and said they'd feature her books at the museum and offer them for sale. And your ma, Aunt Callie, did some paintings of the pictures in the cave. They're big ones, not the sketches she does for the books. So her paintings will be there for sale, as well. Most of the Kincaids went south. They're going to pick up Heath and his family at the Cimarron Ranch and then all go on together."

"Ma's gone?" She'd always been a fine hand with drawing, but she'd rather ride a horse and hog-tie a longhorn than make pictures. Except Julia could be mighty persuasive. Some might say a nag. She was also about the smartest, hardest-working woman Connor had ever known, especially when it came to that big old cave.

"Yep, and none of 'em will be home for a couple of weeks."

Connor frowned. "I should have let them know I was coming."

"You most certainly should have. But then they'd have stayed to see you and missed one of the few trips most of them have ever taken. Pa and Ma are here, but everyone else is gone. Even the young'uns went along on the train."

"The *young'uns* aren't all that young anymore."

"No, though I will always be the oldest, of course. So you all seem young to me."

Connor gave her a wild smile. "I'm counting the two of us as tied."

Maggie sniffed. "Go ahead and pretend if it makes you feel better."

For as long as he could remember, Maggie had been teasing him about their age difference. She was a few months older and never let him forget it. He'd missed her like crazy.

"Pa went along, too?"

Connor's pa, Seth, was Ethan's little brother. Pa lived near Ethan and his big brother Rafe, Julia's husband, on the Kincaid Ranch. Connor was well aware that, while Maggie considered Ethan her pa, Ethan's wife, Audra, came into the marriage with two little girls. Maggie and Connor didn't share a drop of blood.

"Only my folks stayed to do the chores. Ma has a sprained ankle, so she couldn't travel well, and that made picking who stayed behind easy. I'm here helping take care of her."

The tree started rocking back and forth. Connor gripped the wobbling trunk. He looked down to see the buffalo—its hide coarse from a half-shed winter coat—go back to scratching. She'd picked Connor's tree this time.

"I can see why screaming kept you too busy to warn me better." He wrapped both arms around the trembling tree. He held on so tight, the tree whacked him in the face.

"She seems determined to scratch her whole fur coat away." Maggie looked to be calm now. Of course, it wasn't her tree that was shaking. "I suspect every downed tree in this forest can be laid right at her feet."

Watching the buffalo rub her hindquarters, Connor said, "Or laid at her backside."

Maggie giggled. It was about the prettiest sound Connor had ever heard.

He looked around at the thick branches, all intertwined with other trees. "I think with some finagling I can climb from this tree to the one beside me. Then I can go on to the next and the next. I might get far enough away to get to the ground and run for help."

"Don't leave me here." Her smile shrank away.

The buffalo quit scratching and ambled the few feet to Maggie's tree. Connor was surprised how much better he felt without the tree shaking.

Maggie squeaked in alarm, threw her arms around the tree, and forgot about any continued conversation. Which gave him time to climb through the treetops like a giant squirrel. He looked around, saw a path of crisscrossing branches, and picked his way along them to circle around to Maggie.

She gave him a wide-eyed look while she clung to the tree.

"Do you think she's choosing trees based on there being a person in them, or will she go back to the one I was in after a while? That'd get her to stop jiggling you. Then we can get out of here."

The talk drew the buffalo's attention. It stopped scratching and stared up at Connor.

"Climb over here right now, Maggie, while she's distracted. And be quiet about it."

Maggie's hands didn't come loose from the tree. In fact, her whole body seemed frozen in place.

Connor knew he didn't have much time before that itchy buffalo started in again. Continuing his squirrel behavior, he scampered over to Maggie, drew her gently but firmly away from the tree trunk, and then, holding her hand, hurried back to his tree, then on to the next.

The buffalo kept on staring at them—all thoughts of scratching seemed far from her mind. She trailed along, winding through woods that gave before her size and weight, when Connor couldn't see the least sign of a trail.

"We've gotta keep going," Connor whispered.

"Maybe we should split up. She can only follow—" A sudden scream cut her off. Connor dove for her, catching her by one arm. Then his grip gave and he dropped her.

A squall shocked him, and he saw terror in Maggie's eyes as a baby buffalo surged to its feet. It turned and gave Maggie a good solid bunt in the backside. Fierce for one so young.

Maggie sprawled face-first in the undergrowth.

The calf ran to its mother, stumbling and falling, bawling like it was fighting for its life.

The mama seemed to . . . Connor had never heard the sound she made. It was like she was gargling with odd grunts salted in.

Connor dropped to the ground.

Pulling Maggie along, tripping, falling, scrambling up, Connor glanced back to see the cow buffalo charging, blasting through the broken trees and scrub brush. He gave up any plan to run for it.

"Up!" he shouted. "Climb! She's coming."

He shoved Maggie up a limb, but she didn't need shoving. She was moving fast, doing a good squirrel imitation of her own, and he kept right behind her. It was the first time he noticed she had on a riding skirt, and a bag hung over her head and under one arm.

He stepped on a twig poking out of one of the limbs and remembered he was missing a boot.

He didn't pay much mind to it, though, because nothing got a man's full attention like a raging buffalo.

The cow slammed into the tree only inches below his feet. The tree gave an ominous crack, but it stayed upright.

They gained a level far out of her reach.

"Change trees fast," Maggie said. "One more blow and this one might go right over."

The branches were as tightly woven here as they'd been before, so picking their way to the next tree worked.

Connor made it across, but the limbs were slender. His height made it possible to hold on to a branch overhead to lighten his weight and keep him steady.

"We're too high up for these branches to hold." Connor looked at Maggie. Her shining blue eyes were wide with panic, but she turned forward and kept moving. Maggie had always been a lot tougher than she looked.

The buffalo snorted beneath them. Connor had a sudden sick image of what would happen to Maggie if another branch broke, like before, and she fell. That buffalo would use her horns and hooves. Tough or not, Maggie wouldn't last a minute with a cow dancing on her head.

And then Connor would have to get danced on, too, because

he'd have to try to save her—what decent human being wouldn't? And he had a pistol but thought it might only make the buffalo more furious. He'd lose a fight between him and the two-thousand-pound beast. So Connor hung on tight, and when the branch he was on felt sturdy, he towed Maggie to a stop.

He inched forward until he was beside her. They leaned against the trunk and breathed hard for a few minutes, Maggie held tight in his arms. Tight except for a slender tree trunk between them, and her arms securely around him.

"Thank you, Connor." She spoke into his ear and showed no sign of letting go anytime soon. Now the buffalo stood directly below them.

"I think that answers your question about splitting up."

"Yes, it does," she said with the fervor of an oath sworn before God.

"Why are you out here, Maggie?" Might as well visit while they were trapped.

"There are some herbs back in these woods. I use them for medicine. For heaven's sake, I come here all the time. There's never been a buffalo before."

"I've heard they usually stay out on the prairie—but they can be notional. There were a few around Uncle Luke's place in Broken Wheel."

"And this one got a notion to walk in the woods and have her baby. Just my luck."

"We don't need to be this high. Let's go down some. The lower we get, the sturdier the branches, although that gets us mighty close to that cow."

"I didn't think the branches were weak there when I fell on top of that poor baby buffalo."

"The branches where we first stood weren't so wobbly. We must've found a young tree. And the calf is no poor baby." Connor pointed. "He's as tough as they come."

Maggie rubbed her backside and nodded.

Connor forced himself to look away. "He's already forgotten

about being pounced on by a woman. Now he's frolicking along-side his mama, stealing a nip of milk. Look, the baby's not even all the way dried off yet. It really is newly born."

They stood and watched the little calf's antics for a few minutes under the watchful eye of mother cow. Connor spent the time catching his breath and hunting up his backbone.

"Trees ought to be more dependable." Maggie sniffed, then straightened away. "Let's go on away from her and—"

The cow bellowed, and Maggie fell silent again.

Connor finished. "And be more careful about each step."

They descended to the next lower branch, and the buffalo raised her head and grunted. Connor felt hot buffalo breath on his socked foot.

"I think we'd have gotten out of sight if that tree hadn't wobbled so bad. She's moving slow in these woods."

"She charged mighty fast," Maggie reminded him.

"True enough. But you tried to kill her baby and set it to crying."

Maggie glared. "I did no such thing."

Connor jabbed a finger at the buffalo. "Tell her."

Maggie sighed. "Let's try again. Try not to shake the tree and be quiet. Maybe we can leave her behind."

They climbed until Connor glanced back—for the fiftieth time. He whispered, "She's out of sight."

"Shhh . . ." Connor helped Maggie climb down. She didn't need much help. She'd relaxed and was quick and nimble, as steady as he was, if not more so.

The Kincaids had always been a family crazy for climbing. His pa craziest of all, though Rafe's wife, Aunt Julia, was always climbing around in that cavern, to the point that they called it Julia's Cavern.

They finally reached solid ground, and Connor stepped on a sharp stick, remembering too late that he had only one boot on.

"I have to go back," he said.

Maggie's hand wrapped around his arm with the force and sting of a bullwhip. "You will do no such thing."

"I'm half barefoot." He pointed at his sock.

"I don't think going back is a good idea." With a wary eye, Maggie looked between the rock-studded road and the trail leading back the way they'd come.

"I reckon not." He wiggled his toes. Honestly, these were the only boots he owned. "I have to get back my other boot at some point, but for now, considering the buffalo, let's head for home. Later, when we're sure that cranky mama is gone, we'll come back." He hesitated. "Can we find the exact spot?" He hadn't been here in a long time, and the trail had changed a lot.

"I can. My pa can."

By which she meant he wasn't as smart as them. Connor gritted his teeth as he led her toward the trail. He managed to find a sharp twig or a sharper rock with every step he took. This was going to be a long walk. He reminded himself he'd headed home to see his Colorado family. He flinched and hopped on his booted foot a few steps and tried to remember why he'd missed them so much.

Chapter

2

She'd missed Connor so much that she could barely keep from punching him in the nose.

He'd been her best friend while growing up together. Then he'd up and left her. Left her as if she were dirt to be scraped off his boots, as if she meant no more than any other cousin of his. Which she'd finally accepted as the plain truth.

They'd run wild together in the woods, watched more babies come into the family. Learned at a young age to be sturdy little cowboys. Not that big a deal for Connor, a boy. But when Ethan Kincaid had become her pa, he'd also become her champion, letting Maggie go with him everywhere when many girls would've been kept to the house.

Connor's ma was a big influence because she was a top hand, a tough cowpoke, and living proof that a woman oughta know how to take care of herself.

Aunt Callie also taught Maggie to punch. Considering Maggie was a little older than Connor and about half his size, Callie had thought it best that Maggie learn to hold her own.

Connor was a wild man part of the time, and sweet and protective all of the time—yes, even when he was acting wild—and he never punched back. It all added up to her being in love with him all her life, the backstabbing, abandoning rat.

And now here he was. Three inches taller than before, shoulders broad enough to bear any weight, his hair brown and messy, and with those wild blue eyes. Connor was the spitting image of Uncle Seth, funny and teasing and protective as ever, acting like he hadn't been gone five long, dreadful years.

She'd broken herself of the bad habit of punching over the years, but she would've taken it back up in a heartbeat if Connor wasn't about a foot taller than her.

Though he looked like Uncle Seth, Connor had a quiet toughness about him that was more like Aunt Callie, except when that flash of wildness popped out, which was his pa again. And a combination she found captivating.

And here he was saving her from a buffalo, although she would've been just fine without him. Pa would've come sooner or later, and she was sure that tree would've stayed standing and she would've been able to hang on. Pretty sure, anyway.

He walked along, wincing once in a while. She felt herself wincing, too, in sympathy, and hoped he didn't notice. The trail they got on was wide and easy traveling on a horse—and even on foot, unless you wore nothing but a sock on one of them. There were twigs galore and plenty of pebbles.

And she was wasting probably the only time she'd have alone with him. She tried to think of family news to share.

"A neighbor boy's been sparking Lily."

A sharp look from Connor made her wonder if he was thinking overly warm thoughts about Lily. It was a very good thing that Maggie had given up punching.

"And our families are all gone except your folks?"

Did he really mean the whole family, or was he asking about Lily?

"They won't be away long." The asperity of her reply earned her another strange look. She squelched the desire to worry about what his *looks* meant. Then she realized she'd never told him about her brand-new life.

And then Maggie heard hooves on the trail. Connor caught her arms and dragged her into the trees.

"No sense being reckless. It's probably your pa, but I want to see first."

A tall, dark rider came galloping around a curve in the trail with two spare horses tied on behind his mount.

Connor glanced at Maggie. "The cavalry has arrived."

They shared a smile, then stepped out onto the trail. Connor waved. "Uncle Ethan. Howdy."

"Connor!" A laugh broke free, and Pa's face broke into a grin so wide it lifted his hat. He rode right up to Connor, leapt off his horse right before Connor would be trampled, then dragged Connor into his arms.

The two of them started talking so fast Maggie couldn't make out much of what they were saying. There was laughing and back-slapping, then Pa turned to her and slid his strong arms around her and hugged her.

"'Bout scared five years off my life when your horse came in without a rider. Then I found another horse running loose. I've been riding at a tear to find you. What happened?"

Maggie patted Pa on the chest. He wasn't her father by birth, though her earliest memories of a father—her only memories of a father—were of him. She loved him in a way that was deeper than blood.

"A buffalo was in the woods when I went in looking for mint and nettles."

"A buffalo? Around here? In 1883?"

Connor and Maggie took turns telling their buffalo story.

Pa kept giving Connor's foot worried looks.

"Let's see if we can get your boot back," Pa said, "then we'll go on home. I left behind some chores."

"All right, but we need to be careful." Maggie figured that for an obvious statement.

Connor gave her a private smile, the kind they'd shared as children when their parents were doing everything wrong. Maggie had to fake a few with her very nice parents just so Connor wouldn't feel like their fussing was all about his pa.

"Pa, do you have any advice about avoiding a buffalo cow should we happen to run into her again?" Maggie asked with sarcastic sweetness.

"I've heard they've got real bad eyesight, so they don't exactly see you coming, they only see you when you get there. So they'll stand around grazing as you get closer and closer. Then you decide they're just tame, friendly critters. Until they see you. Then they gore you to death so fast no one can avoid it or dodge those horns."

"Weren't nothin' tame about the one we found," Conner said as they rode back to the spot where he'd been treed.

"I reckon I already had her all stirred up." Maggie knew someone would get to where they were blaming her. She was just ahead of them. She really should have yelled, "*Watch out for the buffalo!*"

Connor rode side by side with her and Pa. He gave her that heart-stirring smile. "Long as we live through it, we'll have a story to tell for the ages. Let's get my boot and get out of here alive and then start polishing this story. It'll make a great yarn to tell in the evening when the family comes back."

Connor reined his horse to a halt. "Look there."

Just heading around a curve in the trail, walking away from them, the buffalo and her calf vanished from sight.

"This is the spot." Maggie dismounted. "I didn't exactly notice it before, but now that things have calmed down, I remember something went flying when Connor was wrestling that buff. I know right where that boot went."

"Don't go in alone, Maggie."

She was already going alone. Over her shoulder, she said, "I'll be fine. I figure my excitement is over for the day."

106

She shoved through the thicket and came back in seconds with Connor's boot. He hadn't even dismounted yet.

Maybe he thought they were going to talk things over for a little longer.

Maggie handed the boot to Connor, got back in the saddle as he pulled the boot on, and then she and Pa led the way home.

Chapter

3

"Connor!" Aunt Audra screamed almost as loudly as her daughter . . . no charging buffalo anywhere. Then Audra threw her arms wide and charged. Something else that made him think of the buff.

Then he noticed her hopping, her left ankle bound with a thick wrap.

She landed, laughing and hugging him. "Connor, you're home. I've missed you so much. Your ma will be so sorry she was gone."

Audra was as slender and fine-boned as Maggie, hair white as the sunlight. Eyes blue and wide with joy. "Why didn't you write? She'd have stayed home."

Connor hugged her tight and lifted her right off her feet—or rather, foot—and spun her around. "Now hush, Aunt Audra. I'm home to stay, so a week or two makes no difference. I'm glad she's getting to travel and show off her paintings and see a bit more of the world. What happened to your leg?"

Aunt Audra shook it off like it was nothing. "Sprained ankle. I'm hobbled up some. Maggie's treating me."

Maggie got a hug next. "You're all right?" Aunt Audra asked.

Uncle Ethan started in on the buffalo and how Maggie ended up in a tree. Connor was mighty sure Aunt Audra could see Maggie and Connor both standing right here and healthy, and so, like a wise western woman, she didn't get too worked up. She hopped back to her cast-iron stove and got to work cooking.

"I've made plenty of supper. You're staying with us until your folks get home. I'm so glad you got to see Maggie."

What did she mean by that?

Aunt Audra asked about the lone buff and her baby. They kept talking about herbs. Maggie had gone to gather them, it sounded like to treat Aunt Audra's ankle. Connor's ma had given him something—willow bark?—in a tea to fight sickness. Maybe that was the kind of thing Maggie hunted for.

He heard Maggie chattering about Indian mint, stinging nettles, black snakeroot, St. John's wort. His ma's brother, Uncle Luke, was good friends with Dare Riker, the doctor in Broken Wheel, and Connor had helped Dare some, so he knew a few things about medicine.

Connor quit listening and asked Ethan, "Do I need to ride home and do chores? I could go right now and get back for supper. I want to hear all about the little ones and about Ma's painting and how the ranch is doing and the cave and—"

Ethan laughed and slapped Connor on the back. "I did a whole circuit of the ranches early this morning before I found Maggie's horse. I'd much rather eat Audra's cooking while it's hot. You can ride with me tomorrow, and I can show you a few new stretches of land we bought. We want to keep growing so there's land for all of you young'uns if you want to be part of the ranch. And I'll show you how big the herd is getting. We've brought in a lot of Angus cattle and replaced most of the longhorns in the last five years. We sold heavy on the longhorns when we'd done cattle drives and held on to the black Angus to switch the herd over to Angus faster. Plenty of 'em crossbred, but no longhorn bulls on the property anymore. Angus cattle are beautiful critters."

"Uncle Luke is breeding heavy with Herefords, and he's got a few of those big black cows and a lot of what he's calling black-white faces that are a cross between the two."

"Maybe you can teach us a few things, Connor. It's so good to have you back. Tomorrow, after our chores here and checking your place, we can ride over to Rafe's to work a while." Ethan's eyes sparked with excitement. "Maybe explore the cavern a little. Without Julia here to talk all the time, it's a mighty peaceful place. Not that I mind her talking. She knows things that are really a wonder and I like learning them. But a break from learning would give my brain a rest."

"You're going to the cavern tomorrow?" Maggie broke into the conversation. "I wish I could see it. I haven't been down there in a while."

"Come along," her pa said. "I don't blame you for wanting to go down one last time. You can take a later train. You'll miss this place once you move away."

Connor's brain skidded to a halt. He turned to stare at Maggie. Words seemed stuck in his throat, and his mouth opened and shut like a landed trout's. "Moving away? Going down one last time? One last time? That sounds like you're moving away forever."

"Not forever. Well, maybe not forever. I'll come home when I can—just like I did the last few days. I reckon I can stay one day longer, but if I do, I oughta be helping you, Ma."

"I always like having you here, honey, but I can manage now."

Connor lit up inside, the inner part of him that was so much like his pa. His crazy side.

He'd felt just like this a lot of times before, and he'd heard about the look he got in his eyes—that wild blue flash. Some things he just couldn't control. Worse yet, when he let loose his crazy side, he didn't want to control them.

Maggie had seen that flash in Connor's eyes too many times to doubt he was on the edge of one of his crazy streaks.

He'd never been able to control them. She really should've told him about Denver right away—he could've taken it out on the buffalo.

"When are you going?" He stalked right up to her. "Why are you going? Where are you going?"

And she'd never been able to figure out a way to calm him down.

"I guess we haven't talked about this yet, Connor." She tried to sound chipper, more for her parents' benefit than his.

"I live in Denver now. I'm going to school there. I made a trip home when Ma got hurt, but she's on the mend now and I'd planned on leaving in the morning. I was stocking up on medicine for her when the buffalo cornered me. You got off the train in Colorado City, but there's one out of Rawhide, and it's a short ride from here."

Ma came up and hugged her. "You've been such a great help this last week. It was nice of your school and Dr. Radcliffe to give you the time away. We're going to miss you so much."

"As if you don't have five more children to take all your attention." It was difficult, but Maggie hung on to her easy humor—at least outwardly—again for her parents' sake. If it'd been just her and Connor, she'd be tempted to kick him in the shin. How dare he come home after all these years and be upset at the choices she'd made?

"Hush," Ma said and kissed her on the top of her head before going back to setting food on the table. "I'll miss you, even if I do have plenty of children."

Pa was quick to do all the work he could to get Ma off her feet faster. He paused to rest one of his strong hands on her shoulder. "And we're so proud of you."

"Hey," Connor said, "stop with all the sweetness. Maggie can't leave."

For just one second she'd forgotten all about him.

"Let's sit down. I've made a stew for supper and it's ready. It's a bit early, but I'd think Connor might be very hungry after his travels."

"Aunt Audra, I am not gonna eat when—"

"Hush, Connor. We'll tell you all about what's in store for Maggie. It's something she's dreamed about for years."

Talked about, but not dreamed. Not at first.

Maggie had figured on waiting until Connor came home before she decided what to do with her life.

And he hadn't come.

And she'd started talking about nursing.

And he hadn't come.

And her talking turned into thinking.

And he still hadn't come.

And she'd accepted that he was never coming and got on with her life. That was when she'd begun to dream. She really, finally had. And now she wanted to follow that dream, and here came Connor home. She couldn't give up the blessed opportunity that God had so graciously provided.

After shooing Ma into a chair, she and Pa got the meal on the table. With Connor chipping in too, they were sitting down to a fine supper in minutes.

Pa asked the blessing.

She could see Connor almost vibrating with impatience. Well, she could see him until she closed her eyes and bowed her head, of course.

Pa said, "Amen."

"All right. What's going on?" Connor's words snapped like a bullwhip.

Ma gestured with her open hand to Maggie. "Tell your story."

Pa started eating but kept listening. Ma at the foot of the table didn't even pretend to eat. She watched, her eyes sliding from Maggie to Connor, who sat straight across from Maggie.

Maggie scooped up her first bite of stew but then put the spoon back down. She didn't think she could chew and talk at the same time, and Connor had his eyes aimed at her with a grim expression.

Which began to irritate her, so she told him the bald-faced truth with no interest in how he felt about it.

"I've been accepted into a nursing school in Denver. I started at the beginning of the summer. I wrote to Uncle Heath in New Mexico, and he knows a doctor who's agreed to teach me beyond the nursing so I can safely practice medicine on my own. They've agreed to charge me no fee for the college because a town named Cutler in western Colorado is in desperate need of a doctor. They are paying the cost of my education and giving me money to live on, in exchange for five years of my service in that town."

She swallowed and hoped she sounded calm. "I'm so glad I happened to be home when you got here, Connor. Of course, Denver isn't far, and I'll be there for a year at least. Cutler is impatient, but Dr. Radcliffe in Denver wants to make sure I'm fully trained. The folks at Cutler, well, they've talked of sending someone to check on my progress, and if they're satisfied, I may go by the end of the school term. I'd prefer to wait, but I'll abide by the wishes of the folks from Cutler. I'm taking an intensive course of study, so I won't get home all that often. When I move to Cutler, though, I'll be much farther away, and there are no trains that reach the town, although they hope one is coming so—"

"You're going," Connor cut in, "to some town where you know nobody? Going by yourself to a place so unsettled the train comes nowhere near it? And you'll be moving and settling there for five years?"

"At least five years, yes. I'm hoping to stay the five years and then come back here, closer to family. There's a doctor in Rawhide who said he might be ready for a partner in five years. Right now he's not keeping very busy and he couldn't make a living if he had a partner. If things work out well in Cutler, though, I might just stay."

Connor swept that aside with a slice of his hand through the air, almost hitting his plate of stew. "How settled is this town? What if there's danger? What if men accost you? What if outlaws—"

"Now, Connor," Pa said, always kind, and yet he could be tough if necessary, "do you think I'd let her go traipsing off like this if I wasn't assured it was safe? She'll be living with the town parson and his wife. They have several small children, and the town has agreed to build a new room on the house just for Maggie. Her pay will make it possible for her to help out with food at the parson's, and she can afford her own upkeep of any kind. The doctor's office will be right next to the church and the parson's house. The sheriff of Cutler is a good man. Maggie and I traveled there, and I trust him. The town is a peaceful one. Just because it's remote doesn't mean it's not a friendly town with plenty of young churchgoing families and respectable businesses."

"Why'd she make a deal like this?" Connor quickly glanced at Pa and then turned those wild blue eyes on her. "Your family could send you to school if you have to go. Then you could come back here right away and do your doctoring. You don't need to take charity from a town full of strangers."

"Connor!" she snapped, both her voice and her temper. "Of course my family could pay, but I wanted to stand on my own two feet."

"By taking money from strangers who as good as bought you for five years?"

Maggie stood so quickly her chair skidded back and tipped over.

"By finding a way to pay for this myself." Maggie slapped her hand down on the table and hit the spoon she'd dipped into her stew. The spoon flipped and landed right in Connor's face.

He slowly stood and wiped at his eyes.

Audra jumped up and hopped over to grab a wet washcloth. Connor mopped supper off his face and hands with moves slow and deliberate and furious. He braced his knuckles on the table, then leaned so far forward that Maggie worried he might be coming all the way across.

"You did that on purpose."

"I did not."

"Aw, she didn't either, Connor." Pa rested his hand on Connor's arm. "Now, c'mon. Don't yell at Maggie. That was an accident."

"My family didn't want me to go. I had to push hard to even get permission to write a letter to the school." She'd pushed more than hard, she'd tormented her parents until they said yes. She'd been desperate to get away.

"Well, they shouldn't have given in to you. It's not proper for a woman to go off alone to Denver. Even worse to go off across the state."

"She'll be safe," Ma said. "We made sure of it. And women are becoming nurses and even doctors more every day. It's quite common. And once the train goes through Cutler, she can come home and we'll be able to visit."

"The cost for the school is a good chunk of money," Pa added, "but I would've paid her tuition. I told her I would. Then Maggie contacted the school and they said they could often find money from towns just like Cutler. We would've still paid, only Maggie's a brave and independent woman now, and she wanted to do this without it costing everyone so much."

Maggie righted her chair and sank back into it. She ignored the flying spoon and began eating with her fork.

"And after our visit, we knew what the situation really was. It's a beautiful place. Snowcapped mountains and soaring eagles. A valley so green it's almost blue. Elk and buffalo." Pa's eyes turned to Maggie and sparkled. "You'll be handling buffalo like an old hand by the time you get back."

Maggie's attention was on Pa. Then a sudden movement from Connor drew her eyes. She stared at him as he sat back down, his jaw rigid.

He took a deep breath and visibly relaxed. He pulled his stew plate closer, moving Maggie's spoon aside from its final resting place on his plate.

"We'll talk about this later. And you can tell me about this dream of being a doctor. I didn't know about that." He smiled, but behind that smile his eyes still sparked and his temper simmered.

"Well, you've been gone for five years. You haven't been around to tell."

Connor's eyes flashed but he calmed himself down. He turned to Audra. "Let me tell you about Carrie and Big John. He's the law now in Broken Wheel, Texas."

He went on to pleasantly share his family news. Carrie was

Audra's little sister and they wrote often, but Maggie had only met Aunt Carrie once in her life. The town Maggie was headed for was just as remote as Broken Wheel, sunk deep in the middle of the Rocky Mountains.

She forced her thoughts away from any doubts about the promises she'd made to Cutler and instead focused on her meal. Connor's tone and expression might've been friendly enough to fool the rest of her family, but Maggie knew him too well. When he'd said they'd talk later, that was definitely a threat.

Chapter
4

I just came from the barn. Your pa is busy with a horse that went off its feed. He told us to head on over to Rafe's place."

Connor had announced this at breakfast when Uncle Ethan didn't come in. Now he and Maggie rode side by side. They could've taken a trail that passed his parents' place, but they took a shortcut instead.

His pa, Seth, the youngest of the Kincaid brothers, had a wild streak in him wider than most. Uncle Ethan, the middle brother, was a charming, friendly man who doted on his wife and their crowd of children. Rafe was the boss of the operation. He was a man who liked to be in control. Mostly Pa and Ethan let Rafe take charge. They all knew how to ranch in this rough area by now, so Rafe was just ordering them to do things they were going to do anyway, and it seemed to keep him happy.

They all had homesteads in a sort of curved line around the rugged base of the west side of Pike's Peak. It was a land of heavy woods and wasteland, but there were some open meadows lush with tall grass. The Kincaids owned a whole lot of it.

They worked together as a fine team. Connor figured he'd be

back here working with them for the rest of his life, which was part of the reason he didn't hurry back from Texas. Not the whole reason, or even the main reason. In fact, he was riding alongside the main reason he *did* come back right now.

He'd figured he had plenty of time; he never imagined anything back here would change.

Now here was a big old change.

"Maggie, when—"

"Connor, do you—"

They both spoke at the same time, and both fell silent. Then Maggie plunged on.

"Do you want to go down in Julia's cavern while we're at Rafe's place?"

That sure enough wasn't what he wanted to talk about. "We can go down if you want," he replied.

"I would love to see that cavern again," she said. "I haven't been there in a long time. Between last winter penning us in, then calving and spring roundup, and then moving to Denver—and honestly I had no real need to see it, I've seen it a thousand times, after all—I haven't been down there in close to a year. I miss it."

Connor was afraid to open his mouth. He figured she was mostly talking nonsense to stop him from having his say.

He'd better shock her into listening. "I thought we meant something special to each other, Maggie."

She turned her head so hard he could almost hear the snap. Her eyes flared with a temper she rarely showed. As a rule, she was a sweet little thing. Even when they were youngsters and she was punching him, there'd been no real mean in her.

"You've been gone for five years." There was nothing sweet in her tone now. "I decided you weren't coming back. Nothing very special about that."

"Of course I was coming back. Everybody knew that."

"I knew it, too, for about two years. The third year I decided I'd better figure out what to do with my life. The fourth year I got an idea, and I started learning about medicine and working with the doctor in Rawhide and hunting for herbs, talking with a few Indian folks still around about their natural cures and treatments. The fifth year the idea grew into a real dream. I went from thinking it'd be a decent thing to do with my life to feeling God's leading. I can help people, Connor. I can treat the sick and comfort the dying. Tend families in trouble and in grief. Bring babies into the world. Set broken bones. I can make life better for the folks in Cutler. And after I've been there a while, if I want to, I might come back and help folks here, including my own family. By then I should be an experienced doctor."

Connor watched her and listened to every word. "So you admit you were waiting for me?"

He saw her swallow hard. Quietly, with steady control, she said, "There was never any kind of understanding between us, Connor. We were good friends, close family. I know we share no blood, but we were raised family."

She reached across to rest her hand on his arm. She was being so kind it scared him.

"But you didn't come back. Years and years went by and you didn't come back." She lowered her arm, and her chin dropped nearly to her chest. "The truth is, Connor, you only had these thoughts of me when you got home and saw I'd grown up. That's flattering, I suppose, but don't act like you asked me to wait or that I'd promised to. That never happened. So I grew up and found something to do with my life that will serve the Lord and make the world a better place. I've given my word. I've taken money from the folks in Cutler and signed a contract, one I intend to honor."

Connor waved his hand impatiently. "The worst they could do is sue you, and only then to get their money back, and that'd come from the college because that's where they sent it. If they've paid for a room in Denver, we can chip in to repay it."

"What about the contract I signed?" she asked indignantly. "What about the hands I've shaken? Men and women I've looked in the eye and given my word to. My honor is something I value. I can't legally or morally change my mind. And honestly, the moral part of this means more to me than a signed contract. If a lawyer or a cash payment could get me out of it, I'd reject the lawyer and the money. I'm going."

Connor kept his mouth shut as they rode up to the corral, dismounted, and turned their horses loose. Up here was a hole in the ground that opened treacherously into a deep cavern. They looked at the little building resting over the top. They had both helped build the shed and then installed a ladder that stretched down into the hole. The shed was locked up tight so no one could fall in by accident. There was a much safer entrance across the fast-moving stream they needed to cross. Rafe's herd was over there.

"We can go down from over by Rafe's house." Maggie had grown up running free in the cavern. Connor, too. They knew its dangers, and Pa had made sure there were plenty of torches handy. Maggie patted the little tin of matches in the pocket of her brown riding skirt. She never went anywhere without matches.

"That'll be fine," Connor said and started for the ford. "We'll go exploring if we have time after chores. If your pa shows up and wants to, we'll go down."

They faced a stream that had an almost vertical bank. A line of rocks stretched across the stream, then a steep rocky trail led back up.

Once across, they saddled up a pair of the horses the Kincaids kept pastured on this side. Soon they were riding toward the canyon where Rafe lived.

Up until now, they'd walked the horses. Connor couldn't fail to notice Maggie was galloping. Made it a lot harder to talk. Her rigidly clenched jaw made it hard, too.

"Maggie, slow down! I wouldn't ask you to break your word or to do something you felt was dishonorable." Well, he had started asking her to do exactly that, but once she'd started talking about honor and morality, he'd seen the error of his ways. Besides, she looked stubborn, so he picked another method of persuasion.

She reined in to a walk but didn't say anything. He reckoned it must be his turn.

"What's in my head, well, it came to me last night while I lay awake thinking how much I was going to miss you. I'd hoped you would just change your mind about school and becoming a doctor, but I can see why that's impossible."

Honestly, he'd only been awake a while. He was a man who'd always slept well. But while he waited those couple of minutes, he'd done some thinking and this had occurred to him, and he'd immediately set it aside as . . . yep, crazy.

"It's an idea so crazy it must be right, 'cuz who thinks up crazy stuff otherwise?"

"Uh, your pa."

"Now, Maggie, Pa hasn't been what you'd call *crazy* for a long, long time."

"He has been if you count—"

"And then it never lasts long." Forging on, Connor said, "Ma has a way of shaking him out of it."

She usually threatened to "shake" him with the butt of her Winchester to the head, yet that was a detail Connor skipped. Although she never actually hit him, apparently Pa wasn't that confident she wouldn't because it really did clear his thinking.

"I suppose that's true. He wanted to offer guided tours into unknown parts of the cavern, parts he'd never even been in. He said he'd charge extra if at any point in the tour it looked like they were going to die. For some reason he thought folks would consider that a great experience."

That did sound a little touched.

Connor changed the subject back to what he'd been going to say, which, confound it, sounded crazy. "What if we . . . ?" Then his throat went bone-dry. Though he had his canteen handy, taking a drink in the middle of his sentence would be wrong. Only a galoot even dumber about women than Connor would be foolish enough to do that. He cleared his throat, then cleared it again. "What if we g-get . . . m-married?"

Maggie jerked her horse's reins so hard it reared and neighed. Connor reached out to grab the bridle and pull down on the horse's head to keep it from going over backward. Maggie was a hand with horses so she'd have probably been okay. She quickly got her mount calmed down.

"What if we get married?" she repeated, her voice loud and high.

Connor fought the urge to cover his ears.

"That's how you propose to someone?"

Honestly, he figured the idea itself was outlandish enough without his dropping to one knee.

"I want you to be safe, Maggie. And I want to be with you." Maybe he should have said that first. Although judging by Maggie's mean, narrow gaze, there really was no right way to say this. "If you won't stay, then I'm going with you. And if you won't marry me, I'll follow you to Denver and find some work there and we'll see each other whenever we can. You said the schooling is hard. I'll be mindful of that, just like you're mindful of how busy we are during roundup."

Maggie opened her mouth, then closed it, her forehead furrowed.

Since she was struck dumb, he kept on talking. "But I don't want to *follow* you, live *near* you, see you only once in a while. I want to *stay* with you in Denver and in Cutler. At the end of your day of study or work, I want you to come home to me. And to do that, we have to get married. Honestly, yesterday, after one look at the beautiful woman you've become, added to the great friends we always were, I'd already decided to start chasing you so hard you'd marry me just to get me to leave you alone. This just gets the chase over fast."

Faintly, Maggie said, "*Fast* is a fair enough word."

"I saw it in your eyes yesterday, Maggie. You missed me and you were happy to see me. We were friends, but even back then it was more than that—at least for me. I went away in part because I was feeling things for you that were wrong when we were so young. I left when I was fifteen, and if I hadn't, I think we'd have ended up married when we were sixteen."

A snort from Maggie wasn't encouraging.

"But at sixteen I was too young to be able to take care of you. I'd have been a child myself—a full-grown, hardworking child, but my pa and my bossy uncles would have done everything for us, given us land they managed, built us a house the way they wanted it, and set it nearby my ma and pa so we would have help whenever we wanted it, and a lot of times when we didn't. My whole life, no matter how much land and how many cattle I owned, I would've been nothing but a hired hand. Working for people who love both of us and only want to take care of us, but that wasn't the way I wanted us to live, you and me, the eternal children being cared for by our parents. So I rode away to grow up, and also to learn more about the Texas toughness I love in my ma."

"The Kincaid men are plenty tough."

"They are, but I wanted to learn more. I wanted a chance to grow a sterner spine. I spent plenty of time missing you, Maggie. But I needed to wait until I was man enough to be worthy of you. Once I got back, I figured to start up on my own, make sure I could take charge of my life, and then I was coming for you. All this does is speed the whole thing up."

Maggie's eyes were locked on Connor. She let her horse go on walking, not bothering to guide it. The horses knew where they were going. So Connor ignored his horse, too, and stared right back at her.

"It's too sudden, Connor. We can't know if we'll suit each other. What a terrible thing it would be for the family if we married and then had strife between us. It would spread through all our kin and be worse than if we married outside the family."

"There's nothing sudden about it. Not really."

"There most certainly is."

"We've known each other all our lives. We like each other. I respect you. I know you're a good and decent and kindhearted woman. I know you're plenty smart enough and hardworking enough to make a fine nurse. And if you're a doctor, I'd be proud to have you sew me up and set my broken bones. There is no possible way I can think of where we don't suit each other."

Maggie hesitated as she watched him. Suddenly she pulled her horse to a halt and swung down. "Get off your horse, Connor."

He didn't even consider disobeying her.

They stood between the horses, facing each other. Maggie looked so deeply into his eyes she tugged on his heart.

"Kiss me."

That startled him. Honestly, he'd not given much thought to kissing any woman, and it seemed strange to start with his old friend Maggie. Beautiful, grown-up Maggie . . .

He gave it some more thought, then leaned down until just their lips touched. Something dark and bright, like a lightning bolt in a midnight sky, sent a jagged thrill through him. He felt her slender waist under his hands and gently urged her forward, all without making a single plan. Then he tilted his head just so and found he could kiss her much more deeply without their noses in the way.

Maggie's arms came up to his chest, and for a wrenching moment he prepared to be shoved away and told to forget his clumsy proposal. Then those hands slid on up his chest and wrapped around his neck.

Hoofbeats tore them apart. Connor stepped back so fast he stumbled into his horse, which made the critter prance sideways, just enough to see Uncle Ethan come riding toward them and call out, "Connor, Maggie."

His uncle was still a hundred feet away, far enough that Connor had time to say, "Marry me, Maggie. Let me stay with you in Denver as your husband. I'm coming anyway. I'm not letting you move away by yourself with no family and no one to help you. When you get on the train tomorrow, I'll be on it. Please say you'll marry me."

Her eyes, which had been so fiercely locked on his, shifted then as if looking into his left eye, then his right, then back again. She drew a deep breath. "I—I don't know if getting married to you would be good for you."

124

"For me?" Connor's head was spinning from the kiss, so maybe the fact that she was making no sense wasn't all her fault. "Don't worry about me."

"I'm moving to Denver. It's a big, busy city."

"I've been to Denver. I know what it's like."

"Yes, you've been there, but have you ever lived in a city?"

"No, but neither have you. Not until this summer."

"But before I moved, I visited, stayed a stretch of days. Besides that, I've given this a lot of thought. I've been planning it for nearly a year. Your goal in life is to be a rancher—it's always been that, hasn't it? And you're offering to give all that up for me without really thinking it through. If you can't be a rancher, what are you going to be? It's a huge decision."

She leaned very close to him as her pa approached. "And I don't think we dare make that decision just because we shared a really wonderful kiss."

Connor opened his mouth, then closed it again.

"I'm not going to say yes, Connor, not right now. If you want to follow me, then you do it, but I'm not going to make you take vows for a life you may come to hate. You come to Denver and find work and see if you can stand the strange, bustling life there with never a quiet moment until you swing your door shut at night. No wolves or owls or mountain meadows. No cattle to check or caverns to explore. You come and try it out, then we'll see if you're still interested in marrying me. If you can stand Denver, and think you can stand to leave your family, possibly for good, then I'll be willing to talk more about marriage with you. So I won't say no, but I will say not now. You try it and then think about whether it's a good idea or not. You'll have to be satisfied with that."

With a silent nod, Connor reached out and clasped her hand, then let it go when her heavily armed father rode up.

"Hi, Pa." Maggie mounted up.

"We just stopped for a minute." Connor swung onto his horse without giving Maggie a second look. "Got to talking. It's fun getting to know each other again."

*T*hat stung.

Maggie wasn't sure why exactly. Did she want Connor to go telling Pa he'd proposed? No.

And yet the way Connor had dropped her hand . . . it might not have been too forward just to hang right on, let a hint escape that they had some interest in each other.

As she rode, she got to thinking about just how Connor had reacted when she'd talked about giving up ranching and living in Denver.

At the time she hadn't really let him talk, but now she thought of the way his mouth had opened and closed, the shocked look in his eyes. She'd chalked it up to the kiss. But now she wondered if it was something else. She'd told him he had to live in a big city if he wanted to be with her, and he'd been struck dumb by that.

They galloped on toward Rafe's ranch. Absently she listened to Pa talk with enthusiasm about climbing down into the cavern. Pa hadn't liked the cavern all that much way back when she was little, but since then he'd come to love it. The family now made a fair amount of money giving tours of the cavern, so they were all proud to own it. And they took turns leading tours, so they each had to know it well.

It didn't matter because she wasn't really listening. In her heart, two huge ideas clashed like a couple of bull elks in mating season. Now that she'd kissed Connor and found out how wonderful it was, the side of herself concerned with a husband and marriage had woken wide up and she found she did want to marry him.

And the other side, now that Connor had given just a few moments' thought to living in Denver as opposed to ranching, she feared she'd never hear another proposal—not if Connor couldn't stand to live in the city.

Yes, she needed to know now, before they went through with a hasty marriage and were miserable. But she'd just spoken the exact, correct truth that would, she much feared, resign her to a life alone, with memories of a soul-stirring kiss and a man she would have loved if she'd only turned her whole life on its head to be with him.

That's when another thought occurred to her about the life she had chosen and how a man coming along might be trouble.

Babies.

How could she study and later doctor with a babe in her arms?

Nope, there was no wedding in her future. On some very deep level, she'd known she had to choose. School and doctoring, or wife and mother. When she'd signed that contract, she'd made a decision to remain a spinster all her life.

But doing that hadn't been important enough to bother her before.

And then Connor came home.

She had to think this all through, assume he'd never propose again, and be ready with a reasonable answer if he did. Because her future was set. She'd serve others and serve the Lord with her life. And she'd do it alone.

Connor wanted to spend time alone with Maggie so bad he could barely hold on to his patience as he pitched hay.

She gathered eggs and did the milking, then slopped the hogs with the fresh warm milk because they didn't need it back home. There were plenty of milk cows at Pa's and Ethan's places. Then she went inside the house.

And she did it all while making dead certain she got nowhere near Connor, the little brat.

He wanted the two of them to get away from here and talk. He had to figure out how he was going to survive in Denver, of all places. And none of that was going to happen, because Uncle Ethan wanted to go down into the cavern. Connor did, too, but not as much as he wanted a long stretch of time alone with Maggie.

"Ethan, let's not go down in the cavern." Connor had realized in Texas that part of being a man was talking like one, and he'd dropped the *aunt* and *uncle* when talking to Luke and Ruthy Stone. Now he'd do that for his Kincaid family, too. "I think Audra expects us home for the noon meal."

"We've got plenty of time, Connor." Maggie, finally talking to him when he needed her least.

"Good." Ethan came out of a stall carrying a pitchfork. "Julia found a new room and I haven't seen it yet. There are lanterns inside the mouth of the cave. The new tunnel is in the room with that grizzly stone." Ethan stabbed the pitchfork into the haystack and headed for the cavern.

Connor had all he could do not to start growling like a real grizzly, not that bear-shaped stalactite.

Ethan left them behind. He knew they could find the grizzly room.

Maggie walked past Connor as if he were less interesting than a rock formation. He jogged to catch up.

She went into the cavern, Connor at her heels. They lit a lantern for each of them. Ethan's light was visible as they rounded a bend, then turned to a long, downward tunnel that led into the heart of the massive system of caves.

Connor heard Ethan's footsteps getting more distant, and when he and Maggie reached the bottom of the long slope, there was no sign of light ahead. Which meant they were completely alone. Which was what he'd been hoping for.

"Wait a minute." He set the lantern down with a hard click. "We need to talk."

"We need to keep up or—"

Connor cut her off with a kiss. He pulled the lantern out of her hand before she dropped it and caught them both on fire.

Then, in that kiss, another kind of fire started.

"Stop, Connor." Maggie slipped her fingers between their lips. "You wanted to talk, so let's talk. Pa won't leave us alone here for long. He's too much of a worrier."

Maggie was a little worried herself, because she knew marrying Connor was a mistake, and when he kissed her she couldn't remember why.

"If you're not going to give me time to talk things out, then I'll just say it straight. When you get on that train tomorrow, I'll be on it with you."

She glared at him and that only made her look in his eyes, and they had something a lot like that wild look he sometimes got. Only that wasn't exactly right. It was something different. Something she'd never seen before.

Something just for her.

Maggie moved her hand from between them, feeling her heart soften when she knew it shouldn't. She stepped back and reached for his hand. "Let's catch up to Pa and see what he says about you moving with me to Denver."

What Ethan said didn't bear repeating, and Connor's ears were ringing for a long time after.

Of course, he had waited until Maggie wandered off before he'd done any real talking. Connor told Ethan about the proposal and Maggie's refusal and . . . well, he'd told Ethan every single thing he knew and he told it fast because his uncle didn't approve of their going off together this way.

Neither did Connor, but Maggie was stubborn, so he'd go along with her and work his way around to marrying her as soon as he could.

Audra took it better. She seemed to think Connor tagging along to Denver with Maggie was a fine idea. She had charged Connor last night with keeping Maggie safe, which Connor faithfully promised to do.

There'd been no earthly reason why Ethan had picked breakfast this morning to polish and load his rifle.

Then they'd headed into Rawhide and hopped on a train that was a short spur linked to the same train that ran between Colorado City and Denver. Connor knew that shorter sections of train tracks were popping up all over Texas so he wasn't overly surprised, but Rawhide had been a town near death for most of Connor's growing-up years.

Now it was a town on the rise, with a church and school and businesses that all looked well established. Maybe five years had been too long for Connor to stay away.

Audra hadn't ridden to Rawhide with them. She said her ankle wouldn't hold up to a long ride yet. Ethan refused to cooperate in any way.

Connor tried to load his horse onto the train in Rawhide, but Ethan assured him it wouldn't be necessary. Boarding a horse in Denver was expensive. Maggie hired a carriage to get from the train to her home, then walked to school and back. Connor was going to have to do the same. He felt lost without his faithful horse, but he trusted Ethan.

Still, it was hard to shake the feeling that his horse was being stolen.

Connor kept a close eye on his cranky uncle just in case Ethan decided he didn't need his wallet in Denver, either.

As the train chugged toward Denver, Connor realized he had no idea where he'd live or work once there. Maggie seemed to trust him to figure it out on his own. Which just proved she wasn't half as smart as he'd figured her for.

When they finally stepped down off the train to the platform, Denver about knocked him on his backside.

He'd been to the city before; he'd told Maggie as much. But now Denver had over thirty thousand folks. The crowds rushing past nearly made him dizzy.

Maggie took charge, which pinched his notion of how a man needed to go on. But since he had no idea what to do, he just fell in behind her and made sure to carry everything—a satchel for each of them and his bedroll tucked under one arm. That was all he'd brought back from Texas, and he figured what he held in his arms, along with his rifle slung over his shoulder and his holstered six-shooter, would be plenty enough for him to get by.

He could sleep under the stars and hunt his food until he settled in somewhere. He had a little money in his pocket he'd earned while working for Luke, and that should hold out until he found work. But he couldn't exactly camp out and build a fire in the middle of a big city, and there was no game to hunt.

Maggie had mentioned a boardinghouse, though she wasn't sure where to find one.

Connor found it all mighty confusing. If a man needed a house, he felled some trees and built himself a cabin. If he needed food, he went hunting.

Connor wondered if the parson Maggie lived with had a small yard around his house where Connor could camp.

There was no point asking Maggie any of this. And no point at all in sweeping her up into his arms and marching her right straight back to the train so they could go home to the Kincaid Ranch where they belonged.

He jumped up into the carriage she hailed and sat quietly while it rolled through the throngs of people.

The ways of the city were a mystery.

Maggie was amazed at how everything was so simple in the city. Out in the country, if a body wanted shelter, folks had to fell trees and build a cabin. Here? Rent a room. There, if you wanted food, kill, clean, and fry a chicken, or go hunting. Here, go to a grocery store or a diner.

With a few easy questions asked of the parson and his wife, she had Connor settled in a boardinghouse only a city block away from the parson's house. It was a clean and respectable-looking place, too. They got there just before the evening meal, and the woman serving food offered Maggie dinner for two bits—which Connor quickly paid.

He'd paid for the carriage ride, as well. She'd better warn him to hang on to his money tighter.

They ate chicken and dumplings over warm, freshly baked biscuits, and had custard pie for their dessert. Connor would eat well here.

When the nice lady serving the food turned down Maggie's offer to help with the dishes, they stood from the table and walked out to the front lobby.

"I'm going to head for the parson's house now." Maggie felt awkward leaving Connor here alone. He'd been very quiet since they arrived in town.

"The man at dinner said the blacksmith nearby was hiring. I'm going to find it in the morning and see if I can get the job."

"You should look around for a few days, Connor, before you take a job. Denver has a big stockyard, and you've had plenty of experience with cattle. There are so many jobs in town, you might be able to find one that suits you more and pays better. Have you ever considered working at a desk? In a bank or in a lawyer's office? And there's a thriving land office every few blocks here in Denver."

"But how do I know who needs help?"

And that had Maggie stumped. Then something occurred to her. "Dr. Radcliffe might be able to advise you. He knows a lot more people than I do. If he doesn't know of any jobs, he might be able to send you to someone who is informed of such things.

I'm going to see him first thing in the morning. Why don't you come along with me and we'll talk to him together? I'd like you to meet him, anyway."

"Let me walk you home."

Maggie realized she was lingering, putting off leaving him. "Thank you. It's near, but I'd appreciate the company."

They went outside together, and when they reached the first corner, Connor said, "Wait."

"Why? Did you forget something?"

He turned around to stare down the street they'd just walked. "No, I'm checking my back trail. I want to be able to get back to the boardinghouse."

Maggie turned and stared just like he was doing. "That's honestly a good idea."

The sun was still high overhead on the long June day. She'd better make sure she could get where she was going in the dark when that became necessary.

They headed on, and the parson's house wasn't much farther. Connor would find his way home, and if she needed him, Maggie would find him just as easily.

Connor agreed to come in the morning and walk her to meet with Dr. Radcliffe and maybe get some ideas for a job. When Connor told her good-bye, it was under the watchful eye of the kindly parson and his wife.

So there was no chance for a private moment and possibly a kiss. Maggie was hard-pressed to be grateful for such vigilant chaperones.

Chapter

6

Connor had a job before noon the next day, and his head was spinning at the very idea.

He was working for Dr. Radcliffe, and for several hours a day he'd be right alongside Maggie.

The doctor said he needed someone strong to help him lift patients and handle a few other jobs. Dr. Radcliffe called the job an "orderly." When Connor told him he'd worked for a doctor in Texas, Radcliffe said he might give him a chance at a few other things.

Connor liked the idea of being around Maggie, so he took the job. But it didn't sound like much of a real job to him. By the end of the day, Connor realized he was going to work as hard as he would've at the blacksmith's or back on the Kincaid Ranch.

He walked Maggie home.

"I like having you where I can see you every day, Connor. Do you think you're going to like the job?"

"It doesn't matter much if I like it, does it? I'll do what I'm told and get my pay. It's probably a better idea than being kicked by a horse while I'm trying to shoe it, or working over a blazing-hot forge all day."

Maggie smiled. "You seemed to be doing a good job. You were comfortable around the sick people. Not everyone is."

"I hadn't thought much about it, but one of Luke's good friends in Broken Wheel was the town doctor. I helped him out from time to time. I have a real good idea what Dr. Radcliffe expects of me, and by the end of the day I was starting to know what was wrong with most of the new patients coming in."

Maggie winced.

"What's the matter?"

"Did you tell Dr. Radcliffe that?"

"Yep, he seemed interested in my opinion." From her expression he could tell that bothered her. "Is that wrong? Should I keep my ideas to myself?"

"No, no, that's not it. I just . . . well, that's how Dr. Radcliffe treats me. Asking me if I know what's wrong—like he's constantly testing me and training me. Maybe you'll end up being a doctor the same time I am."

Connor laughed. "Nope, I don't see it. I figure to get back to cattle and horses as soon as I can. But he's paying me well enough that I can live at the boardinghouse without worry. So I'm content to work there for as long as the doctor needs me."

Connor reached over and took her hand. "There's a little park between here and the parson's house. We walked around it this morning. How about we go there now?"

"The parson will notice if I'm very late."

"It's a shortcut, so if we walk slowly and talk a bit, we'll be there at the same time as always. You said I need to figure out if I can live in a city. Well, after one day, I think I can. I miss my horse, though, and I miss the quiet of the country."

"We can rent horses and ride out into the hills. Maybe on Sunday afternoons."

A smile broke on Connor's face. He felt his spirits rise. "That would be a fine thing, Maggie. Yes, let's do that."

He tightened his grip on her hand as they strolled toward the quiet little park. Connor even found a moment to stop and give

Maggie a kiss. "Yes, I think I'm going to like living in the city, so long as you're here with me."

"I like the city a lot more myself now that you're here." They shared a smile, then headed on, hand in hand, until the parson's house came into view. At that point, he loosened his grip on her hand and his fingers slid gently away from hers. His smile was full of longing as they walked a proper distance apart to the front door.

⁊

Maggie spent an hour each morning in a classroom and the rest of the morning tending patients in the hospital with the other nursing students. In the afternoon she went to work with Dr. Radcliffe and now Connor.

For his first week in Denver, Maggie was pleased by how much Dr. Radcliffe liked Connor and how much Connor enjoyed the work. She talked with Connor on their walks home, and he was just as surprised at how well the work suited him. He talked more about his life in Texas and how much he'd worked alongside Luke's friend, Dr. Dare Riker.

Once she admitted how much fun it was to talk with Connor about doctoring and their shared interest, Maggie felt ready to say the word if Connor proposed again: *Yes.*

But then things changed. By near the end of the second week, the whole situation was getting on her nerves. It reached a peak on Thursday, after her morning work at the hospital, when she came into Dr. Radcliffe's examination room to find Connor stitching up a man's arm. First she noticed Connor's steady hand, the blood, the man's gritted teeth, then Connor's quiet, calming voice.

Maggie saw that Dr. Radcliffe was tending another patient.

He'd never left her to stitch up a wound. Oh, she'd taken many stitches while working here, but only under the doctor's watchful eye.

That afternoon, she helped in every way she could. Followed the doctor's orders to the letter. Then a second person came in needing stitches, and Dr. Radcliffe let her do it, but while watch-

136

ing her every stitch. He never once criticized her—and told her she did a great job—but he didn't walk away, either, even when a new patient came in. He told Connor to start the exam while he and Maggie finished. Connor did the whole exam himself and sent the woman on her way without even consulting Dr. Radcliffe.

And then it was time to go home.

Connor took her hand and was walking along, at ease and cheerful.

They'd barely made it out of earshot from Dr. Radcliffe when Maggie said, "When did he start letting you sew up a patient?"

Connor frowned at the sharp tone of her voice. She regretted not asking a bit more pleasantly.

"I've been doing it mostly right from the start. I helped Dare back in Broken Wheel, and that included setting stitches many times. I told Doc I could do it. He watched me once, and since then I've done most of the suturing that comes in. He lets me put a cast on broken bones, too. But that's only after working with him a few times. He's known for doing a fine job with difficult breaks, so a lot of folks come to him. But most are simple fractures that just need a plaster cast. I do those."

"Without supervision?"

With a brief shrug, he said, "If I have any questions, I ask. And he works with me most of the time. It's not often there are two patients in need."

"What else are you doing?" She fought back her rising anger and made her question sound like simple curiosity. Fake, simple curiosity.

Connor's face lit up. "He took me with him to deliver a baby and ended up letting me do most of it. That was a wonderful experience. Dare never let me in on that back in Texas. It was like watching a miracle happen right in front of my eyes." Connor's enthusiasm grew. "And I've been helping him with fevers, and he's got a man with pleurisy who's been in four times now. Doc calls him my patient. I helped tend a man with dropsy. There are three men in a special room here with consumption, and the doctor is very careful how we treat them. I wear a face mask over my mouth and nose, and we wash our hands thoroughly. Dr. Radcliffe has told me what to look for during checkups and so now I do the consumption patients, too. He was talking about—"

Maggie made a sound that reminded her a bit of that angry mama buffalo. Connor quit talking and stared at her. He stopped dead in his tracks, his brow lined with furrows.

"What's wrong?" he asked.

How could he not know? Then Maggie caught herself. How could he know? That was more fair. He was new here and certainly couldn't read what was inside Maggie's head. So she needed to tell him.

"Dr. Radcliffe has never let me do any of that!" Maggie whirled away and stomped toward the park they always passed through together. "I know about the room for consumption patients, but he says it's too dangerous and won't let me in."

"Well, it is dangerous, but if you're careful, I think—"

"I've only set stitches," she said, cutting him off, "under his close supervision, though he's never found fault with how I do it, not since the first few times, months ago. I've never put a cast on a broken bone. And I have never, ever been allowed to go along with him to deliver a baby."

Looking confused, Connor hurried to keep up with her. "I've worked alongside you, Maggie. You're good at all the things I've seen you do. Are you sure it's not just a coincidence? He might feel more protective of you with the consumption patients. And maybe . . . I think the first time he let me set stitches, someone else came in bleeding. He was so busy with that, he left me on my own. He saw I'd done a good job, so he relaxed faster than he might otherwise have done. As for the baby, maybe I was just here and it was at a time when we could both be gone. I know of at least two other times when we had patients waiting in his office and he left me in charge while he went out for a house call."

"He left you in charge?" Maggie started walking faster. She wanted to get away from all this.

Connor looked worried now, and well he should. "He warned me not to handle anything I wasn't familiar with. But I was lucky enough no one like that came in."

"Why is he doing this?" Maggie flung her arms wide and managed to whack Connor in the belly. "Does he see a man as a natural doctor and a woman as someone trying to do a job she's not suited for?"

"I've never heard him say such a thing. He often compliments your work."

"Even if he doesn't outwardly talk like that, his actions tell a different story."

Connor caught her arm and gently but firmly pulled her to a halt. He looked deep into her eyes. She could see his concern. Knew he didn't want to hurt her.

"I'll quit. First thing tomorrow. I won't get in your way, Maggie. And I want no part of hurting you. I have never thought of doctoring for a living. I've just been following orders same as I would at a livery stable, but it never occurred to me Doc might be putting too much of the job on my shoulders, and by doing that, treating you in a way that's insulting. I'll tell him—"

"No. It's nothing you're doing, Connor."

"It must be, at least in part. I never should have told him I'd worked with Dare. I was right there piping up when he had a second patient come in and I was sewing and he was watching. I said, '*I've set stitches before. I'll do it.*' I must have sounded boastful so he thought I was more than I was."

"You're not boastful." Now Maggie had hurt him. None of this was his fault.

"I'll quit tomorrow." Connor towed her to the side of the path. Maggie saw a little iron bench and Connor pulled her to sit beside him, but there was little pulling because she wanted to talk this over.

"I'll get another job. The stockyard is always hiring. And I know how to send a telegram. I learned Morse code in Broken Wheel."

"Whatever happened to make you learn—"

Connor snapped his fingers and looked excited again. "I've

heard they have telephones in Denver. Isn't that a wonder? I'd love to see if the telephone company needs help. It's so new that everyone working there must be training while they work."

It was a wonder how many things he already knew and how eager he seemed to learn more.

"Vince, the lawyer in Broken Wheel, was a friend of Luke. I learned to research law books to find things for him. Maybe a law office in town needs a helping hand. I was a hand as a fry cook, too. Dare's wife owned the diner and was always needing help. She was no hand at cooking so I stepped in there plenty of times."

"Why would a woman who couldn't cook run a diner?" That distracted Maggie from her already waning temper. "Was Dare a terrible doctor? Is that why you helped him? Was Vince an illiterate shyster? Did you have to read the law books out loud to him? Was the telegraph officer a drunk who slept until noon? Could your uncle Luke manage a ranch?"

"They did all right."

Maggie felt her eyes narrow. "They'll probably let you argue cases in front of a judge within two weeks. By the end of the month you'll be a judge."

Connor watched her. She'd probably scared him into thinking every word was a sinful boast. And that was wrong of her, but she couldn't pretend this wasn't a hurtful situation.

She didn't want to be a yelling woman. But right now she wasn't sure what she could say without yelling.

"I'll say this one more time, Connor: This is not about you. It's about Dr. Radcliffe, and he's the one I need to talk to. Don't you even dare think of quitting. That makes me feel like a weakling who can't work with someone who is better than her, and it would be humiliating for me if Dr. Radcliffe believed that." Her body fought for control, until she lurched to her feet and headed for the parson's house, walking as fast as she could.

Connor was beside her in a flash. "Maggie, I want to solve this before you go home. We shouldn't end the evening with this unhappiness between us."

Walking faster, looking straight ahead, Maggie said the only thing she could think of that was the truth . . . that she felt she could say. "We should end this evening as quickly as we can and without saying another word to each other."

Then she turned to look him right in the eye without slowing down even a speck. "If we don't stop discussing this now, I might say things that would end us. And that's a lot worse than ending the evening."

She stormed up the parson's steps and went inside, careful not to slam the door. She didn't look back. She didn't want to see him standing there looking sad. Even more, she didn't want to see him walking away, possibly deciding he wanted no relationship with a woman who couldn't control her temper.

Chapter

7

Connor was chased from sleep by a charging buffalo.
The nightmare sprang him upright in his bed. On his feet before he was fully awake, he raked his fingers through his hair, saying to himself, "I shouldn't have let her go last night. I should have forced her to stay and talk, to clear things up."

After wolfing down breakfast, Connor ran all the way to the parson's house—long before he usually arrived. Charging up the front steps, he banged on the door with his fist. Seconds later, the parson whipped the door open, clearly worried.

It flickered through Connor's head that a parson might get as many frantic calls for help as a doctor. He asked to see Maggie, telling the parson it was really important.

"Sorry, but she's not here," the parson said. "Left a while ago. She had to check in for class ahead of time."

It was too late to catch her. Even if he sprinted the distance to the school, he knew she'd get there and be starting class before he could see her. Fighting the need to barge into her classroom, Connor stormed on to the doctor's office, his thoughts all twisted up.

He should quit.

He had to wait to see Maggie, so he couldn't quit today.

But what about Doc Radcliffe? Suddenly, Connor was tempted to punch him right in the mouth.

What about another job? The stockyard, the livery, blacksmith maybe . . . No, he couldn't go hunting for work until he'd talked to Maggie, who'd be coming to the doctor's office later.

Whatever else he did, it was high time to have a heart-to-heart talk with Dr. Radcliffe. Maggie had been hurt by the doctor's behavior, and Connor wanted some answers.

Stepping inside the doctor's office, he saw three patients waiting. One, Mr. Evans, his dropsy worse than ever. Another, a young man cradling his arm against his chest. The third an elderly woman, hacking into her handkerchief.

"Dr. Kincaid, is that you?" Dr. Radcliffe must've heard the door open. He sounded desperate.

Dr. Kincaid?

"I'll be right with you folks." Connor then rushed through the door that led to an examination room with two narrow cots and shelves full of medical equipment, bottles of medicine, and books. "It's me," he said to Dr. Radcliffe.

The doc was hovering over a little boy wrapped tight in a blanket to keep him from moving while his weeping mother held the child's head. Through her tears, she urged her son to calm down. The father was present, too, using his body to anchor the child. Doc was busy stitching up the boy's chin.

It didn't look serious, medically speaking, only painful for the child, who screamed and fought as the adults tried to help him.

"See to the man holding his arm first. I suspect a break in the forearm. Hope to heaven it doesn't need to be set."

Connor nodded and got to work. No time for a hard talk with the doctor now.

The morning flew by. The doctor finished the stitches and brought in the coughing woman. Connor finished the cast and brought in Mr. Evans. His swollen ankles worried Connor. It was the kind of thing that often warned of a coming heart seizure.

"The doctor . . ." Connor faltered. Dr. Radcliffe had named

Connor as a doctor, and maybe it was so this man would accept treatment from someone besides the real doctor. "I mean, I have a tea that's just come in. We hope it will have a good effect. You've stopped adding salt to your food?"

"Yep, Doc. I've done all you've told me." Something in Mr. Evans's tone made Connor doubt that was the whole truth.

Connor patted him on the arm. "Good. Keep that up and I'll send you a packet of this tea. Brew yourself a cup morning and night. And remember to take long walks. You sit in that chair at the bank for too many hours without moving."

"I'm busy, I don't have time for that."

"I can only advise you, Mr. Evans, but you find time to come in here to see the doctor, and on a day like today when you end up sitting for long stretches waiting your turn. I think a long walk every day would hardly take much longer."

He nodded reluctantly. Connor had little hope the man would change, but he might drink the tea at least. Connor saw the nettles in the tea and remembered Maggie collecting herbs when he found her forced up a tree by that buffalo. Which reminded Connor of his nightmare, which reminded him that Maggie had walked away from him last night, both furious and hurt.

And that reminded him of the talk he needed to have with Radcliffe. Good grief, he hadn't even had time to say anything to the doctor outside of rapidly exchanged words about the patients. He saw the doctor handing a bottle of cough syrup to the elderly woman. Mr. Evans left right behind her, and Connor thought his chance had come.

The office door slammed open. "Come quick, Doc! A horse kicked the blacksmith in the head. He's out cold, and he's bleedin' like a stuck hog."

"I've got to go." Doc looked sharply at Connor. "I'll bring the blacksmith back here as quick as I can. But there are two new patients in the waiting room. You stay and take care of what you're able to. If you can't handle it, just keep them comfortable. I'll be back soon." The doctor slapped his forehead. "I haven't even looked in on the patients in the hospital yet this morning. I'll send a note to the school asking them to let Maggie come to work. It's a bit early, is all. We need another set of hands."

The doctor scribbled a note and gave it to a boy out on the street, along with a coin and an order to run to the school. Then Dr. Radcliffe grabbed his doctor's bag and was gone, hurrying after the anxious man who'd come in shouting about the injured blacksmith.

Connor barely had time to take a breath as he tended the two new patients. Luckily he could handle them. Just as he was finishing up, two men came in carrying a third man, who was fighting them and clawing at his throat.

"Help him, Doc." The older of the two carrying the man kept moving toward a table. "My son got tossed off a bronco and hit a fence. He's fightin' for air. I think he busted somethin' in his throat."

That was something Connor had never heard of before. He rushed to keep up with the two men. One claimed he was the father, the other man his brother.

Connor moved to the young man's side and felt for a pulse. A stupid thing to do, as the man was thrashing around. He found the pulse was strong, in fact hammering. Connor had no idea what to do next.

A commotion in the waiting room drew his attention. Maggie burst in, took one look at the struggling man, and moved quickly to help out.

"Thank God you're here." Connor explained the situation as fast as he could.

"Tracheotomy."

"Trake-what?" Connor asked.

Maggie whirled around to the counter and snatched up a scalpel and tossed it into a steaming pot of water Dr. Radcliffe always kept on the stove.

"Connor, get me one of those eyedroppers and tear off the rubber end so I have a little tube. Drop the tube into the hot water."

The man on the bed began to convulse. He bled from his throat, and no sound, not a wisp of air, not a cry or even a rasp could be heard coming out of his mouth.

The father grabbed at Maggie's arm. "He's dying. Let the doc work on him."

Maggie wrenched free of his grasp.

"Leave her be," Connor said, racing around the bed and blocking the man as he tried to stop Maggie. "If you touch her again, I'll throw you out of here. She's . . . she's just attended a special class to learn how best to treat these kinds of injuries. She's better at it than I am."

Maggie appreciated the help. She coated the man's throat with carbolic acid, then picked up a pair of tongs and fished out the scalpel.

"I need him held absolutely still." Her eyes cut from Connor to the father and brother. "His throat has been crushed. I have to open an airway so he can breathe freely. Connor, you hold his head. You"—she jabbed a finger at the father—"lie across his body."

Her eyes went to the brother next, giving orders, taking charge. There wasn't time for an argument. "Now hold his arms down. I need it done now! He's quit breathing."

All three men obeyed her snapping voice. Maggie bent and cut a swift slash about an inch long in the hollow of the man's throat. Blood bubbled out of the wound.

The men gasped. The father roared, "What are you doing?"

She knew Connor would move to stop the father if he wrestled for the scalpel. "Everyone stay right where you are," Maggie commanded. "He *cannot* move."

Connor stayed put, keeping the injured man's head still, but she could tell he was still braced to jump at the father if need be. But the father did as he was told, holding the son still on the table with his body. Maggie understood his terror. She suspected Connor also was horrified by what she'd just done.

Maggie held a cloth on the cut with one hand while with the other she set aside the scalpel and used the tongs to fetch the thin tube. She lifted the cloth, inserted the tube into the cut, and motioned for the father to step back. She bent low, put her lips to the tube, and blew. The man's chest rose and fell, and he instantly stopped struggling. The man had been fighting for air. Now he had it.

Everyone went still, watching and listening. The sound of air flowing in when Maggie breathed, and out when she moved away, was like a miracle—like she'd breathed the life back into the man. A moment passed, two, three . . . and the injured man's eyes flickered open.

Maggie moved to let the air out and angled her head so that she was eye to eye with him. "Don't move, and don't speak. You've been hurt, but you will be all right."

The man blinked his eyes but remained still as a stone. Maggie bent down again to give him his next breath.

Long moments passed, and finally Connor said, "You saved this man's life, Mag . . . Miss Kincaid. I couldn't have done that. Thank God you're taking those classes."

Maggie gave him a smile that would light up the whole city of Denver. "You'll lie still, now, won't you?" The man blinked his eyes again, acknowledging what she said. "All right, everyone. He understands."

The father, brother, and Connor finally relaxed and straightened.

The waiting room door swung open with a bang, followed by footsteps. Connor stepped back. "Are you all right if I go see who it is?"

"We'll stay and help. And, Doc Kincaid," the older man added with a reverent tone, "we'll do whatever you say."

Connor met Maggie's eyes, and she nodded. "I've got more work to do here but he'll live. Go."

Connor rushed away.

Maggie talked quietly to the injured man and his family, while in the other room she heard shouting.

"Stagecoach turned over, Doc. Ten folks on board, driver and shotgun rider hurt, everyone hurt. Hurry!"

Maggie grabbed the brother, who was closest. "Breathe into this tube. Slow and easy. Check once in a while—he may be able to do it himself. Take over. I'll be right back."

Now in the waiting room, Maggie said, "I heard. I can't leave right now, but I'll come in a bit. Take my doctor's bag."

"Is there anyone else from your class who can help?" Connor asked. "I'll send a message."

"Yes, send it. They'll get help to us if they can. And ask them to send for more doctors."

Chapter

8

*C*onnor wrote the note, ran outside, and found the same boy Doc Radcliffe had sent before. After sending the boy on his way, he turned to the desperate man who'd brought the news. "Lead the way."

The man tore off running, with Connor following close behind him. The overturned stagecoach wasn't far away, about five city blocks. Rounding a corner, they both slowed a bit as the ugly scene came into view.

People lying everywhere, bleeding, some unconscious, some awake, thrashing, wailing, weeping in pain. He had no idea where to start.

For one terrifying second he feared they'd all die right there. And it would be his fault. His arrogance in thinking he understood medicine, which had never been made so clear to him as a few moments ago at the doctor's office.

Ripping past the torrent of self-doubt, he dashed to the nearest victim, a man. He was thrashing around, eyes closed, howling in pain, bleeding from his head and face and arms. Connor dropped to his knees. A quick check told him no broken bones, at least none poking out of the skin. He spun around, seeking the man who'd come for him.

"I need a lot more men to carry the injured back to the doctor's office." There were several standing around the edges of the wreck.

"Grab some of them." Connor pointed to the milling crowd. "I need a stretcher if you can find one. If not, take a door from somewhere and carry this man on that." He nodded, hanging on Connor's every word. "If you can't get a door real fast, then get a couple of men and carry him gently in your arms. But be careful."

Connor jumped up and charged toward the next man down. This one seemed less seriously injured. He was sitting up but looking dazed.

"Where are you hurt?" Connor asked.

"Beat up some, but not too bad. Go on to someone else."

Ten people and he'd dealt with only two so far.

She had to go. She had to go. She had to go.

Connor needed her.

Fighting not to just flat-out leave her patient and run, she carefully worked on the throat blockage. It would heal, but for now the throat was too swollen for air to pass through. She wrapped the man's neck in a clean bandage with the small tube still in place and said to his anxious brother and father, "Help me move him, get him settled in a bed."

How many beds did they have available? How many would be needed for the stagecoach crash? Sending this man home might be for the best, but she had to talk to Dr. Radcliffe first. And Connor needed her. She'd just sent him off with no idea what he'd be facing.

She had to go. She had to go.

"This way." She clamped her mouth shut and tried not to rush things. "Don't jostle him or the tube could dislodge."

She had to go!

Finally, the man was settled and resting again. His family promised to stay at his side and keep watch.

Maggie hurried into the waiting room on her way to the door and to Connor. When she opened it, four men—carrying a fifth man who was lying on a wooden door—almost knocked her down.

"He's from the stagecoach wreck, miss. He's unconscious."

Fighting the urge to scream, she turned back. "Follow me. Now lift him off that door and set him on the table real easy."

One of the men said, "We've got to go back, miss. There are more comin'."

Despite her wanting to go help Connor, Maggie knew she needed to stay where she was. So she turned to the unconscious man and went to work, praying at the same time.

A woman came to Connor's side.

"Maggie?" He hoped it was her. He needed someone smarter than he was.

Instead, it was an older woman. She wore an apron. "No, I'm Mrs. McRay. I worked in a field hospital during the war." She had a lilting Irish accent that worked to calm Connor. "Tell me what to do. I've seen you checking people and shouting orders. Now shout them at me. And if you be needin' a second set of hands, I've got a strong, steady pair."

Mrs. McRay was older than his ma, but solid and calm. He was so happy for the help he wanted to hug her, but he didn't have time.

Crouching by the next man, Connor had no notion of how to treat him. "This one needs to go to the hospital. He's got a serious head wound and a badly broken arm. They took one man away on a stretcher. I need a second one."

"I'll find one and see to it this man gets on his way. Go on to the next patient." Mrs. McRay broke into a run.

Connor quickly moved to the next victim. He nearly turned and ran away, because this was the worst he'd seen yet. Sweat broke out on Connor's forehead. Nausea wrenched his stomach but he fought it down.

Another arm brutally fractured. Right away he thought of arteries. Back in Texas, Dare had once told him that blood spilled out with a pulse if an artery was cut. The blood was driven by the heart pumping, and when a man had an injury like that, there was nothing to do except apply a tourniquet to stop the bleeding and then later they'd likely need to amputate.

The person was bleeding badly, but Connor didn't think the wound was actually pumping out blood. Then he examined the snapped forearm bone, which was protruding through the skin. It was as ugly a thing as he'd ever seen.

He had no idea where to start, but then he remembered a letter he had received a while ago from Uncle Heath. In it Heath had talked about the terrible broken bone his father-in-law, Chance Boden, had suffered. Dare was fascinated by this, so Heath and Dare had exchanged several letters discussing the bad break, and Dare had a long correspondence about it. Connor had read everything Dare had.

That helped, but it was nowhere near enough. Connor turned to the nurse. "Let's get him to the doctor's office. I'll need things I only have there."

Like a doctor. A *real* doctor. Not Connor Kincaid, the fraud.

"We'll be tearin' down every door on the street for stretchers, Doc." Mrs. McRay's calm voice helped to steady him. "We've sent away the man you just checked and have another stretcher ready for this man. And look, here come those men back with the first stretcher already." Mrs. McRay treated him with so much respect, probably fooled by the phony confidence she heard in Connor's voice.

The men held a real stretcher, though it appeared mighty worn and tattered, like something left over from the war twenty years ago.

"I don't dare touch this break here on the street. We have to get him to the doctor's office right away, and we have to be very gentle about it. There are arteries that could be severed."

Nurse McRay gestured to six others standing nearby, who gathered around the hurt man.

Connor looked at them and nodded. "All right," he said, "put the stretcher on the ground beside him. We'll all lift at once, and I'll guide his arm."

Once they had him settled on the stretcher, Connor said, "Go now, men, and watch that arm of his. Move careful."

"He's bleedin' bad, Doc. He ain't got much time."

"Well, go as fast as you can while you keep him steady." Connor watched them as they hurried off toward the doctor's office. Then he forced himself to get back to work on the other injured folks who were still in need of help.

"Put him here." Maggie had one unconscious man on a table. She'd done what she could for him. Now here was another.

The men carrying him obeyed so fast, Maggie wondered at it. "Are there more coming?" she snapped at the closest man.

"Yes, miss, a lot more . . . although some may be dead."

"Take that man into the back," she ordered, jabbing a finger at the first patient. "You'll find an empty bed there."

"We're to go back fast to the wreck, miss."

"Then move him fast. I need him out of this space."

The men carted her first patient away.

How many more? Where was Connor?

She'd barely begun examining the next patient, checking his bleeding head wound and arm swollen to double its normal size, when Dr. Radcliffe came running in.

"I heard about the stagecoach." At that moment, another group came in, bearing a man on a litter.

"I'll see to him." Dr. Radcliffe left Maggie to her current patient. She pressed a damp rag to the head wound, wishing for more hands.

The first of the girls from the school entered the doctor's office. Maggie saw the terrible break on the arm of the man Dr. Radcliffe was treating and knew that would give him all he could do for a while. She took charge of everything else.

Another wounded patient came staggering in on foot, a man on each side helping to support him. Behind them, someone shouted,

"Dr. Radcliffe, what do you need?" Another doctor had arrived, finally.

Before Dr. Radcliffe could answer, Maggie replied, "Two not so badly hurt are in the back, in the hospital. If you could move them to your own offices, we need the beds."

Dr. Radcliffe nodded, and the man charged on through the examination room to the hospital.

With a twinkle in his otherwise grim eyes, Dr. Radcliffe said, "You've got the makings of a doctor, I'd say, Miss Kincaid."

That gave her the energy to get back to work.

Connor had watched the rough western men—men exactly like Connor, in fact—tote away that horribly injured man with the awful broken arm. Those men had moved with great care and tenderness, and the very reverence of it reminded Connor to pray.

In praying, his thoughts cleared and his stomach settled some as he figured out what he needed to do, and no other possible answer would do. He needed to stop thinking he was a doctor and get everyone here *to* a doctor, and as fast as possible.

The next man was dead. He was told this was the stagecoach driver, who'd been thrown off the stage when the axle had snapped with no warning. A second man, not far from the driver, lay dead, as well. He was clutching a rifle.

"He was riding shotgun. Looks as though both of the men on top were killed instantly." Nurse McRay clutched his arm, almost as if she knew he was nearly unable to take his eyes off the dead men.

There were two more men, each unconscious. Connor did a quick examination before sending them away on stretchers.

Someone standing on top of the overturned stage yelled, "There's a woman and a child still inside! Hurry!"

The stagecoach lay on its side in the street. Connor rushed over and peered in through the opening left where one of the doors was torn away. He saw blood everywhere. A young woman was sprawled against the opposite door, a little boy in her arms, also knocked out. Connor wasn't sure who was bleeding, or maybe it was both, but he knew whoever it was . . . there was too much of it.

He slipped through the door opening and carefully lowered himself inside. Looking up, he shouted, "I need two men standing by this door! I'll move these folks to the door. You lift 'em out."

Hearing the clomping of boots approaching the door, Connor turned back to his patients. The boy was five or six years old and had a gash on his forehead that was bleeding liberally. The wound needed a great many stitches. He felt the boy's neck and found a strong pulse. He worried that the boy might have broken his back or might be torn up inside, but Connor couldn't treat the child here in the smashed-up stage.

So he took the boy in his arms and eased the youngster through the door. "Got him?" he asked.

The men on top of the stage knelt and reached down together. They lifted him away and were gone.

Connor moved back to the woman, who was bleeding from her mouth and nose. She had a severe cut on her scalp, and he noticed swelling on her left leg and right shoulder. Her left shoulder was disfigured. Connor suspected it was dislocated. With no notion of how to treat so many injuries, he shouted, "I need two more men! The woman here is badly hurt; she'll need a stretcher."

He gently lifted the woman, brown hair all askew. Her nose looked broken, and the hollows beneath her eyes were swollen and already turning black.

"The stretcher's here, Doc," Nurse McRay hollered back. "One of the men carried the boy in his arms so we'd have the stretcher for his ma."

Connor lifted her, twisting to get her through the door without knocking her against anything. "Be careful, she has several broken bones." She moaned in pain as he handed her up. He prayed he hadn't made things worse.

By the time he climbed out of the stagecoach and jumped to the ground, the wounded woman was gone. He looked at his kindly nurse. "Is there anyone else?"

A groan drew his eyes. The man riding shotgun. "I thought he was dead!" Connor rushed to his side.

"I did, too. Maybe there's hope, Doc." Mrs. McRay at his side, Connor knelt beside the man. His neck was twisted to an impossible angle. Connor had nearly left a man to die with his sloppy doctoring.

They soon had the poor man on his way.

Connor then went to the driver's side. He felt for a heartbeat. The man's body had already begun to cool. "I'm taking him in anyway," he told Mrs. McRay.

Another door was brought over and they sent this one on, too.

"I'm a fool. I almost—what was I—"

"No time for that now." Nurse McRay caught his arm and almost dragged him forward. God had sent this woman for a fact.

"Thank you, Mrs. McRay."

"I'll go with you to the doctor's office. I might be able to help. We sent word out and found two other doctors, and the medical college sent their students over. The last man who came back with the stretcher said the first of them were showing up when he left. He told them to work on the injured because we were as good as done here."

Connor nodded, exhausted as he thought of all the harm he might've done. He'd only kept up his fast pace because Nurse McRay was right there helping him, and somehow that goaded him into finding the strength.

When he and the nurse reached the doctor's office, he saw two bandaged men walking slowly away, helped along by others. He had to give way when a team with a stretcher bearing a man came out the front door. The man following carried a doctor's bag.

He stepped into mayhem. But no, for after a minute he saw it was in fact orderly, just fast-moving and loud. He spotted at least five patients, including two sitting up, being tended by women so young they had to be students.

Maggie and Dr. Radcliffe were here—Radcliffe working on the terribly broken arm, Maggie with the woman. The little boy was

156

still unconscious, cradled in a man's arms. There were no empty beds.

"Connor, Maggie could use some help with that hurt woman," Dr. Radcliffe said. "Multiple breaks. She might have rib injuries. I'll be there as soon as I can."

Thank the good Lord in heaven, someone else was in charge. Connor was so relieved he would've collapsed if he'd had the time. "I brought Mrs. McRay with me. She's a trained nurse."

The doctor glanced over his shoulder. "Mrs. McRay, you're a nurse? Come over here, please."

She rushed to his side.

Connor shifted his attention to Maggie and did as he was told, as fast as he could, thrilled to be able to help—more thrilled that no one expected him to be a doctor. It was someone else's responsibility now.

Chapter

9

Never had such a badly injured patient been Maggie's sole responsibility.

She second-guessed nearly every decision. Even when she knew what to do, like plastering a broken bone, she wasn't sure if she did things in the right order. How to know what the woman needed first?

"Nothing I can see is a deadly wound." Maggie's back cracked as she straightened. Her voice was hoarse from all the orders she'd called out. "There are so many broken bones." She glanced up at Connor, who'd run, fetched, lifted anything she asked for and as fast as she'd asked it. "And who knows about what I can't see?"

Connor shook his head helplessly. "What about the shoulder? You've got a cast on her arm and leg, her ribs are wrapped, and her head's stitched up and bandaged. But resetting that shoulder—"

Dr. Radcliffe approached at that moment. He had a streak of blood on his face and neck. His eyes were red-rimmed, his hair in disarray. But his hands were clean and his sleeves rolled up—a man who meant business. "You've done wonderful work here, both of you. I can reset the shoulder."

"What do you need?" Maggie dropped back and became the assistant.

"Connor, Maggie and I can handle this. Go see if the boy shows any sign of waking up."

Maggie's head came up, and she tried not to reveal her distress. It struck her again that Connor was being sent off to tend a patient on his own while she was kept nearby for supervision by Dr. Radcliffe.

"Because this is more serious and you need better hands here?" Connor asked. He met Maggie's eyes, and she knew he'd understood her thoughts.

"Yes, of course," Doc Radcliffe replied impatiently. "Maggie is possibly the finest pupil I've ever had. She's the first woman I've worked with, and I'm determined she'll be ready for anything." Radcliffe bent over the shoulder and examined it as he talked. "I've been meticulous in watching her bring her skills to the highest level. I'm afraid she'll face doubts among those she treats. The boy just needs a simple check. He got knocked cold and he'll wake up when he's ready. I need Maggie here with me so I can advance her training. I'd let you stay too, Connor, but I need someone with that boy."

Connor hurried away, but not before Maggie saw the smile on his face. Considering the difficult day, finding a smile took some effort.

"Now," Doc Radcliffe began, "normally with an injury of this type . . ."

Maggie snapped her attention back to the task in front of her. Yes. She was on her way to becoming a real doctor.

Maggie stumbled to a halt as she left the doctor's office. "It's still daylight." She glanced behind her at Connor. "Unless we worked overnight and it's actually tomorrow."

"No, it's definitely today. Although today would be today even if it were tomorrow."

Maggie arched a brow. "What does that mean?"

Connor shrugged. "I think it means we're both exhausted."

He rested his hand on her back, maybe to steady her, but it felt so nice she decided to believe he was just touching her because he wanted to be close.

Connor guided her with his strong hand, and Maggie noticed they were taking the meandering path through the park again. Last night had gone badly there, and she wished Connor hadn't come this way.

"It was a wonder watching you work today, Maggie. I'm hoping you're feeling better about the way Doc's been treating you."

Maggie inched closer to Connor, and instead of his hand resting on her back, his arm slid around her waist. "I do feel better."

"You did things today I'd never heard of, let alone seen before. That man with the injured throat—you saved his life, Maggie."

She looked at him, confused. "What?"

"The man who came in first, before all the injured folks from the stagecoach, the one who got thrown from a bronco?"

That wiped away some of her brain fog. "Oh, of course, the tracheotomy. That seems so long ago now. I'd read about the procedure, and we also studied it in class." Maggie went on to explain about what a tracheotomy was, how you could open an airway in a crushed throat to keep someone breathing.

Connor asked more questions as they strolled along, enjoying talking over the madness of the day.

"I think we saved every injured passenger," he said. "Only the driver was beyond help."

Maggie snuggled closer to him and reached across to rest her right hand on his chest. "That must've been an awful thing to see, Connor, that man dead. The others so badly injured. I wasn't done with the man's throat when the first of the injured arrived. I was desperate to come and help you, but I had to stay."

"I understand. And while I could've used the help, I knew what I was sending your way."

"I stuck that poor man with the tube still in his throat in the hospital with only his brother and father there to breathe for him. Dr. Radcliffe got back and found time at some point to go finish

160

what I'd started. I don't know what he did, though. I'll have to ask him tomorrow."

"It was a humbling experience for me, Maggie. My respect for you was already high, but now . . . I feel like a fool for not realizing all there is to know."

She nodded her head toward the little bench where they'd sat together just last night, where they'd fought and where she'd walked away, thinking their romance was over.

They sat on the bench, and he rested his arm across her shoulders and pulled her close. "After the doctor spoke to me so kindly today," Maggie said, "an idea started boiling in my head, and it's been percolating ever since."

"Let's hear it."

"All right, Connor. Tell me what you think about this. I know you're a hard worker. And I can see you're a fast learner, a man who's not afraid to take on something new. What if, instead of you following me to Cutler to build a ranch, we think about what great partners we could be? We could go to Cutler and open an office, one with two doctors."

Connor leaned forward, elbows on his knees, hands clamped together as he turned to look at her. "I honestly have never thought of myself as a doctor—even though I'm working for one and doing a lot of doctoring. But it's hard to get the idea in my head to doctor for a living. And after today, I know how poorly trained I am. I can handle routine things, but that *tractostomy* . . ." He shook his head.

She shoulder-bumped him. "*Tracheotomy*. But I've never done one before today, and the doctor said he'd never done one, either. It's very rare."

Connor looked out across the park. Then, after a long minute, he nodded and turned back to her. "It'll work, won't it? I don't know how exactly. I know I don't need to go to school."

"Yes, you do, but I can—"

"My friend Dare didn't go to school. There's something called . . . I think it's what folks call a nontraditional doctor's license.

Or an irregular license. Something like that. He has such a license because he learned doctoring in the war. Maybe I can get that kind. I'm not sure of the rules, but I think working with a doctor, like I'm doing, is enough."

Maggie squinted at him. "Then why do I have to go to school?"

Connor sat up straight and shrugged. "You probably don't, but look what you've learned already. It's a good idea for one of us to go, and then you can teach me all you know."

"The people in Cutler may object, though. I doubt they'll want to pay for two doctors. And the office they're building for me may not be big enough for two, and—"

Connor touched her lips, and she fell silent. She stared into his sparking blue eyes.

"We'll ask them," he said, "the Cutler folks. You said someone is coming from there one of these days to see how you're doing and decide if they are satisfied with your skills, right?"

"Yes." She moved his fingers away but held on to his hand. "If they don't want two doctors, then I'll be the doctor and you can be my loyal nurse." She giggled. It sounded silly, but she rather liked the idea of her being the doctor and him being the nurse.

"Well then, Doctor, you'd better stay mighty close to me in case some rare accident happens again. And you know the best way we can stay real close?"

Maggie could guess. But she didn't jump in with an answer. She let him do the talking.

Connor leaned forward and kissed her. One quick kiss. "We need to be married. No sense figuring out how we're going to spend the rest of our lives together and not make getting married a part of that plan."

It was Maggie's turn. She leaned in and kissed him back, but not a quick kiss. A kiss that was better than the warmth of sunlight. She pulled back a few inches so she could meet his eyes. "No sense at all."

Connor's eyes went wide. He caught her hands and raised them to his lips, kissing them, holding her. "Really, Maggie? You're ready?"

"Yes, I'll marry you, Connor. I'd be honored to be your wife. I can't take a break to go home for a wedding. Not yet. Normally there's a break at the end of the summer. But I missed too many classes because Ma was hurt, so maybe over Thanksgiving we can get—"

"Tonight."

"Uh, we can have Thanksgiving tonight?"

Grinning, Connor shook his head. "We're getting married tonight. Right now. The parson can marry us tonight, and then you can come and stay with me at the boardinghouse."

"Tonight?" Maggie's breathing turned ragged.

"Yep. Unless the parson has room for us both in his house." He stood and drew her to her feet and started walking fast toward the parson's house, as if he couldn't wait to marry her, which was so sweet. "But I think he's just being kind to give you that room. He'd probably want you to find your own place once you were wed. You can write your folks and tell them the good news. If you think my room at the boardinghouse is too small, we can ask if she's got a bigger one. Married couples stay there, too."

Maggie swallowed hard as she hurried to keep up and Connor planned their life at top speed. Her hand tightened on his.

Connor stopped his headlong planning and turned to her. "What's the matter?"

"You can tell something is the matter? That's sweet."

"But you didn't answer me."

Because she really didn't want to. If she said the wrong thing, he might delay the wedding and she didn't want that. At least not mostly.

Squaring her shoulders, determined to be honest, she said, "I'm just sorry my family couldn't be here for my wedding. I'd like so much to talk to Ma first."

Connor took both her hands and focused on her as no one ever had. "If this is really important to you, Maggie, we will wait. I want to be with you. I don't want to walk away from you every night. But that won't change if we delay getting married. I know you don't think you can get away, but let's ask. We can ride the train down one day and back the next."

"It doesn't go through daily, more like twice a week. I—" Maggie clamped her mouth shut because no more words would come.

Connor pulled her into his arms. "We'll wait."

She buried her face against his chest and shook her head frantically. Finally she lifted it, embarrassed because she knew she had tears running down her cheeks.

"Please don't cry. We'll do whatever you want."

"Hush." She pressed her fingers to his lips. "No, we won't wait. Yes, I wish my ma were here, but she's not, and I'm feeling so lonely right now I don't think I can bear to let go of you. And most of these foolish tears—"

"They're not foolish, Maggie. I wish my family could be here, too."

That made her smile. "I can't have my family right now, but I can have you. Please, Connor, let's go get married. Tonight, if possible."

He bent to kiss her again. She tasted the salt of her own tears as their lips met. When the kiss ended, she wrapped her arms around Connor and let him bear her weight as she wept.

When she had controlled her tears and gathered her strength, she straightened, drew a hanky from the pocket of her dress, and tidied her face. Then she shook back her hair and smiled. "It's been a long, hard day. Let's end it with something wonderful."

Chapter

10

Connor couldn't believe he was walking home with his brand-spankin'-new wife. "Life takes some mighty fine twists and turns, don't it, Maggie?"

Maggie grinned at him. "It does indeed. Although I think we both saw this twist coming for a while now."

She carried a satchel stuffed with clothes and her doctor's bag in one hand, so she had a free hand to hang on to him. He had two carpetbags the parson's wife had lent them. Maggie didn't have much, but there were a few things she needed to collect, including a wind-up clock, heavy winter clothes, as well as a few other things. They would move them tomorrow when they returned the carpetbags. By then Connor would know if he had to find a new place to live.

They reached the boardinghouse, and Connor's hand tightened on hers. "I'm gonna tell someone for the first time in my life that I am married." He let go of her hand in order to sling an arm around her shoulders. In the shadow of a big tree right next to the house, he kissed her. "I can't wait!"

Maggie laughed. "I feel slightly more awkward about it than

that, but I'm honored to be your wife. I'm glad we went ahead and got married tonight."

"The parson seemed a little surprised."

"That didn't stop him from performing the ceremony," Maggie reminded him. "And I thought his wife had a very satisfied expression on her face, as if she'd fully expected this all along."

"She strikes me as a wise woman," Connor agreed. He gave her a firm one-armed hug. "All right, let's go in."

The folks at the boardinghouse were just sitting down to supper. Connor made his announcement, and they pulled up an extra chair so Maggie could eat the evening meal with all the guests. She noticed two other couples, one with a small child, so accommodating families wasn't something new here.

With the soft clinking of cutlery on heavy pottery plates, surrounded by kind words of congratulations, they enjoyed the crisp fried chicken and creamy mashed potatoes. Delicious apple cobbler made a fine finish to Maggie's wedding party.

Connor spoke quietly with the boardinghouse owners, who seemed eager to have a new boarder. His rent would go up a dollar a week, and they'd give them a slightly larger room.

And then the meal was over, and folks began drifting off to their rooms. Connor took her hand and led her upstairs.

Suddenly Maggie realized exactly why she wanted her mother at her wedding.

❧

Maggie woke the next morning with her husband's arms around her. Her head rested on his strong shoulder, her palm open on his strong heart. She lay there quietly, thinking of the wonder of having someone of her very own.

A husband.

And they'd managed fine without her ma.

Smiling, she felt him shift a bit and raised her eyes to see that he was awake, looking at her with the most wonderful joy in his eyes.

"I was just thinking how blessed I am to have such a fine husband."

He kissed her gently. "And I had the same thought, wife. It strikes me as a wonderful thing if a married couple both think they are the one who got the greatest blessing. That's a good way to feel about each other."

"I'd best be up and moving. I've got class today." She sat up, and Connor pulled her right back down. She giggled and nestled against him. "I suppose a few more moments in your arms would be nice."

"A few more moments?" Connor kissed her.

She kissed him back with all the newfound knowledge of a wife. "Or maybe a bit longer."

He walked her to class. He'd always stopped for her at the parson's and they'd gone on together. But the college was a few city blocks on past the doctor's office and she'd always gone herself. Usually there were other students heading that way along with her, most of them she knew. So she was more than safe enough.

But today he couldn't bear to let go of her hand quite yet. They spoke quietly, shutting out the rest of the world.

"It's Saturday," Connor said. "We'll have tonight and tomorrow to celebrate being married." He held back from kissing her, not on a busy street like this, but looked long and deep into her eyes. He was certain that she knew he wanted to.

"I'd like time with only you, Connor. If there's somewhere we can be alone in this city, then it's fine to go rambling. Otherwise let's find a quiet corner of the boardinghouse or just stay in our room. That's the kind of celebration that appeals to me."

"And that is an answer to warm the heart of your husband. I'll see you at the doctor's office." He squeezed her hand and watched her go into the building, then turned to head for work.

There was still plenty to do, left over from yesterday.

"I slept here last night," Dr. Radcliffe said. He wore a clean white shirt and black pants and vest, but he looked rumpled. "I sent all but three patients home. The young mother—her husband came for the boy. The man with the badly broken arm I'm afraid will be here for a long while. And the man riding shotgun is still seeing double. He finally regained consciousness long enough to at least try standing."

Doc ran his hands deeply into his unruly hair. "He told me his name, though. I didn't even know if he was from Denver. But he is, so I sent a messenger to his home. His wife is on the way with a couple of his brothers. I can probably release him when they get here."

Turning to his badly depleted doctor's bag, the doctor began restocking it.

"Maggie and I got married last night," Connor said.

The doctor spun around sharply, his eyes direct. "You did?"

Connor grinned. "Yep, I finally talked her into it."

The doctor chuckled and came to clap Connor on the shoulder. "Well, congratulations. I could see there was a strong affection between you two."

A good part of the morning was gone before they'd finished with all the urgent care these folks needed. There was much to do that'd been neglected yesterday, but before they started with their routine checkups and treatments, Connor managed to get Dr. Radcliffe's attention.

He might as well plunge in with the plans he and Maggie had made.

Maggie rushed in at that moment.

"Is something wrong?" Connor asked.

"No, I'm sorry. I didn't mean to startle you. I'm just concerned about how many patients you might have so I'm hurrying. Most of my class was over here working yesterday, so our teacher let us off from our studies for the day. She said we all learned more nursing yesterday than in a month in her school."

"We welcome your help, uh . . . Mrs. Kincaid, is it?"

Connor reached for her hand. "I told Doc we got married."

Maggie loved the warmth and strength of his touch.

"I'm delighted to hear it," Radcliffe said. "You make a fine couple."

"I'm glad Maggie came now so we can tell you our plan together. We're going to go to Cutler, and I'll work alongside her as a second doctor. I have been training here with you, and while I don't know all you know, Doc, and I've not had the schooling Maggie's had, I think I can get an irregular doctor's license and—"

"Connor, what in the world makes you think you have enough skills to be a doctor? You'd never qualify for an irregular license, not after the few months you'll have worked with me."

"But then if I work with Maggie in Cutler, I can put in as much time as I need to. I can get it then."

"Still, you haven't even begun to have the doctoring skills you need."

"You let me set stitches without even watching me. I've cast broken bones, as well."

"Yes, but after I first made sure they were set. What about the ones that need setting?"

"Maggie can do the more complicated things and teach me as she goes." Connor gave Maggie a nervous glance. She held his hand and nodded.

The doctor scowled and began pacing the room. Clearly upset.

"It was just a notion we had, Doc. You've allowed me a lot of independence here. But I suppose I can find work anywhere. Maggie can doctor, and I'll get a regular job."

Before the doctor could reply, the front door swung open. The doctor's shoulders slumped, and for the first time Maggie saw just how exhausted the man was.

Maggie moved farther into the waiting room toward the door. "Can I help you, sir?"

"I'm here from Cutler to talk to the girl who wants to be a doctor."

"Um, that's me—I'm Maggie Kincaid. I was told someone

would come from Cutler to decide if I was ready to start my duties out there, but you weren't expected quite so soon."

The young man smiled and stepped closer to her. He was short with neatly combed hair and was no older than Connor. He wore a brown suit and a strange hat with a rounded top and a narrow, rolled brim. Removing the hat, he gave them all a cocky grin, blue eyes shining through his gold, wire-rimmed spectacles. "You see, my pa sent me here to tell you that Cutler has changed its mind and wants me to be their doctor instead of a woman. A woman doctor didn't sit well with anyone, but they accepted it because at the time they had no choice."

"What? I don't understand." Just yesterday she'd thought Dr. Radcliffe didn't respect her, and she'd learned different. Now here she was being shown blatant disrespect.

Shaking his head, he narrowed his eyes at Maggie. "I came home from the city to visit my folks, and after talking the matter over, I've decided to be Cutler's new doctor. It sets them back a few months, but that's better than ending up with a woman doctor. The college sent me here. I went there first and made arrangements to start right in taking classes. I'll go through the summer to pick up the classes that are already over and be doctoring by next fall."

"But they begged me to come." Maggie fought to keep her temper under control. "They made me promise I'd stay five years." Her voice then rose a bit. A lot. "I've got a *contract*."

"Yes, well, the contract is canceled." The man waved his hand as if a signed contract had no legal standing. "You can go on home now and . . . I think I overheard the doctor here call you *Mrs. Kincaid*—so there now, you can stay home and tend your family like a wife ought. The town decided you don't even have to repay the money they spent on your schooling." He gave her a smirky smile. "But that's the end of it. You'll have to quit school immediately."

Connor's eyes flashed with a dangerous light, and his body turned all rigid like he was getting ready to fight.

And Maggie had never loved him more. Before Connor could

do anything, though, she glared at the smug man and said, "Now, see here—"

"Mrs. Kincaid *will* continue studying medicine, young man," Dr. Radcliffe interrupted. His voice was calm, and heavy with the authority that came with age and experience. "If Cutler has broken her contract, then I'm going to refer Mrs. Kincaid to a lawyer I know so she can sue your town. She's a fine doctor. She saved a man's life just yesterday through a very difficult surgery I've never even done before myself. So I will not stand here and listen to you insult her."

"It's hardly an insult, Doctor, to say a woman belongs at home."

"It is the way you say it, mister," Connor broke in. "You're as good as sneering at a skilled surgeon—and a wise, strong doctor I would want at my side in any crisis. Your little cow town would be lucky to have her."

Maggie didn't want Connor and Dr. Radcliffe to fight her fights for her. On the other hand, she was hearing lovely things about herself, which made her feel good.

Even so, Maggie held up both hands, palms facing out. "Everyone stop right now." She spoke to the men, one at a time. "Dr. Radcliffe, I appreciate your kind words. I sincerely do. But I have no wish to sue the town of Cutler. This has opened my eyes and I'm delighted I don't have to go there now." Next, she smiled at Connor. "I don't know how we'll afford it, but I would like to finish my studies. Maybe I can get a job in the evening. Maybe I could write my parents and ask if they would help fund my medical training. Maybe—"

"We'll do it, Maggie. I've got money put by. It might not be quite enough, but we'll figure it out."

Then it was the city slicker's turn. She smiled, but it might've been a bit more like she'd bared her teeth. "You have no call to speak to me so rudely, sir. I can tell right now you will make a dreadful doctor. I'd say that town deserves you."

"I'll make a fine doctor," he argued.

"You may learn medical skills, but you will never have the

compassion and wisdom necessary to be a good doctor. Now, you'll have to leave. We have people waiting who need a doctor's care."

The man sniffed at her, rolled his eyes, and said, "Women doctors. What is this world coming to?" He spun on his heel and walked out, and it was a good thing because Connor looked as though he was about to swing a fist.

"I'm so sorry about that, Maggie," Connor said.

She smiled. "I'm not. I do worry about the money, but just think, Connor—instead of going all the way into the mountains to that remote little town, we can go home. If Rawhide doesn't need another doctor, maybe we can settle in Colorado City. We'd be only a few hours' ride from the ranch."

Connor drew her into his arms and hugged her. "You're right. I only heard the insult, but you're right. We can go home."

"It's as if God intervened and is guiding your steps," Dr. Radcliffe added. "Maggie, as of Monday, your hours spent working here will be paid hours. I'll work with you and Connor both to train you as best I can to be doctors."

"I'll keep working here, Doc," Connor said. "But if we go home, I'll probably go back to ranching. So I don't need you to spend too much time with me—I'll just keep doing the simple things. You get Maggie all the learnin' you can."

"That sounds fine." The doctor chuckled. "You may end up being very skilled whether you plan on it or not. And now I'm sending you both home."

"Oh no you don't," Connor said back. "You were here all night, Doc."

"True, but I forgot to tell you that another doctor—one who helped yesterday and took several of the less severely injured patients to his office—came by and told me he released them all. He got a good night's rest and he's coming now to take over here for a few days."

As if on cue, the front door opened and in came the other doctor.

Before Maggie knew it, she and Connor were outside, walking hand in hand toward the boardinghouse.

"I haven't even written home yet to tell Ma and Pa I'm married," Maggie said, although she wasn't too worried about it.

"I reckon I need to do that, too." Connor's smile said that wasn't his first thought, however.

"I think we've got things arranged finally, don't we, husband?"

"Yep, you can have the job you've such a gift for. I can have my ranch, and we can both be near family."

"You know, your willingness to come with me to Cutler helped me to fall in love with you, Connor. I'm glad we had to go through this tangle—it helped me know you better and love you more."

Right out in full daylight, Connor slid his arm around her waist and held her close as they made their way home.

With the rest of the day off, and a full day free after church on Sunday, and important letters to write, it was a wonder really that neither of them got so much as a single word put on paper.

A FORT RENO NOVELLA

Bound AND DETERMINED

REGINA JENNINGS

Chapter

1

August 1885
East of Fort Reno, Indian Territory

I don't want to die on an empty stomach. Oh, please, don't let me die hungry." Private Morris smashed his hat down flat as he leveled his pistol against a shelf of rock.

"I have some jerky in my saddlebag. As soon as they've passed us, I'll get you some. Then you can leave this earth fulfilled." Private Bradley Willis mopped the sweat away from his eyes with his bandanna.

Captain Chandler lowered his field glasses. "They're headed this way. Any word on that gully? Where does it lead?"

Bradley looked over his shoulder at Private Krebs, who was climbing up the bank to join them. The red dust had mixed with his sweat, coating his face in orange.

"It don't go nowhere. We can't get out that way, but at least it'll get the horses out of sight."

Three horses. Not enough for four men to outrun the outlaws, especially with one man injured. And with hiding places scarce in the wide plains of Indian Territory, if you couldn't outrun your foe, you were in a heap of trouble.

"The horses are in the gully? When are you getting me some jerky?" Morris asked. The blood seeping from the bandage on Morris's leg was drawing flies in the heat.

"Can't just now," Bradley said. His throat caught as he tried to swallow. He wasn't partial to being stationed next to an injured man. Fight and win, or die in a blaze of glory—that was Bradley's plan. It wasn't that he was afraid. He just couldn't stand to sit and wait for his fate. They needed to get a jump on these outlaws, and quickly.

"Keep steady. If we're lucky, they'll pass on by." That was Chandler. Avoid a fight if the odds were against you. If the captain had known that the Gunther gang had picked up four more men, he wouldn't have followed them in the first place. Turned out it was an ambush. Now they had to limp back to Fort Reno with a strong gang on their trail, and their odds didn't look good.

Private Krebs took up his rifle on the other side of Bradley. "Do they know we're here?" he whispered.

"Not yet." Bradley squinted against the waving heat rising off the packed ground. "There's still eight of them? I thought we took down two."

"Have mercy," Private Krebs replied. "We fired 'most all our rounds. How'd we not hit more?"

The Gunthers galloped at a diagonal toward them, in plain sight. If they kept to their path, they'd overshoot the hidden cavalrymen by about a quarter of a mile. As Bradley lay on his stomach, propped up by his arms, the ground vibrated beneath him.

"I'm shaky," Morris said. He dropped his pistol and rested his head against the ground. "Tell me when they get closer. I'll save my strength."

The outlaws closed the distance until they were close enough that Bradley could make out the sweat on the flanks of their horses. Pete Gunther's paint trotted past them without pausing. If the rest of the outlaws would just follow him . . .

The younger Gunther boy turned in their direction. With the heat swerving up and the shadow of his hat, Bradley couldn't make out his expression, but his palomino dropped out of the pack as he studied a patch of dried grass that the cavalrymen had ridden through.

No one lying behind the crest breathed a word. The flies buzzed around Morris's leg, but that was the only sound as the gunslinger studied their position.

"Ho!" the outlaw called. With his outstretched arm, he motioned to the path that led directly to the cavalrymen.

His older brother raised his hand, and the galloping outlaws wheeled around.

"That gully might not be a bad idea," Private Krebs said.

"And have them shooting down on us?" Chandler replied. "I'd rather take my chances on flat land."

And Bradley would rather be on his horse, not lying in the dirt like a worm. He looked over at Morris, who'd turned clammy and pale.

If Bradley were in charge, he would've hidden Morris in the gully and ridden for reinforcements. Instead, three able-bodied men were hiding because of one injured. It didn't make any sense at all, but there was no more time for reckoning. They were coming.

"Morris?" Bradley nudged him with his elbow, but the private was out cold.

Chandler caught his eye. "We'll be fine," he said.

Not necessarily.

The calls of the outlaws were getting more excited as they became convinced they'd found their foe. Bradley sighted along his Sharps rifle. "Just tell me when," he said. And then it was time.

With the first volley they unseated two of them, then the ground before them exploded. Bradley fired his rifle twice more. By then, his targets had found cover. Evidently they weren't of a mind to run away.

"We're pinned down," Bradley said to his commander. "What are we supposed to do? Just wait?"

Chandler rubbed the sweat from his eyes, leaving a muddy swipe on his forehead. "They're the ones on the run, not us. They'll move out as soon as they can."

"Doubt it," Bradley said. "They came back for us, didn't they?"

Chandler shoved his field glasses out of his way as he burrowed farther into the ground. "No more of that talk, Private Willis. If Major Adams wasn't family to you, I would have turned you in for insubordination already."

For that remark? Bradley had done much worse. Besides, Major Adams wasn't his kin. Not until he married Bradley's sister, Louisa. And Chandler knew good and well that Major Adams didn't cut Bradley any slack.

Private Krebs fired off a round. "They're coming closer," he said. "See that scrub brush over there? It's got someone in it."

It was only a matter of time. Bradley looked at Captain Chandler, who had grim determination painted on his face. Then there was Private Krebs, whose nervous energy Bradley understood better. And Private Morris, who was resting fitfully and might never know what hit him if they failed.

The noose was tightening around their necks. Good men would be lost if someone didn't do something.

"I'm taking it to them," Bradley said.

Private Krebs gasped. "Are you crazy?"

"Private Willis, you will not abandon your—"

But Bradley wasn't staying to argue. He rolled away and crawled over the rocky ground until he reached the steep bank of the gully. Sliding down it, he reached his horse. Excitement flooded through him at being in the saddle again. Boots in the stirrups—that was how Bradley would meet his destiny. He hadn't joined the cavalry to be killed on the ground. He reached back for his saddlebag and got everything arranged, including his pistol. Taking a deep breath, he spurred his horse. It scrambled for its footing as it rose over the bank, but once it emerged, he charged ahead.

Flying over his enraged captain, Bradley dropped a sack of jerky for Morris and plowed toward the band of outlaws waiting for him.

GARBER, TEXAS

The saber glinted in the morning sun as it swooped through the air. Ambrosia Herald gripped it in both hands and made another daring slice through the dust motes of her father's library. When she and her mother had designed the floor plan of the new house, they'd made sure to include ample room for her father's cavalry memorabilia, but now the medals, spurs, and letters of commendation only seemed to agitate him.

It had been months since she'd heard her father's laugh. Months since he'd felt well enough to take her riding or to work in Mother's rose garden. When he felt well, he sat at his desk and wrote letter after letter, compelled by forces that the rest of the family didn't understand, but most days he wandered aimlessly about the house as if looking for something he'd misplaced.

"You absolutely cannot go." Her mother's voice grew clearer as she descended the stairs, speaking, no doubt, to Father's back. "Why don't you stay home and enjoy your retirement? You've earned a rest."

They were coming her way. Ambrosia barely had time to set the saber back on its stand over the fireplace before her parents entered.

"I've done nothing but rest since winter." And yet his voice sounded weak, strained. "It's time I was out."

"But your health," her mother said. "It's delicate."

That word never failed to annoy her father. "It's not getting any better sitting around here. I've received the letters I was waiting for. Help is meeting me in Kansas."

"What kind of help?" her mother asked.

"A handful of cowboys and a promising young cavalryman from Fort Reno. No reason to delay any longer."

"What are you doing in Kansas?" Ambrosia jumped out of the way as her father went to his desk. She'd always been jealous of his stories, especially now that she was grown and had no such adventures before her.

"It's those camels again." Her mother tried to arrange a blanket over Father's shoulders as he rummaged through his desk drawer, but he shrugged it off. "They'll be the death of him." Never one for understatement, Ambrosia's mother continued. "The last thing he needs is to take on more responsibility. It's not as if we need the money, and I'm not sure what kind of money those animals are supposed to make anyway. Besides, a trip in this heat will probably dry him up like a raisin."

The last time they'd had this conversation, he was doomed to be shoe leather. Ambrosia assumed that was progress.

"We don't need the camels," he said, "but they need us. It's time they come home."

All her childhood, Captain Herald had told Ambrosia stories about the gallant camel cavalry and the Big Bend expedition. He'd always included the names of the camels—Omar, Ruby, and Esmeralda—right along with Lieutenants Echols, Hartz, and Beale, as if they were equals. But however fond he might have been of his long-lost mounts, Ambrosia and her mother couldn't understand his fascination with the beasts.

"Found it." He held up a small leather journal. "Now I can calculate the supplies I'll need and be ready for the train tomorrow."

"Tomorrow?" Her mother gave a sorrowful look out the French doors at her garden. With a determined glint in her eyes, she said, "Ambrosia is going with you."

Ambrosia bounced on her toes. "Really?"

"I wish she could," he said, "because until a person travels with the camels in the summer, they can't truly appreciate them. But this journey will be too strenuous. She'd be miserable."

"No, I won't. It will be an adventure, just like those you're always telling me about." Certainly Ambrosia would miss their new home, the scent of the fresh woodwork and wallpaper, but she couldn't wait to be tested. To see if she had what it took. Swinging a sword through dust motes was a far cry from making a journey on horseback. Or camelback, as it were.

"Once we get started, there'll be no going back," he said. "No matter how rough the going is, Amber, you can't quit."

She'd rarely seen her father so stern. Ambrosia looked to her mother, unsure of her support. But her mother nodded as she nudged her forward with an elbow. For whatever reason, her mother and her father were in agreement. Something was amiss.

"I can keep up," she said finally. "I won't slow you down."

"Fine, but you'd better be ready by tomorrow, or I'm leaving you behind. Now excuse me, as I plan my corral." He headed to the only space they had available, her mother's freshly planted rose garden, and began walking off the length of the north side.

Had her father just agreed? Had that been too easy? She looked to her mother, but she was mourning her roses.

"When I think of all those years spent in army camps, without any permanent home, without a place to plant, and now . . ." She turned to Ambrosia, her eyes alive with purpose. "This is perfect. It's a tall order for someone so young, and your father has already called in reinforcements, but I have full confidence that you can thwart him, the cowboys, and this young trooper he hired."

"Thwart him? He's not even sure I can survive the trip home."

"That's the beauty of my plan. You aren't coming home on camel. You are going to put an end to this madness. If you succeed, you'll come back on the train within the week, and the camel topic will be retired permanently."

Ambrosia might be only eighteen, but she had determination in spades. This was her chance to be just as brave as a cavalryman, and to help her family while she was at it.

"Tell me what you need," she said. "I won't let you down."

Chapter

2

ONE WEEK LATER
OUTSIDE OF ANTHONY, KANSAS

He was still wearing the cavalry blue, but if Bradley didn't complete this mission, he wouldn't be for long.

Instead of congratulating him on escaping the Gunther gang and getting his men home safely, Major Adams had applied harsh words. The major appeared to be of the mind that a private should obey a captain, even if that captain was Captain Chandler. Even if everyone survived. Even if the only damage done was a dent to Bradley's canteen when a bullet ricocheted off it.

Only in the government did you get written up for saving people.

When Bradley had charged straight at the Gunthers, they'd turned tail and run. True, he should've remembered that his saddle-bags held the unit's extra ammunition, but by the time he'd seen it, it was too late. Had he gotten shot while making his charge, Chandler and the others would have been left high and dry. But he hadn't been shot, and that made all the difference.

Following the wagon ruts, Bradley guided a wagon full of crates and kegs that he'd picked up in town out to a farm. Major Adams had assigned him to help a retired cavalry buddy who needed an escort across Indian Territory. As far as punishments went, it wasn't bad. Better than being locked in the guardhouse again. If the retired captain gave a good report, Bradley would be forgiven, and his record would be cleared. He owed it to his sister to try. She'd sacrificed too much for his career for him to lose it.

Besides, Bradley loved being in the cavalry. Though if he had his druthers, he'd druther not go traipsing across the prairie in August. No water, grass all burnt to a crisp, and the sun acting like it had a personal vendetta against you and all your kin. But if anyone could do it, Bradley Willis could.

A slow trip up to Kansas in a stagecoach—why Major Adams hadn't let him bring his horse, he'd never understand—and a slow trip back with the herd. When he'd reached the town of Anthony, he'd been given instructions to bring the wagon of supplies to a Mr. Switcher's farm. Judging from the storekeeper's comments, the old farmer had a reputation for being an eccentric. Judging from the supplies Bradley had on his buckboard, Captain Herald might be, too. Standard chuck wagon fare didn't include fresh apples, horehound candy, and a feather mattress.

Bradley had many questions as he approached the farm, but he'd know everything soon enough. There was always time to worry later.

In this flat, treeless land, the farm was visible for miles, but finally they were close enough to hear the squeaking of the windmill. As they drew nearer, his team slowed. The sorrel's ears pricked. The skin on its hindquarters shuddered in ripples. Bradley loosened the reins. They weren't afraid of a windmill, were they? The sorrel abruptly swerved, pulling the dun with it, and the wagon wheels left the path and rolled into the stubble of the recently harvested wheat field.

"Whoa," Bradley ordered. He directed the horses back onto the trail. Now it wasn't just the sorrel acting up, but the dun, too.

What was wrong with them? They were acting like something at the farm ahead was fixing to ambush them.

It was a nice enough farm. A green roof capped the tidy house. The barn doors yawned open as if so full they couldn't be fastened. A cattle dog dozed on the porch. Nothing amiss, but the horses had stopped. The sorrel's sides heaved. They were spooked, sure enough. Bradley hopped down from his seat and looked over the traces for anything that could be goosing them.

"We're almost there," he said. "Just get these supplies over to the barn."

Wild equine eyes met his. Flared nostrils dripped.

"What is it?" he asked as he stroked the sorrel's neck. "Wolves? Coyotes?"

But the dog on the porch hadn't scented anything. Taking the reins around to the front, Bradley drew the horses forward against their will. Just a walk across the property to the barnyard, and then someone from the house would surely come out.

"Can't have a rancher seeing a cavalryman being bested by an old wagon team," he grunted. "What's wrong with y'all?"

They halted just short of the barnyard. Voices could be heard on the other side. He thought of calling out, but not until he got his horses under control. They were pacing, pulling back against him. The dun gave a little hop. Both watched the barnyard pen. Bradley looked over his shoulder. What could it be? Everything looked just as a farm should.

Until something strange, something he'd never seen before, peered at him from around the side of the barn. It was just a head—foreign, unknown, and floating from up high. His blood ran cold.

The horses just flat-out ran.

"Whoa!" he called, but it was too late. Thrashing against each other, they turned. Bradley had to jump back or be taken down himself. The sorrel quickly found her feet and began pulling away. The dun righted herself to keep stride, and they were off. Bradley chased after the wagon. They cut sharply, but they were going too fast to make the turn. One wheel left the ground as the wagon tilted. The load shifted, and quick as Sergeant Nothem's flapjacks, the buckboard flipped over and spilled its contents. Bradley dodged the apples rolling at him and raced to the horses, which were dragging the destroyed equipment behind them.

Bradley caught a rein and pulled them to a stop. He stroked the frightened horse nearest him. "I don't know what kind of critters they're keeping at this farm, but—"

"Private!" The man coming toward him wasn't dressed in a uniform, but he walked just like those officers at Fort Reno did.

Bradley jumped to attention right there among the spilled goods and tangled lines. He had one shot at keeping his position. He said a quick prayer that wrecking the wagon wouldn't be enough to get him sent back in disgrace. "Private Bradley Willis, reporting for duty," he offered. "I'm reporting for duty, but the horses have other plans."

The man marched through the busted crates and scattered sundries. He put a calming hand on each of the horses. "Captain Herald, here. They must not have warned you at the hotel."

"Warned me, sir?"

"About the horses. As soon as they catch a whiff of the camels, they bolt." Captain Herald's hair was jet-black despite his age, and the loose, double-breasted shirt he wore hung on a frame that was made to carry more muscle.

"Camels?" Bradley looked at the strangely shaped mammal stirring in the corral. "You bought cattle from a camel breeder?"

"I didn't buy cattle."

"But Major Adams said that I'd be accompanying you and your livestock across Indian Territory."

"The camels are my livestock. I'm taking them back to my place in Texas."

Bradley was rarely caught by surprise, but this particular fact knocked him back a notch. "Camels? You're taking camels to Texas? If horses are afraid of them, how are we going to round them up?"

"Who needs horses when you can ride the camels?" The captain's drawn face looked like it hadn't smiled that wide in a very long time.

"Sir," Bradley said, "I'm a cavalryman. A trooper. I ride horses."

But the captain wasn't listening. "Let me introduce you to the herd, and then we need to bring the supplies into the barn. We've got a lot of work to do if we're going to leave tomorrow morning."

Camels? Bradley strained for another look, but the animal had wandered back to the other side of the barnyard. This was his assignment? This was the mission Major Adams had sent him on?

If so, his major was out of his ever-loving mind.

❧

"There ain't no way I'm messing with those creatures." The cowboy's eyes never left the big bull camel. His perfectly white teeth stuck out about as much as the dromedary's. "There ain't no way that God made an animal that ugly."

"I couldn't agree more." Ambrosia adjusted her leghorn hat with the wide, apple-green ribbon as she gazed up at the camel. "And they're dangerous, too. Ill-tempered, with razor-sharp teeth. Their favorite trick is to chomp the foot off a rider when he least expects it."

The cowboy shuddered and took another step back from the corral. Ambrosia hid her smile. When her mother had tasked her with disrupting her father's trip, she hadn't realized it would be this entertaining. Unable to convince her father that the camels were a bad idea, she'd now moved to the next stage, which was preventing him from coming home with the beasts. Without some hired help, they'd never be able to cross Indian Territory, and thankfully the cowboys he'd hired to accompany them were a superstitious lot. At this rate, she'd be able to save her father's health and her mother's beautiful flower gardens in one fell swoop.

Where was her father, anyway? He was jogging out toward the road, the last she saw, and in his condition, he shouldn't be hur-

188

rying about like that. But it had given her the perfect opportunity to send another feckless cowboy packing.

"I'll stick to horses, thank ye very much." The cowboy managed to pull his lips closed, even over all his teeth. "I'll go tell your pa that I've reconsidered my offer."

"No need." She smiled sweetly. "I'll tell him myself."

After a tip of his hat, the cowboy stuck his hands in his pockets and ambled away.

She spun her parasol on her shoulder as she surveyed the camels. The two younger calves loped around the corral with a weird swaying trot, their flat feet splaying out with each step. How in the world could her father have become so infatuated? After listening to his stories for years, she'd imagined them as elegant, noble creatures instead of the awkward animals clowning around before her.

The old bull gazed down over the end of his huge flapping lips, as if he'd read her unflattering thoughts.

Amber stabbed the end of her parasol into the dusty ground as the camel curled his lips back and showed his teeth. "Keep acting like that, and you'll scare them away faster," she said. "Besides, you'll be happier here in a barnyard than in mother's flower garden."

The camels turned their heads in unison. Even after all these years, the older animals seemed to remember her father. They listened for his voice, but this was someone else. Their odd heads rotated away, and they jogged to the other side of the corral.

More men coming to try their hand? Ambrosia gave her parasol another spin. Just a few minutes alone with her next victim, and she'd have another cowboy riding off into the sunset.

But he wasn't a cowboy—he was the cavalryman. She had to look twice for insignia because he strutted like he was at least a sergeant-major, but the lack of chevrons meant he was only a private.

How very disappointing.

"Private Willis, this is my daughter, Miss Herald. She's going with us on this little trip."

She stood tall as the trooper took a full accounting of her. He himself was well built, but not an overly large man. He had a strong jaw, and his lips were uneven, with the bottom lip fuller than it should be. Ambrosia wasn't sure whether it was enticing or not, but she was willing to give it some thought.

"Ma'am." He tipped his black slouch hat, giving her a quick glimpse of some deep-blue eyes. Then he turned to the pen. "Who do we have here?"

And just like that, she'd been dismissed.

"That's Omar. He's my mount," her father said. "And let me introduce you to the other four."

Ambrosia bit her lip as she fiddled with the lace on her collar. A less clever woman would have been annoyed that he was ignoring her. Instead, she was planning his speedy departure. How long would this one last?

"You stay and get acquainted," her father said. "I'll see about getting those supplies salvaged."

As her father left, the trooper crossed his arms over his chest and stood in silence before the dromedaries. Obviously he found them more interesting than her.

Ambrosia moistened her lips and sashayed closer. "Camels," she said. "I guess you weren't expecting that."

The sun reflected off his tanned face and thick eyelashes. "You never know what surprises a day will bring."

She smiled sympathetically. "It's just a pity that my father troubled you for naught."

Now she had his attention, but whatever was going on beneath his handsome face, she couldn't guess.

"You're making this trip with him?" he asked.

She shot a look over her shoulder as if getting ready to impart a secret. Intrigued, he bent forward to hear her whispered answer.

"If our plans hold, I'll go, but so far all of our help has deserted us. The camels are extremely dangerous, and it would take someone with a death wish to handle them. Plus, Father is very unreliable when it comes to payment. I really don't see what the incentive would be."

"Besides getting to spend time with you?" He said it evenly, as if it were a fact that everyone had already acknowledged.

A spark coursed through her veins. He wasn't ignoring her now. "I . . . I . . ." She swallowed, then braved a coquettish smile. "Please don't rely on me to be pleasant company. A journey in sweltering weather across an endless prairie is hardly ideal. Now, maybe if we'd met under different circumstances . . ."

Chapter

3

The camels were sure hard on the eyes, but Miss Herald was another story. She was a beauty, and from the act she was putting on, quite a handful, too. But what did she have to gain with the tall tales?

And what was her father thinking, bringing such a little spitfire on a trip like this? She might talk a tough game, but the scorching grasslands in August were no place for a lady.

"I appreciate the warning on the camels," he said, "but I'm no cowboy. This is my mission, and that means something to me." It didn't matter if he was riding a buffalo and herding catfish, he had to keep the captain happy.

Her parasol rotated slowly. Her smart, apple-green dress looked cool and crisp in the heat. "The camels have teeth like razors, and they chomp off the feet of their riders."

He couldn't keep his face from scrunching up in amusement. Bradley Willis knew when someone was joshing him.

"Then I'll keep my feet away," he said.

"And they're mean-spirited. They'll do anything to throw their riders off. Believe me, you don't want to fall from that height."

"Wouldn't be the first time." Bradley was intrigued. She might look like a proper lady, but she was up to mischief. And Bradley could never resist mischief.

"There's something else, something that I dread mentioning." She lowered her eyes, and her cheeks went pink. "They say that riding a camel can affect . . ."

"Go on."

She twirled an ebony curl around her finger. Adorable, and she knew it. "I really shouldn't say."

"Too late now."

She took a deep breath, as if bracing herself. "If you ride the camels, then you may not be able to sire a family later."

He stepped back to get a better look at the young miss, then burst out laughing.

She frowned. "I don't appreciate being laughed at."

"And I don't appreciate women who try to do my thinking for me."

The coquetry was blinked away in a heartbeat. "What's that supposed to mean?"

"I don't know why you're trying to sabotage your pa, but that's pretty low. Now, how about you stop with the nonsense and tell me something about these animals that's helpful?" Although she was telling him plenty about herself.

Had Major Adams known about the camels? Had he sent Bradley on this farce purposely? No way would a cavalry officer send a bona fide trooper on a mission like this.

Unless that trooper had deserted his unit during a gun fight. And that major happened to be his future brother-in-law who was always looking for new ways to inflict torment on him. Major Adams knew exactly what he was doing.

A rickety wagon pulled by one of the farmer's horses came rambling across the yard.

"Are y'all coming to help?" Captain Herald called.

"Yes, sir!" Bradley took one last look at Miss Herald. She stood in a perfect circle of shade beneath her parasol. The wide green ribbon wrapped around her dainty waist waved gently in the breeze. She would melt away like a stolen sugar cube out on those plains.

Good thing she wasn't as sweet as one.

Her eyes narrowed, as if reading his thoughts. With quick steps, she dashed past him to catch up with Captain Herald, ignoring Bradley's bow as she passed.

They came upon the scattered goods, and Miss Herald paused. She turned to Bradley, her narrow skirt flaring like a gentle fire. "How on earth did you spill a load in a wheat field? Was there a sudden curve you didn't see coming?"

"Oh, Ambrosia." The captain laughed as he pulled the wagon nearer the mess of supplies.

"I wasn't in the wagon when it overturned," Bradley said. "The horses tried it without me."

"They threw you out of the buckboard?" She glanced pointedly at his uniform. "Our troopers are not what they used to be."

"I didn't lose control. I got off—"

"And forgot to set the brake?" She smiled triumphantly. "I suppose cavalrymen aren't accustomed to the responsibility of crating goods. They're usually only looking out for their own hide."

He wondered what it'd take to wipe that smug grin off her face. He had a few ideas.

"Another cowboy backed out on me." Captain Herald grunted as he lifted a bag of beans to his shoulder. "And he was my last one. Good thing Private Willis is made of sterner stuff."

All the cowboys had backed out? Why? Then Bradley looked at Miss Herald. She batted her eyes at him before reaching for an empty gunny sack and collecting the apples that had scattered.

What was she up to?

Bradley grabbed a small barrel and carried it to the farmer's wagon. "Where'd the hotel's wagon and horses go?" he asked.

"I caught that cowboy sneaking away from the farm," Captain Herald answered. "After abandoning the mission, the least he could do is take them back to town for me."

"Can the camels pull this wagon?"

The captain set a crate on the buckboard with a thud. "They

could, but they don't need to. A camel can carry six hundred pounds on its back."

Bradley choked down his surprise. Supply wagons were the bane of the cavalry's existence—having to slow down for them, always looking for a safe crossing. Without wagons, they could travel unencumbered. Then again . . .

"So they're more like oxen?" Slow animals that plodded along. His hopes for a quick assignment and neat resolution to his trouble back at Fort Reno were fading.

"Only their strength. Depending on the length of the race and the terrain, some can travel faster than horses." Giving Bradley no time to dispute that claim, the captain continued. "We'll fit the two younger calves up with frames so they can carry our supplies."

Balancing the sack of apples on her hip, Miss Herald said, "I hate to delay us, but it's going to take some time for Sears, Roebuck to deliver a camel sidesaddle. I doubt they even carry such a thing."

"I swear, daughter. You and your objections, when I know from your mother that you packed a split skirt or two. And I'm going to make saddles for the three of us."

Bradley expected more of an argument, but Miss Herald gave that one up easily. What was going on here? Was her father forcing her to take this trip?

"Why camels?" Bradley asked. "What are you going to do with them?"

"I'm going to keep them for my own enjoyment, and there's nothing you can say to talk me out of it." At this, he cut a quick look at his daughter. "Now, once we get the saddles built, we'll use these pillows to pad them. . . ."

The instructions continued, right along with the absurdity. But at the end of the day, it didn't matter. Bradley needed a good report from Captain Herald if he wanted to stay in the service. That meant following his orders and keeping his willful daughter from ruining their mission.

Ambrosia wrapped cotton batting around the frame of the saddle, just as her father had instructed.

"That's it." He walked across the barn to inspect her work. She had to admit, he hadn't collapsed yet despite the hard labor. "You show an aptitude for this," he added.

"It'd be easier with the right tools. Why don't you rest while I go to town and see what they have available?"

"And lose another day? I'm ready for the adventure. Aren't you?"

She focused on the twine she was wrapping tightly around the batting. Was he ready? So far he'd been well, but she had her doubts that he could keep it up.

That cavalry trooper was watching her again. She wasn't surprised by his attention. Amber knew how lonely troopers were, but no matter how outrageous her behavior and her demands, Private Willis was not discouraged. Had she lost her touch?

"Captain Herald," the trooper said, "I hope you don't mind me sharing my opinion, but I think it's a pity that Miss Herald has to make this trip with us. The heat is unbearable, and there are dangerous men in Indian Territory. Riding across the plains is no place for a lady."

On the other hand, he might be useful yet.

"I appreciate your concern, Private Willis," said her father, "but she insisted that she was up to the challenge. She wouldn't have it any other way."

Private Willis's eyes crinkled. "Sir, are you in the practice of letting your womenfolk tell you what to do?"

The twine tangled in her hands. "How dare you talk to my father that way! He's been unwell."

"Calm down, Ambrosia," her father said. "You've made it no secret that you don't approve of my plans. Maybe Private Willis will appreciate my mounts more than you do."

"That's another problem," the cavalryman continued. "Your daughter seems to have an unhealthy fear of the camels."

Uh-oh. None of the cowboys had stuck around to speak to her

father after they'd decided to bail. Private Willis was going to mess this up. "I'm not afraid," she said. "I just think this is a bad idea."

"You're not afraid of the camels?" Private Willis sat on the table and swung one leg. "According to Miss Herald, they'll bite your feet clean off."

Her father's mouth tightened. "Ambrosia, I told you I didn't need your help. You can take the train home without me."

There was no way she was letting him make this journey with only a conceited cavalryman to help.

"According to Miss Herald, the camels also like to throw their riders," Willis said.

"I—I just assumed . . ." she stammered.

"And what's worse, riding the camels can hurt your ability to . . . what did you say, Miss Herald?"

Amber sputtered in surprise. He wouldn't dare. Not in front of her father.

With a wink, Private Willis said, "Hurt your ability to sleep at night. I think that's what she claimed." His teeth gleamed like a wolf's.

She let out a shaky breath. He hadn't totally humiliated her, but he'd let her know that he could. Ambrosia didn't appreciate the warning. Until now, her father had been patient with her objections, but from the set of his jaw, that patience was running out, and she had Private Willis to thank.

"For some reason, my daughter has made it her goal to terrify every man I've requested help from. Cheers to you, Willis, for calling her bluff. If you can convince her to take the train home, I'm more than happy to arrange it. Listen to him, Ambrosia," her father said as he walked out of the barn to measure the camels for their saddles.

"Ambrosia," Willis said.

"Are you trying to get me into trouble?" she said.

"Why would I do that? I just wanted to verify the information you gave me."

"You're nothing but a . . . a . . . tattletale."

He grinned. "Usually it's me who's getting tattled on. I must be doing something right." He hopped off the table and picked up the mallet lying next to her. "So why are you trying to run everyone away? You need help, you know. You don't want to do this on your own."

She took the mallet from his hand. "It's none of your business."

He dipped his head to the side. "Actually, seeing how I'm assigned to accompany you on this journey, it *is* my business."

"I'm staying with my father, and that's that. I suggest you find another way to employ yourself."

His mouth twitched. "I'm not your father, ma'am. It doesn't matter a whit to me if you get riled up, if you pout, or if you threaten to run away from home. I specialize in reckless, dramatic gestures, and I doubt any of yours would impress me."

"I am not a child." Amber never yelled, but she could speak very emphatically. "You are attributing immaturity to me that I have not displayed." Because she was trying very, very hard not to act her age.

And the shrewd trooper seemed to know it. "All that's missing is for you to pack your bag and stomp off down the road."

Stomping away was her first impulse, and she fought it valiantly.

He leaned close enough that she could see a dusting of blond on his jaw. "What has he done to make you want to ruin his plans? Is he that awful to you?"

Amber slammed the mallet onto the table. The trooper's conclusion was unfair. She had a noble objective, even if her methods were questionable.

"If you want to question my loyalty to my family, then test me," she said. "Try to send me away from my father and watch how I fight you." She'd never spoken to a stranger like this before, and it felt invigorating. Her pulse thrummed; her muscles ached to give action to her words. He'd never try to restrain her physically, but the thought made her want the battle.

Something flickered in his eyes. His voice lowered. "I'm not your enemy."

"If your aim is to separate me from my father, then you are."

"The heat will be unbearable. Water limited. Sickness possible. Will your determination last?"

"The train ride here wasn't much better."

He shook his head. "But this will be slow, and in the sun. And the danger . . . I don't want to scare you needlessly, but there are bad men in Indian Territory—lawless men of every nation. Right now the tribes are at peace, but you never know when tempers will flare."

"Let me guess, the Indians will bite my feet off?"

"I'm not telling stories, ma'am. Your father is a military man. He's faced danger before. You, on the other hand . . ."

"If you can convince him to abandon this endeavor, then do it." The only reason she was still talking to the trooper was that he seemed like he might be listening, after all. That and the bottom lip. It warranted more studying. "Then you'll have an excuse for your commander for why you can't take this assignment."

"I have too much riding on this to back down. Too much to fail."

"Well, so do I."

Their eyes held as each tried to judge the sincerity of the other. Ambrosia didn't know if she was more likely to laugh or cry, but her emotions were roiling.

"Then let's strike a bargain." He extended his hand.

Maybe she was acting like a spoiled child, after all. If he was willing to acquiesce . . . She offered her hand, and he took it in a warm grasp. All the sparks from her anger flared up into something new.

His throat jogged as he studied their linked hands. "I'm going to see that the captain arrives safely home with his camels. You're going to do everything you can to stop me."

"Why are we shaking hands, then?" she asked. "We haven't agreed on anything."

"We're agreeing that we'll behave ourselves like honest opponents and not take it personally."

"I haven't agreed to anything," she protested. "And I take it personally. Very personally." In fact, she was taking this handshake too personally, already. With a huff, she yanked her hand free. "If you're going to oppose me, I don't see how we can be friends."

"That's a pity," he said. "I'd very much like to have a friend like you."

She marched away, but with a tinge of regret. What if she'd treated him honestly upon first meeting him, instead of setting up this rivalry? She was beginning to see that there was more to Private Willis than a quick wit and nervy attitude. There was something strong and determined. Something that made Ambrosia fear she might have met her match.

Chapter

4

Camels had to be the most awkward creatures on God's earth. Instead of sleek lines like a horse, there were bumps sticking out where bumps shouldn't be. Their heads bobbed and swayed like a snake's. Their lips split right down the middle and flopped easily, usually with a long tongue hanging down the side. They might be able to carry more weight than a horse, but they lacked the dignity.

Bradley had yet to sit on one, but the tall saddles didn't look promising. Balancing on the hump looked like the worst place to direct the animal from. And the saddle wasn't fitted to the hump. Instead it was peaked in the middle to accommodate the awkward shape. Bradley couldn't help but wonder what riding tricks he could devise, but standing on the saddle wouldn't be one of them.

The bull named Omar didn't cotton to Bradley. Earlier that morning, when Bradley had helped saddle him, the camel had drawn out those lips like pinchers and pulled Bradley's hat plumb off his head. Maybe Ambrosia wasn't lying about them being dangerous, after all. He walked a wide path around the bull to the smaller female that seemed the friendliest.

"Ruby likes you." Captain Herald tightened the cinch on the

belly of the old cow. "But since she's the calmest, Ambrosia will ride her."

Ambrosia stood off to the side with her parasol perched overhead. Her large blue hat completely hid her dark hair, and her split skirt billowed big and loose. It'd still be a trick for her to balance on that saddle, but he figured she was prepared.

He wasn't. Ambrosia had caught him completely off guard. Bradley was used to being the reckless one, footloose and primed to fire, but Ambrosia changed things. He was responsible for her—responsible in a way he'd never been before. His fellow troopers could take care of themselves, but Miss Herald didn't understand what lay ahead. She was a delightful mess, but beneath the sass was a young lady who bore looking after.

Bradley watched as Captain Herald strapped their packs onto his framework contraptions. Atop the two pack camels, the mounds of barrels, gunny sacks, and a bundled-up feather tick looked top-heavy, but finally the last of the gear was in place, their canteens were full, and they were ready to go.

Bradley's canteen still held water despite the ding it had taken from the Gunther gang's guns. He'd decided to keep it as a souvenir to remind himself that the Gunthers were still out there somewhere, and they'd be looking for him.

"Are you sure all the animals are sound, Father?" Ambrosia called. "If any of them go lame out there, we'll have to leave them behind."

"We aren't leaving anyone behind," Captain Herald responded. "Stop your lollygagging, Amber. Let's go."

With a long riding crop, Captain Herald tapped each animal on the shoulder. One by one, they knelt clumsily, their long knobby legs tucking beneath them.

Captain Herald rushed around, as excited as a bee at a hive, pointing with his prod. "Look at that. Do you see how they sit? Their legs fold and hold them up off the ground. In the desert, that keeps them off the hot sand and lets air get beneath them. It's just one way they are remarkable. No one but God could create such a perfect vehicle for traveling across the desert."

To be honest, Bradley didn't ever want to be in a land so hot that the dirt burned you.

Herald beamed. "Time to start the journey."

Esmeralda was the name of Bradley's animal. Her loose, flexible lips puckered at him like she was trying to kiss him from afar. Or spit at him, which was more likely. He angled his hat against the sun and pulled his gloves from where they were tucked into his belt.

"Hop on up and hold on." Captain Herald pointed to the stirrup, and Bradley settled himself into the saddle.

Perched so high, he felt horribly unbalanced, and the camel hadn't even stood up yet. Captain Herald turned to take Ambrosia's hand. Bradley didn't miss the determined jut of her chin as she approached Ruby. Her hand trembled as she closed her parasol and tucked it into the padded roll on the back of the saddle. Slipping her girly boot into the stirrup, she stretched up on her toes and grabbed the horn of the saddle. He hoped she didn't mind him watching, but someone needed to keep an eye on her.

The camels made some strange noises to each other that sounded like they were gargling soup. Esmeralda shook beneath him as she answered. The captain climbed aboard Omar, then with a whoop, the whole world moved.

With a mighty jump, Esmeralda lurched up to her knees. Just as Bradley caught his balance and kept from rolling off the back, she shoved forward and straightened her back legs. Now Bradley fell forward. Only by bracing himself with locked arms did he keep his nose from smashing into the camel's neck. Before he could get his balance, she rocked her front legs beneath her and stood at her full height.

Bradley felt like he'd just ridden a bucking bronco. He hadn't expected it to be that rough.

"Did you see that?" he asked Ambrosia. "Better hold on tight."

She leaned forward, nearly pressing the horn of the saddle into her chest. When Ruby bounced to her feet, Ambrosia fought to stay as close to her neck as possible, even bumping into the camel, but she didn't fall. Once upright, she tentatively settled into the saddle, her back as straight as the camel's was humped.

"Thanks for the warning," she said.

The captain's camel rose quickly, and he hooted and hollered his excitement. He turned the camel and circled back to Bradley and Ambrosia. "It's been an age since I've been on the back of such a magnificent animal!" Omar peered at Bradley through his impossibly long eyelashes, as if daring him to contradict the judgment. "Thank you, Amber, for understanding. I really do have to do this," he said.

Do what? Get the camels to Texas? Why was it so important to him?

Sitting in the oversized saddle, Ambrosia looked tiny. Bradley looked down, and his feet were a mile from the ground. He wasn't anxious to try any stunts up here. Not yet, anyway.

"Let's go," Herald said. "We've got ten days ahead of us."

Ten days. Not sure what to do, Bradley bumped his heels into Esmeralda's sides. She easily fell into step behind the captain, and Ruby walked alongside her. Bradley turned to look over his shoulder. The two younger camels loaded with supplies were tied in a train behind him. The lines stretched out as they left the barnyard. The farmer and his wife stood on the porch and waved good-bye to their old friends. The black-and-white sheepdog yapped at their big, floppy feet, but the caravan continued.

"He ignores the dog, but takes a bite out of my hat," Bradley said.

"Omar dislikes you," Ambrosia replied. "I think he feels threatened. He's used to being the boss around here."

"He doesn't have to worry about me. I'm just a lowly private. I'm not the boss of anyone."

"Oh really?" Was that a snort from the proper Miss Herald? "You don't take kindly to others telling you what to do."

"Haven't I done everything your pa has asked?"

"Calm down, trooper. I'm taking your measure, not judging your performance." After a long look at him, she said, "I'm right, aren't I? You have trouble with authority."

"I don't know that I'd say that, exactly. I just like to think for myself."

"And not have a woman doing your thinking for you?"

"Not have anyone do my thinking for me." Bradley tried to keep the thinking to a minimum, actually. Too much worry, and you could talk yourself out of what needed doing.

Esmeralda and Ruby stretched their necks out long, enjoying walking in tandem. Bradley was enjoying it, too.

"I'm sorry for not being friendly earlier." Ambrosia shooed away a horsefly. "If we must go, then I suppose it might as well be with you."

He grinned. Sure enough, Ambrosia wasn't as hard-bitten as she wanted him to think. "You're in good hands, Miss Herald. And if you don't watch it, you might end up enjoying yourself."

She tilted her head up so that the sun bathed all the adorable curves and dimples of her face in light. "And yet, just consider what this is going to do to my complexion. Are you willing to jeopardize my looks in this dangerous endeavor?"

While he could spend many happy hours ruminating over her complexion, he wouldn't admit it. "You and your complexion could have taken the train home. I would've looked after your pa."

She rotated the parasol to block his view again, but this time he caught sight of a charming smile before she could hide it. Seemed he wasn't the only one who found orneriness an appealing trait.

Ten days on this journey? It wasn't nearly long enough.

※

This trip was nothing like Ambrosia had expected. The flat prairie was denuded of trees. The hot wind drove sharp bits of dirt into her eyes, which already stung from sweat. She should have brought a scarf or veil. Her wide bonnet and parasol weren't much protection from the wind.

Another thing she hadn't expected was a guide like Private Willis. She'd grown up at western forts, living in the officers' quarters. She was used to handsome soldiers, but this one seemed unaware that he was at the bottom rung of the ladder. In fact, she wondered if he was aware that there was a ladder at all.

Amber could sit a horse, but the camel's canter felt off. Grabbing the saddle, she readjusted, looking for a more comfortable position.

"Sir," Private Willis said, "we might want to slow down. Miss Herald is falling behind."

She wasn't falling behind, but she was tired. How was it that she couldn't keep up with her sick father?

"Amber, are you all right?" Her father leaned forward to scrub on Ruby's neck. "Once you two get better acquainted, we'll have to turn you loose and see what you can do together."

"What?" Her heart skipped a beat. Why would he make such a suggestive comment? "I have no intention of becoming better acquainted with Private Willis or being turned loose with him."

Private Willis coughed into his fist as a gust of scorching air assaulted them. Once the howling wind died down, he found his voice. "I'm sorry, Miss Herald, but I think Captain Herald meant that we should get better acquainted with Ruby and Melda. That's all."

Her father's thick brows pushed together in confusion. "Whyever would you think . . . ?" He shook his head. "She's usually very astute. I don't know what gave her such an inappropriate idea."

"It's probably the sun," Private Willis said.

"It's not the sun. It's . . ." She shrugged. "It's the sun."

Her smiling father, so unlike the desolate man who'd sat in his garden all spring, tapped Omar with his riding crop and jogged ahead, leaving her and Private Willis with the pack camels.

"Ambrosia is an unusual name," Private Willis said. "How'd you come by it?"

"Ambrosia is the food of the gods." She lifted her chin and tried to look sophisticated. "The food was only shared with certain men to whom the gods wanted to convey immortality."

He whistled. "Lucky dogs. I guess a mere mortal like me wouldn't have a chance."

"Absolutely not."

But he didn't look disappointed. "I like steak and taters, personally. No highfalutin fare like that."

"Sour grapes," she said. "Pretending you don't want something because you can't have it."

"Guilty to the pretending, but not convinced on the second part." With a rocking of his saddle, he urged Esmeralda forward.

Amber's jaw dropped. How could she not be impressed by his impudence?

The day stretched long and hot before a town finally appeared on the horizon. "We'll tether the camels under the trees there," Father said. "And I'll walk to town and buy us a hot meal."

"Why walk? Aren't we staying at the hotel tonight?" she asked.

"You can't just ride your camel into town, or every horse in the area goes stark-raving mad," her father said. "We'll stay out here. Are you coming with me for dinner?"

"I just want to get off this camel and rest." Ambrosia wiped her handkerchief across her glistening forehead. "Are you sure you're up to it?"

"I'm feeling stronger every day."

When Omar stopped, all the camels stopped. Her father uttered some foreign word she'd never heard before, and the camels started pacing like dogs arranging their beds.

"Brace yourselves," he said. "It's rough on the way down."

Ruby lifted her front foot and pawed at the ground. Then, as if satisfied that everything below was ready, she dropped to her knees, pitching Amber forward. Finally, Ruby leveled off and rocked gently, making herself comfortable on the leafy space beneath the trees. From there, it was a simple step off the beast's back, and Amber had never been more eager to reach the ground.

Private Willis gave a playful whoop as Melda came to the ground, too. He slapped her on the shoulder and gave her a quick scrub. For a cavalryman, he was adapting quickly to a horse substitute.

Her father got Omar settled and then, with a tug on his hat, waved good-bye. "I'll be back with some supper."

Private Willis stretched. "For the first time in my life, I'm

207

happy to get out of the saddle." He took the lead ropes and tied them to various branches on the trees to give the camels some room.

At first Ambrosia's legs didn't want to straighten and her back felt stiff, but with a deep breath, she stretched her arms over her head and enjoyed the feeling of the blood working its way back into her extremities.

Private Willis was smiling, but for once he didn't seem to be ridiculing her. "Feels good, doesn't it?"

She nodded as she unfastened her canteen from Ruby's saddle and took a long drink from it.

"Should we take off their saddles?" he asked.

"I have no idea." Safely beneath the shade of the trees, she untied the ribbons of her sunbonnet and fanned herself. "If it was up to me, I'd drive the camels off with a stick."

"And that's why I stayed behind instead of going to town to eat a hot meal. I'm protecting your father's investment."

Ambrosia set her canteen on the ground. "I don't see how these things could make anyone money."

"Is he going to breed them?"

"I hardly think so."

"I guess you could eat them. Or maybe you're going to milk them? You wouldn't even need a stool to sit on. You could stand up and—"

"Don't be absurd."

"I'm not the one buying camels, ma'am."

She was too parched to argue any further. She picked up her canteen and held it to her lips. Something warm, wet, and disgusting touched her mouth. She spit in the dirt as she turned the canteen over.

"I've been nice to you, and this is how you repay me?" She shook the canteen. "It's empty, and you slobbered all over it."

"How did I drink your water? I've been talking to you this whole time."

"There was water in it when I set it down."

208

"You probably drank more than you thought. Maybe the heat is getting to you."

She was beginning to regret running off the cowboys. Now she was stuck with the only man in Kansas who had no sense. Amber pushed back her damp hair, frustrated at what a mess everything was. Private Willis's face softened, and he held out his dented canteen.

"No, thank you," she said.

He rolled his eyes and snatched her canteen out of her hand.

"You don't have to refill it," she said as she chased after him. "I can do it myself."

But he ignored the offer and picked up the water barrel. "What exactly is it you do when you're not wrangling camels?"

Watching him handle the heavy water barrel made her grateful that she wasn't doing it herself, after all. She leaned against a tree and watched him at work. "Besides taking care of Father? Well, when he retired a couple years ago, we moved to Garber, Texas, and bought a nice town lot. Right away, Mother and I started planning our new house, from the newel posts on the front porch to the rose garden in the back. It was completed this winter, about the time Father went into his decline, and it is a marvel. Every stick of furniture and every stitch of curtains, drapes, and tablecloths, Mother and I chose."

"You ladies did that on your own?" He scrubbed at the canteen and rinsed it. "That's quite an accomplishment. What's next?"

Good question. Ambrosia had been asking herself that, as well. "One thing I refuse to do is to dig up our beautifully designed rose garden for a camel pen. My mother has spent her entire married life moving from one government post to another. It's about time she has a place to call her own, but those animals will ruin it." The water glistened on his hands, making them smoother and darker. "Our new house is the talk of the town," she said. "Just imagine if we started boarding camels there."

"I'm afraid it's not *if*, but *when*," he said. "But cheer up. With Omar and Ruby in your garden, you'll have even more notoriety."

Was he laughing at her? She tamped down her irritation. He'd cleaned and refilled her canteen, after all.

Once she'd had a good, long drink and arranged her feather mattress to sit on, she felt generous enough to converse.

"And what about you and your family?"

He took a seat and stretched his legs out in front of him. "My sister is the governess for Major Adams's girls back at Fort Reno. They're getting hitched this winter."

His sister was marrying his commander? No wonder he was fearless. "My father thinks a lot of Major Adams," she said.

"I do, too. Now, whether he thinks a lot of me . . ." There was that teasing again, but this time at his own expense.

"Do you come from a military family?"

His smile faded, as if he regretted the question but was determined to answer anyway. "I don't come from any kind of family. My ma wasn't what you'd consider quality, and I never knew my pa. It's only me and my sister, but we've always taken care of each other." He bounced one shoulder in seeming indifference, but she could tell it did matter to him. She could tell it mattered a lot.

"Private Willis, I grew up at military outposts and have known a lot of troopers and officers." He wasn't meeting her gaze, but she held hers steady. "Where you come from before you put on the uniform doesn't matter a jot. It's how you handle yourself afterward."

He raised his eyes, and Ambrosia had never seen anyone as genuinely appreciative for something she'd said. Maybe she had something to offer him, after all.

"I'm trying my best, Miss Ambrosia," he said. "Trying my best to do my duty, even if it frustrates a strong-willed lady."

Before she could answer, he added, "And feel free to call me Bradley."

Chapter

5

The next morning found Bradley rested and excited. They would reach Indian Territory today and finally be in land he knew. He hadn't expected camels, and he hadn't expected Miss Herald, but he did know what to expect in the nation, and it was usually danger.

The camels were sound sleepers, although they snored like Private Gundy when he had a cold. Judging from the birds stirring on the branches above him, daybreak was just around the corner. Bradley trailed his hand over the cool grass just beyond his blanket. He didn't mind sleeping outside. It was cooler than in the hotel, and the ground probably had fewer bumps than the mattress. Fewer critters, too, if he had to guess. He reckoned Ambrosia was comfortable on her mattress, although she and her father had laid their bedrolls farther away from him and the camels.

Bradley had rolled to his back to enjoy the sunrise when he became aware that someone was already up and moving. It was Captain Herald. Not wanting to get caught lying around, Bradley went to meet him.

Bradley saluted casually. "Good morning, sir."

Captain Herald quickly lowered a flask and screwed on the lid.

Bradley scratched at his chest. A stiff drink this early in the morning? He hoped this wasn't a sign of a serious problem.

"I apologize for not being up earlier and ready to go, but frankly I wouldn't know what to do with these beasts," Bradley said.

Captain Herald surveyed the drowsy dromedaries kneeling by the stream. "I'd forgotten how peaceful they are. It's like they're telling us not to worry, everything will be just fine."

Bradley had seen the same expression on a cow's face, but he didn't give them any credit for intelligence. He halfway figured the captain was seeing the message he wanted to see. Fine by Bradley. It was nice having a captain who wasn't worried about running a tight ship for once. No reason to march around all tense if you believed life would go on without you.

Captain Herald motioned Bradley to follow as he made his way to each of the camels, murmuring a greeting and scratching them fondly on the forehead.

"If you don't mind me asking, how'd you get caught up with camels?" Bradley scrubbed on Melda's neck and felt like she probably appreciated it.

"Old Omar here was my mount when I was at Camp Verde, north of San Antonio. These were cavalry camels."

Bradley whistled his surprise. "The US Cavalry rode camels?"

"Only a small number were in the Camel Corps, but we were proud. Ruby and Omar saved our lives back in '60 when we were sent on a reconnaissance mission to map out the San Antonio–El Paso Road and the Rio Grande. We got caught in a rough canyon in July and couldn't find water. It was over a hundred degrees in the shade—not that there was any shade available. There we were, wandering around, hoping to stumble onto some water. The mules died and the horses had to be abandoned, but the camels kept carrying us." His eyes turned misty. "For two more days, we wandered with dry canteens, the camels never complaining. But then they did complain, and boy were we glad."

He gave Omar a playful slap on his haunch. "This old fellow's sire started the grumbling. They'd never been rambunctious before, but they started pulling at their reins. We were too tired to fight them, so we gave them their heads, and you know what? These camels marched straight out of that canyon. Two miles off the trail, they found water. They'd been smelling it the whole time. Just had to wait for us to listen to them before they'd take us there."

The story taught Bradley something about camels, but maybe even more about Captain Herald.

"Everyone survived?" he asked.

"All the troopers and camels, yes. But time hasn't been so kind to them. From what I hear, I'm the last surviving member of that expedition. Me and the camels." Captain Herald's chest seemed to get smaller. His breathing rattled as he absently rubbed Ruby's forehead.

The last one left? Bradley tried to imagine how he'd feel if he was the lone survivor—if Private Krebs, Morris, and Chandler had all been killed. That was what he'd been trying to avoid, wasn't it? That was what had gotten him stuck with these crazy animals to begin with. But obviously these animals meant something more to the captain than livestock. More than an investment.

"When I heard that these poor creatures were stuck on a farm in Kansas," the captain continued, "I decided they wouldn't winter here again. Got to get them somewhere warm. I owe them that."

"And your family? What do they think?" Bradley asked.

Captain Herald gazed out at the early-morning horizon. "They don't understand. I hoped that bringing Ambrosia along might bring her over to my side, but she's as against it as she ever was." He slapped his leg. "Well, we have a lot of ground to cover, Private. Time to get moving."

"Yes, sir." Bradley hadn't had a father, but he knew a good man when he saw one. Captain Herald was a fair man, and Ambrosia was a devoted daughter. Why were they working against each other, and what would it take to change Ambrosia's mind?

※

The sun was punishing, chasing them down, and there was no place to hide. Ambrosia switched her parasol to her other hand

and tried to pull her sleeve down over her arm, but the gathered three-quarter sleeve wasn't long enough. She'd packed this blouse for its light material, not for coverage, and her tiny parasol wasn't doing the job.

"If you wanted me to appreciate the camels, then a trip in the blistering heat wasn't the thing to suggest," she said to her father.

"In the heat is exactly when you appreciate them the most. We wouldn't be making this kind of time with horses. Besides, we'd have to bring along a mule team just to carry our supplies and water."

But his words floated over her head. She was finding it hard to focus. Everywhere she moved, she just encountered more heat. An innocent stretching of her leg brought her in contact with a piece of leather that felt like it was on fire. Changing her grip on the reins would burn through her gloves. Even Ruby's hairy back seemed to radiate heat up at her. How many more days of this?

She looked up to see Private Willis scanning the horizon. His face and hands were as tanned as any outdoorsman's, but she'd wager that beneath his collar was skin as fair as hers. She caught herself watching for a glimmer of exposure, then chided herself. What did it matter? Another line of sweat ran down her own collar, reminding her that she was in no condition to draw a man's interest. While her father generally stayed by her side, the trooper kept his focus far away. After all, he had a job to do.

She moistened her dry lips and reached for her canteen. Even it felt toasty through her gloves. She lifted it to her mouth, but only a trickle leaked out.

"Captain Herald, I think we need to stop for water," Bradley said.

Had he been watching her, after all? At her questioning look, Bradley rattled his own dented canteen, but she wasn't fooled. He always had an eye on her.

Her father said the word, and the camels halted their trek. "We still have two barrels of water," he said as he directed the camels to kneel. "When will we reach the next stream?"

"No streams are guaranteed in August," Bradley replied. "We'll make it to the Cimarron River tomorrow or the day after. I presume the camels will be all right?"

"They haven't slowed down yet."

"I could certainly use a break from the sun," Amber said. Once she'd dismounted, she stomped her feet to get the feeling back and looked around her. Finally, they were off the camels and they could . . . they could . . .

There was nothing. No trees, no shade, no diversion of any kind. Only the endless grass, burnt crispy atop the red, baked soil. Two days in the sun, just two days, and Ambrosia felt like she was drained already.

How was her father surviving? At home, it seemed all he could manage was making it from the house to his seat in the garden. Now he had limitless energy.

Bradley had unfastened a water barrel from one of the younger calves. He hoisted it to his shoulder and brought it over to her. Ambrosia tried to wet her lips, but they felt as dry as the leather saddle she'd helped her father make.

"Canteen?" he asked.

She unfastened it from Ruby's harness. "Poor things. Are you sure they don't need a drink?" she asked as she held out her canteen for Bradley.

Her father answered. "If they did, we wouldn't have enough to give them. They'll make up for it at the river."

Bradley tipped up the barrel, and water gurgled into her canteen and splashed over her fingers and hands. Amber could have sworn that her skin sighed. She rubbed the coolness into her burning forearms, which stung at first, but as the water evaporated, cooled quickly.

"That feels good, doesn't it? If we weren't watching our rations, I'd dump this whole barrel over your head." His eyes sparkled.

"In any other situation, I'd take offense," Ambrosia said, "but I think it sounds delightful."

Bradley laughed, and it was a good, hearty sound. With so

much sorrow and worry in her house for the last months, Amber had forgotten the healing a strong laugh carried.

She gulped down her water while Bradley went to offer her father a drink. Approaching the younger camels carefully, Ambrosia set down her canteen and found the sack of green apples she'd brought along. Riding in the heat had drained her of an appetite, but the fresh crispness of an apple sounded perfect.

She removed one, then decided to get her father and even Bradley one, as well. She heard boots on the ground behind her. It was Bradley bringing the barrel of water back.

"Do you want an apple?" It shouldn't matter if he wanted it or not, but she felt like his accepting would be a gesture of goodwill.

He looked her up and down, his grin growing.

"What?" she said. "What's so funny?"

"If you're not the perfect picture of temptation, I don't know what is." He stepped forward and took her hand right along with the apple. "Yes, I will take and eat." His voice had grown frustratingly, teasingly husky. He was so close that the brims of their hats rubbed. Still gazing into her eyes, he dropped her hand, held the apple to his mouth, and broke the skin.

Where had that chill come from? Anxious to break the spell, Amber ripped off a bite of her own apple. She shouldn't read too much into the attraction that had sprung up between them. He was probably just toying with her. There was nothing else to do, after all.

"How old are you?" she asked.

"Why?"

She shrugged. "I can ask, can't I?"

"You're eighteen," he said.

"Eighteen and a half," she replied. "Did my father tell you? And you didn't answer my question."

"I'm twenty," he said. "You make me feel older, and I didn't ask your father. I just know things." The way he held his mouth, that bottom lip . . .

"A year and a half older than me, but you know things? Like what?"

"Two years older. Things like, if you don't stay out of the sun, you will get burned crispy." He took another sharp bite of his apple.

Amber gently laid her palm against her forearm. Just a little tinge. The water had made it better. "I'll be fine," she said.

"Do you have anything with longer sleeves?"

"Don't worry about me. You're here to take care of my father."

"Your father looks after himself. I'm watching after you and making sure you have everything you need."

Like water. She reached down for her canteen and raised it to her lips. Once again, it was empty. Once again, the rim was dirty.

"You thief! I gave you one of my apples!" Incredulous, she chucked her apple at Bradley and hit him square in the chest. When had he had time to empty her canteen? She'd been standing there talking to him all along.

He started laughing, so she threw her canteen, as well. He tossed his arms up and ducked as it sailed over his head.

"I didn't use your canteen."

"It's hot, but it's not that hot. That water did not evaporate."

"What's going on?" her father asked as he walked toward them. He combed his thick mustache while looking at the apple in the dust and the canteen tossed aside.

"Miss Herald is convinced that I'm sneaking drinks from her canteen when she's not looking. I'm sure there's a rational explanation."

"Of course there's a rational explanation," she said. "He's pestering me."

"Why would I do that?" Bradley asked.

"Stop it, you two," her father interrupted. He grinned like he was fixing to announce the world's greatest prank. "Private Willis didn't drink your water, Ambrosia. It was the calf."

Amber turned to look at the placid mammal hunched down on the ground. "That's impossible. It doesn't have hands."

"It doesn't need hands. Its lips are very pliable. Camels can untie knots, pick a pocket, down a whole bottle, and then set it back on the shelf as if nothing happened."

"The only evidence left behind is a slobbery canteen, right, Ambrosia?"

She glowered at Bradley, and to her surprise, her father didn't seem to notice the trooper had called her by her given name.

"Refill the canteen, and let's get going," he said instead. "No sense in sitting still and baking in this heat."

Refill her canteen? This time they couldn't spare any water to rinse it.

Bradley seemed to notice her hesitation. "Don't worry," he whispered. "You can share mine."

"I'd rather share with the camels," she said, but her smile softened the words.

"Have it your way." He lifted the barrel to refill the canteen one last time. "If only my lips were as skilled as hers."

The chill was back. Even in the heat.

Chapter
6

*L*ook at him—the sultan of Indian Territory. Bradley wished his buddies back at Fort Reno could see him gliding over the grasslands on the back of a swaying camel. If they thought his antics on horseback were impressive, they'd shoot themselves in the foot to watch him now. Just how fast could these beasts go? And how hard would it be to aim while galloping on them? Too bad he hadn't had some time alone with Melda to test her abilities.

Too bad he also hadn't had more time alone with Miss Herald. She was a feisty gal. Extending a peace offering to him one minute, throwing it at him the next. And it had been the camels stealing drinks all along. Didn't that beat all?

He'd spotted some trees along a shallow gorge ahead. It looked as good a place to eat as any. Chances were the water was gone, but they had to have firewood to cook dinner.

They reached the grove and unburdened the beasts while Ambrosia rummaged through the pile of goods, looking for the cooking gear. She found a pot but needed help reaching the water barrel still tied onto the calf's brace. Bradley was only too happy to help, although when the captain wandered off, he had to wonder if that metal flask was coming out again when no one was looking.

Bradley tilted the water barrel for her. "Not too long ago I was fighting for my life against a ruthless gang of outlaws, and now I'm riding a camel. Who would've thought?" He smiled his most charming smile, but she seemed intent on the water gurgling into the pot. What was wrong with her? How could she not be impressed with the outlaw story? Bradley was impressed, even if it was the reason he was in so much trouble.

"Sorry," she said. "I'm just thinking how disappointed my mother is going to be. I've let her down."

"You know, I don't think the camels are an investment." Bradley spoke quietly so the captain wouldn't overhear him. He didn't mean to tell her how to get along with her own kin, but maybe he could help. "They mean something more to him. Nostalgic."

"I wish he'd just keep a lock of their hair or something, because camels don't fit into a memory book very well," she said.

"The best memories can't always be kept in a book."

Ambrosia's dark hair contrasted with her flushed cheeks. Her thick lashes framed striking blue eyes. "Does he miss his job so much?"

"I think it's more than that. But I can sympathize. He's a strong man. Being put out to pasture and sitting by while your daughter and wife build you a house? That doesn't sound like any kind of life to me."

"This is our fault?" The water sloshed in the pot. She was going to lose it if she wasn't careful. "We're taking care of him."

"A man has to have some challenges. If he feels like the best days of his life are behind him, then it's no wonder he's been down. Besides, any fella worth his salt doesn't want to be a burden. He wants to have someone who needs him—someone to take care of."

The sentiment surprised Bradley. He'd never spent much time worrying about himself, much less anyone else, but here he found himself trying to think ahead for Ambrosia's safety and slowing down for her comfort. This trip was changing him, and he didn't credit it to the camels.

Speaking of the strange creatures, their ears twitched. Something wasn't right.

Holding a hand out toward Ambrosia, Bradley said, "Don't move a hair."

Captain Herald had noticed something, too. He motioned to Ambrosia to take cover. There were horsemen, three of them, and they were armed. So was Bradley, but then he saw their uniforms and decided he didn't need his rifle, after all.

"They're friendly," he said. "Cherokees, I reckon." He took stock of their horses, as all troopers did. Two mustangs and a Morgan. But then the horses started acting funny. They slowed. The lead horse reared back, catching the rider off guard and nearly causing him to crash into the rider on the left. The other mustang slowed. Even from here, Bradley could see its flaring nostrils and the whites of its eyes.

"It's the camels," Ambrosia said. "They're afraid."

"These animals make nice guards, I'll give them that." Holding up a hand, Bradley stepped out from around the camels. "Let's see what they want."

Ambrosia crept closer to Ruby, where she could watch from a distance, not sure what to think about the strangers. One of them was a full-blooded Indian, his braids disappearing against his dark coat. The other two were white men, and all had badges. After they'd had a look at the camels, they shook hands with Bradley and her father and walked back to where their nervous horses were waiting.

"What tribe are they from?" she asked.

"They were all Cherokees," Bradley answered. "The Cherokee Lighthorse troops are the same as marshals. They invited us to stay at their lodge tonight. They happen to be on the hunt for the Gunther gang and want to compare notes."

He'd mentioned it earlier, but encountering men on their path made it more real. "Tell me about these outlaws," she said. "Are they dangerous?"

"Very, and they have a particular dislike for me. Twice I've been involved in a showdown with them. Once I happened upon some marshals out of Fort Smith, who'd tracked the gang after a train robbery and found themselves outnumbered. The Gunthers got away that time. Then later, they came after my unit of cavalrymen. Ambushed us when we were on patrol. They've killed, so they know there's no hope for them once they're caught. They're desperate."

Amber thoughtfully arranged some pieces of deadwood for a cook fire. "I feel rather foolish. Here I thought I could scare you away with camel stories."

"You're frightening in your own way, ma'am." He dropped a sack of potatoes next to the pot. "Is there anything else you need?"

But she wasn't finished with the story. "Were you in danger?"

"Pinned down with one of our men injured and the others running out of ammo? Yeah, I suppose that's no Sunday picnic."

"How'd you get away?"

"I didn't run." His jaw clenched. "That is not what happened."

Ambrosia raised an eyebrow. She'd touched a sore spot, and she wasn't talking about her saddle sores. "I wasn't accusing you," she said. "I only wanted to hear the story."

He took a stick and drew it against the ground. If he was hoping to make a mark, the sandstone was too solid to leave any trace. "We were outnumbered. They had us where they wanted us, and the gully at our backs would've been impossible to guard once night fell. I didn't see any way out, so I jumped on my horse and took the fight to them."

"You left cover and ran at them?"

"Yes, ma'am. Winged two of them. The rest scattered, and we were able to get us all home."

Ambrosia looked at him with new respect. It was hard to imagine that the man who was lighting her cook fire had so recently faced death. While she'd been buying rugs and eating her green apples, he'd almost died.

"I didn't know I was riding with a hero." And him only two years older.

He looked up at her. "I ain't no hero. My commander told me to hold my position, but I didn't see much sense in that. Disobeying him is what got me this assignment. If I don't get this done right, I'll lose my living."

"Wait." Amber leaned forward. "You got sent to us as punishment? Riding with me was the worst thing they could think to do to you?"

There it was, the quick grin that told her he was going to be all right, and he thought she was just fine, too.

"If I'd known about you, they couldn't have kept me away," he said. "That I can guarantee."

It was hard to judge at first, but when they reached the Lighthorse troops' lodge before nightfall, Bradley had to admit that the camels were making good time.

"Are you sure it's safe to stay with the Cherokees?" Ambrosia wearily stretched her arm as she passed her parasol to the other hand. Carrying the blamed thing had to be tiring. "I don't want you to stop just for my sake."

Getting her out of the elements was foremost on his mind, but meeting with the men who'd encountered the Gunther gang held a charm of its own.

"We've been crossing the Cherokee Outlet since we left Kansas. Nothing to fear from their lawmen."

The sun was failing before they reached the Lighthorse lodge. Being warned about the camels, the police had left a young man to direct them to a corral where they could leave the camels for the night, away from the stables.

"Do you want me to stay with them?" Bradley offered.

The young Cherokee couldn't keep his eyes off the animals. "Unless they can fly out of the pen, they'll be fine."

"They can't, can they?" Bradley asked.

Captain Herald grinned as he unstrapped their burdens.

A quick shuffling through their bundles to get what they needed for the night, and they were on their way to the lodge.

"I don't know how to act," Ambrosia said. "I don't want to offend them, but I don't know their customs. The plains tribes we were stationed with out west were nothing like this."

Bradley's mouth twitched. After the whoppers she'd told about the camels, he owed her one. "The one rule you need to know is that a woman never sits by the chief or elder of their tribe, or her tribe either. It's considered bad luck."

"But wouldn't my father be considered an elder?"

They'd reached the log structure with a rock chimney and a hitching post in front.

"You'd better play it safe." Bradley deposited her bags at the door. "Just sit by me, and you'll be fine."

She'd entered with her senses as acute as the dry, pricking heat on her skin, ready to face the unusual. Ready to absorb the exotic. Instead, she saw a thickset man standing to greet them. His short, dark hair was parted crisply, and his blue uniform was buttoned up to his chin.

"Captain Sixkiller of the United States Indian Police at your service." Introductions were made all around. Most of the men were dressed in identical uniforms, and maybe only half of them looked like Indians. "We were just sitting down to eat. Won't you join us?"

Ambrosia beamed. Not only was she hungry, but she was curious. And as much as she hated making a fool of herself, she knew she could maneuver the tricky situation with Bradley's instructions.

An officer began setting out bowls on the long table, and another followed, ladling out a chunky stew. Captain Sixkiller sat at the head of the table, and her dad took a seat next to him. The other officers filled in on the benches until Bradley was crammed in near the end. The only spot open to her was next to her father, and had she not had the warning, she would have taken it without thought. Instead, she sashayed to the end of the table and stood behind Bradley and a smooth-faced policeman.

"Excuse me," she said.

The policeman's eyes darted to the top of the table, then he fell all over himself getting out of her way. "I apologize, ma'am. Here, take my seat."

"Very kind of you to join us," Bradley said.

And he wasn't the only one smiling. A few words in a foreign tongue were exchanged along with a few solemn nods. Had she surprised them with her knowledge of their culture? Whatever the case, her father didn't look too happy when the Lighthorse officer took the empty spot next to him.

Captain Sixkiller prayed an eloquent prayer, and after the *amen*, the spoons started their work. Two more men came in, and room had to be found on the benches, squishing Ambrosia right up against Private Willis.

"Pardon my elbow." Bradley switched his spoon to the other hand. "I'll try to eat left-handed so I don't get in your way."

She laughed breathlessly as someone down the table got rowdy, bumping her against him again. "Pardon my whole self," she said. "One more shove, and I'll be in your lap."

"That wouldn't be—" He stopped and cleared his throat. His spoon lowered. "Hey, fellas," he said, "give the lady some room."

The policemen bumped a younger officer off the end of the bench, and he took his food outside. When a basket holding some sort of white pancake was passed around, Bradley took a piece, ripped it in two, and laid half in her bowl.

"You asked about them being Indians," he said. "These men are all Cherokee—some full-blooded, some mixed, and some joined the tribe just like an immigrant might become an American. They're all citizens of the Cherokee nation, though."

Following the example of their hosts, Ambrosia ripped off a piece of the bread and popped it in her mouth. "The Indians we've been stationed around lived in tepees and wore buckskins."

"Many nations do, but the Cherokee had brick houses, businesses, and plantations in Georgia before they were forced to move here and start all over. Financially, many of them are generations ahead of the white settlers just across the border."

Captain Sixkiller motioned to Bradley. "My men tell me you were involved in a shootout with the Gunther gang."

"Yes, sir. I hear you're looking for them."

"They have a hideout somewhere south of here, and we'd like to pay them a visit if we can find it. One of the witnesses of the bank robbery was murdered in Tahlequah. He was going to testify, and now the other witnesses are frightened." Sixkiller paused and then addressed her father. "I don't like you all making a crossing with just two men and no horses."

Captain Herald shook his head. "In the morning, I'm going to get you on one of those camels. You'll see what they can do."

Ambrosia normally wouldn't speak in company where she was so much in the minority, but this might be her last chance. "The camels really are impressive. Your troops might benefit from them. I'm sure Father would consider trading some for your very fine horses."

Captain Sixkiller grunted. "When will the US government stop trying to improve on our ways? No, thank you. You are welcome to our hospitality, but you can keep your camels."

It had been worth a try.

That night the men went to the bunkhouse, while she was given a private room. It didn't matter much what it looked like, because Ambrosia fell asleep as soon as she hit the straw mattress.

But it didn't last.

A rustling outside her window woke her. As quietly as possible, Amber got to her knees and pushed aside the curtain.

"Bradley?" She hadn't meant to say his name, but finding him next to her window, watching the corral, was a surprise.

He was leaning against the wall, not a foot from her. His eyes never left the shadows huddled on the prairie. "Shhh . . . Do you hear that? It sounds like Omar is complaining."

"What's wrong with him?"

"I'm not sure, but something's got him agitated."

"Maybe someone is trying to steal the camels?" A spark of hope made her smile. "Please don't interrupt them."

There was a stir as the big camel pushed to his feet. "Someone's there," Bradley said. "I'm going, but just in case I don't come back, I need to confess something."

Suddenly it wasn't funny anymore. "Don't go," she said. "Not by yourself."

"I'll be fine. You just need to know that I made up that story at dinner."

"What story?"

"The rule that you couldn't sit by your father. I wanted your company, so I made that up. If that annoys you, I'll continue the pursuit. If you're flattered, then I won't do it again."

"I'm not flattered," she sputtered. "Not by your attention."

"Perfect. Then I'll continue."

And he jogged off, taking away her opportunity for a retort and possibly ruining her last chance to be rid of the camels.

Chapter

7

At least Ambrosia had gotten out of the wind for the night, because here they were again under the blazing sun that sapped your energy until you were as useless as potato peelings.

It was tougher than the dickens, keeping his opinions to himself, but Bradley wished the captain had found another way to get Ambrosia home. The conditions were too harsh for a lady of her caliber, and she was having a time of it. The hot, southern wind had battered her parasol until it was a useless, mangled mess of cloth, ruffles, and wire. Declaring herself tired of wrestling with it, Ambrosia finally gave in and let the wind whip it away like a tumbleweed. Now she had only her sunbonnet for shade.

But as brutal as the sun was, it wasn't their only danger.

Last night Bradley and one of the Cherokee officers had chased off two men snooping around their supplies. The visitors had managed to rummage through a few things, but nothing was missing. The only thing of interest was Bradley's canteen—the cavalry-issued one with a bullet dent in the side. It had been pulled from the pile of goods and set up on a post of the corral, almost like they wanted Bradley to find it. Almost like it was a message. Whatever the message, it was full of foreboding.

Bradley had told the captain that they should reach the Cimarron River for their midday meal, and there it was ahead.

"Hanging in there?" he asked Ambrosia. Sweat had left streaks down her face, but her hat seemed to be keeping the sun off.

"I can't wait to get down," she said. "And every step we travel, I think how disappointed Mother will be when she realizes her garden is going to be ripped up and turned into a camel corral."

"Think how pleased she'll be to see Captain Herald revived."

She watched her father on Omar. "I have to admit, he has made a remarkable recovery. You can't imagine how concerned we've been. I only hope it lasts."

The Cimarron River ran nearly even with the rest of the prairie. At some point in the year it would swell and spread wide, depositing soil along both banks. If they'd had wagons, it would have gotten sluggish here, but the camels' wide, soft feet padded over the sand without a hitch.

The slow, shallow river didn't look too challenging, but it was the largest water they'd come across yet.

"How exactly do we cross?" Ambrosia asked. Bradley wondered the same thing. Could camels even swim?

As they approached the bank, the camels showed their first hesitation. They grumbled deep in their chest. Ruby paused as the sand turned damp. She paced sideways rather than go any closer. Captain Herald walked to the edge with Omar, then returned.

"It's not in their nature to be drawn to water," said the captain. "It makes them a bit skittish."

"A bit skittish?" Bradley tugged at the reins to keep Melda from turning. "I've seen cows go to the branding iron with more enthusiasm."

"We'll get them there. They just need some encouragement. Now, stay in your saddle, Ambrosia. It might take Ruby a while to remember." He jabbed at his camel with his heels and shook the reins.

Omar blew raspberries with those massive lips but continued forward. The water swirled slowly around the sandbars. His big feet left giant double prints in the wet sand, which filled up with water from below.

Lowering her head to sniff at the river, Ruby blinked and then contentedly followed Omar into the water.

"Private Willis," the captain called from midstream. "Kindly lead the pack animals across, would you? Now would be the best time, while they're watching the leader."

What Bradley wouldn't give for a horse right now. He turned to gauge the reactions of the pack animals. They weren't as vocal about their complaints but were more hesitant to approach the water. Bradley looked ahead. The water was hitting the captain at the knees, proof that Omar was indeed swimming. Ambrosia looked back at him. Was she afraid to follow into the deeper water? He waved her on. Her father wasn't waiting on her and she shouldn't cross alone. If she didn't hurry . . .

He turned back toward the calves and saw a loose rope on one of their packs. There was a good chance of losing that bundle in the water if he didn't tighten it. With a quick command, Bradley had Melda and the pack animals kneel. The two pack camels balked at being made to wait as he untied the cargo. He didn't mean for it to take so long, but readjustments had to be made, and he wanted to put some thought into which crates should be at the bottom, since they risked getting wet. The mattress should be at the very top.

By the time he was done, Ambrosia and the captain had made it safely to the other side. Ambrosia's split skirt was dripping wet, but she looked refreshed. Bradley couldn't wait for a dip himself.

"Looking for firewood," Captain Herald called. Bradley waved him on and smacked the furry side of one of the youngsters to get him up once the packs were secure.

Turning back toward Melda, Bradley jogged across the sand. His boot sank in a soft patch, nearly causing him to lose his balance. He steadied himself with his other foot, but it began to sink, too.

Shifting his weight from one side to the other did nothing to help. At first he thought if he could slip his boots off, he could climb out, but his boots had tightened around his legs.

Then he realized how much trouble he was in. Quicksand.

Standing absolutely still, Bradley tried to call Melda to him, but she wanted nothing to do with him. He looked out to the river. Could Captain Herald hear him? Maybe not, but Ambrosia was already on her way back.

She was midstream, balancing atop Ruby as she swam toward him. What a lovely sight. Oh, sure, he'd never hear the end of it, but at least she wasn't leaving him to bake under the Cherokee sun.

She slowed Ruby as they came out of the river. "Are you stuck?" she asked.

"Stay back," he said. "There could be more."

"I'm not going to leave you," she huffed.

"No, you're not, but a tossed rope will do the trick. Get the rope off Melda and throw it my way." Although the mud hadn't reached his knees yet, the pressure was incredible. He wasn't sinking and help was right there, but he didn't like the feeling of death being that close.

Pinned down again, but this time there was no running.

She wrapped the end of the rope around her saddle, tied it off, and then tossed it out to him. He had to stretch for it, which sunk him another inch or so. No reason to panic. He wasn't going under. He tied the rope beneath his arms, then got a good grip with both hands.

"Let's go, Ruby," she said. The camel wasn't a roping horse. It didn't know how to back up, but Ambrosia could at least turn it around and walk away.

At first Bradley thought he was going to be ripped in two. The sand held fast until the suction popped both his knees and his ankles, but then he moved. The hardest part was keeping his boots on, but Bradley would be tarred and feathered before he traveled the rest of the way barefoot.

"It's working," he called. Ruby continued until he was free and skidding across the watery sand. "Whoa," he hollered.

Ambrosia stopped the animal and ordered her to kneel.

Bradley lay in the sand and rotated his feet. He pressed his hand on his chest to slow his racing heart. Normally he enjoyed danger, but he didn't like to take it standing still. But now his blood was flowing again, and Ambrosia was next to him.

"You're a mess," she said as she took the hem of her skirt and wiped the sand off his face. The skirt was wet, which made them both laugh.

"Thanks for coming back for me."

"I would never leave someone behind," she said. "Only the camels."

But he wasn't thinking about the camels. He got to his feet and offered Ambrosia his hand. When she pulled herself up, he took a step closer.

"You saved my life."

"Nonsense. The sand wasn't even up to your knees."

"I owe you something." And he knew what he wanted to give her. His eyes wandered to her lips. When she rested her hand on his dripping chest and leaned in, he nearly burst a button.

Her face brushed against his cheek as she moved forward and whispered in his ear, "Do I really have to keep the camels?"

Bradley took her by the waist and snuggled her against him. This had the makings of the most pleasurable argument of his life. "We've been over this before. It's my mission." But it would be an easy mission to forget with her in his arms.

With her finger, she traced a circle above his heart. "He hired you to get us home safely. Forget about the camels. Buy them, sell them, send them scattering to the four winds, for all I care, but we have no place for them." She tilted her face up to him, her sweetness containing an edge of challenge that made her even more irresistible. "I saved your life. Can't you do this for me?"

His heart pounded. He'd kiss her. Just one kiss, because she sure acted like she needed kissing. Her lashes fluttered down, and her chin tilted up, giving him a clear path.

But not a clear conscience. He took one muddy, sandy finger and drew a line on her cheek. "I can't betray your pa."

The sweetness melted into disappointment as she pulled away. "You aren't betraying him. You're helping him, and you're helping me."

"I have to complete this mission to your father's satisfaction."

"What about my satisfaction?" Her hands were on her hips while her wet skirt slapped in the wind.

Bradley groaned. She needed to be locked up somewhere safe until she was old enough to know better. Being the mature, responsible party went against his nature.

And he'd thought the quicksand had been hard to walk away from.

Chapter

8.

No longer counting the steps toward home, Ambrosia had something else to occupy her thoughts. Bradley Willis had refused to kiss her. Stealing a kiss was unforgivable, but refusing a kiss ranked somewhere around criminal. And what was worse, he refused to help her.

She grabbed the frame of her saddle and held on as Ruby made it down another sharp embankment. The brutal sun hadn't slacked, and Amber was paying the price. Without her parasol, she was baking, and her forearms were blistering. Although the heat was the same, the terrain had changed. The ground was broken and chopped up here. Often the smooth, grassy plain dropped off, exposing a red vein of dirt. Here at least was one place that the camels weren't quite as nimble as the horses. True, they endured the heat better and could carry a heavier load, but their large padded feet did better on flat surfaces than steep drops.

She'd saved Bradley's life. Not really, but didn't he owe her one tiny favor? She bit her lip. What if Bradley was right? What if her father *was* getting better, and what if it was because of the camels? She'd never considered how her father might feel with a room full of awards but no challenges ahead. How had Bradley figured it out?

Her father dropped back to ride next to her. "They've handled the gullies pretty well, but I'm curious if we'll find one too steep."

"It seems like we're crossing the same gully as it snakes back and forth. Couldn't we avoid this?"

"What would be the fun in that? Besides, I want you to see what they can do. Let's head over to that washout."

Because they had nothing better to do in the blistering sun than zigzag around, looking for obstacles to cross. Dutifully, Amber followed him. Bradley shrugged a question at her, but she had no answer.

"This will do." Her father sounded like a boy when he was this excited. "Let's see if we've found one that Omar will balk at."

Omar didn't like what he was being asked to do. He extended his long neck to investigate the drop, and his head swung slowly from left to right, looking the situation over. Then, with a strained trumpeting, he began to drop to his knees.

"Hold on," her father cheered. "He's going to do it."

Whatever he was going to do, Ruby was following. She knelt as well, but by now Ambrosia could avoid getting pitched around in the saddle. "I guess we're getting down?" she said. But Ruby didn't stop to let her off. Instead, she rocked and scooted forward on one knee, then on the other. "She's crawling!"

So was Omar. Her father beamed. "They did this in Dog Canyon when we were going across the Guadalupe Mountains. When the way gets too treacherous, instead of slipping, they crawl. Aren't they the most practical, amazing beasts?"

Amber had to admit it was clever.

Once they'd reached the bottom of the gully, up on their feet they went.

Bradley caught up with them. "I've never seen a horse handle a steep like that."

"That was Lieutenant Echols's favorite trick. I wish he could've been here to see it one last time. He always rode Topsy, and he

235

was the fastest crawler. I was at Lieutenant Hartz's funeral when Echols passed away, so I couldn't make it in time for his memorial."

She'd heard this before, but . . . "I didn't realize they both died at the same time."

"Nearly. And then when Edward Beale died in that train wreck this spring, he was the last one to go."

Bradley's face had settled into unusually somber lines. "Your father is the only one left," he reminded her.

She remembered there had been some funerals of people she didn't know, but she hadn't understood the significance.

Her father scratched Omar's hump. "Just me and the camels." He smiled weakly. "You know, I always thought the army turned out rough men, not fit for polite society, but then I realized it fostered a lot of character, too—loyalty, responsibility, the courage to see your friends through. If a man can claim those traits, he's got a lot going for him."

Amber looked at the dry ground passing beneath them. Loyalty? Bradley had proven that he possessed that trait in abundance. Could it be that he and her father understood something about devotion that she was missing? True, she was doing what she and her mother thought best for Father, but maybe they were measuring by a different yardstick.

When they stopped to camp that night, Amber was still bothered by her father's words—that and the burning of her forearms. She hadn't realized how much her little parasol had protected her. Her sunbonnet only shaded her face and neck.

As soon as they'd unloaded the camels, her father had taken them to search for grazing so they could preserve the oats for later. Because of their long, leathery lips, he claimed they could eat cactus with no problems. Amber would like to see it, but not tonight. If it weren't for the burning on her arms, she could've fallen asleep immediately.

She sat next to a charred pile of sticks, evidence that this had been someone else's camping spot as well, and tried to untie her sunbonnet with shaking fingers.

Bradley, having fully recovered from his quicksand event, had kept his distance that day, preferring to ride mostly in silence. But watching her apparently had broken his resolve.

"Who ever heard of bringing a woman across the plains in August?" he said on her third attempt to pry the knot loose. He pushed her hands away and took up the ribbons in his own. He knelt, face-to-face with her. If he didn't smell so much like camels, she might have found his thoughtful blue eyes irresistible.

She was tired. So tired that she'd almost forgotten she was irritated with him.

Bradley fussed like a mother hen as he carefully removed her hat and set it aside. "Hand me your canteen. I'm going to go refill them."

Ambrosia handed it over, and he saw her arms.

"Oh, sweetheart . . ." he whispered. He caught her by the hand and pulled off her glove. A sharp hiss of breath was all the reply she could make as he took in the dry, reddened skin that began right where her gloves had ended. You could have fried eggs in the heat radiating from her skin.

"You should've said something." His touch made her shiver, and not for the good reasons. "We have to get something on this. Do you have any creams? Witch hazel?"

"My father drinks a bit of vinegar every morning for his health. We brought a small flask."

"Vinegar? That's what's in your father's flask?"

"What did you think it was?"

Bradley wagged his eyebrows. "I'll go get it. Don't scratch. Whatever you do, don't scratch."

The heat hadn't gone away, but she was almost too tired to care. She couldn't wait to collapse on her mattress, but the thought of the stiff fabric rubbing her arms made her cringe.

Bradley returned, carrying her father's flask. He started to sit, then paused to push her skirt aside so he wouldn't crush it. He opened the flask and removed his bandanna.

"I'm too tired to mind that your bandanna has been out in the dust all day," she said.

"So have your arms." Carefully, he rolled up her dainty lace sleeves to her elbows.

"I should have been more careful," she said.

He gritted his teeth. "And us here with nothing but another week's worth of travel ahead of us." He upended the vinegar into the hankie. "I'll be gentle," he said.

At the first contact, the cold vinegar on her arms left her light-headed. Her skin tightened and burned, but then came a blessed coolness that spun the world around.

"That doesn't hurt too bad, does it?" His blue eyes held concern, but also assurance that she was going to be just fine.

She let her eyes slide closed. "It feels heavenly."

"Just relax. Let me take care of you," he said as he swabbed the rest of her arm.

"I was worried about your smelling like a camel," she said, "but now I smell like I climbed out of a pickle vat."

"I love pickles," he said.

"And I'm growing fond of camels."

"Is that right?" He grinned slowly. "Only the camels?"

She didn't have to wonder how she'd fallen under his spell. Of course he'd captured her heart. The real question was what he saw in her. Or was she just part of the job? Someone to humor while he completed his mission?

She looked nothing like the spotless, fresh miss he'd met at the farm earlier that week. Her flawless skin showed the effects of the harsh wind and sun. Her hair, although smooth every morning, had been teased out of her braid and now framed her face with dark tendrils. Her clothes were battered and stained. She might not think it was an improvement, but he was impressed. Now she was real. And she made his blood sing.

"I've been thinking about what you said." She held out her other arm for him to swab. "You said a man needs someone to look after, and I've got to ask . . . who are you looking after?"

238

On the face of it, it was a ridiculous question. He was a part of the US Cavalry, a brotherhood that meant something. Krebs, Morris, Chandler—heck, even Major Adams—were who he was looking after. But she was right. Someday they would all go their own ways. He wasn't planning the rest of his life around them.

But Ambrosia Herald was someone he could possibly find room for.

"Until this trip, I never knew that I wanted the responsibility of caring for someone else." The tight feeling in his chest reminded him of the quicksand. He brushed back her tangled hair and anchored it behind her ear. "You don't need me, but I wish you did."

"How do you know what I need?"

Could she be telling the truth? Was there room in her life for a rascal like him? He took her hand and pressed it against his lips. If he'd misunderstood, she'd better set him straight fast.

"You know I'm helping your father." Bradley turned her hand over and watched the thin, blue veins pulse beneath her pale skin. "No matter how sweet you act, you can't persuade me otherwise."

"Mmmm . . ." she purred as he planted his lips on her wrist. "I was wrong. I think the camels are good for him. Mother's garden might get destroyed, but—" She stopped talking when he pressed another kiss higher on her arm.

"I hope that doesn't hurt," he said.

"It doesn't hurt."

"A kiss to make it better, right?"

She dropped her gaze to his mouth. "My lips are sunburned, too," she said.

The wind had died to a breeze, but Bradley felt like the earth had stopped completely. He leaned forward and, just before his lips touched hers, said, "At least they don't taste like pickles."

And then he kissed her good and solid, just to show her that he meant business. To show her she couldn't tease him like that and not mean it. But, have mercy, she did mean it. Her lips softened, willing and inviting. It was easy to kiss her, easy to go forward,

239

but Bradley knew there was no going back. This would change who he was and what he wanted out of life.

But for that moment, what he wanted out of life was pretty simple. More of Ambrosia.

"Private Willis!"

Bradley smiled, which threw off his kissing. He could just imagine Major Adams's shock that he'd fallen in love on this crazy mission.

"Private Willis!"

But that wasn't Major Adams. It was Captain Herald.

Bradley rocked away from Ambrosia and jumped to attention. His elbow bounced into her shoulder and nearly knocked her over. It was a messy affair. He was a mess. He was *in* a mess.

Captain Herald glared at both of them. "I don't know who I should discipline first."

"It's my fault, sir. I instigated the kissing. Ambrosia had nothing to do with it."

"What?" She stood. "I had everything to do with it."

"As the gentleman, I was in the wrong," Bradley insisted.

"As the lady, so was I. You finally kiss me, and now you want to act like I'm too immature to know what was going on?"

Her father held up his hand. "Fine, Ambrosia, you're just as much to blame. Does that make you happy?"

She beamed at Bradley, and he couldn't help but smile back.

"Best kiss of my life. I can't let you take all the credit," she whispered.

Stars above. What had he gotten himself into?

The captain marched between them. "What else have I missed? Do we need to form a firing squad out here?"

"Nothing else, sir," Bradley said. "That was the first time I kissed her."

But it wouldn't be the last.

Chapter
9

The next morning, Ambrosia worried that the trip was passing too quickly. In a matter of days, they would be home, and what then? Bradley was a trooper. He had no control over where he was stationed or how long he stayed. She knew that, and she'd decided to love him anyway.

They hadn't been riding very long when Bradley pointed out a Cheyenne settlement with its white tepees. The camel ensemble steered clear of them and Bradley kept an alert eye, but after half the day, they could no longer see the village and assumed they'd passed by undetected.

Ambrosia breathed a sigh of relief, but then she saw horsemen following them. At first she didn't trust her eyes. Something was back there, but it was too far away to see clearly. But as the figures grew bigger and bigger, she didn't think they were Indians, after all.

Bradley had wisely kept his distance from her, even though her father wasn't nearly as mad as she'd expected. When he turned to scan the horizon, he spotted the horsemen for himself.

"Don't worry." Ambrosia scratched at her sunburnt arm. "I've been watching them, and I don't think they're Cheyenne."

"How long have they been following us?" He didn't act as re-lieved as he should.

"A half hour or so. They seem wary. If they're afraid of us, then we're safe, aren't we?"

"Captain Herald!" Bradley shouted. He dug in his knapsack for a pair of field glasses while her father turned Omar and joined him.

"What is it?"

Bradley held the glasses to his face. Their small meal of canned beans felt heavy in Ambrosia's stomach as she watched his mouth tighten and his lips go white.

"It's the Gunther gang," he said. "That's Pete's paint horse. They've been following us since the lodge, if not before."

"How do you know?" her father asked.

"Because of this." Bradley held up his canteen. "That dent is from the gunfight we had. The night we heard someone messing around our corral, I found this pulled from my stuff and sitting on a fence post. They know it's me."

The horsemen had stopped on a ridge. There were five of them, all men, just looking down at them from a distance.

Regret showed plainly on Bradley's face. "You have nothing of value for them. They want me. I can keep them busy for a while." He slapped his thigh. "What I wouldn't give for a horse right now."

"You can't go," Ambrosia said. "They tried to kill you before."

"Fort Reno is southwest of here. Maybe you'll come across some troopers if you head that way."

Bradley's throat jogged as he looked at her. Was he really going? Would this be the last time she saw him? No. Not like this. Not this sudden. It wasn't fair.

"You've made a tactical error," her father said.

"Bringing you here, or not coming with more men?" Bradley asked.

"Not trusting my camels. How far is it to the fort?"

Bradley squinted. "Forty miles or so."

Her father stared at the western horizon. "They have an angle on us, but we'll give them a race they won't forget. Unload the pack

242

animals and set them free to follow. We'll all lighten our loads and get there early morning."

"Not Ambrosia," Bradley said. "You stay and protect her—"

"Private Willis. We are not every man for himself, neither are we offering up sacrificial lambs. Sometimes bravery involves staying at your post and guarding those who are supposed to be guarded, instead of hightailing it out at the first sign of danger."

"Pardon me, sir, but I am not running from a fight. I'm running toward it."

"And leaving your comrades unprotected. We will stay together. Between the three of us and our superior mounts, we should be able to outmaneuver the enemy."

Ambrosia looked at Melda and Omar, drowsily blinking in the hot sun. She wasn't ready to risk her future with Bradley on the backs of these dromedaries, but it didn't look like they had a choice.

It didn't matter how noble Captain Herald tried to make it sound, what he was asking of Bradley amounted to cowardice. Just because the captain didn't want to rush into the open guns of the Gunther gang didn't mean that Bradley wasn't willing.

Anything to keep them away from Ambrosia.

And if it didn't work, well, Bradley would rather go down fighting tooth and nail and give her a chance than be at her side facing a bleak end. His shoulders felt heavier than the crates he was tossing off the pack animals. He could face his own death, but not hers.

He quickly untethered the camels from each other. Captain Herald was unburdening Melda, Ruby, and Omar of excess weight while Ambrosia filled their canteens one last time before leaving the barrels of water behind.

The Gunthers were still hours from catching them, but they weren't dissuaded. Bradley could only imagine what they thought of the camels. They probably thought the three travelers were sitting ducks without horses. Maybe they were.

"Better get going." Bradley went to give Ambrosia a hand up onto her camel. She looked scared but determined.

"Just remember," she said, "I came back for you when you were stuck in that quicksand. I didn't leave you to face it alone."

"That's right, Ambrosia. And we'll make it through this together, too." He tried to smile.

She settled in as he ran to Melda. Captain Herald gave the order for them to rise. Ruby shook her shoulders, appreciating her lighter load, and Omar let out a bellow as if he'd sensed their urgency.

"Just hold on," Captain Herald said, "and give them full rein to go at their own pace."

He urged Omar into motion, and before they could settle into their walk, he dug his heels in and pushed him faster. Omar stepped it up again and was soon loping in long, swaying strides. Without any prompting, Melda and Ruby joined in, with the younger camels kicking up their heels as they followed.

It was smoother than a trot, and when Bradley looked down, he couldn't believe how quickly the ground was passing beneath them. He looked to the north. They'd still be within firing range before sunset if the Gunthers didn't give up. Their only hope was to encounter some troopers. What he wouldn't give to see Lieutenant Hennessey about now. Or even Major Adams.

Pete Gunther knew Bradley was cavalry and knew where they'd be headed. The gang would probably try to cut them off. If the outlaws got in front of them, it'd be gun against gun. Bradley desperately thought through the terrain between them and the fort. Although he'd never favored building a defense, he'd rather have some time to prepare than meet the Gunthers in the open. Where could they make a stand? Nearby were the Canadian River and a few creeks. At least there were trees there, but nothing that could be considered much cover.

Better to stay in the saddle and try to outrun them.

As time passed, Bradley grew more confident. The camels, although huffing, didn't seem to be in any distress, while the horses had to be pushing with all their strength. Finally, the horses began to lag, even though the camels continued their trot. Captain Herald had been right. There was no way the horses could keep up this pace cross-country. The sun had disappeared, and the riders were getting harder to see in the fading light. Finally, they disappeared altogether into a dip on the plain.

"Where'd they go?" Ambrosia asked.

Bradley scanned the lay of the land. "There's a creek out there."

"Their horses have to stop for water," Herald said. "That's another advantage we have."

"How are you doing?" Bradley asked Ambrosia.

She held up her hands. With an effort, she unclenched her fingers. They were shaking. "I've been better," she said.

"They've been running at full capacity," Captain Herald said. "We still have reserves. By morning light, we'll have them beat easily. Let's eat quickly, rest lightly, then set out at dawn."

Bradley looked over the prairie. They were still too far away from the fort, but so was the Gunther gang. After riding that hard all day, their mounts wouldn't have the stamina to confront them now. Bunking down for the night went against his instincts, but logic told him it would be safe.

Find a low place and get something at their backs. That was Bradley's number one most dreaded position in which to meet a foe, but he was doing the right thing.

That was what he had to tell himself, at least.

Chapter
10

She hadn't slept well since they'd left Texas. Why did she imagine that this night would be any different?

She heard a gurgle from Omar and rolled over, feeling each one of the hard, red lumps of clay against her back and wishing for her nice mattress that they'd left behind.

Omar was babbling again. Was he talking in his sleep? Usually he only talked to her father. Someone must be over there. Ambrosia sat up and looked around. Supper had been some of her apples and jerky that Bradley had traded for at the Lighthorse lodge, so she was already hungry again. She reached for her knapsack, hoping there was something left, but by the moonlight she noticed that her father was gone. Afraid of what she'd find, she sped toward the camels.

"You should be resting," her father said. With his knees pulled up to his chest, he was leaning against Omar and watching the sleeping prairie.

She sat next to him. All year she'd feared that he wouldn't be with them much longer. Now he was healthy again and in more danger than ever.

"I'm sorry I fought you over the camels," she said. "I didn't realize how much they meant to you."

He wrapped his arm around her. "It was foolish of me. In my mind, Omar, Ruby, and Esmeralda were still wandering in that desert with Beale, Echols, and Hartz, and needed me to save them. I have the camels now, but that doesn't bring those men back. We don't always get a second chance."

She snuggled up against him. "But in a way, you do have a second chance. Mother and I thought you'd given up on life this summer, but this trip has revived you. If you come home ready to get back in the saddle, then saving these camels did bring back a person we love. You."

"Do you think your mother will learn to love the camels, too?"

"I wouldn't count on it. Especially if you pen them in her garden."

He sighed. "Then I'll have to find someplace else. Or even sell them. As long as we find someone who understands them and keeps them out of the cold, I'm satisfied." He grunted. "Here I'm worrying over these animals, when I still have to bring you home safely."

"We can ask God for His help, too."

"I am, honey. Believe me, I am."

A rustling made them both turn around. It was Bradley. Seeing it was just them, he let out a long breath. "You had me concerned."

Her father got to his feet. "If we're all up, we might as well hit the trail."

Omar shared his opinion in the form of an extended belch.

What would this day bring? The safety of Fort Reno, or death at the hands of outlaws? Ambrosia had been looking for adventure. After this, she'd never be satisfied swinging a sword around a library again.

Bradley took her hand and accompanied her to Ruby. "Ambrosia, before we go, I just have to say that meeting you on this trip made it all worth it, no matter how it ends."

Her hand tightened in his. "I didn't find you just to lose you this easily. We're going to fight for this." It was hard to be romantic with Ruby pulling at her skirt with those rubbery, clownish lips.

"It's worth fighting for," he said. Then, with a sweet kiss on her cheek—he had promised her father, after all—he handed her up into the saddle.

The camels made striking silhouettes in the dim light, but it wouldn't be dark for long. The scissortails had begun swooping around, and the moon was far in the west.

But by the time the sky lit, a row of horsemen had appeared on a ridge, standing between them and Fort Reno.

"I don't understand." Ambrosia pulled Ruby to a stop. Her throat went tight. "How did they get in front of us?"

"It's impossible." Bradley looked murderously angry. No longer worried or fearful, just angry.

Her father was, as well. He hated being wrong, especially about his camels.

One of the men raised his pistol above his head. A gunshot echoed across the prairie. To Ambrosia's surprise, the camels didn't flinch. They nosed each other, still saying good morning just like they did every day.

"Private Willis," one of the horsemen called from afar, now that he had their attention. "You're outnumbered and practically afoot. Give up now."

Bradley turned to her father. "I could. I would, but I don't trust them to keep their word and let you and your daughter go. Still, if you want me to—"

"They aren't going to let two witnesses go when they kill a trooper. We're all in danger." Her father tightened the reins in his hands. "Yesterday these camels trotted along as they felt comfortable. Today we're going to push them. We're going full speed, and we're bringing it right to those men." His eyes narrowed as he judged the distance between them and the row of outlaws. "Amber, keep your head low. All you need to do is hang on, because you'll be moving faster than you've ever moved before in your life."

"Yes, sir." She'd failed miserably in her quest to leave the camels behind. Now they were her only hope for survival.

"I'll ride in front, to shield Ambrosia," Bradley said.

"We both will. Just remember, speed and surprise are the keys."

"But won't they be able to just stand there and shoot us?" Maybe there wasn't a choice, but Amber still wanted to make sure they'd thought of every outcome.

Her father smiled. "It's hard to shoot straight when your horse spooks. Let's go."

They lined up facing the gunmen. The younger camels joined them, their heads swaying playfully as they tried to figure out the new game.

"That's right," Gunther called. "Turn yourselves in. We'll treat you right nice."

Bradley had never been so mad in his life.

"Walk toward him," Captain Herald said. "Watch his horse."

But what if the horse didn't bolt? The Gunther gang had been following them ever since the Cherokee lodge. According to the captain, horses quickly became accustomed to the camels' scent and appearance. Not only that, but these horses had already traveled a distance at a speed that surprised Bradley. Maybe they weren't your everyday, run-of-the-mill horses.

The morning light spilled over the horizon. They had it at their back—thank God for small favors. And by the light, Bradley saw a most heartening sight. Pete Gunther's horse. Except it wasn't his horse at all. It wasn't the paint that he'd been riding yesterday.

"Those are fresh horses." Bradley kept his voice low. "That's why they caught up with us." He now knew the location of the gang's hideout. And what was even better, these horses had never seen the camels before.

The new horse's ears twitched as it tried to spot them in the sun. Even from this distance, Bradley could see its nostrils flare as it whiffed their unfamiliar scent. Gunther removed his hand from his gun holster to take up the reins. He was having trouble keeping his mount still. His brother said something from behind him. The others laughed, but then one of their horses started acting up, too. No longer were they focused on their approaching enemy. Instead, they were trying to calm their suddenly agitated horses.

"This is it," Captain Herald said. "Run right at them."

"Bust their line and keep going until you see the fort," Bradley answered.

Camels weren't as easy to spur as horses, since they tended to have a mind of their own, but they liked fun, and steaming ahead at a row of nervous horses must have been fun for the camels. If it weren't for the guns the gang was carrying and the fact that he was protecting Ambrosia, it would've been fun for Bradley, too.

The camels' trot smoothed into a gallop. Now they were flying. He looked once at Ambrosia. She'd lost her hat but was sticking in the saddle like an old hand.

The Gunthers weren't as lucky. Two horses were galloping away despite their riders' best efforts to hold them. One man was on the ground, and another was barely holding on as his mount pitched and bucked.

Bradley had looked forward to busting through their line, but by the time the camels breached their spot, there was no line left. Only wild-eyed horses doing their best to get away. Most of the gang realized their miscalculation, and seeing that they weren't in a position to put up a fight with both their horses and the law, they made a run for it. Only the two Gunthers had a mind to stick it out and follow.

Bradley watched over his shoulder as they strong-armed their horses into submission. "Don't be stupid," he muttered, but the Gunthers were all sorts of ignorant and spurred the horses after them.

Bradley had wondered what kinds of stunts he could do on a camel, and now he was fixing to find out. Throwing a leg over the hump and spinning around backward, he slid down Melda's sloped withers and ducked below the high saddle. She didn't seem to mind that he was riding backward and almost sitting on her neck. Maybe she understood that he was protecting their rear.

A bullet whizzed past before he heard the shot go off. The Gunthers weren't messing around. He leveled his gun against the saddle and sighted it on Pete Gunther. As he was pulling the trigger, a ping sounded next to him, and Melda stumbled. His shot went high.

"Is she hit?" Amber called.

"Keep going," he answered.

That had been the younger brother shooting at him. Bradley glanced down and saw water spurting from his canteen. He grinned. That piece of tin was the most useful item in his gear. First it had saved his life, and now his mount's.

He drew Pete into his sights again and knew he wouldn't miss this time. Bradley's finger squeezed the trigger. Fire leapt from the barrel. Pete jarred, then slowly slid out of his saddle. His brother wheeled around, giving up the chase to help him.

Bradley felt like cheering. From here it was clear sailing to Fort Reno. In a couple hours, they'd be home.

Chapter

11

Heading northeast from the fort, a small band of troopers glided over the waving grasslands toward the Arapaho council meeting. Lieutenant Jack Hennessey was the representative for the cavalry, and while he expected the Arapaho meeting to go well, the troopers knew the Gunther gang was in the area. No one would travel alone until they were brought in.

"Sir," Private Krebs called from behind him. "Someone is coming up fast on our right."

Jack shaded his eyes. Was it one of their own, or someone looking for trouble? "Field glasses." He held out his hand.

"Uh . . ." Sergeant Byrd kept the glasses to his face. "You're not going to believe this."

"That's why I want the field glasses," Jack said, prompting Byrd to finally hand them over.

It took his eyes a second to adjust. There was the cloud of dust and what looked like a group of five, perhaps. He thought he saw the blue of a cavalry uniform, so he focused on that rider, but then a bizarre face flashed across the lens. Jack lowered the glasses and squinted, then pulled the glasses up again. What was that? The riders were closer now, and he could tell there was something wrong with their horses. They were giant, with strange heads and absurdly long legs. The riders were sitting way up in the air, like balancing on a pile of saddle blankets, but one of them was turned around backward, shooting behind them.

There was only one cavalryman from Fort Reno who would try a stunt like that.

"Boys," Jack said, "I don't know what they're doing, but that there is Private Willis, and he's one of our own."

"It's Willis?" Word spread like wildfire along with shouts and cheers. "Let's go!"

What would Major Adams say when he found out that his punitive assignment had added another chapter to the legend of Bradley Willis? Jack would insist on being the one to give the report.

Lieutenant Hennessey and his men came to the rescue. Bradley considered accompanying them to round up the rest of the Gunther gang, but the camel and horse trouble made it impossible. Besides, after all they'd been through, he wasn't about to leave Ambrosia and Captain Herald now.

They reached Fort Reno safely, and when Ambrosia saw the stately houses on Officer's Row, she immediately began to fret about being unpresentable, but Bradley thought she'd never looked better.

They soon found themselves standing at the door of Major Adams's house with trail dust, sweat, and camel hair still pestering them. When the door opened, Bradley stood back to allow Captain Herald and Ambrosia to enter before him. He would salute his commander, but he was really watching for his sister. He couldn't wait to introduce her to Amber. Meeting his cultured, refined sister would raise everyone's opinion of him.

"Captain Herald, I'm delighted to have you at Fort Reno. And thanks for leaving your herd outside the campgrounds. I'd rather not make a shamble of our stables," Major Adams said as the two men shook hands fondly.

"I'm only glad we were able to communicate with Lieutenant Hennessey before he and his men came too close. You have a fine command here, sir, and all of my dealings with your troops have been beneficial."

Major Adams stared pointedly at Bradley. "All of them?"

Bradley glanced at Amber. She looked like she'd been through the ringer, but her smile was priceless.

Captain Herald laughed. "When I told you to send a headstrong young man who could endure my daughter's sharp tongue, I never imagined you'd find someone who suited her so perfectly."

Bradley couldn't believe what he was hearing.

"What?" Ambrosia asked. "I thought you sent for someone who knew Indian Territory."

"What good is a guide if he doesn't have the backbone to keep you in your place? You ran off all the cowboys." Captain Herald turned to the major. "This is my dear daughter, the one we named after General Ambrose Burnside. In retrospect, *Ulyssia* would've been more appropriate."

"Ambrose Burnside?" Bradley gawked at Amber. "The one with the, uh, very ambitious facial hair? That's who you were named after? What happened to the food of the gods?"

"I prefer to put my own interpretation on the story." She raised an eyebrow, daring him to contradict her.

"Maybe steak and taters aren't enough, after all," he said, making her smile while leaving the officers to wonder.

The danger of falling in love on a journey was that both parties were adrift in a foreign land. What if he looked heroic when he was the only man around besides one's father? What if he was attentive there, but then completely ignored you when his friends arrived? So many unknowns.

But seeing Fort Reno, meeting Bradley's charming sister—who seemed shocked to realize that Bradley's infatuation was reciprocated—and watching his peers welcome him home and congratulate him on his success only increased Amber's appreciation of the brave man who'd gotten her safely through the journey. But they weren't home yet, and that was her concern.

It wasn't long before that concern was addressed. Over dinner that night with the major, Bradley's sister, Louisa, brought up the subject in her gracious manner.

"Bradley, I'm so glad you're back." Louisa's clothes were very fine for a governess. Even though Ambrosia had bathed and donned something clean, she still felt underdressed. "After all you've been through, I imagine that Major Adams would consider sending someone else to help the Heralds finish their journey."

The look exchanged between Louisa and the major confirmed what Bradley had said about their relationship.

"Yes, I've talked that over with Captain Herald and offered him another escort," Major Adams said. "He has generously decided to allow Bradley to stay here rather than continue on with him and Miss Herald. As far as I'm concerned, Bradley has passed the test. This mission has been completed satisfactorily."

Ambrosia felt hope draining away. A summer romance? Was that all she was? Across the table, Bradley avoided looking at her. She raised her chin. Fine. She could do without him. He'd risked his life for her. He deserved a civil good-bye.

Conversation continued, with the major asking a hundred questions about the camels and Louisa inquiring after lodging for the night. Ambrosia's father had just promised to take them both on a camel ride when Bradley blurted out, "Excuse me, sir, but I think I'll go to Texas."

Her father paused, not accustomed to being interrupted. Major Adams looked at Louisa and shook his head, as if unsurprised by his outburst. "Allow the captain to finish, Private Willis."

But Bradley didn't wait. "I'll go with him. I want to go with him. I want to see the mission completed."

Beneath the table, Ambrosia wadded her gown in her fist. "Is your mission that important to you?"

The light from the silver candelabra reflected in Bradley's eyes.

His jaw was freshly shaven, his hair shiny and clean. "It is," he said, "and I intend to see it completed."

"What if I catch the stagecoach and ride it home? Would you still be as determined to escort the camels?" she asked.

Bradley frowned, and Major Adams cleared his throat. Ambrosia tried to smooth the wrinkle she was making in her skirt. It occurred to her that she might sound combative at this fine table where everyone was being so gracious.

Realizing that something was wrong, Louisa intervened. "Captain Herald, does your daughter play chess?" she asked.

"Ambrosia? No, not at all. Why—"

"There's a lovely chess set in the major's office. Bradley, do be a dear and take Miss Herald to see it. I think she'll be impressed."

Bradley stood. "With her father's permission?"

Captain Herald drummed his fingers against the white tablecloth. "I suppose she'll come to no harm in the major's office."

"If I can take care of her while facing the Gunther gang—"

"Bradley," his sister warned, "don't push your luck."

Ambrosia waited for him to come and pull out her chair. After nearly a week of cooking on a campfire and sleeping on the ground, she wanted to feel like a lady, even if she was out of sorts. He led her to an office with French doors overlooking the parade grounds, but he didn't bother showing her the chess set.

Instead, he took her in his arms. Her gown crushed against his spotless blue uniform.

"What's this about you catching a stagecoach? I thought you were going to stay with your pa."

Amber shrugged "That depends. Are you going because you were forced on this mission or because you want to be with me?"

"You heard the major. No one is forcing me to go. I'm doing it because that's what I want."

"And after that?" She busied herself with twisting a brass button on his coat. Why was she pushing him so hard? She didn't like how she was acting, but she was scared. More scared than she'd been with the outlaws. She was afraid that she'd misunderstood, that she'd grown to love someone who didn't love her back.

His breathing was slow and even, while hers felt rapid and strained. He clasped his hands behind her and let her lean back in his arms.

"After I take you home, I'll have a day or so before I head back to the fort. In that time, I want to meet your mother and spend some time with your father when he's not being Captain Herald. If there's any other family I need to impress, I'll leave it up to you to introduce us."

His words soothed her. The fear was diminishing. "But then you'll leave. I might not see you again."

"I'm commissioned to the army for three more years, but Garber is only a couple of days away. Every leave I get, every time I'm near the border, I'll come calling. And perhaps you could come visit my sister on occasion."

"Then you don't regret it?"

"What? Our time together?" With a gentle tug on her chin, he raised her face to his. "Three years, Ambrosia. I've got a lot of growing up to do, but I'll do it knowing that you're waiting for me."

She stretched her arms up around his neck. She reckoned that she needed a few more years, too. "Just don't outgrow me," she said.

And he promised.

Together they'd finish this journey to fulfill her father's dream, and then would come the test. But sometimes courage meant sticking to your post, shoulder to shoulder with your partner, and sometimes courage was facing the battle alone. As long as they knew they were on the same team and committed to each other, they could make it despite the distance, the years, . . . and the camels.

A TEAVILLE MORAL SOCIETY NOVELLA

Tied AND TRUE

MELISSA JAGEARS

Chapter

1

KANSAS CITY, MISSOURI
SEPTEMBER 1908

The pounding of hammers above them ceased.

Marianne Lister put down her tea and smiled at the widow whose roof was being reshingled by men from their church. "Seems you'll have peace and quiet now."

Mrs. Danby's faded blue eyes blinked as if it were hours after nightfall. "I could hardly hear them, sweetie. But God bless you for coming."

"You're welcome." Not that she'd been much help; she'd simply kept the woman company.

If only she could've done more than rearrange Mrs. Danby's pantry and chitchat while they waited. The widow had even taken over making lunch. Marianne rubbed the back of her hand where oil had left a welt. Evidently there was an art to frying ham if one didn't want to splatter oil everywhere. As heiress to a large fortune, she'd never need to cook for herself, but that didn't lessen her feeling of failure.

The front door opened, and Calvin Hochstetler poked in his

honey-blond head. Her heart pitter-pattered like always whenever he came near.

"We've got your roof finished, Mrs. Danby. And none too soon considering the dark clouds rolling in. Was there more you needed done, or shall I send the men home?"

"Nothing I can think of." She waved her age-spotted hand to encourage him across the threshold. "Why don't you come in for more tea?"

Marianne picked up the nearly empty teapot. At least making tea was something she was good at. Even if this would be the fifth pot Mrs. Danby plied on the men.

"Thank you, but I think we're good." Calvin pressed a hand against his stomach and his eyes grew wide, likely at the thought of downing another cup. He managed to give Mrs. Danby a polite smile anyway, which only heightened his good looks.

"If you don't have anything more for us to do, the men would like to get home before the storm." He looked over at Marianne and then at the clock. "Is your driver coming to pick you up?"

She shook her head. "He won't be coming for another hour. Would you mind walking me home?"

He beamed a genuine smile this time, making her insides warmer than the tepid teapot in her hands. "Certainly, but we'll have to leave quickly. Are you ready to go?"

She was more than ready if it meant spending time with him. "Just let me tidy up."

He nodded and backed out the door.

She put away the tea service, and when she returned to the parlor, Mrs. Danby had fallen asleep. Marianne arranged the quilt over the widow's legs and let herself out.

The other men had already left, and Calvin was throwing away the last of the broken shingles.

So not only would she get to spend time with him, but they'd be alone? Her heart picked up and jitters took over. She looked at the sky. Hopefully the storm clouds weren't in any hurry.

Calvin threw the last shingle into a bucket, carried it to the curb, then came back to meet her at the stairs. "Did you have a good visit with Mrs. Danby?"

"I did." She tucked her arm around his, sighing a little at the tingles sweeping through her at his touch.

"I'm glad you agreed to keep her company." Calvin tipped his hat at someone across the road as they started east. "She said her daughter hasn't been up to see her for years."

The poor woman, all alone with no one to help. And her daughter likely would've been better help today—she probably knew how to cook.

Marianne sighed. Would she ever be able to do anything of value? How was it she'd come to be twenty-one and couldn't do much more than make tea? Wonderful tea, yes, but still nothing more significant than tea. Of course, she could also maintain a smile without it looking fake and nod her head sympathetically when Mother's society friends complained about their husbands' antics or philandering. If only she'd been born Mrs. Danby's daughter, she might be able to do something useful outside a parlor. "I'm glad you let me be a part of your widow and orphan ministry, even if I am rather useless."

"You aren't useless." He rubbed the top of her arm.

"When it comes to actually helping, I'm afraid I am." She stared at the tops of her polished leather shoes. She'd certainly felt so today.

"You underestimate how much some of these widows need conversation. We can fix holes or replace windows to keep their houses warm, but you're the one who warms their hearts." He tucked her arm tighter against his and gave it a squeeze.

Did he see something valuable in everyone? "Might I go with you next Saturday?"

"I'd hoped so. Mrs. Phillips makes terrible tea." He winked.

"But what if I wanted to help tear down her porch?" Manual labor couldn't be too hard. Even children did it.

He raised his eyebrows at her. "What about talking with Mrs. Phillips?"

"I'd chat with her afterward. I know I can't help you build the porch, but today I could've picked up broken shingles. Surely I could pile up rotted wood."

"Sounds fine to me." He waved at someone across the street. "You'll save us time."

She smiled so big it could have lifted her off the ground if not for Calvin's arm around hers. And here she'd thought nothing could lighten her step faster than his dimpled smile.

If she'd told anyone in her social set she wanted to pick up rotted wood, they'd have laughed at her. "What project is after Mrs. Phillips's?"

"Not sure. Her porch will wipe out next month's budget."

She was tempted to promise him extra funding, but she could imagine her father would gripe about how the group conveniently started going over budget once she volunteered. "What will you do for the rest of the month?"

He shrugged and looked back over his shoulder at the threatening clouds. "The others will be happy to spend time with their families, and I've got projects at work to finalize. With David out of the office, I should have enough time to do so before he returns. Other than that, I'll keep my ears open for anything we can do that doesn't require money. What about you?"

If she didn't have anywhere to be, her parents would expect her to throw parties, pass cookies, and smile at eligible gentlemen . . . as long as she didn't smile at any of them more than she did David. Calvin's boss was the gentleman of choice when it came to a desired son-in-law.

If only they knew she and David had already discussed everyone's expectations and chosen not to deepen their relationship. David was probably the only man in her circle who'd not take offense at her begging off his courtship because she had feelings for his secretary. "I don't know what Mother has on the calendar, but I wish I could find something more useful to do than visiting."

"What about that plan you had to help the homeless sell day-old breads?"

He remembered that? That had been an idea Papa had proven silly with long columns of numbers and figures, showing her business plan was unsustainable. "Seems I have to think up something that can be a blessing but still pay its own bills. If I do inherit, hopefully I'll have figured out how to help those in need without bankrupting myself by then."

"*If* you inherit?" He turned to frown at her, a deep wrinkle forming between his brows.

"Yes, if . . ." David had warned her that a relationship with Calvin might cause her parents to disinherit her. Though she'd not meant to bring that up now . . . a lady didn't ask a man to court, after all.

"Are your parents in financial trouble? Considering the amount of business they do with the Kingsmans, I hadn't gotten that impression."

"Oh no, no trouble like that. Just me—being trouble, that is."

"If you cause your parents any real trouble, I'll eat my hat." He flashed her the silly grin that always made her feel accepted, despite how different they were.

And if they could be such easy friends, transforming their relationship into something deeper should be just as easy, right?

Oh, what to say? A lady might not propose . . . but was there anything wrong with hinting? "Well, they've forever expected me to marry David, so there's no doubt they'll find it troublesome I've fallen for his secretary instead."

Calvin stopped midstride, his face suddenly blank.

Her body grew cold as she reviewed the words she'd just said. Seemed she was just as bad at hinting as being useful. Perhaps her unchecked tongue was where the real trouble lay.

His brows drew closer, and his gaze bore into hers. When his hand came up, her heart slammed against her chest and she closed her eyes. Would she receive her first kiss? Maybe bumbling out her feelings hadn't been such a bad thing, after all.

Instead, he twisted her nose.

Her eyes flew open. "What was that for?"

His expression was wide-eyed with panic. "I just . . . In my dreams, I'd never tweaked your nose, and I . . ." He rubbed a hand down his face. "This isn't a dream," he said, as if it were the most horrible thing in the world to find himself awake.

She reached up and rubbed her nose. "No, not a dream. I certainly felt that."

"All right, then, I . . ." He nodded decisively. "I must have heard you wrong."

"So then I didn't just say my parents would be upset about my being in love with you?"

He shook his head, then walked off like a shot, both his hands raking through his hair and stopping at the nape of his neck.

"Wait!" Perhaps this was why her parents were always making her play tea party with the elderly women in her circle. She couldn't get into trouble like this with them. She picked up her skirts and rushed after him. "Aren't you going to say something?"

He wouldn't just leave her to wonder, would he?

He didn't slow, but he did let go of the back of his head and start gesturing with his hands as if giving someone a hesitant lecture. But though his mouth moved, he wasn't actually saying anything. He suddenly stopped, closed his eyes, and tipped his head back to the heavens, hands on his hips.

She came up beside him, her heart hammering against her insides. If this was his reaction, maybe she'd mistaken his warm smiles and long looks to be something they weren't. "I was pretty certain you felt the same for me, but if not, I promise I'll try not to make things awkward whenever we're together." She swallowed and looked down before bringing her gaze back up and forcing out the next words. "But if I'm right, I was hoping we could build on those feelings—"

"Feelings?" He shook his head slightly, his face pale and tense. "Feelings aren't enough."

"Of course they're not." But she couldn't simply ignore how his being near her made her feel at home, how she felt like she was worth something in his eyes. "Though I'd contend they should play a bigger part in choosing one's spouse than a person's assets. My parents married for love back when they were poor, and they're much happier than many of the couples that flit about my set. I do want to make certain the man I marry has integrity, follows God, willingly gives of himself—"

"Marianne." His face was a study in hard lines and tension, nothing like the relaxed expression he'd started off with at the beginning of their walk. "No matter how you feel about me, it won't change the fact that I'm as poor as a church mouse."

"You are not that poor." How could he see value in her, but think himself so low?

He shook his head. "I'm that poor in comparison to you."

She reached up to cup his cheek, but he grew so stiff she let her hand drop. "Though I might've been born to wealth, I don't love it enough to make a poor match, and—"

"I am the epitome of a poor match. You and David . . ." He blinked, then scrubbed his hand back and forth over his hair. "What about you and David?"

David? He wanted to talk about David? She heaved a sigh and her heart slowed. Her parents nagging her about David was about all she could handle, truth be told. "Surely you've seen we love each other no more than brother and sister. You're the closest person to both of us—you have to have noticed."

"Such things don't keep people of your set from marrying."

"As I said, I think it should." Though he hadn't swooped in for that kiss she'd hoped for, he hadn't yet denied he felt something for her. Her heart started beating with hope again. "Do you have feelings for me, too?"

He grabbed her by the upper arms. "It doesn't matter what I feel, Marianne." He promptly let go, leaving her suddenly cold, though she'd not realized she'd been hot.

"A woman of meager means is all I can aspire to marry." He looked away, his voice hushed. "And if she's half as pretty and kind as you, I'll count myself lucky."

"So you're rejecting me because I'm rich?" She swallowed down the quaver in her voice. Who said *no* to love because it would bring them money? "If so, don't worry. My parents will likely disapprove of us enough to write me out of their will. But if not, we could always give the money to charity."

"You don't understand." A man bumped Calvin from behind as he walked past, but Calvin's gaze stayed pinned on her, a sadness she'd never seen clouding his green eyes. "Love won't make up for what you'd lose."

Lose? Did he think money was everything? "But what about what I'd gain?"

He shook his head slightly. "You don't know what it's like for those of us who have to work."

"Then tell me." She settled her hands on his arms, giving him a gentle squeeze. She'd never seen him so uncomfortable.

The wind picked up and ruffled his blond hair. His throat worked overtime. "I can't show you how years of want will affect you before it's too late to escape it." He stepped away from her and turned to look at the clouds rolling in, then tipped his head forward. "I think your driver's coming to pick you up."

She looked behind her, and indeed, her parents must have sent him early in light of the approaching storm. If she had more time, she could convince Calvin he mattered more than an inheritance, especially since he was the only person who seemed to think she mattered in spite of it. "Will you accept a ride home?"

He kept his gaze focused on her parents' carriage. "Thank you, but no, I'm not far from my apartment." He stepped away from her, his eyes averted, as the carriage slowed beside them.

Was the conversation about their future over just like that?

She blinked excessively, hugging herself as she let his rejection wash over her. And yet, he'd not rejected her—he'd rejected her status. The one man she'd thought had seen through her prestigious name to the woman inside. "Would you at least think about a future with me before you say no?"

He closed his eyes, his body losing some of its rigidity. "I already have."

He had?

Her driver jumped down from his seat, and all she could do was stare at the fat droplets making dark marks on the sidewalk and Calvin's shoes. What could she say now? If she said more and he still turned her away, she might cry in front of everyone on the street.

Mr. Fleischman opened the side door. "Glad I caught up with you, miss. Don't want you to get drenched and catch cold."

"No." But she couldn't move. Was this the last time she'd walk anywhere with Calvin? Had she just ruined the friendship she enjoyed more than anything?

Calvin took her hand, and she couldn't help but look up at him despite her threatening tears.

"I'm sorry." He gently led her toward the carriage and helped her inside.

She managed to get up the stairs without tripping on her skirts. When she found her seat, she dared to look back at him.

He stood silently by the open door. "I really am sorry." He stepped back. "More than you know." Then he shut the door with a soft click.

She was sorry, too. Oh so sorry. She dropped the shades, and the second the coach rolled away she let the tears come.

Was hoping for a man who desired to marry her for something other than her money and pretty face unreasonable?

Of course, how could she expect such a thing if all she could offer a future husband was nice conversation over perfectly brewed tea and the bank account of an heiress?

*T*he church organ's last notes and the exiting congregation's chatter kept Marianne from hearing Calvin's cough, though it had distracted her plenty throughout the service. Had his insisting on walking home in the rain three days ago caused him to fall ill? Why had he come to church with a cough like that, anyway?

Though their last conversation had been a disaster, she had to know if he was all right.

After a glance back at Mother conversing with a group of society ladies, Marianne slipped into a gap in the crowd, weaved her way across the aisle, and sidled through an empty pew. She crossed to the far side of the sanctuary but couldn't find his blond head anywhere. He couldn't have gotten out of the building already. He might've sat as far across the church from her as possible, but he'd also been closer to the front. Was he intent on never seeing her again?

From somewhere behind her, two staccato coughs and one long one sounded.

She turned. There. He had indeed passed her and was slipping out the exit. She hustled through the crowd toward the heavy wooden doors the deacons held open to the gray, drizzly day.

"Calvin," she called as loudly as she could without sounding improper.

He looked back over his shoulder for a second but didn't stop. And had he just shaken his head at her?

She slowed a bit. Though he might not want to pursue a relationship with her, they could still be friends, right? Surely they could still work together—even if their easy conversations were lost forever.

Calvin didn't stop, but he did turn his head to look at her as she came up beside him. He pulled his hat brim a little lower and stuck his hand back under his coat. "Good afternoon, Miss Lister."

She pressed a hand to the knot in her throat. He was addressing her formally now? "And to you. I wanted to check on that cough of yours. I felt bad for you all throughout service."

As if on cue, he coughed again, his hand rubbing his chest. But being this close, she'd heard the strangest little whistle in his voice. "Shouldn't you be home resting?" she asked. "It must be hard to—"

He coughed into his elbow, but this time the whistle sounded more like a *mew*.

She screwed up her face. "What did I just hear?"

"Nothing." He sped up, coughing again.

Now there definitely was a *mew* amid those halfhearted coughs.

"What on earth?" She scanned the sidewalk around them but saw nothing. "Did I hear a cat?"

He shrugged and kept moving forward, but the lump under his jacket, which she'd assumed was his hand, started to squirm.

"What's in your coat?" She couldn't help the grin. If there was a man in Kansas City who'd take pity on a cat in this weather, it would be Calvin. But why take it into church?

"Nothing. I'm on my way to see Mrs. Danby, so—"

"Now hold on." She cut in front of him and put her hand on the soft, wiggling lump. "This is nothing?"

He stopped short and his cheeks flushed. His other hand came up as if readying to cover hers, but he clenched his fist instead. "All right. . . . It's a kitten."

271

Laughter bubbled out of her, and she couldn't help but smile. "You had a kitten under your jacket during church?"

Though his lips wiggled up a notch, he tried to shrug it off. "I found the pitiful thing by the back door. Figured Mrs. Danby has been lonely, so she might want to nurse it back to health. I was already late for service, and I couldn't just leave it there."

"Let me see." She moved to pull back his lapel.

His hand caught hers against his chest. "No."

"Why not?"

His breathing hitched. "Just no."

Her palm turned suddenly hot despite the chill in the air. Was she really pressing her hand against a man's chest right next to a busy street where almost anyone could see?

And his heart was beating quite hard . . . unless all men's hearts beat this hard?

"Oh," she breathed. She let her hand fall, closing her fist tightly to banish the feel of his heart beneath her hand.

Though his having a heartbeat shouldn't have surprised her, there was still a cat under his coat. What woman wouldn't fall in love with a man who'd keep a kitten warm under his suit coat during church?

The creature in question let out another pitiful *mew* as it wriggled even more.

Calvin winced. "I'm afraid I need to get this cat to Mrs. Danby before its claws become a permanent part of my chest."

"It's because you're smothering it." She tugged his suit coat open, and the thin little face of a big-eared black kitten popped up, one tiny paw desperately trying to find purchase on the top of Calvin's pocket.

A kitten in his pocket. Could anything be more adorable? She couldn't help but smile up at him.

But he was definitely not smiling back. Oh no, this was the look she'd seen many times over the past year, the one she'd hoped would turn into an offer of courtship and a kiss.

His eyes held hers, and her heart thumped hard enough he could probably see it. A few more inches and their lips could meet. What if, despite his claims, he wanted a kiss, too? She leaned closer.

He pulled back. "Don't look at me like that."

She took a step toward him. "Why not?"

"You know very well why not."

No, she didn't. There was nothing wrong with the feelings between them. "I'm afraid I really don't, or at least I don't agree that my having money should stifle our feelings."

The kitten mewed again. Calvin reached up to rub its little chin and took another step back. "And that's why I think it best I excuse myself from this conversation." He gave her a quick nod and started down the sidewalk.

She turned to walk with him, but he didn't even acknowledge her. Perhaps he didn't want to talk about their feelings now, but they couldn't ignore them forever. Maybe he just needed more time to think. "I heard the men talking about going to Mrs. Phillips's next Sunday instead of Saturday."

"Yes." He pulled his coat over the kitten when a couple turned onto the sidewalk and headed toward them.

Her throat went dry, and she nearly stopped walking. He'd not even planned to tell her? Had he only pretended she was worth something before? "Can I not come help you at Mrs. Phillips's?"

He stopped again, his hand still under his coat pocket, probably petting the kitten if the telltale stuttered rumble beneath his coat was any indication. "Perhaps it would be best . . . if you didn't."

Her heart stopped cold, and she tensed to keep from drooping. She'd not turn into mush.

His face softened a bit. "I—I was thinking about it yesterday and . . ." He scanned her dress, a cascade of turquoise flounces and gray trim beneath her black fur cape. His gaze didn't linger long before meeting hers again. "Well, you don't own an outfit suitable for such work."

That was going to be his excuse? "I have work dresses. I've done chores since I was little—my parents didn't pamper me that much."

"Your parents—"

"Forget about my parents."

"They're coming."

"They're what?" She turned to see Mother bustling toward them, with Papa paces behind.

Calvin took a step away from her and dipped his head in greeting. "Good afternoon, Mr. and Mrs. Lister."

Mother gave him a dignified nod and then cut her eyes toward Marianne. "We've been looking everywhere for you."

"I was just checking on Mr. Hochstetler's cough. Did you not hear him during service?"

Mother deigned to glance at him, but her gaze quickly riveted to the wriggling lump near his heart. "I'm sorry to hear you're sick."

He slid his hand under his coat and coughed, covering up a *mew*, but Mother's brow furrowed, her eyes narrowing as if trying to see under his coat.

"He says he's not sick, so I wondered if we might have him over for Sunday dinner."

Calvin held up his other hand. "Um, no, that's—"

"I'm sorry to say that's not possible." Mother put on her best abashed expression as Papa ambled up beside her. "We've got to eat quickly if we're to make the train." She tilted her head toward Calvin. "We're going to visit some good friends in St. Louis. I'm terribly sorry. Perhaps another time."

"I had no aspirations to a dinner invitation, ma'am." He dipped his head. "And now I must be going." And without a look at Marianne, he turned and continued walking down the sidewalk.

"I swear, Marianne," Mother whispered close to her ear, slipping her arm around hers. "That man is going to catch on to your silly infatuation with him and believe he has a chance with you."

"But he does." Though it seemed he was determined to let the chance go by.

If he'd assured her he had no feelings for her, she'd have melted into an embarrassed puddle, but he hadn't. Not today, and not three days ago.

Mother squeezed her arm as she pulled her toward their carriage, which had stopped beside them on the brick-paved street. "You heard Mr. Hochstetler. He hasn't even an aspiration to dine with us. He knows his place—which is not beside you."

Marianne huffed. "He doesn't have 'a place,' Mother. He's our brother in Christ, like everyone else in the congregation. There is no Jew or Greek, slave or free."

"That's in the Lord's house, Marianne." Mother took Papa's offered hand and, with his assistance, disappeared into the vehicle.

Papa turned for her hand next, his expression at least holding a bit of sympathy for her plight. "The Bible is full of rules on treating the lower classes well, and we do that, but that does not mean we marry them."

She preceded Papa into the carriage. "But you were once lower class."

"*Were*, dear. *Were*." He pulled himself up beside Mother and shut the door. "And we don't plan to return. You don't realize how well you have it."

She braced herself as the carriage veered into traffic. "I'm twenty-one years old. I'm not completely oblivious."

From across the carriage, Mother frowned at her. "If you weren't, you'd have noticed that all the other twenty-one-year-old ladies are already in charge of their own households. I thought you had agreed with me months ago that David is the one you talk to when you're hurting, who knows you better than anyone else, and is the perfect choice for you. Weren't you writing him a letter last night?"

She'd started one the day Calvin had turned her down, but it was nothing more than a mess of feelings and tearstains. "Yes."

"Did you send it?"

No, she'd have to rewrite it if she wanted him to be able to read it. "I realize David's a safe choice for a husband, but I don't—"

"Well, you can't marry Mr. Hochstetler." Mother sniffed as if his name carried a stench.

She threw back her shoulders. "Why not?"

"The question isn't why not, Marianne; it's why would you?"

She turned to look out the back window, but they were too far away to see Calvin. "Because he spends his spare time helping the poor and hurting. Because he thinks of me as more than a doll to be put on display. Because he makes me laugh, cares about my ideas, and truly listens. For goodness' sake, he saved a kitten and kept it in his pocket during church so he could cheer up an old widow. How could I not fall for him?"

Papa leaned across the space between them to put his hand on her knee and squeezed. "Being a good man and being the right man are two different things, dear."

Marianne clasped her hands together and stayed her argument.

"Trust me, Marianne. You will be much happier with David. You might not be able to see it now, but you will." Mother took Papa's hand and intertwined their fingers. She leaned her head on his shoulder and smiled up into his eyes. "Please tell me you're leaving all work behind. You promised me this vacation would be nothing but a few weeks of you and me and relaxation."

So that was the end of the conversation? Her feelings weren't worth talking about for more than five minutes?

"Of course, love." He kissed Mother's temple. "I've been just as eager for time alone as you."

"But with the Peterson account being so difficult . . ."

Marianne turned her head away from her snuggling parents and watched the mix of horses and automobile traffic out her window. For her entire life, she'd seen them look at each other as if they'd married the best person in the world. But right now it made the thought of sending David that letter, where she'd wondered if they should revisit the idea of marrying despite their lack of romantic interest, a touch too painful.

She knew David loved her, and she loved David, but more in the manner of siblings. They'd grown up together, lived on the same block, and knew each other's secrets. But could she feel more for him?

Closing her eyes, she just couldn't imagine David and herself cuddled up in a carriage. Rather, she might dare him to try a handstand in the moving vehicle while he teased her about getting tongue-tied around Calvin.

She could imagine David standing at the front of the church beside Calvin as his best man, but to switch them around? Could she give up her feelings for Calvin when she wanted the same kind of love her parents had?

Though if both Calvin and her parents remained opposed to any type of suit, she might not have a choice.

Chapter 3

*B*ehind his desk at Kingsman & Son, Calvin flipped through the requisitions, making sure all were in order. Mr. Kingsman was in quite the lather this morning. Not that his boss was ever the happy sort, but he'd already barked at Calvin twice, and he'd only been there for fifteen minutes.

A knock sounded on the outer door, and Calvin winced. Whoever was out there would regret his timing. Days like today reminded Calvin of what a godsend Mr. Kingsman's son David was. If he weren't off on a business trip right now, he'd come out to shield the unlucky visitor from his father's thunderous attitude.

But the visitor would not be saved by David today, not unless Calvin could convince whoever was behind the door to return later. He shoved his seat back, but only raised himself an inch before he stopped.

Marianne.

She turned to shut the office door, her rose-colored dress swirling with the action, and then she whirled back to look at him, a tentative smile upon her lips. Just a mere shadow of the grin she'd flashed at him the first day she'd walked into this office.

Of course, on that day, he'd grinned right back.

Two years ago, he'd stood and come around his desk, boldly taking in her frothy yellow dress and the bit of red in her cheeks. How lucky was he to get to talk to a woman this fine? "How might I help you?"

The woman had looked him up and down, as well, then smiled even bigger.

He grinned right back. Strange how she'd made it hard for him to breathe just by walking in—but he wasn't going to complain too much.

A woman this lovely could steal his breath any day.

Now, if she were just as nice as she was beautiful, he might be tempted to give up his commitment to bachelorhood. "Do you have an appointment?" He tried to recall if there were any women's names on the calendar, but he'd been so overwhelmed with his new job duties he'd not looked at the schedule.

In the three weeks he'd been working there, no women clients had come in. He took another glance at the intricate details of this woman's dress, her fancy handbag, and the jewels at her throat. His insides took a tumble. What had he been thinking to smile so boldly at a woman who was clearly out of his reach? Of course no woman of his social standing would have reason to venture into the office of Kingsman & Son.

"No appointment." She looked over his shoulder toward the younger Kingsman's office, then at Calvin's desk. "What happened to Mr. Davis?"

Seemed she was a return client. "He works for Peterson's Hotels now."

Her delicate brows knit in the most adorable manner. "Mr. Kingsman fired him?"

"No, he was offered more money."

She cringed as if she'd just stepped on a hornet. "Oh dear, I can't imagine Mr. Kingsman took that well."

He shook his head. But considering her expression, she knew "not taking it well" was an understatement without him saying so.

"Mari!" The door behind him opened, and David walked out of his office. He threw a file folder onto Calvin's desk, then walked straight over to their visitor, swallowing her in an embrace. He stepped back from her a second later yet kept one hand on her arm. "How was your trip to California?"

Calvin returned to his desk, shaking his head at himself. He'd never had a chance with this woman.

"It was terrible. Spent most of our time on Uncle's yacht."

"Yachts aren't that bad."

"They are when Aunt Martha's on it. You've met her enough times to know."

Calvin stifled a huff. He'd never been outside of Missouri, let alone on a yacht. And he couldn't even begin to imagine being on one enough times to find it tiresome.

"I'm sorry. Calvin?"

He looked up at David, who truly did look sorry for something. "Yes?"

"I didn't mean to ignore you. I just hadn't seen Mari for over a month." He held out a hand toward each of them. "Calvin, this is my friend, Marianne Lister. Mari, this is my new secretary, Mr. Hochstetler."

Calvin couldn't help but let his mouth gape—whether more from David feeling he had to apologize for failing to introduce his lowly secretary to a woman of her station, or the fact that he'd nearly flirted with the heiress to the Lister fortune.

"Would you like to join us for lunch?"

"Wh—what?" Surely David hadn't just asked him to join them. These were two of the wealthiest young people in Kansas City, their fortunes well-known and well-discussed. Did David think he could afford wherever they were about to go?

"Lunch?" David smiled as if making an ordinary request. "Mari's birthday was last week. Since she was out of town, I didn't take her out for her lemon meringue birthday pie. I've made sure she's gotten one since the year she turned twelve."

Not only lunch, but a birthday lunch? He'd known David

was a good man the second he'd met him, but had David forgotten Calvin was his secretary? "Uh, I'm afraid I'm behind on work."

Besides, he wasn't sure he wanted to sit through lunch watching a man he could never compete with flirt with the most beautiful woman he'd ever seen.

"Are you certain, Mr. Hochstetler?" Miss Lister's deep blue eyes looked as if she sincerely hoped he'd reconsider.

"I'm certain."

David stared at him as if he could see into his thoughts.

If David figured out he'd been instantly attracted to a woman who was obviously going to be David's bride one day, he'd likely lose his job immediately.

David looked as if he really were disappointed he wasn't coming, but nodded his head to acknowledge his decision before turning to leave with Miss Lister. She glanced over her shoulder as they walked away and smiled at him again.

He had to be imagining things. There was no way she was looking at him as if she found him intriguing. He was—

"Calvin?"

He jumped in his seat.

Marianne stood in front of his desk, looking at him with one fine eyebrow raised.

How long had she been calling his name? "Uh, I'm sorry. I was lost in thought."

"Good thoughts, I hope?" Though her smile was nothing more than a wisp of what it had been that first day they'd met, his heart fluttered the same way it always did when she smiled at him—in a way it never should have fluttered at all.

She was meant for David, even if they weren't courting as he'd first assumed, and he would not hurt David for all the world. And he certainly didn't want to hurt her—though it seemed he had to. But she'd recover.

He stood, knocking down a pile of folders he'd forgotten were behind his chair. When had he become so clumsy?

Likely when she'd nearly knocked *him* over by admitting she had feelings for him.

Which wasn't supposed to happen. Those were supposed to be all on him.

For he'd not been able to tamp down those initial butterflies of attraction she'd created when she'd walked into the office two years ago, and discovering she was just as lovely on the inside hadn't helped him toss out a single one of those butterflies.

Though he hadn't helped himself one bit by allowing himself to enjoy gazing at her whenever she wasn't looking, breathing in the smell of her soap as she walked past, admiring the way she fancied herself up on Sundays, picking out her voice in the choir, pretending it was possible for a man like him to marry a beautiful songbird like her.

But it wasn't possible. "Miss Lister, what brings you here?"

Please, God, don't let her have come to talk to me. My heart cannot take it.

Calvin gave a side glance toward his boss's door. "David hasn't . . ." He didn't want to talk about David too loudly since he and his father were not on the best of terms at the moment. "David hasn't returned from Teaville."

"I actually came to see Mr. Kingsman."

He grimaced. "You may want to postpone such a meeting. He's not in a good mood."

"That's all right, he should be happy enough with why I've come." At her side, a flash of white caught his attention. Was she on some business errand for her father?

But she was rarely ever involved in his business matters.

Calvin ran a hand through his hair. "I'd advise calling out before knocking. Your voice might halt the bark he'll likely answer with."

She nodded and yet continued to stare at him, her fingers running along the sides of an envelope, around and around as if sealing the edges.

He cleared his throat. "I'll let you get to your business, then." He broke his gaze from hers, but not before glimpsing the hurt expression that crossed her face. He knew she'd feel slighted by his not engaging in small talk, but he had to stop every last bit of the attraction, from his side as well as hers. If his boss sensed any romantic interest between them, he'd be out on his backside faster than one could snuff a candle. Mr. Kingsman was determined David and Marianne would marry someday.

Without a word, she swept past his desk toward Mr. Kingsman's office. Her tentative request to enter was followed by the rumble of his boss's exasperated voice.

Calvin picked up his pen and tried to find where he'd left off on the last requisition, but for some reason his ability to comprehend words had jumped off a cliff. He might as well forget about working until she left. He kept his pen poised, however, so as not to appear open for conversation once she exited his boss's office.

If only she wasn't so kind and eager to help. Women who occupied her level of society normally acted as if he weren't good enough to be the dirt on their shoes. And if they had dared to offer their love to a man of his station and were rebuffed, they would have made him pay.

Yet Marianne had just come in and offered him a fragile smile.

Hopefully her feelings would fade long before his did, if they ever would.

A minute later, she came out of Mr. Kingsman's office, and Calvin kept his head down, hoping to avoid another awkward conversation—one where his heart clogged his throat and her voice got breathy and raw. Hopefully this heavy cloud of stifled feelings would one day lift and they could be comfortable with one another again—just not *too* comfortable.

Her soft footsteps hesitantly padded across the wooden floor, but instead of passing by, they came closer. Her hand slid into view on the corner of his desk.

"Yes, Miss Lister?" He didn't look up while marking the page with a random stroke he'd have to correct later.

"Won't you reconsider?"

His heart thumped hard, and his hand stilled—probably a good thing since he wasn't even sure what he'd been writing. Why did she insist on torturing him with dreams he could not have? "Reconsider what, Miss Lister?"

"Us."

He laid down his pen, keeping his gaze on the page before him, and let out a stuttered breath. "The reasons are self-explanatory," he said as quietly as possible.

She moved closer, her skirt unsettling the papers hanging off the edge of his desk. She stopped beside him.

It was rude to keep from looking at her, but if he did, he was afraid of what he'd see in her eyes.

How long had he dreamed she'd look at him the way she had when she put her hand on that silly kitten he'd stuffed in his pocket? Or when she'd declared her feelings for him?

It was quite possibly the worst thing that had ever happened to him. His dreams had become reality, and he'd had to shove them away.

She crouched beside him, laid a hand on his arm, and leaned forward.

He tried to breathe evenly—and failed.

"Your jaw is tight, your chest is stiff, and you've just written something completely illegible on that paper."

He grabbed a stray page to cover whatever else he'd scribbled.

She leaned closer, her breath tickling his ear. He had to do something other than act witless, something like kiss her—

He gripped the edge of his desk and held on as if he were teetering atop a cliff, which he was in a way, one that had sharp rocks at the bottom where his career would die a quick and painful death.

"The problems with us marrying aren't as self-explanatory as you believe."

He breathed as evenly as he could. "You might have dreamed up a fine wedding, but have you thought much past that?"

"Yes." Her hand rubbed against his suit coat's sleeve, almost making him jump out of his seat.

He couldn't continue talking to the top of his desk, so he turned and saw exactly how close she was. If Mr. Kingsman came in and saw where her hand rested . . .

Calvin scooted his chair to the side. "You couldn't have," he whispered. "Both your parents and Mr. Kingsman would be angry I'd broken up the marriage they've all but arranged between you and David. Not only would your parents likely disinherit you, but they might disown you. You'd not be able to run to them when times got tough." He knew what it was like to be abandoned by one's parents, and he refused to be the reason that would happen to her.

"You know David and I don't love each other like that."

"Maybe not, but if you don't marry each other, your parents will expect you to make comparable matches, and I'm not even close."

The hope in her eyes dimmed, and she put a hand to her heart. "Who says I need a wealthy husband to be happy?"

He wanted to reach out and caress her face, her crestfallen expression hopefully indicating she was at least starting to understand. "You don't know what it's like not to have money." He tilted his head toward the windows, where they could see the mills and factories Mr. Liscombe had built across the street. "You don't know what it's like to live like those men, women, and children who work the cotton and linseed mills. Their shifts begin so early the sun has yet to show above the horizon. If the women are not at home raising a brood of children, they're working long hours in the factories."

He pushed out of his chair and headed toward the window, for the longer she stayed hunkered down beside him, the more likely Mr. Kingsman would see them and assume the worst . . . or the truth anyway.

He walked over to the picture window and pointed toward the cotton mill, keeping his voice low enough that Mr. Kingsman wouldn't be alerted. "If you understood what that life was like— what it could end up being with me—you'd have no feelings for me whatsoever, I assure you."

She stood and crossed over to the window beside him. Why did she have to keep coming so close? If she kept this up, he might be insane enough to admit he wanted her this close for the rest of his life.

"But you aren't that poor, and you've got a good job—"

"That I'd lose the moment Mr. Kingsman realized I'd taken you away from David."

"And so you could find another job."

He shook his head. "That's easier said than done." Especially since Mr. Kingsman was powerful and vindictive enough to keep him from getting another job in Kansas City if he so chose.

He turned to look out the window again. "My father was a lawyer, earned about what I do, I'd suspect. But he got disbarred when a case went wrong for an important client. His name was besmirched, and he couldn't find anything to do but general labor. He couldn't sustain his family. . . . We were torn apart." Which was why Calvin now saved all he could, but his savings would never be big enough to keep Marianne content if he hit hard times—which was practically guaranteed if he ruined Mr. Kingsman's plans for his son to marry into the Lister fortune.

"I'm sorry. I didn't know, but that doesn't mean it'll happen to us." She stepped closer, laying her hand on his arm again. "Are there other reasons you don't want to marry me besides the fact that you think we'll suffer hardship?"

Her voice had gained a hopeful lift to it again, but how? What had he said to encourage her? "The fact is, hundreds of working women wish they were you." His mother certainly would have. "But no one dreams of being them."

"That's not true." Her hands planted on her hips. "No woman dreams of being nothing more than a set of numbers to be transferred from one rich man's portfolio to another's."

He shook his head at her. Why was she always thinking so little of herself? "You're far more than that."

Her stern expression melted.

Oh, if he didn't say something to chase that longing look away, he was in trouble. "Have you forgotten Mr. Kingsman would fire me the instant he sensed anything between us?"

"No. Anything else?"

He sighed and turned to look at her, letting his face soften as he took in her high cheekbones and her beautiful eyes, the color of the shadowy blue that followed the sunset. "What else needs to be said when those reasons are insurmountable?"

She didn't shrug or look defeated but let her gaze roam over his face, as if she could discover something in his expression that could convince her they had a future together.

But she wouldn't find anything. For the past few days, he'd tried to convince himself that he could defy convention and marry her. But she'd only grow to hate him once she realized she'd be forever doomed to live as he did. Just as his mother had grown to hate his father when he'd been unable to provide for her as she'd wished.

And if his father hadn't been able to survive being abandoned by his wife, how could Calvin possibly survive being abandoned by Marianne? How could he live through losing the most important woman in his life a second time?

"Are you an honest man?"

He jerked his shoulders back at that one. "You need to ask?" Didn't she know him well enough to know that already?

"I just want you to confirm."

He gave her a decisive nod. "Everything I've said is true."

"Then tell me, are you pushing me away because you find me repulsive?"

What kind of unfair question was that? His lips stayed in a tight line as she moved closer, invading his space, the smell of her lavender soap making him itch to comb his fingers through her hair.

"Well?"

He swallowed. She was the epitome of everything he found attractive. Her hair had just the right amount of waves so his fingers wouldn't be able to brush through without getting entangled. Her full lips made the most attractive pucker whenever she was lost in thought.

"Any—" His voice squeaked and he tried again. "I don't believe any red-blooded male could be repulsed by you."

Her eyes narrowed. "What if I could prove you wrong?"

"You can't, for you certainly can't ask every man in the world. And even if a man finds you attractive, that doesn't mean he'll marry you. No good man would, if it'd destroy your life."

"That's not what I meant—"

Mr. Kingsman's door burst open. "Hochstetler."

Calvin jumped back and raced toward his desk, his heart pumping overtime. "I'm almost done with the requisitions. Are you in need of something else?"

Mr. Kingsman stopped short at his desk, catching sight of Marianne. "Miss Lister, why are you still here?"

He'd hoped Mr. Kingsman wouldn't notice her, but her pretty rose-colored dress contrasted sharply with the wood walls and gray sky outside the office window.

"I had an inquiry of Mr. Hochstetler, but I got my answer." She glanced at him for a second, nibbling her lower lip. She walked toward them, and his heart nearly burst at the thought of what she might say. She could easily get him fired on the spot.

She stopped in front of him, not even bothering to look at his boss. "However, I plan to come back later in hopes of a different answer." She turned to give Mr. Kingsman a farewell nod, and then with her back as straight as if she were going off to battle, she disappeared out the door.

"What was it she asked of you?"

"Oh, um . . ." He shook his head as he busied himself with the papers on his desk, hopefully looking like he wasn't completely flustered. "She asked when David was returning." Hadn't she done so when she'd first come in? "Do you have a better idea of his return than I?"

"No," Mr. Kingsman huffed, yet a small smile graced his lips— but only for a second. "Well, get me those requisitions post haste and then find me the folder on the Quaid account."

"Yes, sir. And what about the figures I'm compiling with Jenkins?"

"I'd forgotten you'd initiated that. Yes, bring those, too." Mr.

Kingsman marched back to his office and slammed the door, jolting Calvin from his tense posture. Had Marianne truly just told him she wasn't giving up on pursuing him right in front of his boss? He tugged at his too-tight tie.

He was in trouble.

The kind of trouble he wished he could leap into, hang the consequences.

More trouble than he'd ever been in in his entire life.

Chapter
4

The early-morning traffic was busier than the last time Marianne had walked across this part of town, or maybe it only felt that way since her maid insisted on coming this time, and staying together was difficult.

Did Miss Blasdale really think she was in danger? Women of lower stations walked longer distances than this, and today she looked like one. She'd put her hair up in a simple knot, and the dress she'd sewn over the past few days was plain and poorly tailored.

Perhaps she was a little spoiled by her lady's maid, dressmakers, and drivers, but she wasn't as hard to please as Calvin thought. If he refused to think about a future with her because she couldn't grasp how life was for the working class, then she'd fix that.

Besides, she wanted to help people. What better way to become something more than a hostess than to actually work? Marianne looked behind her toward the building where Calvin worked. Though he'd made it sound as if his wife would have to live the life of a lowly factory worker, he wasn't that financially bad off. He even had the respect of quite a few in her social set, though they might never entertain him.

But if she could survive the life of a factory worker, surely he'd see she could be content as his wife.

The rising sun backlit the Liscombe Mill across the very crowded street. She tapped her toes, waiting for an opportunity to cross, and looked at Miss Blasdale, who'd been coaching her on how to act more like the class of women she was trying to emulate. If she wanted this job, apparently she must act a little less genteel.

How did Miss Blasdale get her hair to look so good without any help?

A wagon filled high with crates and pulled by a beautiful team of draft horses passed, and Marianne stepped onto the street, careful of the puddle in front of her.

Miss Blasdale's small hand caught her elbow. "You can't go now, miss."

"Why not?" She looked to the left again and saw no traffic.

She pointed to the right on the far side of the street. "Because that buggy isn't going to stop for you."

"He'll see me in plenty of time."

"That's just it, miss. He'd have stopped for a fancy lady, but you're not a fancy lady anymore."

She shook her head but took a step back since an automobile was about to zip past now. "Just because someone's humbly dressed doesn't mean drivers will run them over. The rich don't think so much of themselves they consider others' lives expendable—at least not any who aren't terrible people to begin with."

"'Tis true of your family, yes, but not all people care so much, rich or poor. Besides, you told me I was supposed to help you blend in. I sure don't expect the driver of a fancy buggy to take heed of me. I've been splashed too many times, grazed too often, and cursed at by enough crazy drivers to believe otherwise. And I'm not exactly keen on testing it, not with those newfangled motor-cars racing about."

Who knew anyone thought so much about crossing a road?

Another break in the traffic opened, and she scurried across, avoiding the low areas where the brick had sunk and filled with water.

"Don't walk like that," Miss Blasdale called from behind her.

She was walking wrong, too? "Like what? I'm taking care to avoid puddles. Surely even the basest of women don't just plow through puddles."

"You're right, they don't," she huffed beside her. "But you're walking like you own the world."

How could she possibly be doing so when such a thought hadn't ever entered her head? Marianne slouched her shoulders as she finished crossing the last half of the road.

Her maid chuckled. "Well, that wasn't good, either. Even a lowborn woman wouldn't walk like an ape."

Marianne shook her head as they gained the sidewalk. "Perhaps these non-lady lessons weren't a good idea. If I just act like myself in this new outfit and hairstyle, they'll only think I'm giving off airs—nothing to keep me from being hired, right?"

Miss Blasdale looked over her dress. Several days ago, she'd outright laughed at her for asking where everyone bought their work dresses. "Well, yes, you did a good job copying my mother's dress and picking out the drabbest of brown muslins. Your shoes, however . . ."

Drat. She'd meant to borrow the head housekeeper's boots but had donned her own without thinking after Miss Blasdale panicked over how much time she'd wasted making her hair look ordinary.

"Hopefully no one will notice." If they did, she'd switch shoes before trying for a job at the next place. But Liscombe's cotton mill was the factory Calvin had pointed to when he'd said she'd not be able to make it through a day of work, so that's the job she wanted.

However, she'd failed to procure it at the beginning of the week. A well-to-do lady asking for a job at the mill, even wearing a work dress, had gotten her ignored by some and looked at with disdain and suspicion by others. The foreman hadn't even let her argue her case; he'd promptly told her no and spun on his heel.

Marianne fingered the crooked pleat she'd accidentally sewn into her sleeve. The women who'd rushed along the street beside her this morning all seemed to have flaws somewhere in their attire, be it patches or too-short sleeves or even ill-fitting bodices—which she'd never noticed before.

Perhaps Miss Blasdale was right; maybe she hadn't really been *seeing* the lower class that surrounded her. But she'd pay attention now. "I'm sorry for being snippy with you this morning, but thank you for trying to help. Now pray I get this job." She'd likely be turned right back out the door again, but she'd try once more before asking for work at the linseed mill.

Miss Blasdale shook her head as if trying to talk a toddler out of her belief that she could fly. "I have no idea why you'd want such a job. I wouldn't even want to work in a factory. But if it's that important to you—"

"It is."

The work bell rang behind them.

Miss Blasdale frowned back at the mill. "I will pray, miss. At least that God helps you get to where you *should* be."

"That's a prayer I'll take."

Her lips tickled up into a smile. "Then good luck, Miss Lister."

"You should call me Marianne. At least while my parents are away."

Miss Blasdale's pretty red lips compressed into a frown. "If someone told your parents . . ." Miss Blasdale continued muttering under her breath.

Something about the rich and their silly games?

Marianne gritted her teeth against reprimanding her, since for the next few weeks she would not be her maid, but an equal. "How about this? If someone informs my parents, I'll tell them I insisted. They'd believe that of me. So I insist."

Miss Blasdale's eyes danced a bit. "I wish you the best, Marianne."

"And you, too, Della."

Her maid's eyebrows winged up at that, but she gave Marianne

293

a small push along with a slightly bigger smile. "Go get yourself a terrible job." Then she slipped back into traffic.

Marianne turned toward the newer mills, and her heart sped up. Now faced with the reality of going back in . . . well, the way she'd been derided the last time was almost enough to push her to seek employment at the ice plant instead. But freezing all day was not exactly calling to her.

The crowd had nearly disappeared, so she marched straight up to the big doors, slid into the dim, cacophonous factory, and weaved through the workers toward the area where the foreman had been at this hour last time. When she'd come before, it had taken twenty minutes to find him with all the yelling over the noise she'd had to do. But he was over six feet tall, so he should be easy to spot now that she knew who he was.

As she walked between the rows of constantly clacking contraptions that were slightly taller and wider than upright pianos, she saw no one with earmuffs to dampen the noise. Did they get used to the racket or did it deaden their hearing? She paused for a second. She didn't want to permanently injure herself to gain Calvin's heart. But surely the banging and whirring wasn't enough to turn anyone deaf or no one would work there, right?

She spied the foreman, Mr. Tomblin, looking over the shoulder of a lady working a machine, her fingers dancing lightning quick as they tied knots in cotton thread and fiddled with levers and knobs.

"Sir?"

He turned and gave her a blank stare.

Did the difference in her clothing really cause such a drastic change that he didn't recognize her? Her heart flew with hope. "I would like a job."

He sighed, though the only evidence he did so was the rise and fall of his chest, since such a sound was impossible to hear above the melee. "Your late arrival doesn't make you an appealing employee, but we've got absences enough, the boss might consider you." He started down the aisle. "This way."

She couldn't help her giddy shoulder jiggle. She might have a chance, after all!

Mr. Tomblin walked faster than a man normally would with a woman beside him, then opened a door and pointed for her to go in. She frowned. He wasn't even going to find out her name and introduce her?

The door shut behind her, barely dampening the factory's noises.

A portly man looked up from the stack of papers he'd been perusing from behind his desk. "Yes?"

"I'm in need of a job."

The man, likely one of the Liscombes, scanned her from the top of her head down to the toes of her well-polished boots.

She tried to stand in a way that wasn't too upright nor too apelike. Maybe she should have practiced this in the mirror last night.

"What do you know how to do?"

She let out a breath. Seemed the ugly dress had gotten her to the next step. "I can sew and mend and take care of a family."

"I mean what factory experience do you have?"

She wrung her hands. "None, actually. I'm expecting nothing but an entry-level position."

"Well, you're lucky I'm shorthanded. We'll see how you do, but don't be late again. I can find a girl to replace you easy enough."

"Yes, sir."

The man just stared at her. "Well, go see Mr. Tomblin and tell him to put you to work."

"Now?"

"Yes, now. When else did you expect?" The man's eyes narrowed. "Don't make me fire you already."

"No, sir." She gave him a stilted little curtsy, not knowing what a woman of her new station would do taking leave of a superior, and backed toward the door. "And thank you, sir."

But he'd already returned to scrutinizing his paperwork.

She let herself out and blew out a breath. A job! But she hadn't even packed a lunch.

No matter, one day without lunch wouldn't kill her. Though next time God answered her prayers this quickly she'd try to be better prepared for it.

She spied Mr. Tomblin and scurried over to him, shouting, "I'm to start today."

"Doing what?"

If she hadn't seen his lips, she wouldn't have understood him. "I don't know." She raised her voice above the machines. "I told Mr. Liscombe I don't know anything about manufacturing. I just needed a job—"

"Fine, we'll have you feed the sliver into the spinner."

Did he say *slimer* or *Iver*? Hopefully someone would explain more about what she'd be doing and speak loud enough she didn't have to ask them to repeat themselves a half dozen times.

Mr. Tomblin walked off without asking her to follow. Would they not even discuss hours or pay? No matter, she'd take it even if they paid crumbs. She rushed to keep up as he traversed the factory, passing more machinery than she'd ever seen in one place. So many of the women working the fancy equipment seemed younger than she. Did they not attend school? When Mr. Liscombe had said he could replace her with a girl, he hadn't meant to demean. Seemed he really meant *girl*.

Mr. Tomblin stopped beside a young lady, who couldn't be more than seventeen, rushing back and forth between two machines. "Georgia?"

The redheaded waif looked over at him, her hazel eyes dull yet wary. She only stopped for a second before rushing to the machine beside it to feed it a white wispy rope of cotton.

Seemed she'd certainly stay trim working here, racing back and forth maybe twenty feet.

"This is—" He lifted his eyebrows to indicate that Marianne should finish his sentence.

"I'm Miss—I mean, I'm Marianne." Oh, what was she going to do about her well-known surname? She didn't want to lie. But then maybe by the time they issued her wages, they'd hear Lister and think nothing of it, considering no wealthy Lister would purposely work in such a place.

"You'll work under Georgia."

"All right." She'd expected some matronly woman to be in charge, not someone years her junior.

"You'll report to Georgia each morning at six thirty sharp. If you're gone more than two days in a row for anything, you may find yourself in need of another job if we fill your position while you're gone. You are not allowed to bring any children. If you do, they will be expected to work. We are not a nursery."

She nodded slightly. So if she caught the flu, she'd be out of a job? Not even a shred of sympathy for her situation?

Georgia's eyes didn't register any emotion. Did the loud, monotonous noise of the factory make being cheerful a chore? Or was she taking the spot of Georgia's friend who'd found herself sick at home or dealing with an emergency?

"I'll check on you on my next round." Mr. Tomblin left with a nod.

"So, what have you done before?" Georgia thrust a wispy rope of cotton fluff into a machine.

Marianne looked at the pile of strange cotton cord. "Nothing that would help me know what to do, I'm afraid."

The young woman picked up a fat strand. "This is the sliver. We feed it into the machine here." She pointed to some place amid the constantly moving parts, and as quick as a bat of eyelashes she thrust the strand into the machine, but exactly where . . . well, hopefully she'd see Georgia do it a few more times before she had to take over.

Georgia inserted another strand, pulling off a wisp of cotton that was not threading into the machine correctly. "Now, to be clear. I have to keep up my quota with or without you. Mr. Tomblin will be angry at me if either of us gets behind, so you will not get behind or I'm docked pay."

Marianne swallowed. She'd figured there was a chance she could fail, but to hurt someone else, too? "I'll try my best."

"There is no time for trying. Either do it or walk out."

No, that'd be like walking out on Calvin.

When she didn't leave, Georgia went back to her machines and beckoned her forward. "Now watch."

After a few minutes, Marianne picked up the sliver from the area she was supposed to man and figured out the best way to feed the fat cotton strand as it rushed into the relentlessly whirring machine. After a nod from Georgia, she was officially on her own to keep the hungry apparatus satiated with a constant supply of downy sliver.

Though it certainly was not the most fun she'd ever had, it wasn't exactly difficult.

Calvin was worried over nothing.

The mill's eating area was filled with voices far louder than necessary for the small room, but Marianne supposed it was difficult to go from shouting at each other to conversing genteelly for their staggered fifteen-minute lunch breaks.

Not wanting to call attention to the fact that she had no lunch, she'd sat atop the wide window ledge and stared out at the city. Though her stomach was growling, at least she was off her feet. Oh, how they ached. Perhaps the work wasn't the most complicated thing she'd ever done, but her feet and back were sure complaining.

Thankfully everyone seemed fine with leaving her alone and hadn't come close enough to hear her stomach's protest. She wouldn't want anyone to offer her something to eat when it seemed most of them had nothing more than a slice of bread, cheese, and a side of something left over from their meal from the night before.

But couldn't someone have offered something to the five girls who only had one lunch box between them? The eldest sister couldn't be more than eighteen and the youngest couldn't be a day over twelve. Or maybe the fact that they were gaunt and pale made them seem younger than they were. But surely any person who toiled in this factory would need more sustenance than what they'd brought to endure the remaining seven hours of the workday.

The past five hours had been quite monotonous, and it seemed there would be nothing more exciting to come this evening, or any day following.

If there wasn't anything but this repetitiveness for twelve hours a day, every day, no wonder Georgia had such a blank stare.

Marianne glanced back at the group of sisters. The youngest leaned against the eldest as she nibbled on the last slice of bread.

Maybe no one offered them food because they refused charity?

She'd bring extra tomorrow and see. If they took it, she'd bring more. This job might not exactly be satisfying, but helping these girls could be. The other women workers seemed decently fed and clothed—perhaps these girls' parents took all their earnings? For why else would they force a twelve-year-old to work these hours instead of go to school?

Though the youngest sister was certainly not the only child in the factory.

She'd known children worked, but eight or ten years old seemed awfully young when they flitted about the machines, especially when they crawled under the gigantic contraptions to catch the flyaway cotton.

She looked at the clock across the hall. Only five minutes until work resumed. Suddenly eager for fresh air, she rushed to the front doors. The moment she stepped outside, she turned her face toward the blessedly quiet sunshine. Flexing her sore fingers, she soaked in the breeze and looked across the grounds and street toward the building that housed Kingsman & Son. How long should she work before telling Calvin? What amount of time would convince him she could survive a life like his? Surely the weeks she had before her parents returned would be enough, especially with how he'd looked at her the day she'd given Mr. Kingsman that letter for David.

She'd decided to send the letter because she'd thought Calvin couldn't be swayed, but during that visit, he'd been so determined not to look at her, bending the pencil in his hand, blankly staring at his papers, jumping when she touched him . . . she'd had to fight the urge to go take the letter back.

She'd been right; Calvin felt more for her than he was willing to admit.

Oh, if only God would've let them fall in love with people closer to each other's walks of life.

The bell tolled, calling her in for the second half of the workday. While she raced back into the building, she snatched a stray wisp of sliver off her sleeve, twisted it between her fingers to make a short piece of cotton thread, then wrapped it around her ring finger.

She would see this through. If she couldn't, her claim to be able to love Calvin, rich or poor, was nothing more substantial than cotton fluff.

Chapter
5

*S*unlight diffused the early-morning mist lying heavy upon the city streets. Despite the work crowd rushing past him, Calvin couldn't make himself walk any faster. The elder Mr. Kingsman was often a bear to work with, but after the letter he'd gotten from his son yesterday, he'd shucked the temperamental grizzly for the ornery dragon he kept squashed and angry inside him.

With David in Teaville, there'd be no reason for Marianne to come and visit the office. Of course, in light of the feelings she had for him, that was a good thing. But without the possibility of her dropping in, the only hope he had for a good day at work was if Mr. Kingsman didn't show up.

He stopped midstride. He'd passed the office. If he couldn't keep his mind off Marianne, he was going to lose his job. He marched back through the heavy onslaught of people, determined not to think of her. For nearly a year now, he'd reminded himself over and over that he would have to deal with seeing her married to David, but now that he knew he had a chance with her . . .

He sped up. Maybe he shouldn't bother subjecting himself to his boss's moods anymore and just quit, for how could he handle seeing David married to Marianne now? Only nineteen days had passed since she'd stopped in at the office, and he was about to leap out of his skin wondering what she was doing, how she was faring. Never mind that he'd hoped she'd stop seeking him out.

"Hey! Watch out!"

Down the street, a woman in a drab, brown dress carrying no fewer than five plump paper bags stopped short as an ice wagon turned out of the Liscombe gate. With her dark hair and high cheekbones reddened by the nippy morning, she looked just like Marianne.

Great. Not only was he still daydreaming about a woman he'd told himself not to think about anymore, he was imagining her, too.

She stood near the gate, waiting for someone to get out of her way, when she looked back toward the second-story windows above him.

Marianne didn't have a twin, but goodness, the woman looked just like her.

But surely Marianne owned no dress like that, nor would she be in this area of town without a driver. Definitely not carrying an armload of things she'd have handed to a servant.

The woman slipped past the mill gate and headed into work, but her grace, her poise, the way she moved . . . he'd recognize her walk whether she wore rags or silk. What on earth was Marianne doing at the mill?

He weaved his way through the crowded sidewalk and nearly ran across the street to keep from losing sight of her. "Marianne!"

She stopped for a second and looked the opposite way, but after a short hesitation she continued on.

"Excuse me." He dodged a group of women.

A delivery truck rattled out of Liscombe's big iron gate. The second it passed, Calvin jogged across the entryway, straight for the prettiest woman heading to work, even if her hair was off-kilter in the back. "Marianne!"

She stopped and spied him this time. The paper packages slid in her arms, stealing her attention.

"What are you doing?" he called, despite being winded. Evidently he needed to get out of his office chair more often.

She readjusted her packages and continued in the direction she'd been going. "I'm going to be late for work."

That stopped him. "Work?"

The Lister heiress would never need to work.

"Yes, at the mill."

"At the mill?" Perhaps he'd daydreamed so much he'd slipped into one, for nothing she was saying or wearing made sense.

She rolled her eyes at him, but the soft smile she reserved for teasing him softened the gesture. "You told me I wouldn't be able to endure my life if I married you, that I was too spoiled or fragile to work someplace like the mill, so I decided to test that out for myself. So far, I'm alive, whole, and not crying myself to sleep. What do you think?" She stopped and smiled so brightly, he wasn't sure if he'd missed something she'd said.

"What do I think about what?" Did this mean she hadn't given up on marrying him?

Stupid heart. No reason to start beating so hard. This bright, young, wealthy woman wouldn't go through with trading her prestigious last name for his.

She stepped closer, causing his heart to ramp up its chaotic motions. "I meant, does surviving two weeks of mill work prove to you I'm not a flibbertigibbet?"

Oh, he most certainly knew she was a woman to be reckoned with.

"No?" she asked. "Then tell me what else I need to do to prove my love is true, and I'll do it."

His body ached to swoop her up and test out that love with a kiss right now, which would cause scandal, and then he would have to marry her. Which suddenly didn't seem like such a bad idea.

He stepped back and rubbed his temples, forcing his brain to focus on something other than his desire to take her in his arms. "What are you doing with those paper bags?"

Her beaming expression dimmed, making it even harder not to gather her up and try putting the smile back on her face.

303

"These are for the Moore sisters." She repositioned the top bag that teetered atop her stack.

Why had he stood there like a dolt and not taken them for her? He took the top three. "Who are the Moore sisters?"

"Five young ladies who work with me, from age ten to eighteen. They have so little to eat, I couldn't possibly sit across from them and watch five girls share one meal while I have more than enough for myself."

His heart ached for her, in more ways than one. She might be able to do without, but she'd not be able to endure watching others struggle.

Her neat little eyebrows quirked. "Why are you shaking your head at me?"

"You only just proved one of the many reasons you can't marry me."

She frowned. "I don't understand how helping people could possibly be a reason for disqualifying me as good wife material."

If marrying her could forever banish that hurt expression, he'd wed her in a heartbeat—but a wedding was only a solitary moment in time. "Oh, I'm certain you'll make an absolutely wonderful wife. You're the most generous person I know—"

"Which means . . . ?" That hopeful look was back on her face.

She had to start hating him sooner or later for all the times he kept wiping that hope away. "Which means, if you marry me, your ability to do charity goes out the window." And if there was one woman who couldn't keep from helping when she saw a need, it was Marianne.

"It does not." Her face scrunched like a toddler being told no. "You're charitable. Last month you spent hours reshingling a widow's roof."

He couldn't help but smile a bit at how adorable she looked. "Only because your parents and the deacon supplied the material."

She lifted her brows as if she'd won a point. "Which doesn't negate that you've done charity work. So why couldn't your wife?"

"Don't you see?" He clenched his hands to keep from touching

her, giving in. "Your heart is so generous you'd burst at having
to see needs go unmet. My budget for giving is small. Mostly all
I have is time. And since marriage generally leads to children,
children who won't have nannies or fat bank accounts to see to
their needs, our time and money would soon be spent feeding and
caring for them."

Her eyes warmed. "And how many children do you see us having?"

He stepped back and cleared his throat. "*We* shouldn't have
any children when there are plenty in need already." There were
countless children unloved, ignored, and forced to work for no real
reward. He knew that better than most. He and his siblings had
been farmed out to extended relatives after their father couldn't
keep them together any longer. And yet just the thought of her
having his child . . . He shook himself and pointed to her lunch
sacks. "How would you feel knowing that marrying me would keep
you from helping the Moores? I can't afford to feed five strangers
every day."

She put her hands on her hips, her expression growing per-
turbed. "That wouldn't keep my parents from helping. They won't
even bat an eyelash over these measly expenditures."

He didn't exactly want to get on her bad side, but if it would
turn her from him so she could continue enjoying the life God had
blessed her with, then perhaps that was a good thing. "Right, you're
helping the Moores with your parents' money—not mine. If you
marry a rich man, you're in no danger of impoverishing yourself
to the point you'll be the one in need of charity—"

"And if I don't want to marry a rich man, but the poor man
I love?" Her voice was suffused with irritation and brokenness.

His resolve to keep from causing scandal and kissing her for
all she was worth was crumbling with each second he stood there
watching determination, utter longing, and fleeting hope fill her
eyes.

He turned to look at the mill, the entrance filling with mostly
women and children as they converged inside. He looked back at

her lunches. "As my wife, there would be little money available to help the Moores and all the other needs you'd see. You might be able to help some, but you certainly couldn't help all. I don't think you could handle that."

Her jaw worked, and she stared at the bags in her hands.

As much as he knew she had to give up this romantic notion of shucking wealth for love, watching her come to terms with it hurt. But she'd rebound. She'd be cherished by whichever man—

"Here." She shoved all but one of the remaining lunches into his arms, her expression grim, her voice warbling. "You're right. I'll have to restrict my charity to what would be within your means." She clenched her own lunch with whitened knuckles.

Well, she could help the Moores for a while if she married him, but if the Lord blessed them with child upon child . . . how could he guarantee his children wouldn't end up in the same predicament he and his siblings had been in?

He couldn't. And that was why he'd determined never to have any.

God didn't always keep people safe. He allowed people to fracture, to implode, to hurt. Marianne believed she could be content in a marriage to him, but his own mother hadn't been able to stand the poverty they'd fallen into and had left him, his five siblings, and his father to face the worst time in their lives alone. And though he knew his father had loved him, without their mother's help, he'd had to abandon them, too.

His aunt and uncle had taken him in and seen to his needs, but not a week went by without one of them reminding him of how he ought to be thankful they'd taken on the burden that he was.

"Are you all right?" Marianne looked up at him.

He shook his head and wiped away the deep frown that had taken over his face. "If you stay with your parents or marry a man blessed with a bank account that can withstand disaster, you'll be far better off than with me. I have enough to survive the good times, but if I hit a rough spot, it'll be nothing like your father's worst year. With me, you couldn't give according to your heart's desire. You'd have no servants to attend you—"

306

"I understand." She shook her head as if she actually did.

His heart heaved with finality, and he tried not to crush the lunch bags in his arms.

She threw back her shoulders. "I understand you haven't seen me live as anything but a wealthy woman and so you can't be sure I value relationships over dollars, so I'll continue on and prove it."

He blinked.

"Since you're right about us not being able to rely upon anyone else, I'll search for a place of my own tonight. Where would you suggest I look?"

All right, he knew she was tenacious, but . . . well, certainly she wouldn't go through with this. Not when she saw what sort of accommodations she could afford. "With what you're likely making, you'd only be able to manage a shared bunk at a boardinghouse or a small apartment in Southtown Village."

"I'll go to Southtown, then. However, I don't know where that is."

Exactly. "It's not anywhere you ought to be, Marianne." The rows of shacks south of the mill were one of the worst areas of town. "You belong at home."

"My home is wherever my heart is." She tilted her chin up. "If you won't believe me when I say I'll be content with you, then I aim to convince you with my actions. I'll work here until then."

She turned, but he dropped everything in his arms to snatch her by the elbow.

She looked back at him, a quiver ticking her lips.

"I'm not worth it, Marianne." His own father and mother hadn't thought him worth this much trouble, so how could she?

"Don't say that." A deep sadness filled her eyes, causing moisture to well up in his own.

The mill's huge clock bell bonged. The crowd around them had already disappeared. And as quick as a puff of smoke, she pulled herself from his grasp and ran faster than a pickpocket who'd swiped a handbag.

On the second ring of the clock, she reached the door, hefted it open, and disappeared inside.

He stared down at the lunches scattered at his feet. One of the things he loved most about Marianne was her generosity. So when she'd shoved those lunches into his hands . . . it was almost as if he'd made her give up what made him love her most.

He stooped to pick up the lunches. Today was not off to a good start whatsoever. He was now late, and his thoughts were a muddle. Whether he ran to the office now or stumbled in later, he likely had no chance at appeasing his boss today.

Setting the last lunch on the top of the pyramid he'd made against his chest, he headed for First Baptist's large stone building that took up a quarter of a city block. There were often many homeless men tucked into the nooks and crannies of the building, seeking shelter from the wind.

Marianne's generosity shouldn't go to waste, so he'd hand out her lunches there.

Her parents were supposed to return in two weeks. Surely she'd give up mill work by then and return to helping others to her heart's content. But if she moved off their estate, would she be safe?

Of course the staff who'd been loyal to her since she was an infant would either keep her from moving out or stand guard until her parents came back and convinced her to give up her notion of marrying him.

Though he was unlikely ever to be loved by a woman so fine again, there were good men with decent fortunes who could make both her and her parents happy. A union with a man like that would not rob the world of the rare and generous heart of Miss Marianne Lister.

Chapter

6

The lunch bell rang, and Marianne stopped her machines and let herself droop. The whine of belt and gears and the clack, clack, clacking that now invaded her dreams lessened as the machines cringed to a stop. Not that she could hear any better once they ceased, since the workers ate in shifts and plenty of machines still ran.

When her parents returned, how would she keep from rolling her eyes when Mother complained about the honking and backfiring automobiles that now congested the streets?

Of course, if she could convince Calvin to marry her, she might never hear her mother's complaints again. She swallowed against the misgivings in her throat. She'd told him this morning she'd keep right on working to prove she loved him, but would it be enough? He'd not seemed impressed, but rather determined to talk her out of it.

But he'd been hurt badly once. She'd seen it in his eyes. He'd told her before that his family had broken up during rough times, but she hadn't realized how hurt he'd been until he told her he wasn't worth her effort.

The last moving part on her machine stilled, but she made no move to leave. She simply stared at the cotton sliver, now limp and motionless. If her parents never got over their disappointment in her marrying Calvin, could she survive the heartache of being disowned?

However, God didn't promise anyone tomorrow. If she abandoned her pursuit of the man she loved but then lost her parents to death or some other tragedy, she'd regret letting him go.

But would she regret her parents' everlasting disapproval more?

Ducking to retrieve her lunch sack from under her machine, she ran her hands along the folded top, wishing Calvin had been wrong about how it would hurt not to be able to help the Moore sisters.

Practicing to become Mrs. Hochstetler might mean getting used to having little, but it didn't mean she couldn't give at all.

On the other side of her machines, Mrs. Smith was heading toward the lunch room. Though she was the oldest woman who worked at the mill, she was always cheerful, even if her expression was often pained—most likely from the tightly wound salt-and-pepper bun at the back of her head. Considering her threadbare clothing and meager lunch rations, she didn't have much. But she was always giving what she had—a mother's listening ear and heart.

And that was exactly what Marianne needed right now.

Forcing her achy feet to speed up, she cut over to catch Mrs. Smith, who'd passed the last machine in her row. "May I ask you a question?"

The woman's green eyes sparkled above her thin-lipped, wincing smile. "Yes, young lady, of course."

Marianne fingered her lunch bag. She'd come up with how to tell the Moores about her sudden lack of provisions, but she'd yet to think up a plan for finding suitable, temporary living quarters. If she asked her servants about a place to live, one would likely wire her parents. "I'm looking for a place to stay. I can't afford much, and I've no family to live with me. I was wondering if you might know of a place that's safe." Mother would worry and fuss no matter where she lived, but hopefully Mrs. Smith could direct her to a place Mother wouldn't worry about as much.

Mrs. Smith's eyes widened in shock. "Oh, if this isn't a fortuitous day. My roommate, Mrs. Norris, remarried this past weekend, and I'm in need of someone to share my room. If you could stand to live with an old woman, that is."

Was Mrs. Smith a widow? She'd assumed someone so happy in a place of such drudgery had a loving family to go home to.

Maybe if Calvin met Mrs. Smith his fears would be allayed about money and status being all that could make a woman happy. "I'd enjoy getting to know you better. You're such a light in this dreary mill."

"Fiddlesticks." The woman's face looked abashed despite her tight expression. "You'll be the one who'll brighten my room. It is only one room, though, with two small beds and a washroom down the hall to share with the others on the floor. But the heating is adequate and there's a breeze off the river that lessens the smells."

If Mother found out the biggest perks of the place she was living were that she wouldn't freeze to death and it didn't smell too badly, Mother would believe her daughter had lost her mind. "And the rent?"

"Two dollars and seventy cents weekly." Mrs. Smith frowned while they passed a particularly noisy machine, then hollered once they passed, "But dinner and breakfast are provided."

With needing to supply her own lunch and other necessities, she'd perhaps have eighty dollars saved by the end of the year. That meant only six dollars a month to spend on others or emergency needs of her own.

Would six dollars a month be enough? Hopefully she was miscalculating, but Calvin's job certainly paid better. "Sounds good. An answer to prayer, actually."

"Wonderful." The woman gave her arm a squeeze. "Meet me at the front doors after work, and I'll show you the place. If you like it, would you move in immediately? I'm not sure how long the landlords would be willing to leave it empty."

"I can move in by the end of the week."

"Excellent. I'm sure they'll wait that long."

They stepped into the lunchroom, drowning in loud voices instead of whirring machines.

Mrs. Smith waved at a woman with dark blond hair across the way. "Excuse me, I must talk to Elspeth."

Marianne didn't bother to call out a good-bye since Mrs. Smith was already several paces ahead and wouldn't hear. She glanced over at the table where she ate with the Moores and several other young girls who worked the machines on the second floor. When they spotted her, their happy faces nearly broke her heart. She was loath to see their old, hungry expressions return since they'd only recently exchanged them for shy giggles and full stomachs.

Her feet grew heavy, as if the stray cottony fluff that flitted about the mill's floors and staircases wound tight around her boots instead of dancing in the drafts.

If only she could eat with Mrs. Smith and avoid their disappointment. But she couldn't. She had to either face the girls or go home.

Though she really *could* go home, quit this grueling work, and go back to a life of ease. Then she'd have enough money to take care of these five sisters and the others in this mill who often went without.

But she couldn't right the whole world alone. Money could only go so far, and even if she married someone rich, he'd control her access to their wealth.

If she let herself think about all the injustices, neglect, and hurt she couldn't fix, even if she spent Papa's every dollar, her stomach would be in such a permanent knot she'd lose all hope she could make a difference in people's lives. She closed her eyes and took a deep breath.

God, what do I do?

What you can.

Yes, she'd do what she could and trust God to answer needs she couldn't—whether she be rich or poor. She gripped the top of her paper bag tightly, marched over to the table, and slipped onto the end of the bench. Her aching feet thanked her.

The youngest Moore sister, Ruth, spied Marianne's single paper bag and lost her smile.

"Good day, Marianne," the eldest sister, Patty, said with a forced happy expression, her gaze visibly resisting the urge to look at Marianne's less than full hands.

"Good day to you." Hopefully it would end up good somehow. She unrolled the bag and pulled out the contents meant for one. "I'm afraid my life has taken a sudden downturn, leaving me with no extra money, but I still have good things to eat." She took out her small knife and cut her bread into pieces so thin they looked more like crackers than slices. "I know it's meager, but I intend to share."

"Oh no, miss." Ruth's voice turned sad. "You just eat it."

"That's very kind of you, but I want to share." She pushed the thin bread slice toward the ten-year-old. "You usually have marmalade in your lunch box, yes? Perhaps you could put a little on each piece."

"Yes, miss." Ruth's eyes dulled, but she fished out the little glass jar of marmalade and handed it to her redheaded sister, Laura, whose lovely face was taut with gloom.

Marianne studied her small wedge of cheese and wondered if she could even cut five slices off it.

A small chunk of ham was placed in front of her. She looked up to see Patty offering her a brittle smile. "It's not much, but . . ."

She swallowed and forced out a simple thank you. These girls had been working here for seven months, and before she'd arrived, they'd worked twelve hours a day on rumbling stomachs. They could survive it again, and she'd learn to do so, as well.

Fingering the short piece of cotton she'd picked off the floor earlier, she slowly munched on her skimpy lunch. Would her love for the man who made her pine for his smiles and dream of his touch grow sour on an empty stomach as he claimed it would? Or could she be content with doing what little they could together?

If love couldn't be sustained in times of want or disagreement, what business had she of saying vows to anyone?

At some point she'd have to move on from Calvin if he refused her love, but for now, she'd do what she could to show him that her love was true, even when it was being tried—and tried hard.

Chapter
7

The sun was still bright in the sky, and the strong, warm wind lifted Calvin's spirits. Getting to leave work early because Mr. Kingsman had left for Teaville on the afternoon train made Calvin feel as if gravity wasn't working as well today. It had felt extra heavy since he'd watched Marianne run into the factory three days ago.

At least without Mr. Kingsman's stifling presence he would get somewhere on the Holdern account he'd procured this past week on David's behalf.

Calvin left the sidewalk for the embankment that sloped to the lower level he rented from the Yandells and waved at his landlady kneeling beside her flowerbed.

He pulled out his keys, but something fluttering furiously in the trellis caught his eye.

Every year, Mrs. Yandell arranged pots of flowers on his porch since she declared bachelors needed plants, too, but what was she doing to his trellis? He stepped toward the dying vine, which traveled up the ironwork to the balcony above him, and fingered the short, roughly made strings tucked in among the yellowed leaves. He didn't care what Mrs. Yandell did to his porch, but this had to be for some purpose other than beauty, for it had neither rhyme nor reason. If not for the wind, he'd not have noticed.

He chugged back up the side lawn and stopped beside his landlady, waiting for the older woman to notice his presence.

She smacked her dirty gloves together and looked up. "What can I do for you, Mr. Hochstetler?"

If it weren't for the other pots waiting to be dispersed, he'd have offered to help her stand. "I was wondering what you were planning with my porch's—"

"Would you like more mums?" She quirked an eyebrow. "A certain color?"

"As always, do as you please, but I'm rather curious about the strings you're tying onto the trellis. What's their purpose?"

She frowned. "Purpose? I figured you knew, though I thought it strange myself. Bruce told me not to get involved since you're not doing anything untoward."

Untoward? How did strings in his trellis make anything untoward? "I'm not sure I understand."

"I'm not the one putting the strings there—some young lady is. I've noticed her a few times, but she's only here when you're not and she never stays more than a minute. I was afraid she was stealing, but all she does is tie a bit of string to the trellis and leave."

He could only think of one woman who had any idea where he lived. "Does she have dark brown hair, pale skin, high cheekbones, and walk with an easy grace?"

"That would be an apt description." His landlady immediately frowned. "I'm sorry. Should I have told you about her? If she's trouble, I can have Bruce keep her away."

"No, she's not trouble." Not in a way Mrs. Yandell would categorize trouble, anyway. The day he'd rented their basement two years ago, she'd made an offhand remark about how he wouldn't need the tiny apartment long since he was too handsome to remain single.

"When was the last time you saw this woman?"

"Yesterday. She's always here right before you come home."

316

Yesterday? She was still coming after what he'd said to her? "What was she wearing?"

"A brown dress."

She was still working at the mill? "A work dress or a fine one?"

"Definitely work, though the shawl was daintier than the weather required."

"Excuse me, but I need to return to town." He called out his thanks as he waved good-bye and trudged back up the hill to the street. If Marianne was still working . . .

He glanced at his timepiece. Just ten minutes until six. With a quickness in his step, he walked back through the neighborhood, the wind at his back pushing him along. His leg muscles protested the pace he set, but he wanted to see if she did indeed still work at the mill.

The day after he'd distributed her extra lunches to the homeless, he'd watched for her. The work crowd was huge, so maybe he'd missed her, but he'd been sure he'd convinced her he wasn't worth so much effort.

The bell announced the end of the workday just as he reached Howard Street. He stood in front of a pair of law offices, watching the workers trickling out of the Liscombe buildings. How long until he'd see Marianne? And what could he say to her that he hadn't already? He'd told her to set her sights on someone better. Had explained the problems their union would create. And with Herculean effort, he'd kept himself from kissing her breathless every time she came near.

Pacing, he walked along the sidewalk, scanning the crowd. The throng of men, women, and children leaving through the main gate swirled and churned in so many directions, it was foolhardy to think he could find—

A group of four blondes and a redhead surrounded Marianne's darker head as she smiled sweetly at one of them, seemingly deep in conversation.

He jogged across the street, dodging traffic, and once he made the other side, he had to relocate the group. Thankfully the carrot-colored hair acted as a beacon. As long as Marianne stayed with that group he'd be able to catch her.

The women's homeward pace was surprisingly quick, but with a sudden clearing in the throng of pedestrians, he sprinted up alongside them. "Good evening, ladies."

The group instantly quieted and stared at him.

He pulled at his tie. "I just—"

Marianne threaded her arm around one of the blondes'. "Don't worry about Calvin. He's a friend."

Everyone's eyes widened. A man in a suit befriending one of their status was certainly surprising—but then, much more so was a woman of Marianne's status befriending them. Though they couldn't possibly know who she was.

"Calvin, these are the Moore sisters." Marianne gestured to each woman as they walked. "This is Ruth, Shirley, Patty, Laura, and Jenny."

"How do you do, ladies?"

They only blinked at him.

"Excuse us, this is our street," the oldest one said, and then the five of them threaded out of the crowd and disappeared so quickly it was almost as if they hadn't been there.

Marianne slowed, the crowd around them breaking behind her as if she were a rock in a stream . . . and it seemed like she was hardheaded enough to be one.

And beautiful enough to stand out despite wearing a drab work dress speckled with cotton fluff just like the rest of them.

"What did you want, Calvin?"

What did he want? A lot of things he couldn't have. "Were those, um, the sisters you bring lunches to?"

"Brought lunches to. You told me feeding those five girls would be beyond a man of your means."

Well, he might be able to help them out a few times a month, but certainly not every day, at least not if he wanted to have any savings. "That's right." He scratched along his hairline, bumping back his hat. "And they're not mad at you over the loss?"

"They understood when I told them I couldn't anymore, but I've continued to share my own lunch with them, and before you get onto me for that, my lunch is no bigger than what I'd normally eat myself."

She was giving up her own food? "But with the hours mill employees work—"

"Nearly twelve."

"Yes." He looked at her from head to toe. She didn't look to be wasting away, but then, it had only been three days since she'd started divvying up her lunch. "Are you not hungry?"

"Not nearly as much as those girls. I had a hearty breakfast and have a good dinner to look forward to, and yes, I'm still eating at my parents' home, but come Monday, I'll be enjoying whatever it is they serve at the row of boardinghouses on Buckeye."

She was truly moving out of her parents' house in an effort to win him?

"Aren't you going to say anything?"

What could he say? *Stop pursuing me because at some point you'll realize I'm not worth the sacrifice and my heart will break.*

He couldn't say it, didn't even want to.

Could she actually be more loyal than his own mother?

He'd only been seven when she'd left, so he didn't truly know her character. All he had was random memories of her cooking, gardening, and holding him on her lap. Could something besides their fall into poverty have caused her to leave? But with his father dead and his siblings forever scattered, he might never know what exactly had made her abandon them.

"How long, Calvin?"

He shook his head free of the memories. "How long what?"

"How long until you change your mind about us? I know you're scared, and I understand. I'm scared, too. But tomorrow my parents could go bankrupt, I might die, or you may well inherit thousands of dollars. Nothing in life is fully under our control, but choosing to love someone—as hard as it might be—is." She turned and left.

He blinked and watched her walk away without even a gesture of good-bye.

But then she turned down West Street, in the opposite direction of her parents' house, straight toward his.

Though he'd been trying to convince her for a month to leave him in the dust, when she actually did, his heart tugged at him to follow.

When she reached the Yandells' house, she walked down the embankment, her head held high and her stride stiff with determination.

He sped up to see her unwind a cotton thread from around her finger and add it to the collection on his trellis.

She turned, the tilt of her chin telling him she'd known he'd follow.

He stepped closer. Her confidence, beauty, and the fact that she was still pursuing him made it difficult to keep his distance. "What are you doing?"

She pointed over her shoulder with her thumb. "Every day I work is for you. I know the hardships I could face might not have fully sunk in, but I think you're worth it. So every day, I'm picking up a remnant of forgotten, useless cotton, spinning it into something stronger, and tying it here to tell you that today, my love for you is stronger than my circumstances."

He closed his eyes and gritted his teeth. Was her love really stronger than any circumstance? "How—" His voice croaked, and he cleared his throat to try again. "How long do you intend to do this?"

"Until you're married."

The melancholy underlying her words forced his eyes open. Though he suspected his next words wouldn't alleviate the sadness, they were true nonetheless. "I've never planned to marry."

She'd one day make a match that would give her all the things she deserved, and he'd only be responsible for his own downfall—no hearts to break, no family to tear apart, no children to fail.

She sashayed forward, but the look in her eyes was not the hurt he'd expected, but fire. She stopped beside him and whispered in his ear, her breath caressing his neck. "Then change your plans, and I'd suggest you choose me."

Oh, there was no doubt he'd choose her if he chose anybody, but he loved her too much to do so.

He turned to face her, taking in the wisps of cotton in her hair, dancing in the wind, begging for freedom. Despite his body humming a warning to back away, he reached up to free some whitish fluff, then let his fingers skim across her hair to behind her ear, his thumb slipping below her jawline to tilt her head up a touch.

With the movement, her eyes fell closed and her tense, confident posture melted.

Oh, God, I really could have her. But it's not fair to offer me this wonderful woman if I'm not going to be enough.

She still waited with upturned lips and soft features, her chin nestled in his hand.

How many men would call him a fool for not kissing her? Of course, many wouldn't care about how she'd feel after they'd played her for all she was worth and still told her no.

He couldn't kiss her, no matter how tempting. If he did, she'd believe things could work between them. If he kissed her, he wouldn't be able to tell her no.

He leaned down, resting his forehead against hers, his eyes closing as he brought his other hand up to cup the other side of her face. "Marianne," he whispered.

She hummed in question, the sound vulnerable yet content, making him press his forehead against hers even harder lest he make a move for her lips. He anchored his fingers in her hair, not hard enough to hurt, but enough to keep him where he ought to stay—though he shouldn't have gotten this close at all.

"I—" No, he couldn't tell her he loved her. He did. Oh, how he did, but hardship would come, hardship they could not walk away from, and then what? Could she truly be content with nothing but his lips against hers? His affection and warmth? His income for the rest of her life? If she tired of the cotton mill, her parents would take her back; if she tired of him . . . there was nothing that could undo it. "Have you told your parents?"

She backed away. "About what?"

"About your job at the cotton mill?"

She shook her head. "You know how they'd react."

He let his hands fall away and gave her a sad smile. "They'd squawk like chickens, but they'd take you back the moment you quit."

"So?"

"Kisses aren't enough to keep you warm, to keep you fed, to keep you from poverty. One wrong step and I'm fired. And we both know your parents aren't going to look kindly on me for taking away the bright future they've planned for you."

"Are you truly afraid I'm that faithless, or are you more afraid of reliving your past?"

He didn't think her faithless, just vulnerable. "You don't understand what it was like."

If his mother, who had never been wealthy, could throw away her family when things got difficult, it was too much to ask of Marianne. "What about David?"

She sighed and put a hand on his arm. "He knows I'm in love with you. That's partly why he left, to allow you to forget about him and start thinking about you and me."

He had? Had David been thinking straight?

"He's willing to stand beside you and be your best man in front of all of Kansas City, if you wish."

A year ago, David had mentioned he wished his father would stop pushing him at Marianne, but Calvin had chalked that up to their being young. David might not be head over heels for Marianne, but the second he lost her, he'd realize they were meant for each other just as their parents believed.

"I . . ." His words failed him at the soft look in Marianne's dusky blue eyes.

"I trust you to provide, Calvin. I realize you can't do so in the same fashion as my father, but I'm all right with that. But more importantly, I trust God to take care of me." She took his hand and squeezed it. "I'll be back tomorrow." She let her fingers slide down his and then turned to walk up the embankment. When she disappeared behind the corner of the house, he walked slowly over to the trellis and counted all the varied lengths of string.

He fingered the last one he could find. Twenty-two. A sad smile upturned his lips. She was more tenacious than he'd thought.

If they were tied together, how could he be assured that when hard times came, their knot would prove tighter than the one that had let his father and mother slip away from each other?

Chapter

8

With both bosses out of town, Calvin had ample time to get his work finished, but finding the ability to focus was nearly impossible. He pinched the bridge of his nose and rested his head against his hand.

He'd not talked to Marianne for four days, but he'd seen her in the crowds around Liscombe Mills twice.

And each day there was another string tied to his trellis.

His mother had never even sent him a letter.

If only he could talk to David. He had tried to write him to confirm that his boss and friend had encouraged Marianne to pursue him, for if anyone knew what they faced, David did. But words had failed him, for even if David had left to give him time to woo Marianne, that didn't mean marrying her was wise.

But if none of the things he worried about ever happened . . . ?

Oh, it had been a mistake to touch her. The feeling of Marianne's skin on the pads of his fingers had yet to fade. He could swear he could still feel how soft she was, like down from a pillow, and the smell of her had been like . . .

He sniffed the air. The smell of smoke kept him from remembering.

Had one of the gas lamps he'd turned up against the overcast day malfunctioned? He got up and peeked into Mr. Kingsman's and David's offices, then stopped short after a glimpse out the front window. Columns of smoke billowed against the sky. He raced over to the glass and nearly cursed under his breath as he watched people leave the mill en masse. The muffled sounds of worry and the crackle of the cotton mill's timbers going up in flame stole his breath.

Pressing his face against the windowpane, he searched the scattering crowd as they parted for the horse-drawn fire engine rushing through.

Marianne was nowhere in sight. She was likely out there. However, he couldn't stand there with nothing but hope. He raced to the outer hallway and zipped past the other businessmen who'd left their offices to see what was happening.

He hit the downstairs door running but was stopped by a wall of humanity. How was he going to find her if everyone was standing around gaping?

"Marianne!" he hollered, knowing full well there were probably many Mariannes in the crowd and she was unlikely to hear him. He headed toward a redheaded girl. He grabbed her shoulder, startling her.

She wasn't the girl who'd walked with Marianne the other day, but he'd ask her all the same. "Have you seen Marianne Lister?"

The girl shook her head, so he raced toward the low stone wall surrounding the Liscombe complex. He darted through the crowd and leapt onto the partition. She didn't appear to be on the street or the road leading to the main gate. Surely she wouldn't have gone home without stopping to assure him she was all right.

Though, of course, he had no right to be the first to know she was well—but surely she'd know he'd be panicking.

Because if he lost her . . .

He ran down the wall, glancing both right and left, trying to keep track of all the brown-headed women, seeking the familiar redhead, anything that might help him find Marianne.

He didn't really need to see her, if he could just be assured she was all right.

Or maybe he did need to see her, to hear her, to hold her, to crush her to himself and insist she stop working in a place fraught with danger. Fires were rare, but he'd heard of one too many who'd lost limbs or fingers in the machinery, of workers who'd gotten their hair or skirts tangled in whatever contraptions they ran.

And he was the reason Marianne was here.

Ah! The redhead. The woman probably loathed her bright orange hair, but it was a godsend. He jumped down and pushed his way toward her.

She'd exited with a bunch of other girls, most of them crying, but none of them Marianne.

Once within shouting distance, he hollered out for her, "Miss!" Oh, what was her name? The closer he got to the building, the more his nostrils filled with smoke. The fire in the southeast section was gaining momentum and ferocity, but it seemed the firefighters were keeping it from spreading.

"Miss!" he called out again, but the bell of a second fire engine drowned out his words. He kept looking around for Marianne but saw no one who looked at all like her. "Miss!"

He forced his way through the group of girls surrounding the carrot top. The blonde she comforted was one of the sisters Marianne had introduced him to.

"Miss." He grabbed her arm, and she tugged away. "Miss!" He grabbed for her arm again. "Have you seen Marianne Lister?"

She looked at him, a spark of recognition formed in her eyes, and she calmed. She shook her head and turned to the woman beside her, who was coughing. "Wasn't Marianne with you?"

The blonde nodded, then coughed again. "I couldn't find Ruth. Marianne told me she'd find her."

"Ruth?" He scanned the crowd as if he could locate someone with nothing more than a name. "Where is Ruth?"

"I don't know," the woman cried, panic in her voice. "She told me she was going to get Edith, though I told her not to."

"What does she look like?"

"She's just ten, blond hair and skinny."

He darted off, going against the current of people that slowed once they'd exited the building. "Ruth!" How he wished she was a bright redhead, for half of these women seemed to be blond and skinny. But ten years old was at least something to go on. "Marianne! Ruth!"

"Ho there!" A brick wall of a man stepped in front of him and stopped him with two meaty paws around his upper arms. "Don't you be rushing in there."

"I think my . . . my friend is still in there." He tried to step out of the man's vise grip, but the man was twice his size and obviously did more manual labor than he.

"Now, you leave the rescuing to the firefighters. 'Sides, everyone I know's leaving. He or she ain't in there dillydallying, waiting for you to come and get 'em out."

"Please." He reached up and peeled the man's fingers back from his arm. "I need to find her."

"She's likely already out, lad. Take a look around."

"I have." He tore himself free and raced for the doors she'd run to only days ago when he'd disappointed her. With only a hundred feet left before he got there, Marianne tumbled out the door, along with tendrils of smoke that flew up over the top of the doorway and rushed past the mill's stone walls toward the dark gray sky overhead. Beside her, a girl cradled her arm and cried loudly. However, Marianne wasn't doing much to comfort her, for she was coughing and hobbling herself.

He raced to meet them and swallowed Marianne up against himself.

She coughed near his ear, making him wince. He pulled back and nearly dragged Marianne and the girl to the side of the path, toward an oak tree that was far enough away that only floating ash accosted them.

He helped them slump to the ground against the trunk. He kneeled and put his hand against Marianne's cheek, but she turned her head away from his touch to look at the girl. "I think her arm's broken." Marianne coughed again. "Help her."

Did Marianne think he knew what to do with broken bones?

Nevertheless, she was feisty enough to be ordering him around, but the girl was hysterical.

Without getting up, he sidled over, shushing as he came closer. "Where are you hurt?"

The girl just continued crying.

"I found her under a machine." Marianne scooted closer. "I think it got knocked over in people's panic to get out."

"This is Ruth, then?"

Marianne nodded, and he swept the girl's hair away from her flushed face. "It's all right. You're alive, and we'll get someone to take care of your arm. Is that all that hurts?"

The girl didn't stop her wailing, but she nodded a little.

He took her arm as gently as he could and thankfully saw no blood, but her overly pained expression made him place her arm gingerly back in her lap. He stood and waved his arms above his head. "Is there a doctor here?" He glanced around and spied the redhead. "I found Ruth!"

A man in a navy sack suit arrived before the redhead. "Did you call for a doctor?"

"Yes." He squatted back beside the young girl. "She's hurt her arm, pinned under something evidently, but Marianne got her out."

The young blond man knelt beside the girl just as the redhead and several other women surrounded them.

"Oh, Ruth, we're so glad you're all right."

"Did you find Edith?"

"Are you hurt?"

Calvin turned to Marianne, who was still coughing, and held out his hands to help her up. Once she stood, he pulled her against him and held on tight.

He shouldn't be surprised Marianne would go back in for someone, but it was all he could do not to yell at her for it.

She doubled over, her coughs wracking her whole body.

"Are you all right?"

Another man came up beside him, this one old enough to be a grandfather many times over. "Did someone call for a doctor?"

"I did, but he's already attending the girl."

"So you weren't calling for her?" He moved toward Marianne and put a hand on her shoulder. "How long were you in the smoke?"

She wheezed, trying to clear her throat, only to cough again. "I don't know, not too long."

The man held her wrist for a minute as Marianne coughed intermittently. After a quick barrage of questions that encompassed everything from muscle fatigue to headaches, he released her. He turned and pointed toward a wagon near the front gate. "I want you to get her to that vehicle there. Dr. Costa is taking care of those who've breathed in enough smoke to be concerning."

"How concerning?" Calvin slipped his arm under her shoulder as she coughed again.

"She's in the open air, so that's good. He'll listen to her lungs for a bit, might give her something to put some air in her stomach, cause her to vomit anything unwholesome. Maybe a stimulant." He patted his shoulder. "Just help her over there. He'll reexamine her and decide." The doctor then forged back into the crowd.

Calvin rubbed her back as she coughed again. She started in the direction of the wagon, and he fought to keep from yanking her to a standstill and holding her again. "You'll be all right." She had to be.

"I'm sure I will." She stopped to cough, and he continued patting her back, though it probably did no good. "Thank you for coming for me."

He tucked her closer as they started back up the slight incline. Her coughs were slowing. That had to be good, yes? "Please tell me you'll go home now. Your home. Quit this job and be safe."

"Have I changed your mind about us, then?" She looked over at him with such hope that even her next round of coughs didn't dim the light in her eyes.

How was he to answer that when his thoughts were in such

upheaval? Had she changed his mind? Some. Enough to get down on one knee and propose?

"I can see the answer is still no." She coughed again, but this time less forcefully. "In that case, I'll come back tomorrow and help clean up."

He looked over his shoulder, and indeed, the firefighters pumping water from the nearby creek were shrinking the fire enough that the whole building wouldn't be a loss. "You mean to tell me this hasn't changed your mind?"

"No." She cleared her throat a few times, the cough she was likely suppressing roughening her words. "Nothing besides you choosing to love another would make me change my mind. Besides, I've done some good here."

He pulled her to a stop. "I can't lie and say I'm not extremely . . . lucky to have your love, but I'm just an ordinary man. Nothing to interest a woman of quality like you. You could have your pick of suitors—your beauty, name, and sweet disposition could unite you to someone far better than I. Maybe you've imagined me to be something I'm not—"

"No, I've seen what you refuse to see in yourself. In the same way you've seen what is good in me. You're not worthless, Calvin. A man should not be judged by how much money he has or even might have. There are men of high social rank and wealth I wouldn't marry because their character is deficient."

"But there are plenty of Kansas City men of both quality and wealth."

"I don't love them." She smothered a cough and then reached up to rub a thumb against the stubble along his jawline. "You are all the things I find attractive in a man. But even more than that, I love you because you think me valuable. You've been trying to keep me away for weeks, yet you just about ran into a burning building to find me. I know that no matter what happens in this life, you'll be looking out for me. Even if I married another, I have no doubt you'd be praying I'd be happy."

"I do want you happy. I really do. That's why—"

She put a finger against his lips, and he closed his eyes, his voice shaky enough not to be trusted to continue.

"I know you think not marrying me is what's best for me. And in all other things, I'd heed your warning because I truly believe you do want to look out for me. But in this, you are wrong. I need you." Her voice turned hoarse, the crackle from emotion, smoke damage, or both. "What better way for you to look out for me than being close to me, with me, beside me? Forever." She inhaled sharply and coughed hard.

He pulled her close and patted her back, not knowing if that would help, but what else could he do but stay beside her, with her, close to her? And he did indeed want to do that forever.

He kissed the top of her head, taking in a deep breath, trying to smell the perfume of her soap beneath the pervasive smoke.

If his mother hadn't been the kind of woman to stay and tend her children through a time of misery, she wouldn't have been the kind to rush into a burning building for a person she'd only known for a month, either.

Marianne was not his mother. He had to quit comparing them.

She laid a hand on his chest. "I'll stop working if you can tell me you have no desire to marry me whatsoever."

Breathing grew difficult as he closed his eyes and held her tighter. He could say nothing of the sort.

"I didn't think so." She backed away to cough again, then looked up into his eyes. "I know there could be hardship, but I think the joy we could give to each other outweighs the risk." She took his hand and squeezed it. "Don't shove away a lifetime of blessing because you fear trials. You'll have them no matter what you do."

The simple act of having her in his arms was a blessing he didn't deserve. Getting to love her for the rest of her life . . . he didn't deserve that, either.

But then, David's friendship, his job, his salvation—they were all blessings he didn't deserve, and nothing would compel him to shove those away.

He'd wanted to save Marianne and himself from heartbreak, but was he keeping them from a joy he would never dare hope for?

She took a step closer, and he couldn't help but wrap his arms around her again.

"I've been thinking about what you said about not being worth my love." Though she coughed, she kept talking. "So I thought about what makes gold more valuable than anything else shiny, like tin or glass—why your treatment of me feels different than all the other suitors I've had. And I decided that what makes something a treasure is its rarity and how it's treated." She put a hand against his chest. "You, Calvin, are the only man I've ever felt this way for, and that means you're rare. As for how I treat you, it's like the Bible story about the pearl. The farmer sold all he had to buy the land where he'd found a precious gem. I think you're a treasure worth sacrificing for. Maybe no one else does, maybe not even you, but I do."

Since she'd stopped coughing, he tucked the treasure that was Marianne against his chest. When he'd stumbled upon this pearl of a woman, he'd been a fool, trying to encourage her to hand herself over to anyone else rather than give up all he had for her, fearing he might mishandle the precious thing she was, that their life together would tarnish her beauty.

But her beauty wasn't a superficial layer on the outside he could rub off. Agitation and trials would likely only make her more resplendent—like she was right now.

Her coughing started again, and he forced himself to move forward with her so she could get medical attention. "Let's get you to the doctor before you get worse."

She nodded, unable to talk after using all her breath to convince him that her love was steadfast and true.

An older gentleman near the medical wagon came and took her by the shoulder. "I'm Dr. Costa." He turned to Calvin. "Is this your wife?"

For some reason, his mouth resisted answering with the truth. "No, she's not. This is Marianne Lister."

"Oh." The man's white eyebrows rose quickly and then fell back down as he took in her clothing. "I didn't expect to find a Lister in this chaos. Come. Let's get you to the hospital. I'll have someone call your family physician immediately."

The doctor took Marianne from his arms. . . . They'd never felt so empty.

He'd always known she was a jewel among women. Now it was time he started treating her as such.

Chapter

9

On the walk down to Calvin's basement apartment, Marianne pulled her shawl tighter and loosed a small cough. Dr. Tallgrass had told her she'd recover, but he'd informed her in no uncertain terms that she was not to return to the factory. Not because he was concerned about her health, but rather because he'd been alarmed she'd stooped to such work in the first place.

She had little hope her family's physician would not contact her parents, but she still planned to move into the boardinghouse with Mrs. Smith. She could help the older woman save on rent and have more time to convince Calvin of her love. She was getting close to allaying his fears, wasn't she? But if she couldn't, at least she could mourn the loss of a future with him at the boardinghouse without her parents chastising her for it.

But to do so, she'd have to find another job, since she'd been fired this morning.

Probably Dr. Tallgrass's doing, expecting a reward from her parents for looking out for her well-being.

After she'd left the cotton mill, she'd tried to get a job at the linseed mill and the ice plant, but any place run by the Liscombes would not hire her. So she'd headed to the area surrounding Mrs. Smith's boardinghouse to look for work, but there were no open positions.

Dusk had arrived before she'd gotten any leads, and she'd tried not to think about how Calvin had said poverty was always lurking around the corner when one needed work to survive.

Not that she needed to work, and doing so would make her peers consider her a fool. But the Bible story of the pearl and the farmer had whirled around in her head as she'd searched for employment. Though it was a parable about finding salvation, not love, that farmer had inspired her to keep going. He'd sold everything dear to him, knowing it was possible that by the time he returned, the owner could've already sold the land and he'd have lost the pearl.

But the risk had been worth it.

While turning the corner behind the Yandells' house, she fingered the last piece of cotton she'd taken off the mill floor after saying good-bye to the Moore sisters and handing them her lunch. She walked toward Calvin's trellis in order to tie on the last thread.

But the closer she got, the slower she walked. The trellis stood empty of everything but the dying vine.

Had he taken down all the strings she'd tied to prove her love? After the fire, she'd thought she truly had a chance with him, that if she could hold steady, he'd realize love was a blessing worth shucking fears to attain, but instead, he'd torn down every last memento of how much she cared, the evidence that she willingly lived humbly for a chance at his heart.

She fingered her last cotton thread. Perhaps it no longer mattered that there would be no more cotton string to tie to his trellis. Perhaps there was no reason to upset her parents by moving out. Perhaps her pearl was lost forever.

Her throat clogged at the thought that Calvin had counted the risk and ultimately found her unworthy.

But even so, she still loved him.

She let out a deep sigh and moved forward to tie on the last string she'd bother to put up, blinking back tears she would not shed.

Calvin's apartment door banged open and he burst through, shrugging on his coat as the door slammed behind him. "I was beginning to think you'd finally given up."

Was he coming out to tell her once again that she should? One of the tears she'd chosen not to loose rolled onto her cheek, betraying her.

He stopped in front of her, his gaze roaming her face. "I just got back from your house. They assured me you were all right, but that didn't stop me from shaking my head at you when your maid informed me you went to the mill this morning."

She didn't trust her voice to small talk. Who cared about her health or where she worked, anyway? She glanced over at the trellis, bare of anything but the dying vine. "I see that the trellis has been . . . cleaned up." She swallowed hard against a cough she was afraid might turn into a sob if she weren't careful. "Are you trying to tell me something?"

"Yes." He pulled something white from his pocket, took her hand, and placed it in her palm. "I made this for you."

She frowned at the small crocheted item. A terrible bit of needlework, the end threads loose and the item lopsided, though it looked like a . . . heart, sort of. She blinked against the confusion and looked up at him. "What is this?"

"I took all your strings, tied them together, and crocheted a heart."

She couldn't help the look of disbelief. "You crochet?"

"No, rather, Mrs. Yandell told me what to do with her hook and I did it, since I wanted to be the one who actually made it."

"You made me a heart?"

"Yeah." He tore his gaze off the cockeyed item in her hand and looked into her eyes, his own mesmerizingly vulnerable and soft. "I'm not that farmer in the parable you told me about yesterday. I don't have anything worth selling, and I don't know how long it will take me to save enough for a decent house in a good neighbor-hood, but I hoped you'd be all right with me saving what I'd spend on an engagement ring and accept this heart instead."

"In place of an engagement ring?" she breathed, her own heart-strings feeling like they were being yanked in several directions at once.

"Yes." He curled his hand around hers. "If you'd offered your love to another man and he'd shoved it away, I'd have considered him a fool. I don't want to be a fool anymore. I love you. I've loved you for years. I just couldn't hope for your love in return, because you deserve so much better than what I can give you."

She blinked, attempting not to cry at the words she'd longed to hear.

He caressed her cheek. "It might be a while before we can marry, though. I realized yesterday that I can trust you to stay through good times and bad, but I'd like to start out as well as we can. Once Mr. Kingsman learns I'm the reason you won't be marry-ing David he'll fire me, unless David can save my job. But even then, I'm not sure I should stay since I'd cause him problems, so I'll need to search for another job, and then we'll have to save up for a house—"

She pressed a finger to his lips, her heart too full to hear any more of the obstacles he'd set up before them. "I'd marry you today, but if you need to feel more secure, I'll wait, as long as you know that"—she leaned forward, only a breath away from his lips—"I intend to do whatever I can to hurry you up." She tiptoed to close the distance between them. "I don't need that much," she whispered.

The second her lips touched his, he dug his hands into her hair and kissed her with such passion, she couldn't help but drop the heart in her hand. Though he may have told her to find someone more worthy to love only days ago, the longing in his touch and the hitch in his breathing proved the chemistry she'd felt for the past two years had been real.

When he pulled away from her lips to place a line of kisses along the soft spot behind her ear, she leaned against him. "I do believe, Mr. Hochstetler, that you've just made my dreams come true."

He pulled back and laughed. "If I'm your dream come true, you should've dreamed bigger."

"Don't you be laughing at my dreams." She pulled back a little and thumped his upper arm. She couldn't help the smile that stole over her face at him teasing her again, like he'd done before she'd almost messed everything up. "And since you've suggested I dream bigger, I shall." She tiptoed up and put her nose against his. "I'll pray God helps us get to the next part of my dream faster than you believe possible. Because I want to be your wife by Christmas."

"I'd forgo all Christmas presents for the rest of my life if that's what I get this year." He pulled her into an embrace. "I'm sorry I treated your love for me as less than the treasure it is. I assure you it wasn't because I didn't want it, but my whole life has been a study on why I wasn't worth sticking around for. But you did stick around, even when I wouldn't have blamed you for giving up. I'm sorry you had to go to such lengths to prove it, but I knew—still know, actually—that I'm not worthy of the extraordinary woman you are, but if you're willing to love me anyway, I'm going to thank God and enjoy the gift."

"I'm nothing special," she said, her words muffled by the thick layers of his coat.

He scoffed, but that didn't stop him from kissing her forehead. "There's not a single man in Kansas City who believes my future bride is no one special."

Future bride. How often had her mother talked to her about her wedding, dreaming up lavish plans for tying the Kingsman and Lister fortunes together? And yet, none of those conversations had made her feel as happy as Calvin's declaration that he planned to make her his.

She wrapped her arms around him. "If you take away my wealth and my name, I'm nothing but an ordinary woman in love with an ordinary man, in pursuit of an extraordinary love."

"No longer a pursuit, Marianne." He took her left hand and laid it upon his chest, where his heart thumped hard enough for her to feel it. "You long ago won my heart, and now you've convinced me I can truly have yours. So if God wills, every bit of the rest of me will follow in time."

Epilogue

CHRISTMAS EVE

*Y*ou should've let me get you a new dress instead of wearing this old thing." Mother swiped at the flounces as if dust still clung to the twenty-seven-year-old gown.

"It's fine, Mother." Marianne turned, trying to catch a glimpse of the back of the burgundy dress in the full-length mirror. "It's very sentimental, and what better dress to be married in than one that started a marriage I hope will be as fulfilling as my own?"

"I've been telling all the ladies you wanted it for your 'something old,'" Mother grumbled as she stood back and looked at her again. "It wasn't more than my Sunday best back then, certainly not what you should be wearing."

Thankfully she stopped short of telling her Calvin wasn't who she was supposed to be marrying, either.

But thanks to David, upon his return from Teaville, he'd not only saved Calvin's job but had promoted him to chief executive at Kingsman & Son—taking away much of Calvin's fear and lessening her parents' worry about becoming the laughingstock of their set.

Plus, David had recently married a woman from Teaville, taking the teeth out of their parents' favored argument about them belonging together.

David's new bride, a tall, dark-headed woman, entered the little room at the back of the church just as the "Wedding March" started. "Here you are." Evelyn rushed over with her hand extended, a penny in her palm. "You can't imagine how many people have no pennies in their pockets."

Marianne smiled and slipped the coin into her shoe. She then grabbed the bouquet of silk roses her mother had made her. A new blue ribbon anchored a borrowed handkerchief around the flowers' stems.

Papa poked his head into the room, and his smile stopped halfway. He swallowed and sniffed, seemingly stuck just inside the doorway of the room, causing Mother and Evelyn to have to squeeze their way out around him.

Marianne grabbed the gift she'd fashioned for Calvin and gave her father a reassuring smile. "Oh, Papa, it's not as if I'm leaving and never coming back."

"No, it's just . . . my little girl has disappeared, and in front of me stands a woman as beautiful as her mother."

She tiptoed up to kiss his cheek. "Thank you."

He shook his head a bit as he helped pull the veil in front of her face. He knew she wasn't just thanking him for the compliment, but for how they'd paid and arranged for this wedding without much fuss. "I'm just sorry we gave you so much grief early on. He is as fine a man as you've always said."

The way her throat constricted made it impossible to talk, but thankfully she didn't need to. Papa swept her out into the corridor, and she looked down the holly-decorated aisle to the man who stood front and center.

Calvin was pale and fidgety, but when the crowd hushed, he looked up and locked his eyes on her.

If she'd had any doubts, they all disappeared at the completely enamored look in his eyes. She couldn't help the smile of peace and happiness that welled up from within, knowing this man was going to be loving her for the rest of his days. She'd been right not to postpone the wedding for a "more appropriate" gown, for being his bride had nothing to do with what she wore, but everything to do with how they'd live. And she couldn't wait another moment to be his.

At the altar, she caught a quick wink from David, who stood behind Calvin as best man, and listened to her pastor ask Papa to give her away.

Once Papa lifted her veil, she could see the tears shimmering in Calvin's eyes.

She slipped her hand into his, and he frowned down to where she'd pressed his gift into his palm.

He pulled his hand away slightly to see the little engagement heart he'd crocheted for her, now with a pearl bead sewn onto its middle.

"You're worth everything I have," she whispered.

He squeezed the handmade heart between their hands. "And you're worth more than I could ever acquire."

But it would be their love that would make them rich.

About the Authors

Christy Award finalist and winner of the ACFW Carol Award, HOLT Medallion, and Inspirational Reader's Choice Award, bestselling author **Karen Witemeyer** writes historical romances because she believes the world needs more happily-ever-afters. She is an avid cross-stitcher and shower singer, and she bakes a mean apple cobbler. Karen makes her home in Abilene, Texas, with her husband and three children. To learn more about Karen and her books, please visit www.karenwitemeyer.com.

Mary Connealy writes romantic comedies about cowboys. She's the author of THE CIMARRON LEGACY, THE KINCAID BRIDES, and TROUBLE IN TEXAS, as well as other acclaimed series. Mary has been nominated for a Christy Award, was a finalist for a RITA Award, and is a two-time winner of the Carol Award. She lives on a ranch in Nebraska with her very own romantic cowboy hero. They have four grown daughters and several grandchildren. Learn more about Mary and her books at www.maryconnealy.com and facebook.com/maryconnealy.

Regina Jennings is a graduate of Oklahoma Baptist University with a degree in English and a minor in history. She's the winner of the National Readers' Choice Award, a two-time Golden Quill finalist, and a finalist for the Oklahoma Book of the Year Award. Regina has worked at the *Mustang News* and at First Baptist Church of Mustang, along with time at the Oklahoma National Stockyards and various livestock shows. She lives outside of Oklahoma City with her husband and four children and can be found online at www.reginajennings.com.

Much to her introverted self's delight, ACFW Carol Award winner and double INSPY finalist **Melissa Jagears** hardly needs to leave home to be a homeschooling mother and novelist. She lives in Kansas with her husband and three children and can be found online at Facebook, Pinterest, Goodreads, and www.melissajagears.com.

Books by Karen Witemeyer

A Tailor-Made Bride

Head in the Clouds

To Win Her Heart

Short-Straw Bride

Stealing the Preacher

Full Steam Ahead

A Worthy Pursuit

No Other Will Do

Heart on the Line

A Cowboy Unmatched from *A Match Made
in Texas: A Novella Collection*

Love on the Mend: A Full Steam Ahead Novella
from *With All My Heart Romance Collection*

The Husband Maneuver from *With This Ring? A
Novella Collection of Proposals Gone Awry*

Worth the Wait: A Ladies of Harper's Station Novella

The Love Knot: A Ladies of Harper's Station Novella from
Hearts Entwined: A Historical Romance Novella Collection

Books by Mary Connealy

THE KINCAID BRIDES

Out of Control

In Too Deep

Over the Edge

WILD AT HEART

Tried and True

Now and Forever

Fire and Ice

TROUBLE IN TEXAS

Swept Away

Fired Up

Stuck Together

THE CIMARRON LEGACY

No Way Up

Long Time Gone

Too Far Down

The Boden Birthright: A CIMARRON LEGACY *Novella from* All for Love: Three Historical Romance Novellas of Love and Laughter

Meeting Her Match from *A Match Made
in Texas: A Novella Collection*

Runaway Bride: A KINCAID BRIDES *and* TROUBLE
IN TEXAS *Novella from* With This Ring? A Novella
Collection of Proposals Gone Awry

The Tangled Ties That Bind: A KINCAID BRIDES *Novella from
Hearts Entwined: A Historical Romance Novella Collection*

Books by Regina Jennings

LADIES OF CALDWELL COUNTY

Sixty Acres and a Bride

Love in the Balance

Caught in the Middle

OZARK MOUNTAIN ROMANCE

A Most Inconvenient Marriage

At Love's Bidding

For the Record

THE FORT RENO SERIES

Holding the Fort

An Unforeseen Match from *A Match Made in Texas: A Novella Collection*

Her Dearly Unintended: An OZARK MOUNTAIN ROMANCE Novella from *With This Ring? A Novella Collection of Proposals Gone Awry*

Bound and Determined: A FORT RENO Novella from *Hearts Entwined: A Historical Romance Novella Collection*

Books by Melissa Jagears

UNEXPECTED BRIDES

A Bride for Keeps

A Bride in Store

A Bride at Last

TEAVILLE MORAL SOCIETY

A Heart Most Certain

A Love So True

A Chance at Forever

Love by the Letter: An UNEXPECTED BRIDES *Novella
from* With All My Heart Romance Collection

Engaging the Competition: A TEAVILLE MORAL
SOCIETY *Novella from* With This Ring? A Novella
Collection of Proposals Gone Awry

Tied and True: A TEAVILLE MORAL SOCIETY *Novella from*
Hearts Entwined: A Historical Romance Novella Collection

Sign up for the Authors' Newsletters!

Keep up to date with news on book releases and events by signing up for their email list:

karenwitemeyer.com

maryconnealy.com

reginajennings.com

melissajagears.com

More from the Authors

When Grace Mallory learns that the villain who killed her father is closing in, she has no choice but to run. She is waylaid, however, by Amos Bledsoe, who hopes to continue their telegraph courtship in person. With Grace's life on the line, can he become the hero she requires?

Heart on the Line by Karen Witemeyer
karenwitemeyer.com

After a terrible explosion at the mine, the Boden family is plunged deep into the heart of trouble yet again. As they try to identify the forces against them, Cole is caught between missing his time back east, and all that New Mexico offers—namely, his family and cowgirl Melanie Blake.

Too Far Down by Mary Connealy, THE CIMARRON LEGACY #3
maryconnealy.com

When dance hall singer Louisa Bell visits her brother at Fort Reno, she is mistaken for the governess that Major Daniel Adams is waiting for. Between his rowdy troops and his daughters, he's in desperate need of help—so Louisa sets out to show the widower that she's the perfect fit.

Holding the Fort by Regina Jennings, THE FORT RENO SERIES #1
reginajennings.com

Evelyn Wisely works daily to help get children out of her town's red-light district, but she longs to help the women as well. Intrigued by Evelyn, David Kingsman lends his support to her cause. Though they begin work with the best of intentions, complications soon arise.

A Love So True by Melissa Jagears, TEAVILLE MORAL SOCIETY
melissajagears.com